BOONE COUNTY LIBRARY

2040 9101 223 482 0

D0886370

Aced

K. Bromberg

BOONE COUNTY PUBLIC LIBRARY
BURLINGTON, KY 41005
wwwbcpl.org

MAR 0 5 2020

Copyright

This book is a work of fiction. Names, characters, places, and incidents are the product of the author's imagination or are used fictitiously. Any resemblance to actual events, locales, or persons, living or dead, is coincidental.

Copyright © 2016 – Aced by K. Bromberg

All Rights Reserved. In accordance with the U.S. Copyright Act of 1976, the scanning, uploading, and electronic sharing of any part of this book without the permission of the publisher or author constitute unlawful piracy and theft of the author's intellectual property. If you would like to use material from this book (other than for review purposes), prior written permission must be obtained by contacting the publisher at kbrombergwrites@gmail.com. Thank you for your support of the author's rights.

FBI Anti-Piracy Warning: The unauthorized reproduction or distribution of a copyrighted work is illegal. Criminal copyright infringement, including infringement without monetary gain, in investigated by the FBI and is punishable by up to five years in federal prison and a fine of $250,000.

Editing: Making Manuscripts
Proofing: The Proof is in the Reading, LLC
Cover art created by: K23 Designs
Formatting by: Champagne Formats

Except for the original material written by the author, all songs, song titles, and lyrics mentioned in the novel Aced are the property of the respective songwriters and copyright holders.

ISBN: 978-1-942832-01-0

Other Works by K. Bromberg

Driven

Fueled

Crashed

Raced

UnRaveled (a novella)

Slow Burn

Sweet Ache

Hard Beat

Aced

Find my hand in the darkness
And if we cannot find the light,
We will always make our own.
-*Tyler Knott Gregson*

Prologue

COLTON

"**R**Y?" I CALL HER NAME the minute I clear the top of the stairs. The little note she left me on the counter is in my hand. "Your nothing-but-sheets date night starts now," it reads. Curiosity rules my thoughts and fuels my actions.

Well, that and the image of her naked and waiting for me. My day's been for shit though, so I'm not going to push my luck and expect a miracle like that to turn it around. But a man can sure as fuck hope.

SoMo is playing as I walk onto the upper patio of the house where our original nothing-but-sheets date took place a long-ass time ago. *Sweet Christ.* My feet falter when I find Rylee. She's leaning back on the chaise lounge, dressed in some kind of black lacey thing that I don't pay much attention to because it's see-through enough for me to tell she's naked as sin beneath it. Her hair is piled on top of her head, her lips are bare, and her knees are spread so her feet are on either side of the chair. And I'm distracted momentarily—my eyes searching for a glimpse of the something more between those thighs of hers—before realizing sky-high heels complete the outfit.

Fuck me. I can already feel the spikes of those heels digging into my ass as her legs wrap around me. That's a pain any man can find pleasure in.

"Hey," she says in that raspy voice of hers that calls to my heart, my dick, and every nerve in between. A coy smile plays at the corners of her mouth as her eyes narrow, one foot taps, and eyebrows rise. "I see you got my note. Glad you knew where to find me."

"Baby, I could be deaf and blind and I'd still find you. No way in hell I could forget that night."

"Or that morning," she says, and damn, she's right. It was one helluva morning too. Sleepy sex. Just-woke-up sex. Sunrise sex. I think we tried all of those and then some. And I love the flush that crawls up her cheeks from the memory. My sex-kitten wife greeting me after work in lace and heels is embarrassed. The irony isn't lost on me. I love how she can be this way for me, when I know, despite her confidence, it still unnerves her.

"Definitely a good morning," I agree, as I stare at her. She's always drop-dead gorgeous but there's something new, something different about her tonight, and it has nothing to do with the lace. I can't tell what it is but it's knocked the breath right out of me.

Shit, what am I missing? Panic flickers inside me that I've missed something major. Could it be one of those dates guys have to put in their calendar with five alerts, so they don't forget it? I run through the usual suspects: It's not our anniversary. Not her birthday.

I move to the other shit a guy usually doesn't notice. Her hair's the same color. It must be new lingerie. Is it? Fuck if I know. If it is, can a scrap of lace really change her demeanor?

Damn. I know lingerie changes mine, but that's for a whole different reason.

What else can it be, Donavan? Bite the bullet and just ask. Save yourself the guessing game and the trouble you'll be in if you guess wrong and hurt her feelings. No need to get the hormones she just got back under control—after all those years of fertility shit—to get all out of whack again.

"Something's different about you . . ." I leave the comment open-ended so she can respond.

But of course she doesn't take the bait. I should have known my wife is smarter than that. She'll make me work for the answer, so we just stare at each other in a battle of wills before her smile slowly widens into a full grin.

Give me a clue, Ry.

Nope. She's not going to. I should've guessed as much. Might as well admire the view anyway: cleavage, lace, a whole lotta skin, and thighs I can't wait to be between. The smirk on her face tells me she knows exactly what I'm doing when I finally meet her gaze. When her eyes flicker to the table beside her, she *finally* gives me something to go off.

The table is covered in takeout boxes from our favorite Chinese restaurant. There's a galvanized bucket of ice with some bottlenecks sticking out of it and paper plates and chopsticks piled on the side. Truth be told, I was so busy looking at her, I hadn't even noticed the food.

But now, my stomach growls.

"I got your favorite," she says, fidgeting with the hem of the lace so my eyes are drawn back to the V of her thighs, where it's dark enough I can't see anything. But fuck if it's not from a lack of trying. "I hope you're in the mood for Chinese. I thought we could eat out."

I can't hide the lightning-quick grin that flashes across my face because the type of eating out I'm thinking of has nothing to do with chopsticks. And from the purse of her lips, she knows perfectly well what I'm thinking. And yes, I may be hungry, but I don't really give a flying fuck about food right now because there's the taste of something else I'd rather have on my tongue.

"I know you've been working hard, stressed about the race next week. Sonoma has always been a tough one for you . . . so I thought I'd treat you to a date night with your hot wife," she continues with a lift of her eyebrows, taunting and daring me all at once. Goddamn tease.

"Does my *hot wife* think that when she greets me on the patio in a getup like that, I'll give a rat's ass about the dinner, the cold beer, or the sunset we'll get to enjoy while eating it?" I ask as I cross the distance; the need to have my hands on her growing stronger with each passing second.

"For starters . . . yes."

"I like starters." I reach out and trace the line of her collarbone with my fingertip. After all this time, there is still something so damn sexy about her body moving ever so slightly into my touch, telling me she wants me as badly as I want her. "And I also like dessert . . ." I say, my voice trailing off. The air is thick with sexual tension as I drop to my knees on the chaise between hers. She's crazy if she thinks she's going to greet me like this and not get fucked good and hard before we leave this patio. "But you forgot one very important thing."

Her violet eyes widen as I lean in. "What's that?" she asks, her voice breathless. My every nerve is attuned to the sound of it.

"You forgot to kiss your husband hello." I catch a flash of a smile before she tilts her head back so our lips are in perfect alignment.

"Well, let me correct that right now, *sir*," she says, knowing damn well that term will only turn me on more. Shit. Like that's a hard thing for her to do. It's Rylee, isn't it?

Before I can finish thinking about what more I want her to do while calling me sir, she leans forward and closes the distance between us. And fuck yes, I want all of her right now, but I'll take what I can get. Besides, the way she kisses me is so damn sexy. It's that kind of kiss guys hate to admit they love: the soft and slow kind that causes that ache deep in my balls before it slowly spreads up my spine and tickles the base of my neck. It's the kiss that comes two steps before I lose control and panties are torn because the need to bury myself in her tight, hot pussy is the only desire I have.

When she pulls back to end the kiss, I groan in complaint and fist my hands to prevent myself from reaching out and yanking her against me. I'm ready to say screw the dinner, regardless of how hungry I am.

"Better?" she asks, sass on her lips and seduction in her eyes.

"Hmm . . . there are other parts of me that still need to be welcomed home properly." I fight the grin I want to give her because I love when she's like this. Feisty. Sexy. Mine. Shedding her reserved nature in the way she only does around me.

"What a poor, deprived husband you are," she says, her lips in a sexy pout while her fingers walk up my thigh. I watch the ascent of her hand, my dick definitely wanting those fingers to move faster. "And I promise to welcome all of those parts home properly, but first . . . *you need to eat.*"

Buzzkill. *Seriously?* She thinks she can tempt me with her touch and then stuff an egg roll in my mouth? Does she not know me by now? That when it comes to her I have no restraint? Well, unless of course those restraints are tying her to a bed.

"You tease." I lock eyes on hers the same time I reach out and grab onto her hand. I place it exactly where I want it: my cock. "Why wait? We can have dessert first."

"Nice try, Ace, but dinner's going to get cold." She cups my balls, fingernails scraping ever so softly that the minute my head falls back and the moan falls from my lips, she tugs her hand from my grip. "Let's eat."

"Oh, now that's cold." I laugh. What else can I do? Like always, the woman has me by the balls. I stare at her, smirk on my lips and disbelief in my eyes, as I swing my legs over the edge of the lounge chair. "You can't greet me wearing that and expect me to focus on Kung Pao chicken."

"But it's your favorite," she says, voice playful. With determined actions, she starts to open containers.

I'm hungry all right, but not for Chinese.

I reach out and tug her against me, so her back is to my front, and the feel of her warm body against mine strengthens my resolve. I've decided Chinese food is much better reheated. And if I have any say in the matter, that's exactly what's going to happen to ours.

"I beg to differ. You're my favorite," I murmur against the curve of her shoulder as her curls tickle my cheek and her vanilla scent fills my nose. My let's-always-stick-to-the-schedule wife's body stiffens in resistance at first, but when I press a kiss just beneath her ear in that clothes-immediately-fall-off zone, her body melts into mine and she relaxes. "I want dessert first."

"Rule breaker," she sighs, lacing her fingers with mine on her chest. She's trying to figure out how to rein me in when she should know by now it won't do any good. I always get what I want when it comes to getting my fill of her.

"You wouldn't like me any other way."

"True."

"How about we compromise?"

"Compromise?" she asks, as if she's shocked to hear that word coming from my mouth when discussing sex.

"Yes, it means you give some and I give some."

"I have a feeling what you want to give and what I want to give are two entirely different things," she teases. "Don't forget that I know you, Donavan. I know you like to play dirty—"

"Damn straight I do, especially when it comes to having sex with you."

She just smiles and shakes her head at me. "But I have a plan."

"You always have a plan," I say with an exasperated laugh. "Bet my plan is better."

"Lay it on me," she deadpans and then realizes exactly what she's said. I can feel the laugh she tries to hide vibrate from her back into my chest.

"How about we have sex first and then eat?" I suggest, knowing I'm driving her crazy. Her laugh rings around us, but for the first time since I've been home, I hear something different in her tone.

Before I can give it much thought, she continues.

"Nope. That's not the plan. And definitely not a compromise. Food first, then sex," Rylee says as she shifts away and moves to face me. She crosses her arms over her chest and nods, trying to take a hard line with me.

"I love when you get all demanding." I lean forward with a half-smile on my lips, knowing my comment will get her all riled up.

She narrows her eyes, and I can see her mind working to figure out a way to negotiate so she gets what she wants. And for the life of me, I can't figure out what that is. I've been so absorbed in work—the narrow lead I have in points over Luke Mason going into Sonoma and all of the other shit that goes with it—I've obviously missed something.

"It seems we're at an impasse," she finally says. Her prior confidence, which had momentarily wavered, is back, and I'm more than ready for action.

"Good thing I drive a hard bargain," I say with a quirk of my eyebrows as I glance down at her outfit.

I'll drive more than a bargain, sweetheart.

"Oh, I know you do, Ace, but I think we need to leave it up to the fortune cookies to decide what we do next." Her eyes light up with challenge while I start laughing at how ridiculous that sounds.

"The fortune cookies? What are you talking about?"

"Well . . . you said you wanted dessert first so I'm just trying to compromise," she says with a bat of her eyelashes.

"Not that kind of dessert," I state. There's nothing I can do but shake my head at her and her asinine suggestion, but fuck, I'll take any help I can get to speed up this process so I can slow it down with her. Come to think of it, I'm sure I can twist any of those stupid little fortunes to my benefit. So be it. *Game on, Ryles.* "It's ridiculous, but you planned this so you get to make the rules. Let's just hope those fortunes say you need to have hot monkey sex with your husband."

Her face lights up and her lips curve into a grin. She leans forward and grants me a great view of her cleavage as she starts rummaging through the plastic bag on the table. My eyes shift and focus on the dark pink of her nipples just beneath the sheer fabric, until she starts waving the cookies in front of my eyes with the smuggest of smiles.

She knows exactly what she's doing, and has no shame in playing it up as I work my tongue in my cheek, bide my time, and let her have this moment.

"Only three?" I ask when she sets them on the table in front of us. "How are we going to decide who gets the third one?"

"Since we're learning to compromise . . ." Her voice trails off as she elbows me in the ribs. And just as she starts to pull away, I grab her arm, pull her into me, and press a chaste kiss on her mouth. It's already been way too damn long since I kissed her. She swats me away when I try to slip my tongue between her lips. "Are you trying to sway me for the third cookie, Donavan?"

"Did it work?" A man can always hope.

"Here. You go first," she says, leaving me hanging without an answer as she holds the cookie in front of me by the cellophane. When I take it from her, she shifts so she sits square to me, her bent knee against my thigh, giving me a perfect view of her pussy. In a glance, I can make out the trim strip of her hair down there, and fuck if it doesn't turn me on even more.

Fortune cookie gods, please be kind. Sex is needed.

"Okay. Let's see," I say as I pull the cookie out of the bag and break it with a dramatic flair, praying it's a fortune I can work with. I pull the strip of paper out and shake my head as I read the words. *Really? How fucking perfect is this?*

"What does it say?" she asks as I laugh.

"*It's been a long race, but you've finally crossed the finish line.*" I look up and she seems as amused as I am.

"I'd say that's a fitting fortune," she says, eyes narrowing as she contemplates the words. "I guess the real question is what race are they talking about?"

"*Life?*" I shrug. "Fuck if I know."

She laughs and fidgets with the cookie in her hand. Why does she seem so on edge all of a sudden?

"You're trying to figure out how that gets you sex, and I don't think that helps you out in any way, shape, or form."

Shit. She's right. There's no way to parlay this into me getting sex before food because if I've already crossed the proverbial finish line, it doesn't bode well for me.

"Damn it. That's a food-before-sex one. Don't get cocky, Donavan. I'm primed for a comeback," I say pushing her cookie toward her and taking a bite of mine, hoping this silly game will end soon, but am enjoying myself all at the same time. "Your turn."

The things I do for my wife.

"Okay," she says as she breaks the cookie and stares at her fortune. "It says *your lucky numbers are six, nine, and sixteen.*" She looks up from her fortune, eyes guarded, teeth worrying her bottom lip.

"That's random. Nothing else is on there?" I ask as I grab it from her. Yep. It says exactly that. Must be a misprinted fortune, but hell, I'll take it because I can use it. "Sweet! This is a sex-before-food one because it says your lucky number is six and nine . . . *sixty-nine.* And guess what? I happen to like doing certain things pertaining to that number too . . ."

"You're incorrigible," she says, playfully pushing against my chest, before uncharacteristically fisting her hand in my shirt and pulling me into her. Our faces are inches apart, the heat of her breath is on my lips, but there is something in her expression that stops me from kissing her.

And I never stop myself from kissing her.

"What is it?" I ask. She just shakes her head, trying to blink away the tears welling in her eyes despite the smile on her lips. "Talk to me, Ry. What's wrong?" My hands are cupping her face as I wait for her to explain. Tears make me fucking panic. How'd we get from sexy to flirty to funny to tears?

"I'm being stupid," she says, shaking her head as if that is going to help clear the tears from her eyes. She must sense I'm freaked the fuck out because she pushes against my hands holding her head, and presses her lips to mine. "I love you." Her voice is soft as her lips move against mine, and something about her tone makes my heart beat a bit faster. "Like head-over-heels, butterflies-in-my-stomach kind of love you . . . that's all."

Her words dig deep down into the places that rarely get paid attention to these days: the goddamn abyss where the demons from my childhood live. The ones that used to rule my life until Rylee came along using her fucking perfection and selfless love to help brighten that darkness, and chase away the doubt that occasionally rears its bitch of an ugly head.

I lean back to make sure this woman who means the whole god-damn world to me really is okay. Because if she isn't, I'll do whatever it takes to make sure she is. When she bites her bottom lip, smiles and nods she's fine, I smooth my thumb over the indent her teeth just left, before trying to lighten the suddenly serious moment. "You scared me for a minute. I thought you were upset about the prospect of sixty-nining, and that would mean I'd be in a whole world of hurt with this death-do-us-part thing since I kind of like when I get to do that with you."

"You perform that number exceptionally well, so no, that number stays in play," she says with a cute wink. She bites the inside of her cheek and eyes the third and final cookie in my hand before flicking her gaze back up to mine.

Thank fuck for that, but there is something most definitely off with her. "Here," I say as I hold out the last fortune cookie, hoping to make whatever wrong I've done, right.

"No. You open it." She shoves it back toward me, smile back in place. "It's the tie-breaker."

When I try to make her take the cookie, she just pushes it into my hands and scoots back. "Sex before food, sex before food," I chant and we both chuckle. But my laugh dies off when I read the fortune, and try to make sense of it. "*OVbunEN.*"

What the fuck? I read it again before I look up to meet Ry's eyes. The sight of her—tears welling, that smile so goddamn big on those perfect lips—knocks the breath out of me. And, suddenly, it all clicks into place.

It's like everything is moving in slow motion—thoughts, breath, vision—everything except for my heart. Because it's pounding like a fucking freight train as I glance back down to the jumbled words on the paper, before looking back up to her.

There's no fucking way.

Can't be.

"*Really?*" I ask. I don't even recognize the awed disbelief in my voice as I ask about the one thing I thought we'd never get another chance at again.

The first tear slips over and slides down her cheek as we stare at each other, but this one doesn't make me panic like they usually do.

"*Really,*" she whispers.

Disbelief turns into the best fucking reality. Ever.

OVbunEN.

Bun in the oven.

"You're pregnant?" I can't even believe the words I'm saying as I pull her toward me, and onto my lap.

She can't get the words out to tell me yes so she just nods her head as tears fall, and her arms cling to me. And fuck, her hands digging into my back feel incredible because I don't think I've ever felt closer to her. Not even when I'm in her.

I have one hand on her neck and the other on her lower back. Air's not even welcome in the space between us as we hold on to each other on this patio where so many firsts have happened for us. Telling me here of all places makes perfect fucking sense, now.

My face is buried in the curve of her neck. And if I thought my heart and soul had been lost to her before, I was so fucking wrong it's not even funny. Right now, in this moment, I've never felt more connected to her. My fucking Rylee.

My mind flickers back over the years of agonizing fertility treatments when emotions ran high, and hope always gave way to heartbreaking disappointment. When we finally acknowledged last year that having a baby the traditional way was never going to happen for us, Rylee lost herself for a bit. Fuck yes, it put a strain on our marriage, but it was more devastating for me to watch the woman I love more than my own soul slip away day by day, bit by bit, and not be able to do a goddamn thing about it.

The helpless feelings I had during that time can take a hike.

When I lean back and move my trembling hands to her face, I don't think she's ever been more beautiful than in this moment: eyes alive, lips in a glowing smile, and a tiny part of us growing inside her.

"We're gonna have a baby," she whispers. And although I already know it, hearing her say it causes my breath to catch and my heart to summersault. "June ninth."

Six. Nine.

Fuckin' A.

We finally crossed the finish line we thought we'd never reach.

Chapter One

COLTON

Six months later

"**I** WAS A LITTLE WORRIED when you told me to come over today that you'd lost control of your balls, but this?" Becks asks, as he takes a measured look at the empty beach around us. "This is just what the doctor ordered."

"Where's the faith, brother?" I slide a glance over to him behind my sunglasses. "Can you see me at a baby shower?" I ask. He snorts in response. "I assure you my balls are firmly attached. There is no way in hell I'm setting foot anywhere near the house right now." I mock-shiver at the thought of all those women who'd gladly leave lipstick on my cheek.

"A whole new definition for the estrogen vortex."

"Damn straight." I reach over and tap the neck of my beer against his. "And not in a good way."

"And for that reason alone, I think the baby's a girl," he says with a laugh, causing me to grunt at his logic. "Dude, you've played women for so damn long, it'd be funny as fuck and serve you right to watch one play you for the rest of your life." He holds up his pinkie telling me if we had a little girl, I'll be wrapped around her finger. Fucker's probably right, but I'm not telling him that. Besides, the smarmy grin on his face is wide enough to earn the bottle top I throw at him.

"No one is playing me. That you can be sure of." I tip my bottle to my lips, as Becks laughs long and hard at the words he knows are a lie.

"I don't think you have any idea what's about to hit you, brother."

He's right. I have no fucking clue. Zip. Zero. Zilch. All I know is the closer the due date gets the more I feel like I haven't had enough time to get ready for it. *It?* More like a complete overhaul of our life. Scary fucking shit.

"So, how are you doing with all of this?"

"Shit's getting real," I muse with a slow nod of my head.

"Considering there's a baby shower up at the house right now with women dressing themselves in toilet paper—in some ritual I pray I never understand—and talking about crowning that has nothing to do with the kind a king wears . . . and diapers . . . yeah, it's definitely real. But uh, nice try, Wood. You never answered my question."

"I'm good." *Back off, Daniels.*

"We've known each other how long?" he asks, and I know he's going in for the kill here. I just wish I knew what the fuck he's hunting for, so instead of giving him the answer he already knows, I just concentrate on peeling the label on my beer bottle.

"Pussy," he mutters under his breath. Baiting me. Fueling a fire I'd rather not light.

"What's your bag, Becks? You want to know that this whole baby thing scares the shit out of me? That it's fucking with my head?" I pick up a shell and huck it at a pile of seaweed to the right of me. "Feel better, now?"

I want to shove up and walk down to the water, get the hell away from him, and yet he knows me well enough that if I do, then he's gotten under my skin. Pressed the buttons he's been waiting to push.

How the fuck do I explain that everything already feels the same and so goddamn different, and yet I wouldn't want to change it even if I could? He'd be bringing out the damn straight jacket.

"Me feel better? No." He chuckles, grating on every nerve. "But I think you do." I glare at him from behind my lenses. "Wanna talk about it?"

"No," I snap. Leave the shit I don't want to talk about alone. But the silence eats at me, taunts me to speak. I can trust Becks; I know I can. Yet as the words form, I choke on them. *Man the fuck up, Donavan.* "Yes. Fuck. I don't know."

"Well, that simplifies things," he teases, trying to draw a laugh out of me.

I take my hat off, scrub a hand through my hair, and put it back on to buy some time. "I'm having a kid, Becks. And all of it's scary as shit. Diapers and futures and expectations and . . . I don't know what else, but I'm sure I'm missing a million other things. What the fuck qualifies me to be a dad? Not just any dad, but a good one? I mean, look at my fucked-up childhood. It's all I know. How in the hell do I know when I'm stressed and tired that I'm not going to revert to the only thing I've ever known?" I end the question, my voice almost a shout, and realize everything I just said.

Have another beer, Donavan. You sound like a sap.

Becks laughs. And not just any kind of laugh but a chiding chuckle that scrapes on my nerves like 60-grit sandpaper.

"Thank God! It's about damn time you start acting like you're freaking out because sure as shit I'd be too. Look, no one qualifies to be a good parent. You just kind of learn as you go, mistakes and all." He shrugs. "And as for the last one . . . dude, look how you are with the boys at The House. You'd never hurt them. It's not in your make-up regardless of the fucked-up shit you grew up with."

Hearing his words I nod my head, finding some relief that the shit that's been bouncing around in my head is normal. But my normal and Becks's normal growing up are polar opposites. So while I appreciate the sentiment, it doesn't stop the freight train of fear I'm going to fail epically at this parenting shit. That Rylee will be so head over heels in love with the baby she'll forget me. That I have the same blood running through my veins as my mother who'd had no regard for me. That I have the same blood running through my veins as my father who hadn't stuck around.

"Dude, it's totally normal to be freaked," he says, as I open the cooler and grab another beer to drink away my stupidity. "You'll fuck up sometimes, but that's how it is. There's no manual on how to be a good dad . . . you learn as you go. Kind of like the first time you had sex. Practice makes perfect type of thing."

I laugh. Fucking Becks. He's the only person I know who could compare parenting to sex, and I'd completely understand the parallel. He gets me.

"And sex? *Now that's something* I've practiced a lot."

"By the look of Rylee's belly, I think you finally mastered that skill. So, see? No need to worry. You've got this."

"Damn." The word falls from my mouth as images of earlier today flood my mind. I was supposed to be moving the couch in the great room to make space for the rental tables and chairs being delivered for the shower. Rather, I found myself looking down at Ry's cheeks hollowing out as she sucked me off. The look in her eyes and smirk on her lips as she ran my slick cock up through the V of her cleavage until it met the sweetness of her wet mouth. My balls tighten remembering how her lips looked stretched around me when she teased my tip before sliding it back down again.

"That good, huh?" Becks asks, dragging me from the images of my hot wife.

"Fucking perfection." It's futile to fight the smug grin on my lips.

"So, is it true then?" I glance over to Becks, my beer now stopped halfway to my lips as I wait for him to explain. "That pregnant women are really that horny?"

My eyes flicker back toward the house at our backs. Laughter from the estrogen invasion floats down to us and I nod my head. "Brother, let's just say that voodoo doesn't hold a fucking candle to pregnant pussy."

"No shit?"

"Nympho." I draw the word out.

The look on his face right now—the raised eyebrows, slow nod of his head, slack jaw—is classic. "Damn. Just damn."

"You have *no* idea," I say with a laugh. "Shit. All the guys were warning me about hormones and mood swings, and I'm sitting over here with a cat-ate-the-canary grin on my face because pussy is my friend. Dude, the only pregnancy craving she's having is for my cock, and I'm more than willing to help her out."

"You lucky bastard."

"Don't I know it."

"Aren't you afraid you're going to . . ." His voice trails off but I can hear the amusement in his tone. "Never mind . . ."

"Finish what you were going to say, Daniels."

"Well, I was going to say, aren't you afraid all that sex is going to hurt the baby—poke it in the head or something? But then I forgot you're only about three inches long so there's no need to worry about that." He stifles the chuckle.

"Fucker." It's my go-to comment with him and even with the dig, I can't help but laugh because I wouldn't expect anything less from him. Besides, I could use the distraction since I keep questioning whether I should have made the call to my private investigator, Kelly, this week.

Ball's already rolling. Too late to stop it now.

I know nothing good can come from it. No happy endings to be had in this situation. In fact, I'm sure it'll fuck me up before it makes me better. But maybe, just maybe, I can lay this one last thing to rest. Close this final circle before the baby comes and move on.

Full circles and shit.

At least once this one's linked together; the goddamn ghosts can just chase each other over and over like a hamster on a wheel while I'm putting the pedal to the metal one hundred miles per hour in the opposite direction.

"Dude," Becks says, pulling me from my thoughts, "you need to take advantage of the sex while you can because after the baby comes, you won't be getting any for a while."

"So I've heard," I groan. How I'm going to go from my wife being a nympho to a nun is not lost on me. "Changes, man. They just keep happening. One day I'm single, the next I'm getting married, and now I'm about to have a baby. How the fuck did that happen?" Despite my words, the smile is wide on my face.

"Not sure how you found a woman who's willing to put up with your crap but she deserves a damn medal for it."

"Thanks for the support." I tip my beer his way in a cheers motion.

"Always. That's what I'm here for . . . but with all of these changes happening, I need to ask you, what's gotten under your skin? Something's up with you and I know you well enough to know it's more than what you've just said."

Here we go again. *Let the Becks psych evaluation begin.*

I refuse to look at him, not wanting him to know I'm not okay. That this banter is all a front because my head feels like it's been put in a blender: too much, too goddamn fast, with too many doubts, and too many unknowns. My fucking past that never goes completely away.

Goddamn ghosts.

"Colton?" he goads.

My beer stops midway to my mouth as irritation fires anew and sarcasm becomes my friend. "Are you asking as my crew chief, my best friend, or my shrink?"

"I've got lifetime privileges for two of the three, so does it really matter?"

Fuck. He's got me there. Why is he pushing the goddamn issue?

Does he really want to know the truth? Because I sure as fuck would rather stick my head in the sand. Ignorance is bliss and all that shit.

"I'll get the job done. No worries there," I say way too easily and immediately curse myself because Becks will see right through that response in a heartbeat. I just wonder if he's going to let sleeping dogs lie or if he's going to jingle the leash so they come out to play.

"Ah . . ." he says, drawing the sound out. "But you forget, I do worry. It's my job. You've got a lot of shit going on, and I need your head straight before you even board a plane to the Grand Prix."

"Jesus Christ, Becks. Always worried about the track. Well, there's other shit to life besides the goddamn track!" I snap at him, pissed he knows just what to say to set me off and at the same time hating that he's right.

Baited hook? Meet line and sinker.

Motherfucker. You'd think by now I'd be immune to Becks pushing buttons, and yet every damn time I react on cue like a puppet.

"No worries. My head will be just fine," I say, trying to gain some traction. "You satisfied?"

"You think I care about the fucking track, Donavan? You think racing rules my every thought? No. Not hardly. What does though is having to pick up a phone and call your wife who's nine months pregnant and tell her I put you in a car knowing you had a fucked-up head, that you crashed and died because you were distracted and couldn't focus on the task at hand. Now that? That's what I worry about . . . so you can take out whatever it is you don't want me to know and tell me I'm a selfish asshole for thinking about racing. What I really want to know is that your head is in the goddamn game enough that I don't have to watch some medic put you in a fucking body bag because you can't focus and won't tell anyone why. Call me selfish, call me whatever the fuck you want to . . . talk to me, don't talk to me . . . *Christ* . . . just make sure you're good to go so that doesn't happen." And then in perfect Beckett fashion, he ends his tirade as quick as he starts it.

Silence returns. Eats at me. Pulls from me the truth I don't want to confess.

"I'm trying to find my dad." Fuck. Where did that come from? I wasn't going to tell anyone until I had something solid—like concrete-barrier solid—and yet there I go spilling secrets like a leaky faucet.

Wanting to see his reaction, I glance his way from behind my mirrored lenses; he takes a deep breath and nods his head twice as he digests what I've just said.

"I'm not going to pretend I understand the why behind this . . . but man, aren't some things better left for dead?" There's understanding in his tone, but at the same time, there's no way he can understand. No one can. My shoes have walked through the proverbial Valley of Death more times than I care to count. Maybe I need to go there one more time to finally shake the shadow so I can move forward without it hanging over my head.

"That's just it though—he's always been a loose end. I need to tie it up, cut the strings for good, and never look back." I take a long tug on my beer and try to wash away the bitter taste thinking of him leaves. "It's a shot in the dark. Kelly probably won't find him. And if he does? Maybe just knowing where he is will be enough. Maybe not." I sigh. Feeling more stupid for calling Kelly now than I did before. "Fuck it. Forget I said anything."

"No can do. You said it. I heard it. At least that explains what's crawled up your ass lately. Does Ry know?"

"There's nothing to tell yet." I ignore the twinge of guilt. "She's already stressed about the new kid at work and the baby . . . The last thing I need is for her to worry about me."

"That's what you've got me for."

"Exactly," I say with a definitive nod of my head.

"And your pops? What does he say about all of this?"

Guilt: the gift that keeps on giving.

"Same thing. I'll tell him if something comes of it. Besides . . .

he's my dad, if I need to do something, he always supports me." *And yet if that's the case, why aren't you telling him?*

"Exactly," Becks says, and the simple word validates my guilt.

Why in the world am I looking for the piece of shit who never wanted me when I have a man who took me in battered and broken and never looked back?

Exactly.

Thoughts. Doubts. Questions. All three circle the other. But only Kelly will be able to confirm if I'll ever find the answers.

"I promise my head will be clear when I hit the track." It's the only thing I can say to my best friend. My fucked-up way of apologizing.

He nods his head and adjusts the bill of his ball cap. "Well, I hope you find what you're looking for, brother, but I kind of think you already have." When I glance over to him, he tips the green neck of his bottle toward the deck over my shoulder. Confused, I follow his line of sight and look up to see Rylee standing at the railing talking to guests.

Our eyes lock. That goddamn sucker punch of emotion hits me like a battering ram, because for a man who thought he'd never feel anything, she makes me feel everything. The whole fucking gamut.

I remember to breathe. That pang of desire just as strong now as that first time I saw her. But there's so much more that goes with it now: needs, wants, tomorrows, yesterdays, and every fucking thing in between.

Becks is most definitely right.

My father's not the endgame. Just another ghost to exorcise from my soul.

I'm a lucky fucker because I *have* found what I never knew I was looking for. Thank fuck she's looking right back at me.

Chapter Two

Rylee

THE FEAR STILL HOLDS MY heart hostage.

I try to push it down, not think about it, and go about my day to day with work, the boys, and Colton, but every once in a while it rules my thoughts. It doesn't matter that I'm seven months along now. The worry this will all be taken away from me like it has the two times before still sits in the back of my mind with each twinge of my belly or ache in my hips.

And so here I sit in the nursery amid piles of onesies, diapers, and receiving blankets afraid to open a single thing in fear I'll jinx this. That if I open one package of clothes, pre-wash one load of laundry, put sheets on the mattress of the bassinet, I'll cause my long-awaited dream of motherhood to come crashing down.

The rocking chair is safe though. I can sit here and close my eyes and feel the baby move, enjoy the ripples across my hardened belly that allow me to breathe a little easier each and every time I feel a kick. I can rest my hands on my abdomen and know that he or she is a fighter, is healthy, and can't wait for me to hold him or her in my arms. I can sit here and feel the love surging through me for this baby

Colton and I made together, and know without a doubt, this perfect little being will only cement and make stronger the love we feel for one another.

And I try to maintain this feeling to will away the worry when I rise from the rocking chair and run my hand over the mattress on the crib. I can't believe this is really happening, that in less than three months' time, there will be this new addition to our life and everything and nothing will change all at once.

Moments in time. How easily we shift from one role to the next and never question the butterfly effect of these transitions. How will this one event segue into the next? Or will it?

A baby. *Our baby.* Even though the life is growing inside me, and I can feel him or her move every now and again, I'm still staggered by the reality of it.

Carefully, I sink to my knees to sort through the baby gifts stacked on the floor. By the looks of the stacks, our friends and family are excited to meet and spoil Baby Donavan. I reach out and pick up a fuzzy yellow blanket, my smile automatic as I hold it up to my cheek to feel its softness.

"Does a baby really need all this stuff?" Colton's voice startles me. He's leaning with his shoulder against the doorjamb, thumbs hooked in the pockets of his shorts. Every inch of his toned, tanned chest all the way down to that V of muscles, calls to the pregnancy hormones that have been ruling my sex drive these past few months.

And even without the hormones, I'm sure I'd still be staring because there is no shortage of want on my end when it comes to him. Just the sight of him gets my blood humming, my heart racing, and makes my soul content.

I take a moment to appreciate my handsome husband. My gaze scrapes over every inch of him before lifting to take in that cocky smirk on his lips that tells me he knows exactly what I'm thinking. And when I lock onto his emerald irises, the amusement I expect to be there isn't. Instead Colton's eyes are a mixture of guarded emotion

I can't quite read. It's reminiscent of those first months of dating, when secrets were kept, and I hate the feeling of unease that tickles the back of my neck from its reappearance.

Forcing aside the innate need within me to ask and fix, I tell myself if something's wrong, he'll tell me when he's ready. I shrug off the niggling worry. It's probably just pre-baby jitters. He's been handling this all so much better than I thought he would, but at the same time the past few weeks he's withdrawn some. And while that concerns me, I know he's bound to have some fears and reservations like most impending parents.

"I'm not sure if it's all needed. It's definitely a lot of stuff for one little baby." I finally answer as I glance at the piles of gifts around me.

"You're gorgeous."

The unexpected comment has my eyes flashing up to meet his and love to swell in my chest. Disbelieving he can see me as beautiful when I feel like a beached whale, I let the soft laugh fall from my mouth as I shift onto my butt, brace my hands behind me for support, and stretch out my legs. "Thanks, but I don't really think that a huge stomach and toes swollen like sausages qualifies me for the *gorgeous* category."

"Well, in that case, maybe just the beautiful category," he teases with a flash of a grin as he enters the room. He looks around, picks up a checkered flag baby quilt that causes his eyebrows to lift in amusement before he moves to where I'm sitting.

"Hmm," I murmur, nowhere near agreeing with the beautiful consensus. But when I look back up to meet his gaze, I can see that when he looks at me, beautiful is what he sees, and I'll take it, because when a man sees you at what you feel is your worst and thinks you're at your best, you don't question it.

"You're working too hard, Ry," he says as he lowers himself to the floor in front of me. I force myself not to sigh at the refrain, but it's the one thing we've argued about lately, his want for me to take maternity leave. "You need to stop doing so much. Let others help you."

I look down to the blanket in my hands, hating he's right and that he can see how much I'm struggling with ceding control. "I know, but there's just so much to do before the baby comes that only I can do. With the new project coming online and Auggie struggling at The House and . . ." My voice trails off thinking of the newest addition to the brood and how much attention he needs that I'm not going to be able to give him. Everything on my invisible task list is screaming at me for it to be done—like yesterday, done—and there are not enough hours in the day. Becoming overwhelmed by the mere thought, I blow out a breath as tears sting the back of my eyes. My internal struggle about letting people down resurfaces; I already feel I'm dropping the ball, and I haven't even started maternity leave.

"Breathe, Ry. I know your type-A personality wants to have all your ducks in a row," he says, "but it's not possible. Other people can do things. It might not be just how you want it, but at least it's help. And if it doesn't get done, it will still be there after BIRT comes."

"Colton!"

"What's wrong with BIRT? Baby In Rylee's Tummy," he states innocently, knowing damn well he's just trying to irritate me. *Or make me smile.*

"Stop calling him that." I smack a hand on his leg as he laughs out loud, and he grabs my hand before I can pull it away.

"Him? Did you just say *him*?" Our long-running debate about the baby's unknown gender just became front and center. He pulls my arm, and I move forward at the same time as he leans in. He presses a tender kiss to my lips that sends a shockwave of desire way down to my core. I can feel his lips curve into a smile as they remain against mine.

"Yes, I said *he* . . . but that's just a pronoun," I murmur, loving being close to him. The past couple days he's felt so far away. I've just chalked it up to him feeling as overwhelmed as me but for different reasons: the points lead he's barely hanging onto with the Grand Prix coming up next month, the baby shower today with over fifty women filling his sole private place on earth, and the impending changes in general with the baby's birth. It's a lot for any man to adjust to, let alone a man who never expected to have most of them in his life.

Is he still okay with all this? Saying he's ready to have a baby and really meaning it are two completely different things. I know he has no regrets—wants our baby as much as I do—yet I can't seem to quell my concern about how he'll adjust to the inevitable changes to our lives.

He holds my hand idly in his lap. The need to connect with him and ease my worry rides shotgun beside my want and desire *for* him. And the impulse to sate both is just too great to not give in to, so I graze my fingertips across the fabric covering his dick and love his quick intake of air.

"Are you trying to distract me, Ryles?"

"Never," I tease, my mind now fixated on the temptation just beneath my fingers.

"We were talking about pronouns, remember? *He* is just a pronoun?" he asks trying to get back to the topic at hand. He swears I should know the gender because after all, I'm the one carrying the baby. *Men.*

And while I have a fifty-fifty chance of being right, I know it's a boy. Has to be. The little boy with dark hair and green eyes who has filled my recent dreams. A freckled nose that scrunches up when he causes mischief and melts my heart just like his daddy. But that's all an assumption, mother's intuition, and is not something I'm going to verbalize.

"Uh-uh." His fingers tighten on my arm as I try to cop another feel of him, distract him from becoming fixated on a pronoun that may or may not be right. "*Pronouns.*"

"Well, if you want to talk grammar . . . I seem to remember that wet and willing are adjectives," I murmur, knowing damn well he'll be able to read both mischief and desire in my eyes. *Two can play this distraction game, Ace.*

He throws his head back and laughs, and I know he has caught my reference to the words he teased me with the very first night we had sex on Sex. He pulls me even closer this time and doesn't hold back when his lips meet mine. We kiss like we haven't seen each other in weeks. Need mixes with greed. Passion collides with want. My body vibrates with desperation because how can it not when he can push every one of my libido buttons with such a simple connection?

His kiss is like gravity, pulling at every part of me until I want to cling to him and hold on so I'm never taken away. Our tongues meet, demanding at first, before the kiss morphs into a tender reflection of love and desire. His free hand comes up to cup the side of my face, his thumb running over my cheek as he ends the kiss despite my protests. And at first I take the look in his eyes as one of amusement over me wanting some form of physicality with him *yet again*, but when he speaks, I know it's because he is seeing right through my attempts.

Damn him. He knows me too well.

"Did you forget I'm the master of the game of distraction, Ryles?" He lifts his eyebrows and a cocky, lopsided grin pulls up one corner of his mouth. "I see what you're trying to do here."

"Are you turning down sex?"

"Oh baby, I'll never turn down sex with you . . . I just want to get back to pronouns." He grants me a lightning-fast grin as he cuffs both of my hands and laces our fingers, presumably to prevent mine from wandering and tempting him further. For a man who doesn't want to pick a name, he sure seems set on clarifying his parts of speech.

He wants pronouns? I'll give him pronouns, all right.

"Like stick *it* in *me*, type of pronouns?"

He shakes his head and chuckles. "Not those specifically, no."

"You'd rather talk grammar than please your wife?"

That flash of a grin is back. "No, I'd rather discuss why you hate the name BIRT."

"You're exasperating. And a tease," I say, knowing I'll get the sex eventually if the tenting of his shorts is any indication of his state of mind. He may be resisting now, but I know sex will win out in the end. It always does.

"So you think the baby is a boy?" he asks, eyes wide, voice excited. And the lighthearted tone tugs on my heartstrings.

"Does it matter what I think, considering you won't even discuss names with me? I mean we're getting close to the wire here, Donavan."

"I love when you *Donavan* me," he says then squeezes my hand when I try to pull away. "C'mon, Ryles, fly by the seat of your pants. Let the moment rule us. Live dangerously," says the racecar driver to the social worker. All I can do is sigh in exasperation.

"Our baby's name is permanent. It's not a decision to be made on the spur of the moment." I still can't believe he's sticking to his plan of naming the baby after we meet him or her. I thought this strategy was a joke the first time he brought it up but now know different.

"Look, you have names you like and I have names I like. Why don't we just wait and see what BIRT looks like when he or she is born and then we'll both say them and go from there?" I narrow my eyes at him, desperate to know the names he prefers or if he likes any of the ones I've thrown out at him over the past few months. His silence on the topic is killing me. "Live dangerously with me, Ry." He chuckles as I shake my head, trying to feign irritation and hide my own smile.

"I already do live dangerously. I married you, *remember*?"

"Oh baby, I remember. No man is going to forget the things you did to me this morning," he says with a wicked gleam in his eyes.

I blush immediately, momentarily embarrassed by my very needy *and very horny* self, that didn't resist him despite knowing the caterers would be arriving at any moment. And of course the thought of his eyes heavy with desire and his cock thick and hard in my mouth makes my body ache to have him *again*. This time for my pleasure though, and I don't think he'd have a problem delivering on that demand.

I have to force the image from my mind because I think he accomplished exactly what he was hoping for with the comment.

"Now look who's trying to distract whom. BIRT's name?" I arch an eyebrow as his laughter rings around us. The man is relentless. "What if I don't like any of the names you pick and you don't like any of the names I like?"

"Well, that's easy." He shrugs. "I'll distract you."

"That must be the word of the day. Nice try, but that's not easy to do when it comes to something this important . . . oh God, that feels good," I moan as he takes my foot into his lap and starts rubbing its instep. Everything I have been overdoing the past few days between work and getting ready for the shower has manifested in the size of my swollen feet, so this feels like absolute Heaven. I sag against the wall at my back, eyes closing as I welcome the pleasure he's giving me.

Screw chocolate, forget sex with Colton, and forgo paradise, because *this*, a foot rub after being on your feet all day when you're pregnant, is absolute nirvana. He uses his adept fingers to push and press and rub to put me in a pleasure coma.

I lift my head and open my eyes to find him looking at me with a huge grin on his face. "What?"

"See?" He shrugs. "Distraction. All it takes is changing the subject, shifting gears somehow, and I can get what I want."

He thinks he's so crafty that I'll fall for it every time, but when it comes to Colton Donavan, I learned a long time ago that he likes to play dirty to get what he wants. Good thing I've learned from the master because I know all his tricks and will put them to good use against him.

"Magic hands," I murmur breathlessly, as his thumb presses against a pressure point that feels like it mainlines an electric current to the delta of my thighs.

"Your feet are so swollen." His head is down as his fingers rub their way up to my calf bringing me much more joy than they should.

"There are other things on me that are swollen," I deadpan. And the reaction I want from him is almost instantaneous when his eyes flash up and hands still momentarily. That lopsided grin of his—part arrogant bad boy, part eager lover—graces his lips as he holds my gaze.

"That so?" He tries to feign nonchalance and yet his reaction already told me he's willing to play my game. Time to see how quick he will take the bait because this woman is desperate for more than just his touch on my instep.

"Mm-hmm. Swollen means super sensitive. And sensitive means intense." I run my hands over my breasts that are spilling out of the cami tank top. His eyes follow and take notice of my nipples hardening from my touch against the thin fabric. I may have a huge belly, can't see my ankles, and would never have thought in a million years I'd be seducing my husband at seven months pregnant, but the way he looks at me—with a predatory gleam, not to mention the hitch in his breath—tells me he doesn't care. He finds me sexy. He still wants me. And that provides the confidence I need to give me the wherewithal to keep going.

"Intense is good."

"Intense is incredible," I all but moan as our eyes lock in a playful war of wills over who is going to make the first move. "Swollen means tight. Responsive. Multi—"

"I think I need to inspect," he says as he shifts onto his knees, his gaze never leaving mine. His hands slide up my thighs, feather-light touches laced with intent, moving my loose knit skirt with them as they go.

"If you inspect, you must try out the goods," I taunt. His touch tests my resolve, the sight of his tanned chest and scent of cocoa butter in his sunscreen bending my restraint.

"Demanding, are we?" He stops and lifts his eyebrows, a smile playing at the corners of his mouth.

"Haven't had any complaints yet," I toss back at him as he leans forward and presses a whisper of a kiss to my mouth. When he starts to pull away, I move with him because I want more. Always do when it comes to him.

Mirth flashes through his eyes because he knows he's caught me in a catch-all: trying to be the seductress when all I want is him, in me, on me, doing something to me, and very soon.

"Do you want something?" he asks, as his fingers continue their tantalizing ascent to the apex of my thighs. I love the hiss he emits when his thumbs brush over the swollen flesh, discovering I'd taken my panties off when I changed into more comfy clothes after the shower. His touch falters, a small show of the desire and need to control warring within him before he moves his fingers back down toward my knees.

"You." Why beat around the bush when that sweet ache deep in my lower belly is already flashing with heat and the one and only person I know that can sate it is sitting before me?

"*Me?*" He dips his head down and presses a kiss to first my left and then my right thigh. From beneath his thick lashes, he looks up at me then slowly wets his bottom lip. "Is that why you're not wearing any panties? What specifically do you want from me?"

His hands begin to move again, seducing me with his contact and mesmerizing me with the knowledge of what he's withholding.

My laugh is low and laced with suggestion. "Well, it's not just what I want from you per se but more where exactly I want you that's important."

"Do you want me here?" he asks as the pads of his fingers graze ever so softly over the seam of my sex. Even though I try to stay still, I arch my hips in a nonverbal begging motion.

And then he removes his fingers.

"Don't tease me, Donavan." My body aches on the verge of pain for him to touch me again. His chuckle fills the silence of the room as he leans forward, his eyes on mine, and then uses his tongue to trace around the outline of my nipple through the fabric. Just enough to let me know what it feels like but not enough to let me succumb to the sensation of it.

"Oh, I'm not teasing, Donavan," he says back, mimicking me with mirth in his eyes and purpose in his touch. "I'm just getting the lay of the land."

"I'm pretty sure the lay of the land is that you need to fuck me soon."

I love the lightning-fast grin that flashes over his features and the slight stutter in his movement from hearing me demand like this. He tsk-tsks with a shake of his head and another taunting tease of his fingertips.

"Rest assured, I intend to fuck you, sweetheart, but I'm all about equal opportunity."

My muscles clench at the first part of his statement while I'm trying to figure out just what he means by the last part, because now is not the time to be witty. Now is the time to give the hormone-riddled woman exactly what she wants.

"Equal opportunity?" I sigh in frustration and then gasp in surprise when Colton uses his knees to press my legs a little farther apart and at the same slides his fingers between the lips of my sex. If it were physically possible, my body sags in relief and tenses at the same time because I've finally gotten his touch and now I just want more.

"Yep," he says as he lowers his head, the warm heat of his mouth closing over my clit his fingers have exposed. My head lolls back against the wall as a ripple of pleasure washes over my body. My hands are in his hair, fingers gripping, and hips lifting to tell him I want more from him. Cool air hits when his mouth releases the skin he's sucking on. My hands try to keep him in the cradle of my thighs and a chuckle falls from his mouth, the reverberation heightening the nerves he's just brought to the surface. "Equal parts pleasure here," he says, dipping his head down again so his tongue slides up and down the cleft of my sex . . . and here."

An incoherent moan falls from my mouth as Colton slides his fingers inside me and curves them to hit the nerves within. And my God . . . thoughts escape me and sensation overwhelms me as the combination of his fingers and tongue begin to satisfy my insatiable need for sex.

He creates a rhythm all his own: the slide of his tongue, the skillful movement of fingers inside me, the soft sucking on my clit. My body reacts: muscles clench, back arches, hands hold tight as he causes the ebb and flow of sensations needed to climax.

"C'mon, Ry," he murmurs. The heat of his breath against my slick skin makes me writhe and buck into his hand. "Come for me so I can fuck you when you're still coming. Coat my cock with your cum while its sweet taste is fresh on my tongue."

His words are like that last lick of gasoline thrown onto a smoldering fire. Incendiary. Provocative. Inevitable.

I give into the moment—the feeling, the *everything* with him—and crash over the edge into that free fall of white-hot heat. It sears up my spine, out to my fingers and toes to gain strength, before slamming back into my core where he's continuing to push my climax to beyond bearable. Intense is too tame of a word for what he's made me feel.

Every. Time. The simple thought flickers how he gives me nothing less than his best every single time.

My muscles are so damn tight—my mind so lost in that post-orgasmic wash of pleasure—and my nails are digging so hard into his shoulders that I'm not sure how he escapes the confine of my thighs. But when he does, with my arousal still glistening on his mouth and hunger burning in his eyes, I can't help but stare at him and thank every damn lucky star in the sky that he's mine.

Because Colton Donavan on any day is drop-dead handsome, but when his waist is framed between my thighs, his chest bared so every inch of bronzed skin is shadowed for effect, and the look in his eyes says he's going to take me as he sees fit—no holds barred—he's indescribable.

Rogue. Rebel. Reckless.

The words flit through my mind, memories colliding from another place, another time, but still so fitting all this time later as he undoes his shorts and pulls his dick out. It's thick and hard, ready to claim, and hell if my mouth doesn't water at the sight, my damn hormones kicking into overdrive again despite having just come.

"Colton." His name on my lips is a plea and a demand all at the same time that causes his arrogant smirk to return.

The crest of his dick presses against my pleasure. His tongue darts out to wet his bottom lip. His eyes flash to mine one last time before he looks to where he's slowly pushing into me.

"Fuck," he moans. "I love watching your pussy stretch around me. Love how it pulls tight when you take me in."

His words hit my ears but my body is completely focused on him filling me, stretching me, drawing pleasure with each and every tilt of his hips. So many sensations and emotions flush through my body. All I can do is close my eyes, lay my head back, and lose myself in the onslaught of desire I know is coming.

He's gentle yet demanding, drawing all the way out before taking his hand and guiding his cock so its head can rub right where I need it most. My nerves are so sensitized that when I shift my hips, my eyes open in shock at how damn good it feels.

And the look on his face tells me he knows my reaction well enough to know he's hit the spot perfectly. So much so he's determined to do it again. Pull me to the surface from my post-orgasmic state so I can momentarily catch my breath before he shifts into high gear and pulls me back under the next wave of pleasure.

He begins to do just that, picking up the pace, looking down at me with concentration in his eyes and pleasure etching the lines of his face. The muscles in his neck and shoulders are taut, and his mouth is pulled tight as he pushes us both beyond the edge of reason.

My pulse speeds up but my mind slows down. The sting of the

carpet into my back. The press of his fingers into my thighs. The feeling of oblivion as he swells inside me. My name on his lips. The sight of him coming undone.

"Colton," I cry out, my back arching as I let his action dictate my every reaction. Anything else I say is incoherent because my second orgasm is always so much stronger. This one is no exception. I fumble for something to hold onto and instantly Colton's hands find mine, lacing our fingers as I succumb to the sensations he's drawn from me.

Now that he knows I've had mine, he begins to chase his own release. And even though I'm still coming down from my high, it's impossible to drag my eyes away from him: teeth biting into his bottom lip, hips bucking harder into me, and his head falling back, lost in his own bliss.

"Goddamn it, Ry . . ." he moans brokenly, the sexiest sound in the world to me because *I put it there*. When he empties himself into me, he stills—his hands, his hips, his breath—lost in the wash of pleasure. And then slowly he lifts his head up as he unlaces our fingers, and that satisfied grin turns up the corners of his mouth as his eyes meet mine. "Damn, woman."

"Mm," I murmur, groggy and sated and completely enamored with him.

"Intense enough for you?"

Like he has to ask. "I think I'll keep you."

He laughs, deep and rich, as he withdraws from me and crawls over my legs so he can lean over me on his hands. He looks at me long and hard, so many things in his eyes I can't decipher. The one I can is the one that's most important. It's the look that tells me I am his whole world and hell if I'm going to argue with that. What sane woman would? He's the total package: sexy, thoughtful, generous, mischievous, and most importantly, all mine. Love isn't a strong enough word for what I feel for him.

"I don't think you get a choice in that matter."

Chapter Three

Rylee

"**B**AXTER'S NOT GOING TO BE very happy with you."
I look up from the dog at my feet—lying on her back spread-eagle—with a smile on my face and know my dog is definitely not going to be happy when I come home with the scent of another on me.

"Hey bud. You're right," I say to Zander as he leads the charge of the middle school boys through the front door. "How was school today, guys?"

My question is greeted with an array of *fine, good, boring,* from the four of them as their attention shifts to Racer who has scrambled up from my feet to meet her boys. I love seeing how excited they all are to lavish attention on the newest member of the house.

Rubbing a hand over my belly, I lean against the counter and watch them sitting on the floor with the ball of fur. They've all enjoyed taking on the responsibility of having a pet better than I thought. Thankfully. I just hope she does her job as a therapy dog and helps out the latest boy, Auggie, assimilate into our madness.

I glance over to where he's coloring quietly at the table. His head is down, but I can see his eyes angling over to watch the boys and their camaraderie from beneath his shock of sandy-blond hair. He takes in their teasing, the elbowing of each other, their comfort, and I can see him desperate to make a connection. So many things hold him back. He wants to be a part of the crew, but the PTSD, along with a plethora of other issues living in a violent and abusive home ensued—things that skated just beneath the radar of social services for so very long—hasn't provided him the coping skills needed to assimilate. When your parents keep you locked in a dog crate for hours, if not days on end, as a punishment without any outside social interaction for year upon year, knowing how to fit in just isn't something you can do.

To say it breaks my heart is an understatement. The therapists suggested we bring in a therapy dog for comfort, with the hope Racer will eventually create the opening for him to have a connection with the other boys.

And of course, Auggie's part of the reason I'm so stressed about the lack of time before the baby is due. I desperately want to see him connect with someone here as much as he has with me before I go on maternity leave. If he doesn't, then I worry he'll feel as confined as he was in his parents' self-imposed prison at home.

The baby moves beneath my hand, my constant reminder of how lucky my child is going to be to never have to even remotely experience any of these horrors.

"Hey Auggie? Do you want a snack before I leave for the night?" He looks over to me, a ghost of a smile on his sweet lips as he nods ever so slightly. The sight of a smile, regardless of how faint, gives me an inch of hope in this marathon we're running together. "Oreos and milk?"

His smile becomes more surefooted at the same time Scooter pipes up, "Dude, I'm all over that!" *Perfect.* Just what I wanted to happen. A table of boys eating cookies and milk together. All different walks of life, making their own path together.

"Dude," I mimic him with a grin on my face, "put your backpacks away and it'll be waiting for you."

"Rad," one of them says as my phone alerts a text. As I reach into the pantry, I glance over to my cell sitting on the counter and see it's from Colton. I'm not sure what he needs but my shift ends in fifteen minutes and this opportunity with all the boys together is way too important to break up the moment.

"Okay," I say, as I pull out two packages of Oreos and cups. "Snacks get doled out in the order of who tells me something good about their day."

"Pit and the peak!" Ricky says with exasperation. He likes to pretend he's too old for this tradition we started a few years ago, but I secretly know he enjoys it.

"Yep." I start filling the plastic cups as Kyle passes out napkins.

"Auggie goes first," Zander says, surprising me. I think both Auggie and I startle at the comment but for completely different reasons. Zander slides me a glance that says he knows exactly what he's doing. It may be almost six years since he was in similar shoes, but he remembers the anxiety like it was yesterday and is trying to help Auggie in the only way he knows how.

My heart swells with pride at the kind heart he has, and I'm reminded of how very far he's come. And the knowledge that Zander could overcome and thrive encourages my hopes that Auggie will be able to have the same success.

"Z's right. Auggie gets to go first," I say.

And the best part about it is that in a house constantly full of bickering, they just showed it to be one weighted more heavily with love and compassion.

"Hello?" I answer the phone as I crawl along the highway, traffic moving at a snail's pace in the last few miles to the house. I'm so exhausted. Presuming it's Colton calling me back, I answer on the Bluetooth's first ring, not waiting for caller ID to pop up on the Range Rover's GPS screen. My calls have been going straight to his voicemail since I've left work so when I answer, I fully expect to hear the lecture right off the bat about how I need to take my maternity leave now. And I'm lucky because as vocal as he is on it, he understands the reasons behind why I haven't. I have a feeling the compassion is waning the more out of breath I am and the more swollen my feet become.

That's exactly why I've been telling him I'm perfectly fine to go to my checkups without him so he doesn't hear Dr. Steele tell me I need to start taking it easier. And maybe that's why I answer right away, so he thinks everything is okay instead of the actual throbbing in my rapidly swelling toes and ankles.

"Rylee Donavan?"

"Yes. Who's this?" I try to place the female voice on the other end of the line but come up empty.

"This is Casey at TMZ and—"

"How'd you get my number?" I ask, cutting off the tabloid reporter, my guard instantly up.

"We'd like to know if the tip we received is true and how you're dealing with it all?"

Curiosity and unease meld into a ball of discord. I stutter a response I know I shouldn't even ask. "Wh . . . what are you talking about?"

"The video proving your husband's infidelity."

And it's like my ears don't hear what she says over the roar of disbelief and flash of hurt that burns in my chest. "Video?" And I reiterate the word more to myself, lost in my own world of upset than to her.

"The sex tape."

I know it's not possible but I gasp and stop breathing all at the same time. I disconnect the call instantly. My heart drops into the pit of my stomach. I struggle to catch my breath. Luckily I'm turning off on Broadbeach because my thoughts are so scattered and the adrenaline is pumping so fast that my hands are shaking.

Normally I don't let bullshit like this get to me—after all I am married to a man who was once known as one of the racing world's top playboys.

Colton wouldn't do that to me. He loves me. He loves us. We're each other's world.

And yet despite knowing this, something about the phone call unnerves me. Staggers me. Resonates in my ears when it shouldn't.

How did they have my number? What video is she talking about?

I'm too close to the house to call and even if I wanted to, I don't think my fingers are steady enough to push the right buttons.

Calm down, Rylee. It's all I can tell myself because this isn't the first rumor that has been spread about Colton and whatever hot woman he's been in the same vicinity as. But it's the first time I've been sought out to give a response before I knew anything about the *scandal.*

When the gates on the driveway shut behind me, I sigh, equal parts relief and anxiety, and scramble out of the car as fast as my pregnant body can. When Sammy opens the front door before I even put my key in the lock, I know way more than a purported rumor from TMZ is going on.

Even worse, he just nods at me without saying a word and steps outside closing the door behind him so Colton and I are alone. Not a good sign at all.

"Colton?" I call his name as I drop my purse on the table before following the sound of his voice in the office. So many things run through my head as I cross the short distance and none of them are welcome. I'm ready to barrel into the room and demand answers regarding the rumored cheating that the *rational* part of my brain knows must be wrong.

"They're fucking crazy if they think I'm going to believe them," Colton asserts, fist pounding against the desk. My feet falter and my demands die on my lips when I see him: back to me, broad shoulders framed against the window, head hung down, body visibly tense. The scene beyond him of the ocean is serene but in just the instant I've been in the room, I know Colton is anything but.

The sight of him physically upset like this isn't normal. It throws me for a second and makes me fear the phone call I received might just be real. The uncertainty I felt in the car comes back with a vengeance, vibrating through my body in a flash of heat and wave of dizziness. The words I was determined to say when I saw Colton are lost to worry as I try to wrap my head around the sudden assault to my perfectly imperfect world.

"I don't care what you think you're seeing, CJ, it's not fucking possible. Zip. Zero. Zilch." Anger vibrates off him and slams around the room's walls as he listens to his lawyer on the other end of the line. Leaning against the doorjamb, I attempt to steady myself, my emotions caught in turmoil as I try to read into the conversation without knowing any additional information. "I don't need a fucking road map . . . What you don't get though is that I've never even put myself in the situation where someone could even imply such bull-shit!"

He hangs his head and blows out a breath as CJ talks and as much as I want him to get off the phone and tell me what in the hell is going on, I also want him to carry on his conversation without him knowing I'm home. I *need* to hear the non-sugarcoated version I'm sure he'll give me. Hearing Colton without a filter will allow me to believe the extensive explanations I'm going to need to hear the minute he gets off the phone.

"You're not fucking listening to me," he grits out exasperated. "They can Photoshop it however they want. It's NOT true! Guys like me only get one chance at this shit. I got my chance. I got my Rylee.

Why in the hell would I fuck that up?" His words are barked out with spite to prove whatever point he's making and yet they weave around my heart and squeeze tight because the way he says it—like it's the simplest truth in the world—only helps fortify so many things: my belief in how my husband feels about me, that the rumor is pure bullshit on a slow gossip news day, I'm going to have to thicken my skin to weather whatever storm is bearing down on us.

"Fuckin' A! Do you . . .?" Colton's words trail off as he turns around and sees me leaning against the doorjamb, one hand on my belly, the other covering my mouth. Our eyes lock, uncertainty passing between us as my name falls from his mouth in a hushed whisper. "Ry . . ." And even if I didn't know whatever was going on was bad, the etched lines on his face and taut carriage confirmed it. "I want to see the entire thing. Not just the ten-second snippet you have. If they want their money, CJ, they'll show me their bargaining chip now, won't they?" He walks toward me, gaze never wavering despite the worry it holds.

When he reaches me, he pulls me into him without saying another word and wraps his arms around my shoulders, burying his head in the curve of my neck despite the phone still at his ear.

And this show of emotion freaks me out. My heart thunders. My stomach churns. My eyes close as I absorb his familiarity and try to hold on to it as best as I can. Because if he's worried, then I know I'm going to be freaked.

"I'm at my computer. I'll be waiting for the email." I hear the clatter of his iPhone as he tosses it on the table beside us moments before he gathers me tighter into him. My hands are on his back, my lips against his neck, his all-familiar scent in my nose, and yet it suddenly feels like so very much is different.

We stand like this for several moments despite the anxiety rioting through my soul as I let him breathe me in because I fear what he's going to say when he lets go. Is he going to apologize? Confess to something I don't want to hear that will shatter our ideal little world?

"Just tell me," I finally breathe out, my chest aching with worry and fear. His body tenses as he grabs my shoulders and leans back to look at me, the reporter's words repeating in my mind.

"Ry . . ." My name falls from his mouth again and as much as I want to beg him to say something besides it, I'm also almost afraid to. I welcome the silence but hope for some noise. "Someone is claiming to have a video."

"So it's true," I state, trying to keep my voice void of emotion as tears immediately sting the backs of my eyes. And when I'm afraid they're going to leak over, I close my eyes and shake my head, as if I can rid my mind of the bad dream I feel is sucking us in its clutches.

"What's true?" he demands.

"The phone call." It's all I say, purposely trying to draw a reaction from him so he has to explain what's going on.

"Phone call? What in the fucking hell are you talking about, Ry?" He takes a step back and runs a hand through his hair as he leans a hip against the desk behind him.

"I think you need to be the one to start explaining, Colton, because I'm a little freaked out. Something's going on here and I should have found out from you . . . not from TMZ calling to ask me if I'd like to make a statement about the rumored video proving my husband cheated on me!" I yell, hands flailing, voice escalating. The disbelief I want to feel doesn't feel so certain anymore when his jaw falls lax and hands grip the edges of the desk.

He blinks his eyes a few times, hurt I don't understand flashing in them, as he digests what I've said before shaking his head. "Fucking Christ, Ry. You actually believed I'd cheat on you?" The shock on his face staggers me—unfettered disbelief I'd even consider his infidelity to be true—and knocks me from my momentary lapse. I can see the man in front of me, feel his love for me, and know I'm crazy for even considering it.

"I didn't know what to think," I whisper, my confession hanging in the air between us. And then his words to CJ hit my ears again, and I know I was wrong to even let the idea find any kind of purchase in my conscience. I shift so I can sit down, my body as tired as my head all of the sudden.

"Someone is trying to blackmail us."

"*What*?" I'd laugh at the ludicrous claim if I weren't sitting here right now, sick to my stomach. "Who?"

Colton shakes his head. "CJ doesn't know who for sure. He, she, they are hiding behind a lawyer right now." So many questions race through my mind as I wait for him to continue.

"Blackmail is illegal, isn't it?" I ask, wondering how someone could be hiding behind a lawyer and do this.

Colton emits a self-deprecating laugh that gives me no comfort and only results in making me feel stupid for asking. "Money in exchange for an item they claim is mine is considered a transaction," he states using his fingers to make quotation marks over the last word, which leads me to believe this is something he has argued about with CJ. Just as I'm about to ask more, he says something that makes my ears buzz and changes the direction of my thoughts. "They say they have a video of me having sex with another woman."

And even though I knew as much from my short-lived conversation with TMZ, I still suck in an audible breath when I hear him say the words and automatically start shaking my head as I try to reject them. Everything I know I should say or ask is stuck in my throat because as much as I believe him, why is dread sifting through my body weighing every part of me down?

Dread. Curiosity. Unease. All three swirl in an eddy of discord as I try to process this.

I can tell my lack of a response makes Colton worry. He steps forward and then steps back. Antsy and irritated. "Do you doubt me?" he asks, voice rising in pitch with each word. I don't answer him. I'm too inside my own head, too overwhelmed by every single thing about this.

"No." I mouth the word, unable to find my voice.

"Don't you ever doubt my love for you!" I jump as his voice thunders through the room; his palm hits the desk to reinforce the words. And I can see he immediately regrets the reaction by the fisting of his hands and how his head falls back to try and rein in his anger. When he lifts his head back up, he meets my eyes with a determination I've never seen before. "Ry, I swear on the life of this baby that I have not so much as touched, kissed, or anythinged another woman, let alone put myself in a position to be videotaped having sex with them."

I force a swallow down my throat. I believe him. Have no doubt. And yet . . . "I want to see it," I say with more certainty than I feel.

"You walked in just as the full video came across to CJ. He's emailing it to me." He scrunches his nose momentarily and in that instant I can see how worried he is about this. And not about the existence of a tape, but more so what this is going to do to me. To us. "You don't need to see it."

"Don't tell me what I need to do, Colton. If you didn't do anything, then it shouldn't be an issue, right?" I slowly stand and walk over to the desk so I can sit at the computer while Colton remains with his hips against the desk and head hung down, no doubt preparing himself for whatever we're about to watch.

I click alive the computer screen, and my breath hitches immediately when I see the email sitting in the inbox from CJ. The subject line of "Video" taunts me as I wait for Colton to come over.

"Please, Ry," he begs. "I don't know what's going to be on here . . . and you're not going to be able to unsee it once you do. I know for a fact it's not me but at the same time, whatever they have on tape, I don't even want that image in your head so you doubt me." He hangs his head down again before looking back up to me with determined clarity. "I would never cheat on you, Ry. *Never.*"

I worry my wedding ring around my finger, knowing what he's saying to be true but at the same time, needing to see for myself. My only response is to move the cursor and open the email. The fortifying breath he draws in disrupts the silence in the room and rides shotgun to the sound of my own pulse thundering like a drum in my ears.

I double-click the file.

Snow fills the screen, gray, white, and black grain that holds my attention hostage. I will for it to clear and *not* want it to clear all at the same time. And when it finally does, it takes me a second to believe what I'm seeing.

"Oh fuck!" falls from Colton's mouth the exact same time as the thought flickers through my mind.

The image is dark, grainy, but *the what* and *the where* are unmistakable. The memory zooms back in high definition color in my mind as I watch the one person that is unmistakably clear in the video, Colton, unknowingly look up toward the camera as he holds a woman's hips and drives into her over and over.

Not just any woman though.

One in a dress, which is pulled up over her hips and bunched down around her waist, so she is completely exposed.

And even though the video is black and white, I know the dress is red. Fire-engine red to be exact.

Because the woman is me.

In the parking garage.

On the hood of Sex.

And in case I wasn't sure, the concrete wall of the parking garage is painted with the hotel's name. There is no mistaking the where or the what. *Or the whom.*

Both of us lean in closer out of reflex as we watch the video unfold, second by second, thrust after thrust, and I'm not sure if I'm more mesmerized or horrified at first before the realization sets in with what exactly this means. There is no audio on the security cam's footage so the office weighs heavy with the silence until the clip goes dark and the video ends.

We're both stunned, unsure what to say, not certain what to do. I feel like a thousand-pound weight has been lifted from my shoulders because Colton was right: he wasn't cheating on me.

That weight has been replaced with an anvil teetering on the edge of a cliff, waiting to fall off and harm anyone in its path.

And we're standing in that damn path.

Someone has footage of Colton and me having sex.

I think even if I watched the video replay one hundred times I still wouldn't believe it.

"They're on crack if they think I'm going to pay them three million dollars for that," Colton says, breaking the silence, voice resolute, and staggering me in more ways than just one. Dumbfounded with my hand over my mouth, I force myself to look away from the black square on the computer screen and over to him.

And if I thought he was angry before, he's livid now.

"What did you just say?" I finally stutter, not sure if I'm more shocked at the three million dollar figure or that he doesn't care that a video of us having sex has been made.

"You heard me," he growls at the walls. He shoves off from where he's sitting atop the desk and starts pacing the room. I need to understand what he means, but I'll wait him out . . . wait for him to temper his anger. There's no way in hell we're not paying this. That's me. And him. Naked. Having sex. For anyone to watch. Oh my God!

He doesn't answer me, just keeps muttering to himself as he paces, working something out in his head. I'd much rather he shares than remain silent. After a few minutes, he waltzes back to the computer and frames his body above mine as he reaches over the back of the chair. "Watch it again."

"Did you call the police? Did you—"

"That's futile," he snaps at me. "It's not our property. Wasn't stolen from us or our house so it's not ours to claim."

"But it's us!" I reiterate my voice breaking and eyes widening.

"Play it again," he demands, in a voice I've only ever heard when he's at work. It's the do-not-fuck-with-me tone that tells whoever he's dealing with to do as he says without question.

I hesitate, confused as to why he wants to watch it again, prompting him to move his hand over mine on the mouse and click the play button. Our images spring to life once more and again I'm transfixed. It's like a car accident: I know I need to look away and yet I'm mesmerized. As much as I'm appalled, there is something about watching the two of us together, stepping outside of the moment, and seeing how fluidly we move in sync. Undeniable proof we were meant to be together.

"CJ believes it," he murmurs, more talking to himself than to me. I try to follow his train of thought, but replaying it has caused deafening panic to strike again. Every single breath—each thought—takes an enormous amount of effort. *How are we going to fix this?* "So will everyone else."

Exactly, I want to scream at him. Everyone will believe it's us. How could they not?

Colton turns my chair around so I'm facing him. "Do you trust me?" he asks, and I'm already shaking my head no because *that* gleam in his eye means he's about to tell me something I don't want to hear. And God yes, I trust him, but this isn't a normal, "can you trust me?" type of question. "CJ watched this. He *believed* what they said."

"Huh?" I'm not following him.

"Don't you get it, Ry? They have no clue the woman is *you*. Your face . . . it's not identifiable in one single frame."

"But every other part of me is," I shriek, as the sudden knowledge of where he's going with this forms in my head. He can't be serious. My stomach knots, forcing me to focus on breathing for a moment as my eyes look deep into his and question what I see there.

"Watch it again."

"I don't want to watch it again," I shout, shrugging his hands off my shoulders and not liking what he's suggesting one bit. "And I refuse to entertain whatever idea is in your head." Panic returns with a vengeance.

"Hear me out, Ry," he says, getting down to eye level with me as

I avert my eyes to where my hands are resting on my belly. "Please look at me." I take a moment before I raise my eyes and I'm glad that when I do, he seems as conflicted as I feel. "Do you really think that if we pay off whoever this person is they won't keep an extra tape for insurance? That they won't get their money and *accidentally* let the tape end up on the Internet?"

"Colton . . ."

"No, Ry. You just told me TMZ called you. They've already contacted media and planted a seed. Do you actually think they'd do that if they'd planned on taking the money and then disappearing with the video for good? Something is off here, and I can't figure out what the fuck it is."

His comments weigh down the atmosphere around us and it takes everything I have to blink, to breathe, to think, because this just can't be happening. He's right. The fact they've already contacted a tabloid tells me it's something more . . . and hell if I know what the more is or why the video is surfacing right now.

"I've been wracking my brain, have some ideas, but that's beside the point, right now. The point is they want money, want to make us panic . . . want to tear us apart right when we're about to be happiest we've ever been with the baby coming." His eyes soften momentarily as he looks down to where my hands rest before looking back up to me with more resolve than I want him to have. "Think about it, Ry," he urges, and I hate that he makes so much sense.

He can tell my mind is spinning and my ears are tuning him out. I grit my teeth and fight a wave of nausea. "What exactly are you thinking?"

His chest rises as he takes in a deep breath, and I fear he's preparing himself for the backlash from whatever he has to say. "It's not as bad as it looks."

"What's not? The video? The situation? The idea in your head?" My voice rises with each word.

"All of it," he states.

"Are you fucking kidding me?" I ask, eyes wide with disbelief. "There's a video of you screwing me on the hood of a Ferrari!"

"No. There's a video of me fucking *somebody* on the hood of the Ferrari. Your face is never shown. The only people who know that dress is red are you and me. The only people who know you hold your hands over your tits when you're about to come, or that you reach out and scratch your nails over my hip like that when I come, are you and me. No. One. Else."

I just keep shaking my head, eyes blinking, pulse pounding in my ears. "You're out of your goddamn mind." I throw my hands up, helpless and astounded. "So easy for you to suggest when the video is so dark you can barely see your dick but you sure as hell can see all of me, laid out and spread-eagle."

"Listen to me, Ry. I couldn't care less if my dick was on display or not."

"Stupid me. I forgot you're used to being seen by the masses. After all, you were the playboy once upon a time. You had your dick on display for more women than I care to count." I take a dig at him, wanting him to be as upset as I am over this whole thing.

"That's exactly my point. I'm the notorious playboy. The player. People expect this shit from me."

"But they're going to think you cheated on me," I say, completely dumbfounded by the turn of events. And while I may have learned not to care what people think, I do care about that.

"I don't give a fuck what people think about me . . . you know that. The only person that matters is you. You know I didn't cheat on you—"

"This is a bad idea, Colton."

"I'm not paying some bastard three mil so he or she can turn around and release the tape anyway. I don't bow down to threats, Ry. Never have. Never will." We stare at each other in silence and his words sink in, take hold, and as much as I want to reject the idea immediately, I fear that what he says is true.

"But what about your parents? My parents? The baby?" I say, each passing moment adding more panicked dread to my voice. "There's going to be a video out there, documented for them to google and know about." I have to stop. A gasp falls from my lips because as the baby moves into my ribs my breath doesn't come fast enough.

"Calm down, Ry. Please." He sits on his knees again and pulls me against him. I close my eyes, attempt to wish this all away, yet know there is no way that's possible. "We'll tell our family it's not what they think. That it's Photoshopped. We'll have Chase issue a press release to the media. It'll say something like we were sent this tape that's been tampered with. That we were being blackmailed for a ridiculous amount of money and we won't entertain paying for it because my image has been cut and pasted into it somehow, and it's not true."

I push him away and just stare at him, seeing the logic but at the same time, that's *us* on there. Him and me. "No one's going to believe it, Colton. You know better than anyone the press is going to run with the story and report it in the worst light possible. Sensationalize it. Try to document how distraught I am. Dig up old photos of you with other women, plaster them all over the pages to show that's how you are."

"Who cares?"

"I do," I scream, causing his head to startle while I stare at him with blank, disbelieving eyes. Surely it's not possible that what I'm thinking and what he's saying is the same thing. "I'd care that people think you are fucking around behind my back. I'd hate that people would think I'm this meek woman holding on to her famous husband because she has this new baby and can't get any better so she stays." The first tear falls over my cheek and I shove it away, hating that it fell and despising I just admitted that.

"No! All that matters is what you and I know," he emphasizes but it falls on deaf ears. "The press isn't going to—"

"That's what they do."

"Rylee—"

"Don't *Rylee* me! Do you want some sick fuck somewhere jacking off to images of you and me having sex? I mean, seriously? Doesn't that make your stomach turn, Colton? I'm your wife. Not some whore you slept with and discarded for God's sake." I push myself out of the chair needing to get away from him and get some perspective. He's talking crazy, and right now, I have enough crazy in my life.

I move through the house, his frustrated sigh behind me, and walk onto the patio overlooking the beach below. Alone, I can think without him clouding my thoughts. I can breathe without him and his logic that I fear is one hundred percent correct in how things will go if we do pay whomever it is off.

We're in a no-win situation. Damned if we do, damned if we don't.

I sink down into a chair on the edge of the patio and pet Baxter's head when he sidles up next to me. My mind flashes back to those images that are etched in my mind with crystal-clear precision. Good images. Personal images. Intimate images. The fight in the garden after hearing Tawny's comments in the bathroom. How I'd gone from thinking I was losing Colton to finding out he was willing to try and have a relationship with me. The exhilaration that had ruled my thoughts as we'd entered the elevator. The disbelief as we'd walked toward the red Ferrari and the knowledge of what Colton had wanted to do with me on it. My desire overwhelming my senses, giving into the emotion and having sex with Colton on the hood, cementing that bond we shared and feeling on top of the world.

All the while, a camera had been capturing our moment. And someone behind that camera had been watching.

My skin crawls. The ball of acid sits in my stomach, the acrid taste of incredulity on my tongue.

This is so screwed up I don't even know what to think, where to go, what to do. Of course, the one time I stepped out of my perfectly modest box look what happened. And as much as I want to be pissed at Colton because the whole sex on the hood of the car thing was his idea, I can't. I didn't say no. I went along with the idea, was persuaded by passion, got lost in the moment, and had loved every minute of it, simply because it was with Colton.

Who would have thought almost six years later, this would come back to haunt us?

"Hey," Colton says from behind me and I don't respond because I don't even know what to say or think anymore. "I'm sorry."

"Who would do this to us, Colton? Why all this time later? It doesn't make sense." And even after I say the words, the justified spite that's still within me after all of these years comes back with a vengeance when I think of the one person who would want to ruin our happiness. "Tawny."

Colton blinks his eyes slowly, telling me he already has considered this. "I don't think so."

"What?" My back's up, ire already boiling in my blood as he bites the inside of his cheek and holds my stare. "How dare you defend her," I accuse, even when I know he hasn't and that I'm being completely irrational.

"I'm not defending her," he says in that placating tone of his that is like oil to my water. "Tawny isn't stupid enough to cross that line. She may be a vindictive cunt, but she wouldn't cross me. Not after the paperwork I made her sign when I fired her. The consequences of fucking with us again were laid out quite candidly, and I assure you she's not that stupid . . ."

"Oh." It's all I can say. His eyes hold mine. I had no clue that he'd done that. "But she knew we were there that night, knew what we were doing. When we came back up I told her about . . ." My voice trails off as the memory flashes through my mind. My immediate thought when I saw her of *here comes the rain to fuck with my parade,* and how victorious I felt telling her that Colton and I had just fucked on the hood of Sex. How for the first time, I was confident in where we stood in our relationship.

Oh my God. Did I bring this upon us?

"No, Ry. This isn't on you. Please," he begs, because he knows me well enough to know what I'm thinking. "I've crossed a lot of people in my life. In racing. In dating. In business. *By surviving.* It could be any one of the many."

"Who else knew about that night then? Parking garage staff? Sammy?" I go through the names out loud and see the anger flicker in his eyes when I mention his most-trusted person.

"Sammy had to sign the same agreement Tawny did plus about twenty more. It wasn't him." And I know he hates the narrowing of my eyes because he explains, "Not him, Ry. If he wanted to blackmail me, he has much better dirt on me than that."

A flash of anger fires through me. It must be the volatile emotions and uncertainty weaving around us because I can't remember the last time Colton's past playboy status bugged me. Yet *that* simple comment causes me to more than bristle at the thought. "Charming," I say, sarcasm rich in my voice.

"It's no secret. I used to live a little, Rylee. I won't apologize for who I was but rather be thankful for the man you helped make me. *Understood?*" The bite in his tone hits me where intended, and I feel guilt for my snarky comment. Our gazes connect. So many emotions swim in his eyes and it hits me just how upset he is. He probably feels he brought all of this upon us somehow and yet his first thought was to protect me. How could I have doubted him? I worry my bottom lip through my teeth and answer him with a nod of my head.

"Who else then? The valet or parking staff? Security?"

"Mm. Not likely. Not after all this time. It feels too timed, you know?" I murmur in agreement. "My gut instinct says it's Eddie or someone connected to him. It's a long shot but there could be a possibility there . . . I just don't know." He blows out a breath and scrubs a hand over his face, and the sound of the chafe against his stubble fills the silence. "I've already called Kelly to try and sniff him out but I doubt we'll find anything."

His eyes will me to believe him but my heart says this is on me. Somehow, someway, Tawny told someone along the way and now, whether she knows it or not, she's going to get her one last dig. I can't look at him, can't face him, knowing that our one night of pleasure— the catalyst of so very much for us—is now going to come back and haunt us.

"Fuck me!" he says, eyes widening as he holds his finger up in the just-one-minute motion before jogging into the house. By the time I've followed him into the office, he already has the video replaying and is pointing at the screen. "Right there," he shouts, a strained smile spreading on his lips. "Give me my phone," he demands, his face lighting up while I'm left in the dark, handing him his cell.

I watch him as he flips through his phone for something, my eyes drawn to the screen to the frozen image of his hands gripping my hips in all their naked glory.

"Look at the date," he says, excitement woven in his tone as he looks down at the calendar app on his phone. I look at the timestamp on the video and realize it has been tampered with because the date is wrong. It says last year, not six years ago. I was so busy getting lost in the frantic feeling of watching our images on the screen that I never thought to look at the timestamp. "That's the date of the Iowa race last year."

"Okay." I draw the word out, ideas forming of where he's going with this line of thought.

"The exact date, Ry. If we don't pay him and the jackass releases the tape, we have proof the video was tampered with. There is no way I can be in that parking garage in Los Angeles on that date because I was *in* the goddamn race. And we will have proof at the office that we flew home the next day."

I put my hands on both sides of my head as I try to take this in. "But Colton . . . that is *US*," I say, incredulity in my voice.

"I know," he says, not realizing how much the thought bugs me. "But whoever has this tape, either tampered with it to make the dates more recent to try to cause problems, or this is the one they found . . . I don't know, but I know we have everything we need to prove that's not me if they were to release it to the press."

I drop down into a seat opposite him, my head spinning, my chest hurting, as I try to figure out the best plan of attack. It seems to me like this is an ambush with no way to escape. "There is no way out of this," I murmur.

"I'm trying to find one that doesn't affect you," he says, and I can hear the self-deprecation in his voice.

"I know . . . I'm just having a hard time wrapping my head around it all. I just need time to think this through without the shock warping my reason, you know?"

"I do," he says, walking over to stand in front of me, and leaning down so we're eye to eye.

"Did they give you a time frame in which to respond?" I ask, not even believing that question has to leave my mouth.

"Seventy-two hours."

Reaching up, I run my hands over the stubble of his jaw to weave in the hair at the base of his neck. I can't believe how much he has grown as a person over our time together. He's learned to make good choices, has great instincts, and has always kept my best interests in mind. Why should I doubt he's trying to do that right now as well?

Trust me, his eyes beg.

Trust him, my reason tells me.

"Let's see what Kelly finds out . . . then I'll trust your judgment on what you think we should do from there, but I've got to tell you that doing nothing doesn't sit well with me."

He nods his head and leans in, brushing a soft kiss to my lips. When he steps back, his eyes are serious and intense. "I'll never let anything happen to you."

I close my eyes and lean my forehead against his.

Every knight has a weak link in their armor.

I fear I just might be his.

Chapter Four

Rylee

"THE BABY'S GROWTH IS ON par. The heartbeat is strong and within normal range . . . but I'm a little concerned about your blood pressure, Rylee," Dr. Steele says, as she looks back down at the chart in her hand.

"I know. It's just . . . we had something unexpected happen last night and it's still kind of crazy and . . ." I stop and blow a breath out, trying to calm myself yet again and not worry about what Colton says he'll take care of, but know is futile. I can't rid my mind of the grainy images or the fear that this is all going to spiral out of control. "Sorry." I shake my head to blink away the threatening tears.

"It's okay. Sometimes things can be a bit overwhelming with your first baby coming. A lot of women get stressed over feeling their life is going to change so drastically and they can no longer do it all." She reaches out and squeezes my forearm. "I'm inclined to put you on modified bed rest at this point."

"No!" The word falls out in a shocked gasp, my eyes flying up to meet the concern in hers as my blood pressure starts to elevate again.

"Don't think I don't know that's why Colton hasn't been coming in. We both know he wants you off your feet, and you fear if he hears me suggest it, he'll pressure you." The stern warning in her voice is unmistakable. And there's no use denying it, so I just nod my head and worry my hands together. "I'll trust you'll use good judgment or I'll be forced to put you on bed rest for the remainder of your pregnancy. The longer the baby is in utero, the better all around for him or her. Delivering early because of preeclampsia isn't an option I want. Try to make Colton deal with whatever situation came up last night so you're not involved and your blood pressure can stay on an even keel."

"I will," I say, knowing I can't. Her intelligent eyes assess the truthfulness of my statement. She nods her head. I guess I was believable.

"Okay. We'll see you in two weeks then. Take care," she says as she pats me on the shoulder before walking out of the examination room.

My drive home is consumed by unwanted thoughts of last night, when I shouldn't be thinking about it. Doctor's orders. But the images of Colton and me in the garage keep coming back to mind. The real ones. The ones I remember. Not the cheapened black and white version, which seems so classless, but the ones that will forever be etched in my subconscious because they meant so very much to me. I blow out a breath, still not believing how a night that was the spark of so many good things for us has now come back in such a malevolent way.

Driving onto Broadbeach Road, I'm so preoccupied with what I'm going to tell Colton about the doctor's visit that when I turn the bend in the street leading to our driveway, I'm shocked to see the melee; the road clogged with paparazzi. As I pull closer I notice two of the big dogs—Laine Cartwright, Denton Massey—and I immediately know something is going on. Through closed windows I hear words like "video" and statements of "how does it feel?" The baseless hope I had that it was something completely different than the video vanishes instantly.

The assholes released the tape.

My first thought is that Colton told them to fuck off and die without telling me. My next thought is he wouldn't do that without telling me. He promised he'd see what Kelly learned before making any decisions.

My heart drops as I do my best to keep my head down while I drive through the gates. Memories flood back to the last time the entrance to our house looked like this. Tawny had been involved that time so doesn't it fit that she'd be involved this time too? But at the same time, it's been six years. Why now? Why this? What's the damn purpose behind it?

Nothing makes sense and the simple fact is driving me crazy.

My hands are shaking by the time I put the Range Rover in park. And as much as I want to bolt out of the car and find out what the hell is going on, I've learned to wait until the gates close at my back before I open the door so the vultures can't get a shot they can sell. Once they do and I'm protected from sight, Sammy is already at my door opening it.

"Sammy?"

"Rylee," he says with a nod of his head and an aversion of his eyes, ignoring my questioning look. My feet falter on the short distance to the front door when it hits me. If the video has been released, Sammy knows who is on that tape. He arranged the car to be where it was that night. He's seen me naked. And having sex.

Oh fuck.

And when I stop, he stops, only ratcheting up my embarrassment. When he places his hand softly on my lower back to help usher me to the door, I realize just how bad the situation is. He's shielding my body just in case someone has managed to get me in their long-range lens.

This time I'm glad when he opens the front door for me and then steps outside because I can't look him in the eyes. I'm mortified with embarrassment but at least he'll be the only person who will know. I drop my purse on the table and go in search of Colton.

He's not in the office or kitchen, and I'm surprised when I find him upstairs on the upper patio, elbows resting on his knees, glass of amber liquid in one hand, phone to his ear with the other, and his head hung down in concentration.

"We were obviously played, CJ. Fucking full-court press without a goddamn ball." The resignation in his voice causes the hair on my arms to stand on end because why does he sound so defeated when he figured this was going to happen in the first place? That the ass-hole was going to release the tape anyway? "I know, but . . . fuck this is a clusterfuck. I didn't see this coming. Not from a million miles away." He pauses as CJ says whatever he's saying. "There is no con-trolling it. Don't you get that?" he shouts. By the shake of his head, he obviously disagrees with what is being said. "This conversation is done before I say something I'm going to regret and that you don't deserve."

He drops the phone on the chair next to him and without even looking up, downs the rest of the alcohol, meeting my eyes in a fleet-ing glance before concentrating back on the glass he's just emptied. "I'm assuming you didn't get my zillion texts?" he asks, irritated and agitated.

"I was at the doctor." *Oh shit. I was so stressed about how I was going to relay Dr. Steele's warning to Colton, I completely forgot to turn my ringer back on.* "Sorry," I say, cautiously stepping onto the patio. "What's going on, Colton?" I ask, although by his conversation with CJ, I already know.

He scrubs a hand over his face and when I get a little closer to him, something about his movements tells me he's a little buzzed. And I hate that he can't look me in the eye.

"The fuckers released the video," he says, words mirroring the thoughts I had when I saw paparazzi outside. The grimace on his face only serves to heighten my sense of dread.

"Okay," I say with a slow nod. "Well, you were right then." What else can I say?

The low chuckle he emits is anything but amused, and I will him to look at me so I can see what he's thinking. But he won't. Instead he just purses his lips, eyes focused on the bottle of Jack next to him, and pours himself another drink.

"But I was so very wrong." The words hang between us as he slowly raises his eyes to meet mine. And the look in them—absolute and utter apology mixed with regret and concern—causes more than just feelings of dread. Something is so very wrong.

"What do you mean?"

"They never wanted the money." Another long pull on the whiskey and the fact he never even winces tells me he's had more than a few already. "Nope. Not even close." He shakes his head when all I want to do is shake the answer out of him as the silence stretches. "In fact," he says as he raises his glass toward me, "they one-upped us."

"What do you mean they one-upped us?" The teeter-totter of uncertainty we are standing on starts to crash without a stopping point.

"They reeled me in, Ry, like a fucking fish on a hook. Doctored the time stamp like they knew I'd notice it. Made me think that was the only video of that night . . ." His voice draws off as he finally meets my eyes. "But there was one more. Another angle."

And that simple statement hijacks my breath and makes my heart thunder. "Another angle?" My voice is barely a whisper.

"Fuckin' A straight," he barks out, his self-deprecating laugh back that sounds equal parts sinister and lost hope.

"What the fuck do you mean, Colton?" I ask, my own mind running a million miles per hour now. I'm scared, worried, uncertain, and it all comes through in the words. *Another angle?* What do paparazzi know out front that I don't?

"Sit down," he orders, as he reaches out to grab my hand and tries to make me.

"*Don't!*" I warn him as I shrug out of his grip, letting the single word mean so many things. Don't coddle me. Don't bullshit me. Don't tell me to calm down because I'm not an idiot. I know something is very wrong here.

His eyes hold mine while the silence that feels like hours stretches between us, unnerving me more and more with each and every second that passes. He starts to speak a few times and stops; the words he wants to use not coming to him.

"Just tell me," I implore.

He closes his eyes momentarily before running a hand through his hair and taking a long swallow of his drink. I wrack my brain to remember the last time I saw him this stressed. It's been so long that I feel completely out of practice in what to say or how to soothe him.

"They played me. Knew I was going to say 'fuck them' and not pay. They never wanted the money, Ry," he says. Even though I'm not completely following him, I'm also mentally begging him to get to the point because I need to know why he's this upset. "Nope. They wanted to prove what an arrogant son of a bitch I am. Prove that even when I do what I think is best for my family, I still can't fucking protect you."

"What's on the tape, Colton?"

"Close-ups. Your face. Your body. Us together. The correct date," he says so quietly, it takes me a second to realize what he is actually saying.

"No!" I shout. He reaches out for me but I step back. The pressure in my chest mounts and the buzzing in my head grows louder.

"Ry . . ." My name is a plea on his lips and even though I hear it, I can't respond. My discordant thoughts are colliding together like a kaleidoscope—fractured images of unfinished thoughts that overwhelm me and confuse me all at once. "How was I supposed to know?"

The emotion in his voice pulls on every single one inside me, and yet I'm not sure which one to hold on to for a reaction. I want to rage and scream while at the same time I want to run and hide and pretend I didn't hear a thing.

I brace my hands on the patio railing; my eyes focus on the tranquility of the beach below, but all I feel inside is a dissonant storm of turmoil. "There's no mistaking it's me?" I ask, hoping against hope he's going to tell me what I need to hear.

"There are close-ups of us getting off the elevator and walking toward the car. Of you during," he says, voice empty, because how else can he possibly sound, "of us leaving after."

I press the heel of my hand on my breastbone, the pressure mounting steadily as I try to fathom how the situation he swore to me was under control is more like a tornado about to touch down.

And then it hits me. I've been so dumbfounded listening to him and trying to get what is wrong out of him that it didn't compute to me the real reason paparazzi are outside. It's not just because it was a sex tape where they thought the Prince of Racing was cheating on his do-good wife. No. Not in the least. They are out there circling like sharks with chum in the water because they've seen the tape where the Prince is actually fucking said wife on the hood of a car.

Oh. My. God.

I have a sex tape. That's been made public.

Oh. Shit.

Even through his whiskey-fogged mind, Colton must sense it's all clicked for me because when I turn around to face him, a deep exhale falls from his mouth. He watches me warily, possibly wondering if I'm going to rage and scream or go into my no-nonsense, let's-fix-this business mode.

"How bad?" It's all I can say, the only question I can think to voice.

"I already have Chase on it."

"That's not what I asked." His response gives me all I need to know though. If his publicity rep is already responding, that means it's public. Like majorly public. Like it's beyond controlling, public.

"How bad, Colton?" His chuckle returns in response. I start to pace one way then stop and forget what I was doing. I can't focus. "How is this even . . .?" I can hope, although the dread I feel already tells me what the answer is. The anger festers but is held at bay by disbelief. "Like viral bad?"

"The public loves their celebrity sex tapes," he says, sarcasm thick in his voice and the look I've learned to hate on his face. The one I've seen so many times during our fertility journey that says there's nothing he can do to make it better besides put one foot in front of the other and try to put this all behind us. And that's not what I want to see right now. This is the last thing I need.

I want to dig my heels in instead of putting one foot in front of the other.

His eyes, usually so full of life, are deadly serious. I just shake my head back and forth as he starts to speak because I don't want to listen any more and yet need to hear everything.

"I have our lawyers on this, Ry. We'll find out—"

"Does it matter, Colton? Does it?" I throw my hands up, my body vibrating with anger, my soul hiding in embarrassment. "It's not like CJ is going to be able to get it taken down from the Internet. Because that's what you're not telling me, right? That's why you won't answer me when I ask how bad it is because you're afraid to say that a video of us having sex is being uploaded left and right to computers all over the goddamn place and there's not a fucking thing we can do about it."

I feel violated in so many ways right now, and not just because I'm naked. But more so because someone took an intimate, meaningful moment between him and me and exploited it. Demeaned it. Made it sleazy.

Made us sleazy.

This is not some sex scandal. *It. Is. Us.* A married couple. We're not cheating on each other. We're not into some weird taboo sex. Loving each other to the point where the outside world faded away and we became caught up in each other was our only fault.

"Please calm down, Ry. It's not good for the baby."

"Calm down? Are you kidding me? *THIS* isn't good for the baby. Not in the goddamn least," I say as I try to control the anger that's raging out of control. "You're the revered playboy who has lived your life in the public eye. Shit like this is good for your popularity, right? I mean this may elevate you to rock-star status with your groupies. *But. Not. Me!*" I scream as the shock finally gives way to anger. And I know I'm being mean and irrational but I don't care because this isn't fair.

"Ry . . . C'mon. That's not—"

"Not fair?" I yell, finishing his words that mirror my thoughts. "You want to know what's not fair, Colton? What this is going to do to me. I'm the good girl who works for a non-profit with little boys who look up to me. How am I going to explain this to them? *Fuck.* I'm the face of a company who asks for donations to fund our projects. So when you want to talk about fair, think about how in the hell this is going to affect me."

I have to move to abate my anger, the fire in my veins reflected in the aimless and erratic direction of my feet as I move from the doorway to the railing and then back to the doorway. Colton stands there watching me without saying a word. "Oh look, Bob, let's give money to Rylee Donavan. She's the class act who spread her legs and taped it for the world to see. Maybe we can ask her to do a video for us while she's at it because that'd sure as fuck raise some money for the organization."

"Rylee!" Colton barks out my name, trying to get me to stop my misplaced rage, but I don't care because it's not his professionalism at stake. *It's mine.* One I've built with years of hard work and sweat and tears. "How will anyone ever look at me again without seeing the look on my face when I come with my legs spread wide?"

We stare at each other now, but I can't hold back the spite in my tone or the accusation in my glare any longer as the detailed visual of that night fills my mind. The one of him standing before me with his pants unzipped and every other part of him completely clothed while I looked up at him from the hood of the car, my dress bunched up around my waist, breasts exposed. "I was naked for the world to see. *All of me.* Do you know how that feels? Do you have any clue? Fuck, Colton! This is who *you* are. You live your life in front of the masses and—"

"And what? You think this doesn't bug me?" He steps into me, chest heaving, anger palpable. "That I'm not devastated that a special moment between you and me is now on display for everyone to see? You think I give a rat's ass about people seeing my dick? I don't, Rylee. Not in the fucking least. I feel violated, and it's not because of me but because of you. I care because it's YOU. I worry because it was my idea and you went along with it when I knew that wasn't your norm, and now what? Now you're going to blame me for this and do *I don't know what* to our relationship?" The muscle in his jaw pulses as he clenches his teeth, his hands fisting, and eyes begging me for forgiveness that isn't his to ask for. I went with him willingly. I let him fuck me on the hood of the car and now years later look what's happened.

"I don't know," I whisper. Too many emotions are overwhelming me and pulling me in so many directions. He stands, the glass clinking as he sets it next to the bottle of Jack Daniels, before taking a few steps away from me, running his hand through his hair, and then stepping back toward me.

"If we let this get to us, we're letting them win. Giving them exactly what they want," he says, an unspoken plea for me not to shut him out right now.

And as much as I know his words hold truth, when he reaches out to me, I step back. The pressure in my chest increases and my head starts to hurt. I feel vulnerable, and I hate that feeling.

"My dad," I murmur, my heart beginning to pound so fast I become dizzy. "My dad's going to know about this. And Tanner." I'm not sure why the idea is so very devastating to me when I know they'd never watch it when a public of voyeurs will, but it does all the same.

The tears well as I think how embarrassed my parents are going to be. When I think of how my mom is going to have to answer questions at work or how my dad's going to react when his buddies at his weekly poker match ask him if that's really his daughter on the tape.

The sharp pain comes out of nowhere and despite immediately knocking the breath from me, I gasp out in pain. Colton's at my side in an instant as I brace one hand on the back of the lounge chair while my other one holds onto the swell of my belly. The immediate thought of '*No, it's too early,*' fills my head . . . and terrifies me.

"Ry." The fear in his voice matches how I feel. "Please sit down."

I roll my shoulders to get his hands off me. As much as I want him to pull me close right now, I also don't want to be touched at all. Don't want to be coddled. Don't want to be soothed. My nerves are raw and abraded; my emotions have been raked over the coals. When I sit down and stare at my hands folded in my lap, I will the baby to move to tell me he's okay while I try to calm down the riot of instability inside me.

And of course as I slow down, I'm forced to think, to let reason seep through the disbelief, and I hate when I feel the tears begin to burn in the back of my throat.

"Who would do this, Colton?" I finally look up and meet his eyes. I hate seeing his suffering, but I can't find it within me to comfort him like he is me. I know that makes me a bitch, but all I can think about is my job. The boys. My parents.

Us.

I know we can survive this, know we've weathered storms before, but we are now in such a different place in our lives than the other times. We are on the cusp of bringing this new life into our world. How do we manage the chaos from the outside when our inner circle is shifting too? Even the smallest of storms can cause damage, but how can you repair it when you can't even see it coming?

He sits down on the table in front of me and the look on his face tells me he's waiting for me to tell him to leave me alone. We stare at each other for a few seconds, so many things pass between us in the gaze and yet I can't say a single one of them.

"I don't know. I'll find out and try to fix this." It's all he can say and yet I know there is no fixing this. There is only fallout and that in itself scares the crap out of me because there is no parachute to help us float above the chaos this video will create.

"I know," I say quietly. I shake my head trying to stop the imminent tears I don't want to shed.

"Are you okay?" he asks and I know he means about everything, but I don't have the wherewithal to lie to him.

"The baby kicked." I can't tell him I'm okay, because I'm not. I have too many things going on in my head, and I just need to process it all. He won't stop looking at me and right now I don't want to be stared at. Currently, too many people online are gawking at me, and yet the one who can see the deepest into me is the one I don't want looking. All I want to do is crawl in a hole and be left alone, and therein lies the problem.

My privacy is nonexistent.

"I just want to be by myself for a bit."

"Ry, please."

"No. I just need to wrap my head around this."

I can see him want to tell me not to go, to stay here and talk to him, but I can't. I don't even know what to say to myself. I can't comprehend where I go from here or how I can rebound from this to claim my life back.

The waves crash onto the beach below. I watch them, know the breeze is hitting my face by the way my hair moves with it, but I can't feel it. My thoughts run wild, images in my mind that were so meaningful now turned into someone else's sick, twisted pleasure. I'm nauseated to think that somewhere, someone might be getting off right now on a video of us having sex. Creating fantasies in their own mind, making their own sound effects to it.

My stomach churns as I imagine some dark, seedy room with a creepy guy and a box of Kleenex. I know I'm overreacting but the image keeps repeating in my mind.

Feeling so exposed, so vulnerable, I curl into a tighter ball on the lounge chair where I'm sitting on the lower patio. These feelings are so foreign to me that I'm struggling to accept that this situation is actually real. Since we've been married, vulnerability has been absent in my life. That feeling of helplessness is nonexistent. Colton has never made me feel that way. Besides the random articles here and there, we've been able to keep our life *ours*, unaffected by the outside world. I have never doubted in his ability to smooth things when they go awry. We've turned to each other, reassured each other, taken care of each other.

And I know that those three actions aren't going to fix things now.

We can't say it's a bullshit story—someone out to make a name for themselves—because their name is irrelevant when it comes to sex in the public eye. It's going to be *our* names splashed around, twisted into some sordid story so I'm made to be some whore because let's face it: the men usually get hero status while the women are left with the tarnished reputation.

Normally I'd be in auto-fix mode by now. That's what I do, who I am. If there's a problem, I attack it with a clear head and try to mitigate damages and get it taken care of. I don't think there is a single way to mitigate anything when it comes to this situation and that's what's staggering me. Even worse, I'm sitting here, wanting to sink into oblivion but have my phone in my hand, fighting the urge to see how bad things really are. I have a feeling the fact that I had to turn my ringer off an hour ago to get some peace and quiet is already telling me the answer.

"Hey," Haddie says. The cushion next to me dips when she sits down and puts her arm around me. I should be shocked she's here, but I'm not. She always seems to know what I need to hear. Whether Colton called her because he feels lost that I don't want to speak to him right now or because she came on her own accord, doesn't matter. And as much as I want to be alone, wallow in whatever pity I have for myself that is useless anyway, it also feels good to have her beside me. The one person who will know what I need or don't need to hear right now because she knows me inside and out.

Out of habit, she reaches out and rubs her hand over my belly and deep down, beyond my embarrassment, I know the baby is the real reason I'm lost in a fog. I can't even process the thought that one day our son or daughter is going to google their mom or dad and come across us having sex on the hood of a car. In a garage. In public. How do you explain that?

My whole body tenses at the thought, the burn of tears back with a vengeance. "How bad is it?" I ask for what feels like the tenth time today. Again, I don't really expect an answer as I reach up to wipe away the tear that escapes and slides down my cheek.

"Well . . ." she starts and trails off, trying to find the right words. "When I told you to have some wild, reckless sex with the man, I guess I should have added the caveat to have some wild, reckless sex where there weren't any cameras."

All I can do is sigh, thankful she's trying to infuse some humor into the situation but not really feeling it. "Not funny."

"C'mon. That was a little funny," she says, holding her thumb and forefinger an inch apart.

"There's nothing funny about this whatsoever. Just tell me," I say again, wanting to know how bad it is because I'm too chicken shit to look myself.

She blows out a breath, and I close my eyes wanting to crawl inside myself. "It's bad. Like Internet frenzy, social media everywhere, reporters will be at the gate for some time, type of bad."

"*Fuck.*" One word says it all for me.

"That's kind of what got you in this position so maybe we should choose a different word."

I turn my head to look at her, not amused at all despite the exasperated smile turning up the corners of my mouth. "How about *bullshit*?"

"That's a good one. You've definitely stepped in it."

"Did you watch it?" I ask, because she is the one person who's going to give me the truth and not sugarcoat things. She nods her head slowly, serious eyes holding mine. "And?"

"It's definitely you and Colton, if that's what you're asking," she says, cutting straight to the chase and causing my stomach to churn. I know she is holding back a flippant comment—"a damn, girl" or "a holy hotness"—and I appreciate her restraint.

"Did Colton tell you about the whole . . . everything yesterday?"

"Yes," she states matter-of-factly and looks back toward the ocean beyond.

"Why? Why would someone do this to us, Had?"

"If I had one guess, I'd say money," she muses, "but that's what I don't understand. If it was all about the money, wouldn't the person sell the tape to make a bazillion dollars? The only thing that makes sense is someone seriously wants to fuck with you guys."

I want to cry. I want to sob. To rage. However, I push the heels of my hands over my eyes and just press them there, hoping they miraculously hold back the tears. Because as screwed up as it is in my mind, I feel like if I cry—if one tear leaks over—then this is really real. This isn't a nightmare I'm going to wake from.

"This can't be happening," I say to no one and everyone.

"Colton's worried about you," she says softly. "Wants to talk to you."

"He should be," I snip and then wince. "Look." I sigh. "I know he is but I need to clear my head for a bit before I talk to him. I mean, I have my parents calling and Tanner, and God only knows who else is leaving one of the million messages on my phone. I don't want to talk to anyone right now."

"I get it," she says, as I rest my head back on her shoulder. "But you're going to need to talk to everyone at some point or else you're going to explode."

"I know," I murmur, closing my eyes and wondering how I'm going to face anyone again. Exploding sounds like a more viable option.

But I can't.

The baby. I have to focus on our little miracle and not let any of this affect my stress, my health, or my blood pressure because it's still too early for him or her to come. I have to keep it together. Bury the emotion. Hide from the embarrassment. Push down the pain. Do what it takes.

I have this baby depending on me.

I'm a mom now. My needs come second.

Chapter Five

COLTON

"WHO THE FUCK IS IT, Kelly?" I pinch the bridge of my nose as I stare at my computer screen. Fucking Google and its far-reaching fingers. Pictures upon pictures of Rylee stare back at me. Stills taken from the video. Her body on display for the world to see, and all I can see is red. Rage in my blood, revenge on my mind. Finding the bastard who did this is my only thought so I can plow my fist into his face and then ask why if he's still conscious.

"I'm on it."

"Well, while I wait a few thousand more downloads will occur. No biggie," I say, sarcasm front and center, even though I know this isn't *his* fault. Shit, it's only been hours since the video appeared and it's already everywhere: TMZ, Perez Hilton, YouTube, E!, fucking CNN. You name it; it's there. "I want this bastard found the fuck out."

"And then what, Colton? It's not like they stole it from your house and then uploaded it. It was a random video taken in a public place. It's fodder for public use."

"I don't give a fuck," I shout into the phone. It alerts another call, and I cringe when I look down to see who it is. Dad. *Fuck.* "I gotta go. Keep me up to speed." I stare at the phone for a fleeting second, not wanting to tackle this just yet, before I switch the call over. "Dad."

"Hey," my dad says. In that single word I can hear him searching out how I'm doing. He never fails. No matter what curveball my life has thrown, my dad has always had my back.

"I take it you've seen the big news." Sarcasm is my friend today. Well, that and fucking Jack Daniels, but I had to cut myself off to prevent getting plastered. I need a clear head so I can deal with this crap. And so I can be there for Ry, my only focus in this whole shitstorm.

Even with valid reasons to abstain clear as fucking day, my eyes veer from my empty glass over to the bottle sitting on the kitchen counter. The sight of the whiskey tempts me. Sings to me like a siren luring me to crash and burn.

"Just wanted to check and make sure you and Rylee were okay." Thank fuck he finally speaks, pulling me from the temptation to drown my problems away. I swivel so my back faces the kitchen—and the bottle—while I wait for him to say more, ask the questions I know are on his tongue. Yet I'm met with silence. Rolling my shoulders, I blow out a breath as I try to let in the one person who matters most when all I want to do is shut people out right now.

"I'm worried about her," I confess as I look out the window. She's still curled up on the chaise lounge where she's been since Haddie left. The food next to her untouched. It's fucking killing me to not go out there and talk to her, but I'm the reason she's hurting.

I'm not going to let her pull away. Don't think she will. But she asked for space, and I'm giving it to her. *For now.*

"It takes a lot to catch me off guard, Dad," I say finally as my mind runs faster than I can say the thoughts, "and this . . . fuck . . . this just blindsided us."

"I don't want an explanation, son. I've lived this life too long to know how people twist and manipulate things to hurt others. I'm just calling to let you know we're behind you. I'm here if you need to talk and to make sure you take care of her."

"She told me she trusted me to handle this, and now? Now, I don't even know what the fuck to say to her."

"How about you start by using her name."

My knee-jerk reaction is to yell at him for the comment, but it dies on my lips when I click another link with the mouse and more images of Ry fill the screen: close-ups of her face, her tits, her spread legs, her goddamn everything.

I'm sure my dad can hear the sound of my fist hitting the desk through the connection and yet he says nothing. The drywall calls to me. It's so much more tempting to hit—satisfying—because the destruction is there, visible, and yet helps fucking nothing.

"*Her name*? Easier said than done, Dad. I brought her into my public world, pushed her, and now this is what she gets for loving me?"

"I bet she gets a whole lot more than that, Colton, or she wouldn't be with you." His words hang on the connection as I struggle whether or not to believe him. Is *the more* worth enough for her to stick with me through all of this?

His words repeat in my head.

I sure as fuck hope he's right. Everything's been too perfect as of late. Is this the other shoe dropping to put me back in my place and remind me how cruel fate can be?

"Remember, son, marriage isn't about how madly in love you are through the good times, but how committed you are to each other in the bad times."

And as cheesy as my dad's advice sounds, I hear it. Hold on to it. And hope to fucking God it's the truth because the shit has most definitely hit the fan.

"She won't even speak to me." I chuckle in frustration and force myself to turn off the computer. If I see one more image I have a feeling the drywall will be too tempting to resist. Unclench your fists, Donavan. Shove down the urge to hit something.

"I probably wouldn't want to speak to you right now either," he says. "You grew up in this world. As much as your mom and I tried to shelter you from it, the cameras were always there. You're used to them, the intrusion. She's not. She's always been a private person and now the two worlds have collided in such an intrusive way. You need to give her some space, let her come to terms with feeling violated, and then you need to do something to remind her how very special that moment was to you two so you don't let the vultures take that away from you."

Yeah. Because once they take a part of your soul, they only want more. And fuck if I plan on letting them have another piece of it.

"Thanks, Dad."

"I'm always here if you need me. Let's hope a huge story will come along and brush this under the rug sooner rather than later." *One can hope.* "You can't control this, son. The only thing you can do is to turn your wounds into wisdom."

My phone beeps again as I glance back to Rylee and her unmoving figure so very close but who seems so far away. "Yeah. Thanks, Dad. I'll talk to you soon. Chase is on the other line."

"Chase."

"You need to make a statement, Colton." As much as I love my publicist's straight-to-the-point manner, right now I don't really want to hear a fucking thing she says.

"I shouldn't have picked up," I say drolly, the only warning to her of the mood I'm in.

"Or the both of you need to make a public appearance and show you aren't fazed by any of this. The Ivy or Chateau Marmont?" she asks, knowing me well enough to ignore my comment.

"You're reaching for pie in the goddamn sky if you think I'm going to let Rylee anywhere near a public place right now."

"I get it, but you need to face the chaos head-on."

"Out of the fucking question. Now tell me how bad it is on your scale."

"Well, no publicity is bad publicity," she says, causing every part of me to bristle with anger.

"I'm going to pretend you didn't say that."

"Look, I'm not going to sugarcoat it, but it's what you'd expect from the fickle, sex-starved masses. You look like some sex god where *attaboys* will be handed out, and Ry looks exactly the opposite."

"But we're married," I shout, pissed off they're treating her like a whore.

"That's how I'm spinning it. Intimate moment between husband and wife. You didn't know about the cameras. Sell the story that some sick fuck is taking advantage of you two caught in a passionate moment. Make him out to be the bad guy and that you are the victims."

But I'm not a victim.

Never again.

Baxter's collar jingles as he follows me through the darkened house. My eyes burn from staring at the computer. Keeping it turned off didn't last very long. So many images, so many comments, and every single one of them was like a personal attack on me because they were all about Rylee. And it's only been hours since the video has been released. I fear what the morning will bring.

Turn wounds into wisdom. My dad's words ring in my ears and yet right now I'm not quite sure how that's possible. Wisdom won't punish the fucker who did this. It won't let me sleep better at night. It won't suffice as an apology to Rylee.

When I enter the bedroom, my feet falter and my hand with my drink stops halfway to my mouth when I see her. She's lying on her left side, body pillow tucked under her big belly and between her legs, sound asleep. Every part of my body tenses and relaxes simultaneously at the sight of her: perfection I don't deserve in any way, shape, or form.

Fucking Rylee.

My breath.

My life.

My kryptonite.

And now I've brought whatever the fuck this is down on her.

I sit in the chair across from the bed in our little sitting area that overlooks the beach darkened by the night beyond. It takes all I have not to crawl into bed and pull her against me and reassure her that everything is going to be fine again when she wakes up. Because it isn't. Far fucking from it.

Silence is much better than bullshit.

So I sit in silence with my legs propped on the coffee table in front of me and pour myself another glass of whiskey. I can drown in it now—let it sing me to sleep—since it's way too fucking late at night for anyone to need me.

I take a sip and watch Baxter go plop down on his bed. Shit, if he had a doghouse, I'd be in it tonight. And for good reason.

The alcohol burns but doesn't dull the ache in my gut or take the edge off the unknown and worry. Only Rylee can do that, and she's still not speaking to me.

I've done this husband thing for almost six years now. Thought I was doing a pretty damn good job at it. But then something like this happens and I'm reminded how little I can actually control, especially when it comes to taking care of those around me. There's no stopping the crazy we are going to wake up to in the morning. In my heart of fucking hearts—the one she brought back to life again—I know this for a fact.

Just like I know we can withstand this tornado we're in the middle of. It won't be the first. I sure as fuck hope it will be the last. Such optimism when I'm used to living by the *hope for the best, expect the worst* approach.

Who the fuck did this to us? And why?

Thoughts, theories, speculation. All three circle in my head and none of them make sense.

Rylee. My goddamn perfection in this whirlwind of chaos and bullshit. She is the only thing still crystal clear to me. My spark. My light.

My chest constricts. *We're introducing a baby into this mix.*

That lick of panic that's been on standby is dulled by the Jack, but it's still there.

Still flickering.

Still telling me there's no turning back.

Chapter Six

Rylee

I WAKE WITH A START. It's more than just the baby resting on my bladder. It's that sudden awareness when I reach out to find cold sheets, realizing Colton's not beside me. And then before I can shift to see if he even came to bed, yesterday comes flooding back to me.

In full 3D effect.

My whole body tenses. I want to pull the pillow over my head and hide, and in fact, I do just that for a brief moment to collect my thoughts and try to find the me that's hiding underneath layer upon layer of humiliation and mortification. But I can't live like this—hiding in shame—so I allow myself a momentary pity party before I get up to face the feared chaos.

The phone call to my parents last night comes back to mind. How supportive they were amidst my apologies for the embarrassment caused, and the promise that this footage was not something Colton and I even knew about. How my mom kept reiterating they were sorry someone was trying to exploit us in the worst way, but that the most important thing was to take care of the baby and my health.

Who thinks they'd ever have to make *that* apology to their parents? Ugh.

The baby shifts and reminds me how very hungry I am and how full my bladder is. I rise slowly from the bed, take care of my morning business, and then set off to find Colton and food. We need to talk. I shut him out last night so I wouldn't take my disbelieving anger out on him when this whole thing is just as much my fault as his.

I prepare myself before I look out our bedroom window to the gates at the front of the house. Being on the second story allows me to see the street clearly and of course the minute I move the curtains, I wish I hadn't.

Paparazzi lurk there, milling around, waiting for any movement from our house. They're vultures waiting for the tiniest bit of flesh they can tear away and use to their liking: to sensationalize, to vilify, to exploit, and to manufacture lies.

And it's not like they haven't seen enough of my flesh already.

My stomach tightens at the sight. Too much. Too fast. I wince, worried what this is doing to my blood pressure. The room around me becomes foggy as dizziness overwhelms me momentarily. I fear what I'm going to find when I go downstairs to my laptop, which adds pressure to the constriction in my chest.

I sit on the edge of the bed and attempt to calm myself. The welfare of the baby my only thought as I try to regain the determination I felt ten minutes ago to face head-on whatever the day brings. A few deep breaths later, my cell on the nightstand vibrates. The name on the screen causes me to cringe. With quiet resolve, I have no choice but to answer him.

"Hello?"

"Are you okay, Rylee?" My sweet boy—now grown man in college—coming to the rescue.

"Hey, Shane. I'm okay. *I'm sorry.*" The apology is off my tongue in an instant. Two words I feel like I'm going to be saying a lot in the coming days.

"Do you need me to come home?" The simple question has tears welling in my eyes. I'd like to blame it on the hormones but I can't. Yesterday showed me how cruel the masses could be to no one in particular and yet today, this moment, I'm shown once again how much good there is still in the world. That a boy once lost, who I spent a lifetime comforting and trying to help heal, has taken to me like I am his own. And there is something so very poignant about the thought that it's exactly what I needed to receive.

"You have no idea how much that simple question means to me, Shane. I appreciate the offer more than you know, but there's not much anyone can do. More than anything I'm mortified . . . It's just . . ." I exhale audibly into the connection because what exactly am I supposed to say? I know he's an adult now, that he understands as much as anyone the fishbowl world I now live in, but that doesn't take away any of the awkwardness.

"It's okay. You don't need to say anything. Colton and I talked last night. He explained everything." I breathe a slight sigh of relief because that saves me from having to take a step in this dance of discomfort. Well, at least when it comes to Shane.

I'll still have to address the boys at The House at some point. The thought causes me to roll my shoulders in unease.

"Are you sure you don't want me to drive down?" he asks again. "I can skip some classes tomorrow."

"No. Thank you, though. I don't want you skipping any classes. Just hearing your voice has made me feel better."

"Okay. If you're sure."

"Positive."

"Okay. Speaking of classes, I've got to get to one right now."

We say our goodbyes, and I sit on the bed with my phone clutched in my hand. All I can think about is Shane and the little ray of sunlight his call afforded me. How that little boy I took in at The House way back when has grown into this incredible man who worried enough about me to call Colton to make sure I was okay.

There is right in this world. And I helped make it. I hold on to that thought. I think I'm going to need it in the coming days.

I make my way down the stairs listening for sounds of Colton in the kitchen. That flutter of panic happens when dead silence greets me. When there is no response to my whistle for Baxter, I head toward the downstairs bedroom that houses our workout equipment to find the door shut, the beat of Colton's feet hitting the treadmill coming through it.

And as much as I need to talk to him, I also need to face the reality of what my world now looks like through the microscope of public scrutiny. Besides, by the way he's pounding the belt of the treadmill, I have a feeling Colton needs the release the exercise will bring.

I grab an apple on the way to the office but don't even bother to take a bite of it once the screen of the computer flickers to life. Images upon images of myself litter the monitor. Good images. Bad images. Violating images.

No wonder the treadmill sounded like it was going to break. Colton must have been surveying the damage before he ran.

The pictures suck the air from my lungs so it takes me a moment, my eyes wide with horror, before I can even my breathing. And as much as I know I should turn the computer off and not click on the links to see the public's perception, this is me. My life. I have to know what I'm facing.

With a reluctant hand, I click on the first Google link and am brought to a massive gossip news site. An image of some of the boys and me from a promotional event a few months back dominates the page, but it's the title that owns my mind. "Risky Business: Sex tape vixen leads our troubled youth."

My hands start shaking as I read the article and the comments that don't have merit gracing the pages. "Rylee Donavan surely knows how to land the racing world's most eligible bachelor. I wonder just what she'd do for you in exchange for a donation." Or "Is this how we fundraise nowadays? Is Corporate Cares struggling to fund their next project so their most prominent employee decides to take matters in her own hands to raise awareness? She's been known to say *anything for her boys*. We didn't realize this was her anything."

Link after link.

Comment after comment.

I don't want to believe what I'm reading and seeing so I keep clicking, keep reading, keep being shocked by the cruelty of others.

Oh. My. God. This isn't possible. It's just not. Can't be. I'm not *that person*. The media whore needing to further my career. Yet *that's* what they've made me out to be.

My eyes burn as I search and scrutinize and look for some kind of good in the links, but I'm fooling myself if I actually think I'm going to find some. And when I do, the positive and supportive stories are buried four pages in by the sensationalized crap that sells.

I'm horrified by the images I'm not yet familiar with. The ones from the new version of the tape. And yet I can't stop clicking the links and reading the bylines. I can't stop seeing all of my hard work and dedication to a worthy cause dragged through the mud because some asshole wants to prove a point none of us are privy to.

I replay it again. Paralyzed. Lost in the images. Mortified. Wondering for the first time if there is more to this than just an attack on Colton. The obvious go-to answer. *What if this is about me?* What if someone has a vendetta against me because I was the person taking care of their son?

It's a ridiculous thought. I shake my head to clear it from my mind. It's not possible. Even if it were, they'd have no clue this video even existed.

But the thought lingers. Worries around in my head. Draws my eyes back to the video on the monitor and the final image frozen on screen when the video ends. I close my eyes and sigh because the lasting image is more damaging than the sex itself. It's a close up of

Colton and me as we leave the garage. He is looking over to me and I am looking ahead, almost as if I'm directing my face toward the camera. Like I knew it was there. The worst part is that I have the happiest of smiles on my face. Emotions I can still feel all these years later rush back to me, but this time they've been tainted. Because with the grainy quality of the video, the smile I have on my face can now be misread.

I look smug, calculating, manipulative. Like I knew exactly where the camera was, and was telling anyone watching, "*Look who I landed.*"

Lost in thought, I stare out the windows beyond and try to figure out what we need to do and where we need to go from here because my worst fear is that this will hurt the boys somehow. Boys that have had way too much happen in their short lifetimes to be affected by this too.

"Ry?" Colton calls to me from the doorway where he's standing with a towel draped around his neck, both hands pulling down on it. His chest is misted with sweat from his workout, and a cautious expression plays on his face. And there are so many questions in that single syllable. Are you all right? Are you going to speak to me yet? Do you know how much I missed you?

And just the sound of his voice quiets the turmoil within. Whereas last night all I wanted to do was lash out at him—blame him when it's not his fault—today I just want him to pull me into him and hold on tight.

"Hey," I say as I stare at him in a whole new light. This is the first real problem we've encountered since we've been married, and yet he was able to step back and give me the space I needed when I know it was killing him not to rush in and try to fix what can't be fixed. "Good run?"

He shrugs. "Just trying to work off some shit," he murmurs as he moves into the room behind the desk where I am, and clicks the computer screen off. "Please don't read any more."

"Look, I'm the good girl. I don't do things that get attention so this is . . ." I blow a breath out not sure what I'm trying to say. "I needed to know how bad it was," I explain quietly, as my eyes follow his when he leans a hip on the desk in front of me. We sit in silence for a moment, until I reach out and he meets my hand halfway, our fingers lacing in an unexpected show of unity that sounds stupid but feels so very significant.

Us against them.

"And . . ."

"It's bad," I say as I look up from our hands to meet the somber expression in his eyes. When I just purse my lips and nod my head because there is nothing else I can say, he just squeezes our fingers.

"I talked to my parents. To Tanner. To Shane." My voice fades off as the disbelief I have to take stock and let him know the damage control I've done takes hold. Unsure how to respond to me when he's always so sure, he just nods his head as our eyes hold steadfast. "Our baby is going to grow up knowing this is out there." My voice is so soft, it sounds so very different than the storm of anger that rages inside me, and yet I can't find it within me to show my emotions. I can feel his fingers tense from my comment, see his Adam's apple bob from the forced swallow, and notice the tick of muscle as he clenches his jaw.

"We'll get through this."

The condescending chuckle falls from my lips, the first break in my fraudulent façade because it's so damn easy for him to say. "I know." Voice back, emotion nonexistent, tone unsure.

Colton stares, willing me to say more but I don't. I just match him stare for hollow stare as images of myself from Google flicker through my mind. Finally he breaks our connection and reaches his fingers to pinch the bridge of his nose before blowing out a sigh.

"Scream at me, Ry. Yell. Rage. Take it out on me. Do anything but be silent because I can't handle when you're silent with me," he pleads. All I can do is shake my head, dig down within myself to will the emotion to come. When I can't find the words or the feeling behind them, it unnerves him, worries him. "I'm sorry, baby. Were we stupid that night? Maybe. Do I regret that night?" He shakes his head. "I regret all of this, yes, but that night in general? No. So many damn things happened that put you and me where we are now. So for that? I'm not sorry. You pushed me that night, made me question if I could give someone more of myself." He reaches his free hand up to brush a thumb over the line of my jaw. His touch reassuring, his words helping soothe the sting of our situation.

"It's not your fault," I say, trying to ease the concern in his eyes.

"Maybe not directly . . . but I made you color outside of your perfectly constructed lines . . . do something against your nature, and look what happened. I'm so sorry. I wish I could make this right," he says, dropping his head as he shakes his head in defeat. "All I can try to do is mitigate the damage. That's it." He throws his hands up. "It's killing me because I can't fix this." The break in his voice and the tension in his body would have told me everything I needed to know even if he hadn't uttered a sound.

I look at my achingly handsome husband, so distraught, so desperate to make wrongs right that aren't his to be held responsible for. And seeing him as upset as I am makes me feel a little better and allows me to dig into the deep well of emotion. I finally find the words I need and want to tell him. The decisions I came to last night when I sat on the deck and considered the life-altering situation we were in.

"Stop. Please quit beating yourself up over this. I don't blame you." I pause, my teeth worrying my bottom lip as I put words to my thoughts and wait for him to hear that last sentence. "Thank you for giving me space last night. At first I was pissed at you . . . just because you are the one here to lash out at. But the longer I sat and thought, I realized that more than anything, my fury is aimed at whoever did this. *They* took a moment between the two of us and made it something for others to judge and ridicule."

Colton pulls on our hands so the chair I'm sitting in rolls toward him. He leans forward, our faces inches apart, and looks into my eyes. "No one knows us. No one understands why our relationship works but us. I know the real you, Rylee Jade Thomas Donavan. They don't have a clue how fucking incredible you are. Only I get the privilege of knowing you like ice cream for breakfast and pancakes for dinner. I'm the only one who gets to know that when you scream and rage you get that little crease in your forehead that's so fucking adorable. I love that you love those boys like they are your life and would never do a goddamn thing to hurt them. I know you're disciplined and modest and hate coloring outside the lines, but that you do sometimes just for me. The fact that you do means the world to me. And more than anything, I love that you raced me even when I didn't have any wheels on the fucking track."

His words hit me and wrap around my heart like a bow on a package that's wrapping is tattered and torn. They crawl into my soul and take hold because they are exactly what I need to hear to reinforce the love I have for him. My gruff, arrogant husband can be the man I need him to be when I need it the most and that says volumes for what I mean to him.

He leans forward and presses a kiss to my lips so tender it makes me adore him more. When he leans back he rests his forehead against mine, our noses touch, his exhale my next breath, and I feel a bit steadier even though nothing's changed.

"We'll get through this, Ry. Just like we have before. Just like we always will. What we have between us," he says, voice thick with emotion as he pauses to find the words, "is a beautiful thing."

"A beautiful thing is never perfect," I murmur.

"You're right. We're far from perfect. We're *perfectly imperfect.*"

If I wasn't already madly in love with my husband, that two-word description would win me over. It reinforces the arrow shot through my heart. Words I used once to describe him have now come back to represent exactly what we are as a couple. And the fact he realizes, accepts, and acknowledges it, makes it that much more meaningful.

"You're right," I say with a shaky voice. He presses a kiss to my nose and leans back, hands smoothing my messy hair out of my face before holding my face in his hands so I can see the intention in his eyes.

"I promise you, I will find out who did this and make them pay." His statement means a lot to me but I know even if he does find them, the damage is done. We'll never be able to get those images, the privacy of that moment back, and so I just nod my head in response.

"I need to talk to the older boys about this somehow." Although I'm at a loss for words of what exactly I'm going to say to them. Everyone but Auggie is a teenager. Teenagers and their long-reaching fingers into social media will find out about this. The thought makes my heart fall.

"No, you don't." He scrubs the towel through his hair and shakes his head like I'm crazy.

"Some of the pictures splashed all over the Internet are of them, Colton. Of course I have to." A tinge of hysteria laces the edges of my anger. "Kids at school are going to talk. They need to hear it from me. Have to. I can't let them think I'm some kind of . . ." My voice trails off as I try to figure out what exactly I think they are going to think of me now.

"Ry, listen to me. They love you. You don't have to say any—"

"Yes, I do."

"I'll speak to them," he states matter-of-factly, causing my head to whip up at the response since I know how uncomfortable he is with that kind of thing.

"You what?"

"You're not leaving the house right now with the press out there. I'm not letting them take pictures of you to have fodder for their lies. They can have me . . . let them vilify me. Not you. No way." I'm shocked by his words and yet shouldn't be. "Chase is issuing a statement to the press for us. Hopefully that will help all of this die down."

"Mm-hmm." I must look at him like a doe in the headlights because as much as I know this will die down, people will forever know what I look like naked. That's not an easy thing to swallow. Not now. Not ever.

And even when Chase issues that statement, it will do very little to dim the sparkle of the sensationalism.

"I've got to go take a shower. Then I'm going to work from home the rest of the week," he says as he rises from his seat, his comment causing my stomach to churn in anxiety.

"I have my shift tomorrow," I say, suddenly realizing reality needs to continue amid this storm of chaos. "Can you and Sammy figure out how to get me out of here so I can get there?"

The minute his body stills, I know a fight's coming. He doesn't disappoint but goes straight for the kill. "Dr. Steele called this morning." I'm immediately irritated and defensive before he even says another word. I feel like he's been waiting to make this point. Inwardly I groan because that means he knows about my blood pressure issues.

"Yes?" I say nonchalantly even though inside I'm already preparing for World War Donavan.

"The way I see it, you're staying home tomorrow."

"That's bullshit!" He just quirks an eyebrow to say *try me*.

"Well, seems to me she called to check on you. Said she was worried about your blood pressure . . . with all of this." I avert my eyes to my hands folded in my lap.

"I'm fine." I nod my head with a forced smile on my lips in hopeful reassurance.

"That's not what she said," he says, making said blood pressure feel as though it is rising.

"Colton, I'm going to work tomorrow, with or without your help. If you want my blood pressure to stay low, you'll help," I fire back, lips pursed, eyebrows raised. Two can play this game. We stare at each other, both daring the other to back down but neither budging.

"Exactly. I'll help. I'll go instead and talk to the boys about it," he lifts his eyebrows, "while you stay here."

"Don't push me on this," I warn.

His chuckle fills the room. "That's rich, Donavan," he says with a shake of his head as he walks toward the door. "I need to take a shower but this discussion is over."

I snort in response. He stops abruptly, back still to me when he speaks. "I love the boys, Rylee. More than you know. I said I'd never come between you and them . . . but you, and that baby of ours you're carrying, are my first priority. Numero Uno. You'd better start making both of them yours too, or we're going to have a huge fucking problem. End of discussion." And he doesn't even give me a chance to pick my jaw up off the floor to respond before he waltzes out of the office, tossing, "Don't look at the computer anymore either," over his shoulder.

Staring at the empty doorway, I'm not quite sure what to think so I lean back in the chair and blow out a slow and steady breath to calm myself. Colton's never said anything like that to me before, and while everything he just said holds serious merit, I'm still astounded he said it. And while a small part of me warms, knowing he wants to take care of me, a larger part is irritated he's laying down the law. The irony.

It doesn't mean I have to abide by it though.

I look toward the ceiling and close my eyes momentarily. The many things I need to do run through my head, but I can't do any of them because I can't leave my house, can't carry on my life like normal. I'm stuck here and that thought alone makes me feel claustrophobic.

I'm exposed to the world but trapped in my house.

Feeling defeated, my eyes flutter open to see the beach beyond the windows down below. And for the first time since we've met, I truly understand why Colton finds such refuge in his beloved beach—the crash of the waves, the feel of the sand beneath his feet, and the sense he's this tiny blip on Mother Nature's radar.

A soft chuckle falls from my lips as it hits me. On the beach, he feels *inconsequential*. How very fitting for a man who once told me I would never be that to him to have the need to feel that way at times.

My mind shifts back to that place and time. A ghost of a smile turns up my lips of the welcome memory of the Merit Rum party: dancing in the club followed by him chasing me into the hallway. Angry words. Contemptuous kisses. Hungry eyes. An elevator ride to the penthouse with a promised threat to decide. *Yes. Or. No.*

I find comfort in the memory. Without that night, there most likely wouldn't be this. No Colton. No baby on the way. No chaos to want to hide from.

My eyes are drawn back to the beach. To the temptation of Colton's place to escape. Sadly, right now, I couldn't escape down there if I wanted to. At least he can get on his board and paddle out beyond the break to get some distance from the photographers. I'm not so lucky.

What I'd give to be inconsequential right now.

And yet deep down, no matter how hard I try, I know I will never be that to Colton. He'd never allow it. My handsome, complicated, and very stubborn husband takes too much pride in the two things he never thought he'd have—a wife and her love—to ever let me feel inconsequential again.

Chapter Seven

COLTON

"**G**RAB A BEER, BOYS."

The looks on their faces? Fucking priceless as I motion to the cooler sitting beside the table. Aiden's mouth is hanging open, waiting to catch flies. Both Ricky and Kyle's eyes look like they are bugging out of their heads. Zander and Scooter shift uncomfortably on the bench, glance over their shoulders like they don't want Jax to walk in and get them in trouble.

"Go on," I encourage and lean over and open the lid myself.

Aiden sees it first. His laugh rings across the room. "It's root beer, guys." His voice is part relief, part disbelief as he shakes his head and passes down the silver cans of soda.

The others join in. Eyes flicker from the cans back to me, looks of curiosity over why I'm here and what's going on. The crack of the tops of the cans fill the room. I wait for them the take that first sip before looking back to me.

"I need to have a man-to-man talk with you guys so I figured you could handle having a beer or two while we chat." I nod my head to reinforce my point and get five more nods in return.

"Are we in trouble?" Ricky asks, hands fiddling with the tab on his can.

"No, but I need to talk to you guys about something." Fuck. Fuck. Fuck. Why am I nervous? I look down at my hands. *Buck the fuck up, Donavan.* They're all under fourteen. How am I going to do this? Crap.

"What?" Zander asks, eyebrows raised, voice innocent.

And shit. Innocent is the keyword here. Did I know what sex was at age thirteen? Hell yes, I did. Thought I did, anyway. A messy French kiss with Laura Parker was the extent of it. The sheets I'd balled up in the morning, mortified for my mom to find, had been my reality.

"So . . . you guys might start hearing some stuff at school or see stuff on TV or the Internet about Rylee and me." Brows furrow. Lips quirk. And my palms sweat. I clear my throat. "Sometimes adults do things in the heat of the moment that leads to . . . er . . . uh . . . consequences."

"Heat of the moment?" Aiden says with a snicker. I swear to God I blush for the first time in what feels like forever.

"You know sometimes you do something without thinking—"

"Like that time you climbed on the counter to get the cookies on top of the refrigerator and—"

"No. Not like that," I cut Kyle off. Sweet Jesus this is going to be difficult. "More like when two married people love each other they—"

"Do they have to be married?" Scooter asks.

Seriously? Do I have to go here? I feel like I'm sitting on hot coals. My balls are burning and I can't sit still.

"For the most part, *yes.*" I'm going to be struck by lightning for saying that. For lying through my teeth.

Aiden snickers again. I guess at age fourteen he knows where I'm going with this. And is enjoying watching me struggle.

"Anyway, there is going to be some talk about us and I wanted to say that you know Rylee. You know the person she is. So please don't believe any of the crap you hear being said."

There. Maybe that will be enough.

"But why? What's on the Internet?"

I just fucked this up. If I were their age and someone said this to me, I'd immediately go and online and search for it. Curiosity and all that.

The snicker again from Aiden. The one that says he either already knows because someone said something at school today or is assuming.

Don't lose your cool, Donavan.

"Five Three X," he murmurs under his breath, confusing the fuck out of me but making perfect sense to the four of them by the way they whip their heads his way and their mouths fall open like they know perfectly well what he's saying.

"*What?*" I ask.

Five pairs of eyes look down at hands on soda cans and leave me lost in the goddamn dark.

"Someone going to explain what the hell five three X means?"

Snickers times five now.

"Aiden?"

He looks up, meets my eyes, and the look he gives me tells me he knows exactly what I'm here to tell them about. A single scathing look that tells me he's pissed at me for whatever it is he's read about Ry—like it's all my fault—and all I can do is sigh and run a hand through my hair. And try to figure out what the fuck he's talking about.

A part of me loves this glare he's giving me. He's pissed with me because he's protective of Ry, but at the same time . . . really? I'm being eye-scolded by a fourteen-year-old?

And then it hits me. The visual of what Five Three X looks like.

53X

SEX.

Jesus fucking Christ. When did I get so old I don't know that lingo and when did these kids get so old when they're not?

I jog my knee. Take a breath. What the hell am I supposed to say now? I wasn't really going to go into the sex part of it. Was I? I don't even know. I thought this was going to be a cinch. A little chat. Don't believe everything you see or hear on the Internet type of thing.

And now I'm stuck with birds and bees and son-of-a-bitch Aiden just threw a whole goddamn hornet's nest on me when I wasn't looking.

Can anyone say fish out of water?

"Dude. It's totally cool," Aiden says, taking point for the brood despite the two youngest, Zander and Scooter, blushing.

"No, it's not cool," I say, finding my footing. "Rylee's super concerned that you will be affected by this and she doesn't want you to—"

"Look, we're not going to click on anything, okay?" My eyes bug out of my head. "No one wants to see you bumping uglies . . . especially us."

That's one way to put it. My mouth goes dry as snickers fall, red creeps into cheeks, and eyes are averted from mine.

"Well . . . then . . ." Shit. *Great job, Donavan. You've got Aiden pissed at you but you still haven't made them understand that this is about more than just sex.* I scrub a hand over my face and try to figure out what the fuck I need to say to get the point across. "Listen, guys, you love Rylee like I do, right?" All heads nod and each pair of eyes narrow as they wait to see what else I'm going to say. "That's what I thought. So I need you to understand that there have been some mean, ugly things said about her because of the images out there of us. She's upset and really hurt by them. But more than anything, she's worried it's going to affect all of you. So when I ask you not to click on anything online, don't click on anything. When I ask you not to believe anything crappy said about her or her reasons for supporting The House, don't believe them. You guys are her world, and she'd hate herself if you were hurt in any way from this. So can you do that for me? Can you ignore all of this and pretend like it didn't happen so Rylee doesn't have to worry about you guys?"

For fuck's sake, please understand what I'm asking here.

Aiden's gaze meets mine. Gone is the immature smugness from moments before. It's been replaced with an understanding that seems to go well beyond his years. He nods his head once to me, eyes relaying his unspoken words: *we promise.*

I shift in my seat when all I really want to do is sag in relief. *Thank Christ.* I start to talk and then stop, unsure what to say next.

"Dodgers," Aiden says, recognizing my uncertainty and owning this conversation like nobody's business. "Let's talk about last night's Dodgers game."

All I can do is shake my head.

I'm not ready for this parenting shit.

Chapter Eight

Rylee

"WHAT THE FUCK DO YOU mean early parole?" Colton's voice ricochets off the stairwell and up into the room, shocking me from the case reports I'm trying to complete on my laptop and indicating he is home. Within an instant, I set my computer aside and move downstairs to find out what's going on.

"I know, CJ. I know," Colton says, one hand fisted at his side, posture tense, as I walk into the great room, his back to me framed against the open doors to the patio. "But it's too much of a goddamn coincidence, don't you think? The timing, his vindication . . . all of it adds up."

Colton must sense me and turns to meet my eyes, holding one finger up requesting I wait while he finishes the conversation. I watch the emotions play over his face as he listens to our lawyer. He moves to abate the restlessness of whatever CJ is telling him, my eyes following him pace, my mind trying to figure out what's going on. They say their goodbyes, and he turns again to face me.

"Eddie."

It's all he says as he smacks his hands together. That simple name—a blast from our past—and Colton's reflex reaction cause details from three years ago to flood back to me. The CD Enterprises patent for an innovative neck protection device being denied because someone else was already in the process of getting a very similar one approved. Almost identical in fact. Investigations to find out that the other patent applicant had CDE's same exact blueprints for the device, followed by digging into the layering of the corporation applying to find Eddie Kimball on the board of directors.

The same Eddie Kimball who Colton had fired for stealing said blueprints.

As I look at the fire lighting up Colton's eyes, I think of the two-year legal battle that ensued over the right of ownership and future revenues from the device the blueprints made. I'm reminded of the stress, the lies, the accusations, the mediation meetings, and offers of settlement to buy time on Eddie's part. After spending a fortune in legal counsel, the judge eventually ruled in our favor and convicted Eddie of numerous charges—fraud, perjury, false witness—and sentenced him to a four-year jail sentence.

"How?" I ask, making calculations about someone I mentally told myself was out of our lives. The trial ended three years ago. He had a four-year sentence.

"Early release. Good Behavior. Jails too crowded from the three-strikes statute." He answers my unspoken questions as he runs a hand through his hair, his head nodding, and I can see him trying to put the pieces of the puzzle together in his mind.

"Tawny knew where we were." It's all I say, voice quiet, gaze fixed on him. He looks up, narrows his eyes, and grits his teeth, not wanting to hear me say it again.

"I know," he says with a sigh, "but I'm trying to figure out how it all fits together. What? Did Tawny go up and get the video of us that night? If she had it way back when, then why keep it and release it all this time later?" He slumps down on the couch and puts his head in his hand while he tries to make sense of it.

I move and sit down next to him and rest my head on his shoulder.

"I can't give you the answers but it all seems too convenient for her not to have had a hand in this." My voice is calm but anger fires in my veins at the thought that either of them have had a hand in this. And yet I shouldn't expect any less from them.

Bitches can't change their stripes. Oh wait, that's *tigers*. Hmpf. Doesn't matter because I refuse to give her a second thought. If she did do this, then Lord have mercy on her when Colton gets done with her.

The idea doesn't take the sting out of our public humiliation any less, but at least with this newfound information about Eddie's release, we might have some place to start looking.

"Kelly is trying to track him down through his parole officer," Colton says, pulling me from my thoughts. He reaches out and squeezes my knee to show me he's present although I know mentally he's a million miles away.

"This is all just so fucked up," I murmur, speaking my thoughts aloud and garnering a sound of agreement from him. We sit like this for a few moments. The silence is comforting because we know outside this bubble we've surrounded ourselves with, there are people waiting to tear us apart.

My cell phone rings from the kitchen counter causing me to sigh because I'm sure it's some intrusive person from a tabloid. "I need to change my number," I groan.

"I'll handle this," he says, beating me to the punch and getting up from the couch. Besides, with the time it would take to get my pregnant self up, the call would probably go to voicemail.

I sink back into the couch and wait for Colton to answer and unleash his temper on whatever poor soul thinks they are calling me, so I'm surprised when I hear him greet the person warmly.

"Hey, good afternoon," Colton says. "She's right here, Teddy.

Hold on."

And there is something in that split second of time that causes my brain—that has been so overwhelmed by everything today—to fire on all cylinders. I thought of my parents and the boys. I've read articles denouncing my motives and implying I released the tape for my own benefit. I called Jax and had him cover my shift at The House. And yet not once did I pick up the phone and call my boss. Not once did I think of damage control or how this man I greatly admire is going to look at me now.

Pregnancy brain.

Oh shit.

Scenarios flicker through my mind as I take the phone from Colton. Our eyes meet momentarily, and I can already see he's thinking the same thing I am.

"Hey Teddy," I say, my voice ten times more enthusiastic than I feel.

"How you doing, kiddo?" he asks cautiously.

"I'm sorry I haven't called you," I say, immediately using those two words again even though I technically haven't done anything wrong.

"No need to." It's all he says and the awkward silence hangs through the connection. I can sense he's trying to figure out how to approach this conversation, an awkward dance of unspoken words. "But we do need to talk."

And the angst I had shelved momentarily returns in a blaze of glory.

"What do you need from me, Teddy?" I feel the need to rise and walk, subdue the discord I already feel, but don't have the energy. Colton steps behind the couch and places his hands on my shoulders and begins to knead away the tension there.

My boss sighs into the line and it's the only sound I need to hear to know my fears about why he's calling are warranted. "Some benefactors are raising their hypocritical highbrow hands and protesting your lead on the project."

I take a deep breath, biting back the comments on my tongue. "I see. Well, take me off as the lead then. Let me have my shifts at The House, and I'll work behind the scenes on the upcoming project."

When he doesn't respond immediately, I bite my bottom lip. "I wish I could." And then silence. We sigh simultaneously, the singular sound a symphony of disquiet.

"What do you mean you wish you could?"

"Ry . . ."

And it hits me. It's not that he wants me to take a back seat on the project. He wants me off the project entirely. And out of The House.

"Oh," I say. Colton's fingers tense as he feeds off my physical reaction. Right now I'm so glad he can't see my face because he'll see how devastated I am. He already feels guilty enough for things he can't control. "I won't risk the project. The boys, the mission, everything means way too much to me. I've put my blood, sweat, tears, and heart into this and I can't risk it for the many more we are going to be able to help. I know this is hard for you and I won't make you ask me so I'll just say it. I'll take an early maternity leave. I'll hate it. It'll kill me to leave Auggie right now just as we're making progress and a breakthrough is on the horizon . . ." My voice trails off, ending my ramble as I struggle to articulate how hard this is for me. In the same breath, I know it was ten times harder for him to pick up the phone to call me and ask this of me.

"They want more than an early maternity leave, Rylee."

"What do you mean?"

"The Board wants me to place you on an indefinite leave of absence."

"Indefinite?" I stutter, voice unsteady, disbelief tingeing its edges as I prod him for the answer I want. "As in three-month type of indefinite?"

"You know I respect you. You know *I* know this project is a continued success because of you and that the boys are contributing members to society because of all the time and hard work you've put in." I hate that all of a sudden Teddy sounds like he's speaking to a room of stiff suits instead of me, the woman who has worked for him for over twelve years. However, I understand his protective wall of detachment more than he knows because I'm fortifying mine too right now. I have to. It's the only way I'll be able to get through this conversation when he tells me I am no longer mother to my boys. To my family. When I don't respond, he continues, trying to find his footing in a world where he is boss, mentor, and friend. "I swear to God I went to bat for you, kid . . . but with the board vote coming up," he says, shame in his voice but I get where he's coming from. The annual vote to approve his position is next month and if he fights too hard, he might not get renewed.

Teddy losing his position would be a colossal mistake; the boys would lose both of us—their biggest advocates. I bite back the bitterness, the want to argue, because with him still in the mix, I know there will at least be one of us working with them.

"It's temporary. I promise you that. Just until the attention dies down."

Yeah. Temporary. The bitterness returns. Disbelief overwhelms me and shakes loose a new thought: what if his contract isn't renewed? Would *I* still have a place at Corporate Cares?

The fear replaces my rage, allows me to calm down and realize fighting him is like preaching to the choir. I just need to fade into the background regardless of the fact I feel like I'm bathed in a neon light. It will be hard as hell but I don't want to rock the boat for him any more than I already have.

"Okay," I respond softly, my voice anything but certain. And I want to ask him how he knows it's temporary—need some kind of concrete here—but know it's useless to ask. This is hard enough for both of us as it is, so why throw false promises in there too?

"I feel like I'm selling you out for the donations—"

"No—"

"But we need these funds," he murmurs.

Desperately. Non-profits always need funds. I've been doing this way too long to know there's never enough and always so many we can't help.

"I won't risk the project, Teddy." And I know he's having a hard time finding the right words to ask me to step down. And the fact it's hard for him shows just how much he believes in me, and that means the world to me. "I'll step down effective immediately." I choke on the words as tears clog in my throat and drown out all sound momentarily, my mind trying to wrap itself around what I just said. Colton's reaction is reflected in the tightening of his fingers on my shoulders, and I immediately shrug out of his grip, push myself up off the couch, and walk to the far side of the room. It is almost a reflex reaction to feel the need to come to terms with this on my own. Yet when I turn to look at Colton and the unwavering love in his eyes, I know I'm not alone. Know together we are a unified front.

"Ry . . ." The resigned sadness in Teddy's voice is like pinpricks in an already gaping wound.

"No. It's okay. It's fine. I'm just . . . it's okay," I reiterate, unsure whether I'm trying to assure him or myself. I know neither of us believes it.

"Quit telling me it's okay, Rylee, because it's not. This is *bullshit*," he swears into the phone, and I can hear how he feels in the single word that keeps coming up over and over.

"But you're handcuffed. The boys come first," I say, immediately hearing Colton's earlier words said in such a different way. "They always come first, Teddy."

"Thank you for understanding the situation I'm in."

I nod my head, unable to speak, and then I realize he can't see me. The problem is that I *don't* understand. I want to rage and scream, tell him this is a railroad because the video does not prevent me from doing my job whatsoever and yet, the die is cast. The video is viral. My job is not mine anymore.

Holy shit. The one constant in my life for as long as I can remember is gone. Talk about going from having a sense of purpose to feeling completely lost in a matter of moments.

How can one video—a single moment in our lives—cause this gigantic ripple effect?

"I need to see the boys one last time." It's the only thought I can process.

"I'm sorry, Rylee, but that's probably not a good idea right now with . . . with everything."

"Oh." My plans for them before I took maternity leave are now obsolete; the bond I was building with Auggie will be non-existent when I return.

If I get to return.

The thought hits me harder than anything else. With Teddy still on the line, I drop the phone and run to the bathroom where I empty the contents of my stomach into the toilet.

Within moments I feel Colton's hands on me: one holding my hair back and the other rubbing up and down the length of my spine in silent reassurance as dry heaves hit me with violent shudders.

"I'm so sorry, Rylee. I know your job and the boys mean the world to you," he murmurs, as I sit there with my forehead resting on the back of my hand atop the toilet seat.

The first tear slips out; the only show of emotion I allow. I can feel it slide ever so slowly down my cheek. With my eyes closed and the man I love behind me, I allow myself to consider the endless uncertainty.

Is this all about me? And if so, whoever did this just got exactly what they wanted. To devastate me. To take my heart and soul—my boys—away from me. To hand me a punishment capable of breaking me.

Taking Colton or the baby away from me would be the only thing worse they could do. And that sure as hell isn't going to happen.

I may be down, but I'm not out.

Chapter Nine

COLTON

"LET'S HOPE WE NEVER NEED it."

"It's strictly a precaution," I say about the restraining order Rylee just signed at the police station against Eddie Kimball. I flip on my blinker, eyes scanning the rearview mirror to make sure we are still paparazzi-free, as I turn onto the unfamiliar street.

"I still disagree though. You should have one too."

Nope. Not me. I hope the fucker comes face-to-face with me. Welcome the thought, actually. I'm jonesing for a chance to beat the truth out of him.

"I can more than handle myself," I state calmly.

Her huff of disapproval is noted and ignored. I drive slowly through the tree-lined streets occasionally leaning over the console toward the passenger seat so I can read the house numbers on her side of the car. And in doing so, I've drawn her attention to figure out where we're going and provided the perfect distraction to get her to drop the topic. For now, at least. I'm sure she'll bring it up again but for now she's diverted.

"Last stop," I say as I pull up when I've found the correct house.

"Where are we?" she asks, curiosity in her tone as she cranes her neck to look around us.

"Proving one of us right," I tell her. "Sit tight."

I open the door and get out, shutting it on her questions, and walk around the car to the sidewalk. She opens her door and I glance over to her before she can get out. "*Don't.*" A single word warning her to stay in the car. Our eyes lock, her temper flashing in hers, but my bite's bigger and she knows it. So after a moment she mutters something under her breath but shuts the door without getting out.

Fuck if I'm not being an asshole. Like that's something new. But at the same time, if I'm laying all my cards on the table, it has to be face-to-face. I can't have the catfight bullshit I'm sure Ry would initiate if she were at my side: a distraction when I'm trying to call Tawny's bluff.

I check the address once more as I walk up the concrete path, the daggers from Rylee's glare burning holes into the back of my shoulders. The house is nothing special—a little run-down, flowers in the planters, a red wagon on the porch—and I can't help but think it's a long-ass way from the high-rise condo she had the last time I visited her.

I knock on the door. A dog barks nearby. I shift my feet. Take my sunglasses off because I want there to be no mistaking what I'm saying and how I mean it. Let's get this done and fucking over with. Problem is when all's said and done, I have a feeling I might be eating a little crow for Rylee, and I've heard it tastes like shit.

I should know better by now. Ry's usually right when it comes to this kind of thing. Only one way to find out.

I knock again. Look over my shoulder to where Rylee sits in the car, window down, head tilted to the side as she tries to figure out what in the fuck I'm doing.

C'mon. Answer the damn door. I don't have time for this shit. Wasted minutes.

Did she or didn't she? That's the big fucking question of the hour. *Tawny.*

I grit my teeth at the name. At the person who has been dead to me. She may have been one of my oldest friends, but she tried to play me for a fool, tie me to her with her bullshit lies, and more than anything, fucked with Rylee. End. Of. Story.

My hands fist. Memories return. Temper flares.

The door swings open. I jolt seeing someone I don't know at all anymore.

"Colton!" Her blue eyes widen in shock. The lines etched around them tell me life's been tough. Too bad, so fucking sad. The beauty queen's lost her crown. You fuck with people, you reap what you sow. Her hand immediately flies up to pat her hair and smooth down her shirt.

Don't worry sweetheart, I wouldn't even touch you with a ten-foot pole.

"What the fuck are you and Eddie trying to pull, Tawny?" I want to catch her off guard, see if I can glimpse a flicker in her eyes. Something. Anything. A goddamn clue whether she had a hand in this whole situation.

"What are you . . .?" Her voice fades as she shakes her head, eyes blinking as if she can't believe I'm standing here. The feeling is mutual.

Cat got your tongue, T?

"Colton . . . please, come in." She reaches out, puts her hand on my arm, and I yank it back in automatic reflex. Does she think I'm here for her? That maybe . . . fuck, I don't know what she could be thinking, but obviously from the hurt that flashed in her eyes she sure as shit didn't expect my rejection.

Good. At least the stage is set for this conversation. Her hopes dashed. All expectation out the damn door.

"No thanks. I've got better things waiting for me in the car," I say with a lift of my chin. I then step to the side so she can see Rylee.

And so Rylee can see her. Understand why we're here. That I listened to her, heard her, and am trying to get some answers. I just hope like hell Ry stays put so I can up the ante. Take the pot and finish this on my terms. Because I need to do that.

"Oh."

Yeah. *Oh.* Glad we got the fact I'm still married out of the way. *Happily.* Now, back to business.

"Tell me about the tape." Images flash in my head: Ry crying on the phone with Teddy, Ry on the patio all by herself, the vulgar comments made beneath the video on YouTube about what other sick fucks want to do to her.

"What tape?" She shakes her head back and forth, eyes narrowed in confusion.

"Cut the crap, T. I fell for your lies once upon a fucking time, and I'm a little short of change to buy them now." I cross my arms over my chest and raise my eyebrows.

"I'm sorry, Colton, but I have no idea what you're talking about."

I'm not buying the innocent routine. "Did you watch TV at all this week? Go to the store? Read People magazine? *Anything?*"

"My son's been sick for the past few days so unless you mean Scooby Doo on TV, no. Why? What's going on?" she asks, tone defensive, and I purposely don't answer. I want to use the silence as a way to make her nervous. She fidgets, shifts her feet, works her tongue in her cheek.

Goddamn it. *Ry was right.* She knows something. Fuckin' A.

"Shit, I haven't seen Eddie in over four years," she finally says.

I stare at her, eyes determined to find some kind of deception in her words but all I see is the woman I used to know, curves a little fuller, clothes messy, and eyes tired.

And I don't care how rough it seems life has been for her. Looks can be deceiving. I still don't trust her. Not one bit. Not after what she did to us way the fuck back when and what I'm pretty sure she had a hand in now.

"Video footage has surfaced of Ry and me from six years ago. You're the only one who knew where we were and what we did that night." I let the comment hang in the space between us. She tries to hide her reaction—a lick of her lips, a quick look to the car driving down the street—but once you've had a relationship with someone, you can read them like a clock. Tick fucking tock. And I know she has more to say. "The Kids Now event. When Ry and I had sex in the parking garage. Footage of us is plastered all over the media, Tawny. You're the only one who knew."

She forces a swallow down her throat. A glance behind her where there are Hot Wheels all over the floor. A shift of her feet. A bite into her bottom lip. All done before she finally has the courage to meet my eyes again.

"Care to change your answer, now?"

"Oh my God," she murmurs more to herself than to me. And something about the way she says it bugs me. It seems genuine, full of surprise, real. I call bullshit. She's just playing the part without dressing up for the cameras. "I completely forgot about that video."

"You forgot?" I sneer, sarcasm rich in my voice. "That's awfully convenient."

"No, really," she says, reaching out to touch me, and then stopping presumably when she remembers my reaction the last time she tried. Smart woman.

"I'm losing my patience," I say between gritted teeth.

"That night after I left the party, I met up with Eddie. We had some drinks. Too many. I told him about the charity event, seeing you and Rylee there, and what she had said about you guys on the hood of Sex. I was feeling angry, rejected, and didn't think twice about it until after he was fired. That's when he called me, livid and unhinged. Said he knew the perfect way to get back at you and that he had gotten hold of a video from that night. Had it in a safe place."

Bingo. Dots connected. A confirmation. Now let's try to complete the picture.

"And you never thought to tell me?" I shout. My hands flex as I resist the urge to grab her shoulders and shake her in frustration.

"It was a different time. You fired me shortly thereafter and I was furious, ashamed, disowned by my mother . . . so no, I'm sorry, Colton, I didn't. I was so busy worrying about myself, being selfish." She sighs, clasping and unclasping her hands in front of her. And I fucking hate when she looks up at me with clarity in her eyes I've never seen before. I don't want to see it but I can't ignore it either. "I was a different person back then. Time . . . things . . . kids, life, it changes you."

"Kids?" I snort out, holding my anger in front of me like a shield as I remember her shocking blindside all these years later. "You mean like the baby you lied about and tried to tell me was mine? Used as a pawn in your fucked-up games?" I take a step forward, fists clenched, anger owning me.

"Yes, as in that one," she says her voice barely audible. "I . . . I'm so—"

"Save the apologies, Tawny. Your bullshit lies and accusations almost made me lose the most important person in the world." The acrid taste of revulsion hits my tongue. "That's something that doesn't deserve forgiveness."

My words hit her like a one-two punch—hard, fast, and bruising. Does she think her quivering bottom lip will win me over? Make me forget the past?

Not hardly.

"I know," she says giving me whiplash. I expected denial and defiance, attitude and arrogance, and she gives me neither. Our eyes hold for a long moment and fuck, all of a sudden I feel like I'm seeing her for the first time in a different light. *Don't fall for her act, Donavan. People like her don't change. Can't. It's not possible.*

But you changed.

The voice in the back of my head so very quiet, barely audible, sounds like a scream, causing me to bite back the snide comments as the unwelcome tang of doubt replaces them.

The look on Rylee's face flashes in my mind from the day Tawny came waltzing in the house to tell me she was pregnant with my baby. A manipulative game by one of the masters. Too bad for her I was a master at it myself. Had no problem going up to the plate against her curveballs. But Rylee . . . she didn't even have a bat in her hand.

I hold onto that thought—Ry's tears, the nasty fight, the break we took—all of it, and tell the tiny ounce of pity I feel for Tawny to take a fucking hike. She brought this upon herself. Not me. Not Rylee. Just her.

Tawny starts to speak and then stops. "If I had known that Eddie really had a tape . . . or what he was going to do, I would have told you."

I stare at her, leery of the sudden decency that doesn't fit with the memory of the woman I used to know, and deliver a visual warning: *You better not be fucking with me.*

"Tell me what you know." My voice is gruff, incapable of believing her or that the years have changed her enough she'd actually look out for me. She'd have told me, my ass.

Would she have?

Does it really fucking matter, Donavan? Get as much info as you can, turn your back, and walk away. You don't need to know if she's changed, wonder if life has been rough for her, because the only thing that matters is the woman sitting in the car behind you.

"Honestly—"

"I'd like to believe that honesty is something you're capable of but you're not the one dealing with . . ." I let my words fall off, catch myself from letting her have a glimpse into my private life. Don't want her to know about the butterfly effect this video she knew about is having on everything in Rylee's life. Because if she's playing me and is behind this—somehow, someway—then she'll have gotten exactly what she was looking for: hurting Rylee, which hurts me. And while I may be sympathetic at times, it's only toward my wife, only with the boys, and only with those I care about. Tawny and I may have a past together, but she is most definitely not any of those people.

"Look, I know you don't want to hear it but I fucked up. Was in a bad place with pressures you have no idea about and I won't use as an excuse . . . but it was a long time ago. Like I said, I'm a different person now, Colton. I don't expect you to believe me . . . to know I'm sorry for the games I played, but I am." We hold each other's gaze, my jaw clenched tight, pulse pounding.

I expected to come here, fight with her, and threaten her to get some answers. Not in a million years did I expect her to be like this: apologetic, decent, sincere. And so the fuck what if she is? It changes nothing. Top priority is getting answers so I can try to make my wife whole again.

"At first I thought he was lying about the tape," she says, breaking through my warring thoughts. "I thought he was trying to get in my pants by feeding my spite over you choosing Rylee, because . . . well, because it was Eddie. You know how untrustworthy he was."

She leans her back against the doorjamb and I shift my feet, wanting to rush this, get the fuck away from here, but I need more. Seeing her causes the memories to resurface. The lies she told. Her manipulative ways. How I thought she'd been in cahoots with Eddie in stealing the blueprints way the fuck back when. Despite investigators and depositions, and every other legal means under the sun CJ couldn't find shit to prove she was involved. To say I had a hard time believing she was innocent is an understatement. But I did. Had no choice.

The question is, do I believe that now?

"Did you ever watch it?" And it's a stupid question, but the thought of her of all people watching Ry and me have sex seems ten more times intrusive than the other millions of people who have.

"No. Never," she says definitively, earning her a rise of my eyebrow in disbelief. "Really. That's why I never thought twice about it."

Great. Now I've given her the idea to go watch it. *Brilliant, Dona-*

van. Fucking brilliant. But then again, I had to ask. Had to know.

I blow out a breath, roll my shoulders, and ask the one question left that makes no fucking sense to me. "If he had the video though, why wait all this time?"

She angles her head as she stares at me, feet shifting, arms crossed over her chest. "I don't know, Colton. I just don't know."

Impatient, uncomfortable, and still a little thrown by this new woman in front of me that looks the same but sounds so very different, I just nod my head, turn my back, and stride down the walk to my car. I don't know what else to do. There is no good in goodbye here. There's just the closing of a door on another chapter of my past.

"Colton."

Every muscle in my body tenses—feet want to keep walking—yet curiosity stops me dead in my tracks. With my back to her, I wait for her to say whatever it is she wants to say.

"It's good to see you happy. It suits you. I know now that's because of Rylee."

I lift my eyes to meet Rylee's at the same time Tawny speaks. I hear her statement, take it for what it is, and don't try to find a hidden meaning or an underlying dig. With eyes locked on Rylee's, I nod my head in acknowledgement and walk toward the car.

Time can change people. The woman with violet eyes staring back at me? She's my living proof that I've done just that, *changed.*

Tawny might have changed too, yet I don't have the effort to care right now. I have a wife that is more important than the air I fucking breathe, and being this close to Tawny, I'm starting to suffocate.

I need my air.

Chapter Ten

COLTON

"TALK ABOUT BLINDSIDING HER," BECKS says.

"Which one?" I ask with a laugh followed by a hiss as I throw back the Macallan. The shit's smooth but burns like a motherfucker.

"I was talking about Tawny but you've got a point there," Becks says with a smirk. "I imagine Rylee got whiplash when she saw Tawny open the front door."

"I'm sure she did, but thank fuck she stayed in the car or who knows what would have happened."

"You're a brave fucker taking Ry there after everything she did to the two of you," he says as he lifts two fingers to our waitress for another round.

"Brave or stupid. But this right here," I say, holding my left hand in the air and pointing to my wedding ring, "means I didn't dare visit Tawny without her. That would have been *no bueno*. Besides, she had a right to know since she called it."

"Dude, I still can't get over the fact you saw Tawny after all this time."

"Yeah . . . well . . ." I shrug, thinking of all of the shit I said way back when about how I'd never step within a hundred yards of her again. "Sometimes the promises you make to yourself are the easiest to break. And shit, we were on the way back from the police station so I figured why not kill two birds with one stone since we'd dodged the vultures?"

"I can't believe the paps are still all over you. Is Ry okay after yesterday?"

I blow out a breath. Fucking assholes. "A little shaken but she's scrappy." I clench my fist on the table as I recall her phone call yesterday. How she tried to take a walk on the beach to get some fresh air but paparazzi shifted from the gate to the sand and swarmed her before she could even reach the waterline.

And I know how she felt—needing the fresh air—because I feel the same way. Isn't that why I'm here right now? Decompressing. Grabbing a few minutes while she's taking a nap after the excitement of my visit to Tawny today, to hang with Becks, shoot the shit, and get a change of scenery to make me a better man. Sitting in your own house day after day can wear on any man. Make you feel like an animal in the zoo: caged, pacing, and constantly toyed with by those on the outside looking in.

I grit my teeth and thank fuck the back entrance of Sully's pub was paparazzi-free so Sammy could drop me off and I could slide in and meet Becks without being mobbed. After yesterday and how they treated Ry, my fuse is short and ready to ignite at the slightest misstep.

"Was it strange seeing her again after all this time?" Becks asks as he lifts his beer to his lips.

"Is the sky blue? Fuck, man . . . it was weird. But she gave me what I needed to know so maybe she's changed some."

"Don't give her that much credit," he murmurs.

"I don't give her any."

"Smart," he says and slides the cardboard coaster around on the table. "Should have known Eddie would be the one to pull shit like this. Fucker."

"Fucker," I repeat because anything else would be a waste of breath. I glance at my phone to make sure Ry or Kelly hasn't texted since the noise in the bar is getting louder the longer we sit here.

"Everything okay?"

"After ten more of these it will be. Need to drink to forget," I say, rolling my shoulders and letting out a frustrated sigh. Too much shit, too damn fast. I want my happy, baby-crazed wife back. Her job back. Our life back. "It's not gonna help shit and I'll be sicker than a dog in the morning, but sometimes, it's just what the doctor ordered."

"Truth. And I've got just the prescription for us," Becks says as he motions to the waitress again to head over to our regular table tucked in the back.

"What can I get you boys?" she asks, smile wide and cleavage jiggling.

"Bottle of Patron Gold. Two shot glasses, please. We need to forget," Becks says.

"That'll sure do the job," she says with a lift of her eyebrows. "Looks like you're going to be stuck here for a while anyway with the way paparazzi are stacking up outside."

"Shit," I mutter under my breath.

"Sorry, hon. We find out who in here called, we're kicking their sorry asses to the curb," she says louder than normal so those around us can hear her. She starts to walk away and then stops and turns around. "And we'll stick 'em with your tab."

I throw my head back with a laugh. "I like the way you think."

She returns within minutes, our ongoing tab and prior large tips always earning us the best service. "Here you go, boys," she says, as she sets two full shot glasses in front of us, and the bottle in between us. "May God rest your souls."

"Amen to that," Becks says as he lifts his glass. "What's the first thing we need to forget?"

"Paparazzi."

"Cheers," he says as we tap our glasses against each other's. "Fuck you, paparazzi."

We toss the shots back. My throat burns as the warmth starts to flood through me. Becks lifts a lime from the bowl on the table and I mutter, "*Pussy*," under my breath, earning me a flip of his finger. "Umm." I think of what I want to forget next. "Fucking CJ."

"Okay," he draws the word out as he pours us another shot, "but if I'm drinking to forget something, I need to know what I'm supposed to forget since I sure as hell hope you're not fucking CJ."

"No. I'm not fucking CJ." I belt out a laugh. My mind is starting to spin as I glance around the bar. "Because my goddamn hands are cuffed and not in a good way. He called earlier, said that in the eyes of the law, the tape was public. Eddie didn't steal it from us per se. He uploaded it for free . . . isn't making any money off it and so we can't do shit about it. He gets his kicks fucking with us and we have no legal means to get back at him."

"Sure as shit there are other means though," he says with a smirk and a raise of his fist.

"Now that," I say as I hold up my shot, "I'll drink to. Cheers, brother."

"Cheers."

Our glasses clink. The tequila burns until it warms. Our laughter gets louder and our cheers get sloppier and take longer to come up with.

But I begin to forget.

About Eddie. The pressure to fix it all. And the thousands of men jacking off to the image of my wife holding her tits as she comes. And the rage over how she lost her job. And becoming a father. The need to win the next race. Being told to bite my tongue with the press.

And God does it feels good to forget.

I'm lost in thought, trying to figure out how many shots we've downed, when my phone rings. I fumble with my cell before answering.

"If it's good enough to make me sober, Kelly, I just might forgive you for ruining my buzz," I say into the phone with a laugh.

"You drunk?"

"Well on my way."

"Understandably," he says in his no nonsense tone. "Eddie checks in with his parole officer once a month."

"Mm," I say as visions fill my head of waiting for him outside the social services office and greeting him with a fist to the face.

"Don't even think about it, Donavan. You got the restraining order for Rylee. Leave it at that. Just like I've told you all week long, you touch him, he's going to sue you like he owns the Fluff and Fold and take you to the cleaners. It's not worth it."

Quit fucking telling me what to do.

"Let him try," I sneer, admitting to myself he's right but also knowing revenge gives its own special satisfaction. I begin to say something else when the thought hits me that I might be able to get him back and not lift a fucking finger. The problem is I want to lift more than a finger at him. I want a whole knockout fist.

"Thanks, Kelly. Keep me up to speed." Thoughts try to connect through my fuzzy mind on how I can make this all work to my advantage. Fuck Eddie over. Redeem Rylee. Get back the happily ever after.

My plan could work.

"Everything okay?" Becks asks, as he looks up from his own phone.

Later, Donavan. Figure it out later. Right now? Drink.

"Fucking peachy," I say, copying one of his go-to sayings. "Kelly's got a line on Eddie."

"And that pisses you off, why?"

"Just thinking."

"That's scary," he teases and I slide my glass across the table so it clinks against his in response. "What is it?"

"Bad juju, man," I finally say, trying to put into words what I think's been bugging me the past few days. The drinking to forget didn't numb this. "I've got this feeling that won't go away."

"I'm not following you."

"Things have been too goddamn perfect for us. I have the fucking fairy tale, Becks. The princess, the castle, the—"

"Jackass," Becks snorts as he points my way, causing me to laugh. Asshole. "Sorry. I couldn't resist," he says, putting his hands up in a mock surrender. "Please, continue."

"Nah. Never mind." Shut it down, Donavan. You sound like an idiot. A drunk one at that.

"No. Seriously. Go on."

I concentrate on drawing lines in the ridges of the worn tabletop. "Shit in our life was just too good. Too perfect. And now with the tape and Ry's job and . . ." My voice fades as I try to explain the feeling I don't understand, but that all of a sudden feels like it's clinging to me like a second skin. "I just keep waiting for the other shoe to drop to make this fairy-tale life of ours come crashing down. It's a shitty feeling."

"Feelings are like waves, brother. You can't stop them from coming but you sure as fuck can decide which ones to let pass you by and which ones to surf."

"Yeah, well, let's just hope I don't wipe the fuck out by picking the wrong one."

Becks and I decide we're looped enough to brave the chaos.

We push open the back door of Sully's and are met with blinding flashes of light and a roar of sound. I wince. The alcohol makes the clicking shutters and shouts of my name sound like they're coming through a megaphone. They stagger me. Blind me.

Anger the fuck out of me.

Sammy's here. Pushing people back to let Becks and I inch toward the Rover. But each step, each push of the mob against me fuels my fire.

Take a step. A camera hits my shoulders. My fists clench.

"Colton, how does it feel to be the most downloaded video on YouTube in over five years?"

Another step. Questions shout. Sammy's hands moving people back.

"Colton, are you and Rylee thinking of making a porn soon?"

One more step. A single thought: Rylee dealt with this on her own yesterday on the beach. Motherfucker.

"Colton, how is Rylee handling all of this?"

Another step. The car within reach. Flash in my eyes. Fury in my veins.

Fuck Chase's *no comment* advice. Fuck everyone. *I'm done.* Shoved way too far one way, and now I'm coming back swinging.

"You want a comment?" I shout. Silence is almost automatic. "Well, I'll give you one." I glance over to where Becks is standing in the open car door, eyes full of pride, telling me I'm doing the right thing.

"The question is, do you really want to know how we feel or are you just interested in twisting your story because sex sells so much better than the truth? I get it. I do. And if you take the selfless do-gooder who's spent her life helping others and turn her into a whore who makes sex tapes in exchange for funding . . . well shit, that sells ten times more. But that's not who Rylee Donavan is." I take a breath. My body vibrates with anger. My thoughts slowly click together.

That revenge I was looking for just found the most perfect stage of all.

"How about I give you a better story? How about you focus on the sick bastard who released this video of a private moment between my wife and me? How about you go harass the bastard who did this rather than harass my wife? I'll even give you a head start. *Eddie Kimball,*" I say, putting my plan in motion. "Focus on why he tried to blackmail us, because I assure you, he definitely had an agenda releasing this video. Sex sells. I get it . . . but uncovering the story behind his bullshit attack on my wife's reputation would make much better copy."

Good luck hiding now, you fucking weasel.

The night erupts in sound. But they give me a wide berth because I gave them something. I nod my head in goodbye.

The cameras flash. Each one causes me to feel more and more sober. Makes me realize what I just did. Slide into the car beside Becks and catch his nod of approval. Rest my head back on the seat with a sigh.

Fuck. You. Eddie.

You want to play hardball? I've got your number, you spineless son of a bitch. Right now some little nosey reporter is digging for the story. They'll connect the dots with your early release from prison. They'll use your name in the press and it'll shine like a fucking neon sign, notifying the many you owe a shitload of money to.

Oh, and how they'll come. I have no doubt about that with the amount of money you owe people. Plus three years worth of interest. They'll flush you out of hiding and right into karma's long reaching arms.

The best part is if I don't want to, I won't have to lift a single finger to give you what you deserve, because I just did.

Social media can be a bitch when you have shit to hide. Good thing I don't. *Good thing you do.*

Revenge can be a mean, nasty fucker sometimes.

"You good?" Sammy asks as he pulls out of the alleyway, leaving the flashing cameras behind.

"Yup." I sigh, long and loud as I meet his eyes in the rearview mirror. *It's crazy how much I need Rylee, right now.* "Home please. I miss my wife."

Chapter Eleven

Rylee

"DAMN IT," I SHOUT IN frustration as the flour flies all over the kitchen because I forgot to put the guard around the mixer's blade. Tears sting the backs of my eyes as I look around at the mess. Normally I'd find this amusing, laugh it off, but not right now. Not with how this week has gone. Nothing can seem to pull me from this funk I'm in.

I squeeze my eyes shut and ignore the voices in my head telling me I'm going crazy because I fear that I am. The video's ripple effect just continues to knock me on my ass. Gone are the things I normally use to center myself: my boys, my freedom outside this house, my work. Even Colton's visit to Tawny derailed me momentarily. Yes, I felt validated Colton believed enough in my assumption that he went and talked to her, but at the same time, it still knocked me back a step seeing her again.

Shake it off, Rylee. It's temporary. Enjoy playing the domesticated role, take advantage of the quiet time now before the baby comes, and life is turned around with lack of sleep and two a.m. feedings.

I pick up the carton of eggs on the counter and blow the flour off them so I can put them away and start to clean up this disaster. Mind focused on the mess at hand, I don't notice Baxter on the floor behind me. When I step on his paw, he skitters up and away from me with a yip causing me to lose my balance. I catch myself from falling by grabbing the edge of the counter, but all nine eggs in the carton fly across the kitchen making a distinct symphony of splats as they land on the tile floor, counter, and against the refrigerator door.

"Fuck!" Adrenaline begins to rush through my body, and just as quickly as it hits me, it morphs and changes into a rush of so many emotions that I'm suddenly fighting back huge, gulping sobs. And it's no use to fight them because they already own my body, so I carefully lower my pregnant body to the flour-ridden floor beneath me. Leaning against the cabinet behind me, I let them come.

Wave after wave. Tear by tear. Sob by sob.

So many feelings—anger, humiliation, despair—come forth before being replaced by the next in line that have been waiting all week to get out. And I just don't have the wherewithal to fight them anymore.

"Rylee?" Colton's voice calls from the front door, and I just close my eyes and try to wipe the tears away but there's no way I'll be able to hide them from him. "What the . . .? Ry, are you okay?" he asks as he rushes to my side where I just shake my head, tears still falling, the agony all-consuming.

He drops to his knees beside me, and the concern etched in his face as he looks me over, ignites my irrational temper.

"Leave me alone," I say between sobs.

"What's wrong?" he pleads, reaching out to wipe flour from my cheek, causing me to cry harder.

"Don't," I tell him as I shake my head away from his hands, making him lean back on his haunches. And I can feel his eyes on me, assessing me, trying to figure me out, and for some reason that thought sets me off. I've had enough eyes on my body judging me this week—scrutinizing me—and the notion causes the distress to come to a head. "You want to know what's wrong with me?" I yell unexpectedly, startling him.

"Please," he says ever so calmly.

"That!" I yell, pointing at him. "You walking around this house like everything is all right when it's not. You treating me with kid gloves and avoiding me every time I get emotional because you feel guilty about the video when it's not your fault. I'm sick of trying to pick a fight with you because I'm going stir crazy in this goddamn house and you won't take the bait. You just nod your head and tell me to calm down and walk away. Fight me, damn it! Yell at me! Tell me to snap the fuck out of it!" My chest is heaving and my body is trembling again. I know I'm being irrational, know I'm letting the hormones within me take charge, but I don't care because it feels so good to get it all out.

"What do you want to fight about?"

"Anything. Nothing. I don't know," I say completely frustrated that now he's giving me the option to fight with him, I don't know what to fight about. "I'm mad at you because I'm worried about you racing next week. I'm freaked out that all of this is going to distract you and you're not going to be careful and . . . and—"

"Calm down, Rylee. I'm going to be fine." He reaches out to take my hand, and I yank it back.

"DON'T tell me to calm down," I scream when he does exactly what I told him I hated. Visions of the crash in St. Petersburg flash through my mind and cause my breath to hitch. I shove it away, but the hysteria starts to take over. "I miss the boys. I'm worried about Auggie and how he's doing. *I miss my normal.* Nothing is normal! Everything is up in the air and I can't handle up in the air, Colton. You know I can't." I ramble, and he no doubt tries to follow my schizophrenic train of thought.

"Let's make our own normal then. Why don't we start by getting the baby's room set up? That's one thing we can do, right?" he asks, eyes wide, face panicked. But his words cause fear to choke in my throat.

"Look at me," he says. "Putting BIRT's room together is not going to make something happen to him, okay? I know that's why you haven't done it yet . . . but it's time. Okay?"

With those words, the fight leaves me. Those body-wracking sobs I had moments ago are now quiet. Tears well in my eyes but I refuse to look up at him and acknowledge what he's saying is true. The nursery *is* incomplete because I'm frozen with fear that if I actually finish it, I'm jinxing it. That fate's cruel hand will tell me I'm taking the baby for granted, and reach out and take him or her away from me again.

When I can finally swallow over the lump in my throat, I look up to meet the crystalline green of his eyes and nod, just as the first silent tear slips over and slides slowly down my cheek.

"It's all going to be okay, baby," he says softly. I don't deserve his tenderness after how I just yelled at him. And then of course that sets me off even further and another tear falls over.

"You're absolutely beautiful," he murmurs reaching forward to move hair off of my cheek, and I squeeze my eyes shut.

"No, I'm not."

"I'm the husband, I make the rules," he says with a soft laugh.

"How can you say that? I'm covered in flour because I tried to make you cookies, which is normally simple, and I failed so epically at that including dropping nearly a whole carton of eggs. And my belly is so big I can't reach my toes to paint them and they look horrible and I hate when my toes look horrible. I tried to shave today and I can't even see between my legs to do that and I'm going to go into labor and have all this hair and look like I don't take care of myself and . . . and . . . we're having a baby and what if I'm a horrible mother?" I confess all of this as we sit on a flour-covered floor with a dog licking up broken eggs, but the way Colton looks at me? He only sees me.

I take comfort in the thought. That even amid all this chaos swirling around us, my husband only sees me. That I can still stop the blur for him. That I'm still his spark.

Be my spark, Ry.

We sit in silence for a moment, the memory of that night in St. Petersburg clear in my mind, his hand on my cheek, our eyes locked, and it hits me. With him by my side, everything is going to turn out how it's meant to be. It always has. He knows how to calm my crazy even amidst the wildest of storms.

Colton leans forward and presses a kiss to my belly before placing a soft one on my lips. "C'mon," he says, grabbing my hands and starting to pull me up when I'd rather just stay right where I am, wallowing in my own self-pity.

"Why?" I ask as I look up at him beneath my lashes, lips pouting.

"We're going to go make our own kind of normal." Between the comment and grin he flashes me, I can't resist him. *I never can.* He gently pulls me up and before I can process it, he has me cradled in his arms and is walking toward the stairs. "Colton!" I laugh.

"That, right there . . . I've missed the sound of that laugh," he murmurs into the top of my head when we clear the landing.

He carries me into the bedroom and sets me down on the edge of the bed, fluffs a bunch of pillows against the headboard, and then helps me lean back against them. Our eyes hold momentarily—violet to green—and I can tell he's trying to figure something out. My curiosity is definitely piqued.

"Red or pink?" he asks. I look at him like he's crazy.

"What?"

"Pick one."

"Red," I say with a definitive nod.

"Good choice," he says as he turns around and disappears into the bathroom. I hear a drawer open, the clank of glass against glass, and then the drawer shut again. Carrying a bath towel in one hand, what appears to be a bottle of nail polish in the other, and a huge grin on his face, he climbs up on the bed and sits at my feet. "At your service, madam."

I just stare—a little shocked, a lot in like—and absolutely head over heels in love with him and the completely lost look on his face over what in the hell he should do next. And while the Type A in me wants to tell him the answers, I don't. My husband is trying to take care of me regardless of how awkward he feels and that's a very special thing.

He lays the towel out over the comforter and then gently lifts my legs so my feet are positioned atop of it. And I stifle a laugh as Colton holds the bottle up of fire-engine red nail polish and reads the instructions on the back, his eyebrows furrowed and teeth biting his bottom lip as he concentrates. He chuckles and shakes his head as he grabs my foot.

"I must really love you because I've never done this for anyone before." His cheeks flush with pink and his dimple deepens. All I can do is lean back, smile wide, and appreciate him all the more.

"Not even for Quin when you were kids?" I ask, thinking back to how sometimes Tanner would help me with girly stuff as long as I'd help him with icky boy stuff first.

"Nope," he says as he concentrates on painting my big toe. He grimaces as I feel him wipe at the sides of my nail. I fight the grin pulling at my lips because I have a feeling I am going to have more polish on my skin than on my nails. But *that's* okay. It doesn't matter. He's trying and that's what matters most.

I stare at my husband—gorgeous, inside and out. He listened to my rant, and picked the thing he could do something about to try and help me. I've always known I'm a lucky woman to have found him, but never realized just how fortunate until right now.

I watch him concentrate as I try to let go of the chaos of the last week.

Angered shock: What I felt when I found out my picture was on the cover of People magazine. Inside, a blow-by-blow story about the video and a million other lies about my purported sexual preferences. Psychologists giving their two cents about the heightened arousal that some people get when they have sex in public with the risk of being caught. I wanted to scream—to rage—and tell them to stop telling lies. To explain it was a moment of heated passion that got carried away. Two people loving each other.

Two people who still love each other.

Confinement: How I felt when Dr. Steele made a house call—something she normally doesn't do—because I couldn't leave the house without paparazzi following me to her office. A doctor, whose clientele includes a high ratio of celebrities, is not too fond of photos being taken of her office as other patients come and go.

Exposed: Not being able to turn on the television, open my email, go onto Google without knowing there was a chance of seeing an image of myself.

Lonely: How I feel without seeing my boys daily. I miss their laughter, their bickering, and their smiles.

Validation: Watching Tawny come into view over Colton's shoulder. Knowing he'd considered my feelings, confronting her in my presence when he'd promised he'd never see her again.

Hurt and hope: Colton's unexpected speech last week as he left Sully's Pub. Using my name and whore in the same sentence stabbed deeply into my resolve and stung enough that I'd picked a fight over it. But at the same time, I appreciated the fact he was saying something, *doing something*, to try and expose Eddie.

So many things, all unexpected, have caused my head to be in a constant whirl and our lives in upheaval even though I've never left the confines of our property.

"I wonder if your little speech the other night caused reporters to start digging up info on Eddie?" I murmur as I watch the top of his head.

He looks up and meets my eyes. "Not now, Ry. I don't want to talk about any of that right now. I want to spend time with my wife, paint her toes, talk to her, and not let the outside world in, okay?"

He nods his head to reinforce what he's saying. "It's just you and me and—"

"Nothing but sheets," I finish for him, causing a huge grin to spread on those lips of his.

"I haven't heard that phrase in a long time," he says with a reflective laugh as he screws the cap onto the nail polish. I notice how much red is on his fingers from trying to fix his overage. He looks back down and shakes his head. "Not as good as when you do it, but—"

"It's perfect," I tell him without even looking at my toes. The overage of paint on my skin is almost like an added badge reflecting how much he loves me. "Besides, the part on my skin will come off in the shower."

"It will?" he asks as he spreads his fingers out and looks at his own speckled with nail polish. My bad boy marked by the deeds of a good husband. "Thank Christ, because I was worried how I was going to get it off. I thought I was going to have to use carb cleaner."

A giggle falls from my mouth and it feels so good. All of this does: his effort, his softer side, seeing him look so out of place, and simply spending time together.

He blows gently on my toenails to help them dry, and I find so much comfort in the silence. I lean my head back on the pillow and close my eyes as he moves from one foot to the other.

"I know you'll do good at the race next week," I murmur eventually, not wanting him to think from my whirlwind of emotions earlier that I'm as worried as I let on.

"I promise I'll come home to you and the baby safe and whole," he says, eyes intense and heart on his sleeve like the tattoos on his flank. And I know that's a promise he really can't make. After all these years together I know he can't control what others do or don't do on the track, but I hold dearly to the fact he's cognizant of it because that's all I can ask. "And with apple pie a la mode."

The laughter comes again because that's my go-to craving right now. Well, besides sex with him. "You know a way to a woman's heart."

"Nope. Just my woman's." His eyes light up as he shifts off the bed, and I immediately become saddened because I fear our time together seems over. I know he has a lot of work to do since he's so behind staying home with me, so I won't ask him to keep me company any longer. Besides he's been more than sweet enough to me after how I acted in the kitchen.

So I'm taken by surprise when Colton reaches behind my back and under my knees and picks me up off the bed. He's seriously trying to throw his back out by carrying my pregnant ass again but the only protest I emit is a startled gasp as I look into his eyes to find a mischievous gleam.

"Hold tight."

"What are you . . .?" I ask, confused as he sets me down on the edge of the bathtub. I look longingly at the tub and think of what I'd do to climb in it and let the hot water swirl all around me. But no can do being pregnant so I just sit silently and wait to see what Colton is up to.

He steps over and into the tub and one by one picks my legs up so they swing into the oval haven. I stare at him, partially wanting him to tell me to break the doctor's orders and take a bath, but also surprised that my husband—the man who never follows rules except for when it comes to what the doctor tells me I can and can't do while pregnant—seems to be going rogue.

And of course I kind of like it.

"Stand up," he says as he grabs my hands and helps to pull me up so we are both standing barefoot and fully clothed in the empty tub. With his eyes locked on mine, he drops to his knees and very cautiously pulls my shorts down. His eyes light up and a smirk plays at the corners of his mouth as he carefully pulls each foot out of the leg holes to avoid messing up my polish. When he's done and I'm staring at him like he's crazy, he looks up at me and orders, "Scoot back on the edge with your shoulders against the wall."

I do as he says, my butt on the lip of the tub and my back pressed against the chilled wall behind, and watch with curiosity as he drops to his knees before me. With his tongue tucked in his cheek, he scoots closer, hands pressing my knees apart as he moves between them.

I suck in my breath, eyes flashing up to lock onto his. My need for him still stronger than ever, but hidden beneath the layers of emotion this week has brought upon us, resurfaces. My body re-acts viscerally to the thought of his hands on me: a warmth floods through my veins, my nipples harden, my heart picks up its pace, and my breathing evens.

"Do you trust me?" he asks, snapping me from the visions in my head of his fingers parting me and his tongue pleasuring me.

"Always," I stutter, knowing the last time he asked me this, the video was released. I hold my breath as he moves the towel from the edge of the tub to uncover a razor blade and shaving balm. Well, maybe not so much. My eyes widen as I realize he's trying to fix the second problem I complained about in my childish rant downstairs.

I bite back the immediate recant of my instant agreement about trust, because

a razor blade on my nether regions should allow for a reconsid-eration of the question. And I know he can see my hesitation because his eyes ask me again.

He wants to shave me. I'm nervous but at the same time feel a rush of heat between my thighs at how hot the simple idea is. I nod my head ever so slightly, my eyes on his, because yes, I've been mar-ried to the man for six years, trust him with every part of me . . . but shaving me? That's a whole helluva lot of trust.

And the old me would be massively embarrassed about sitting on the lip of the bathtub spread-eagle in broad daylight while my husband squirts shaving lotion into his hand, but for some reason I'm not. The world has seen me naked like this by now. However, the idea is so damn intimate and personal that when I look down to watch his hand disappear below my belly seconds before the cool, moist lotion is spread into the crease of my thighs, I feel a new connection with him, a new intimacy that restores some of what was lost with the video.

He turns the faucet of the tub on and lets it run a bit as he warms the razor under its flow. He looks back at me with an encouraging smile in place and then slowly moves the blade below the swell of my belly. We both hold our breaths as he begins to shave me; the only sound in the room is the soft scrape of metal against flesh and the trickle of water into an empty tub.

After a few minutes I allow myself to relax, the inability to see what he's doing only serving to heighten both the intensity and the sensuality of the whole act. He continues to shave, face etched in concentration on areas I can't see but can sure as hell feel. And it's not the bite of pain I expected. Instead it's the soft press of his fingers as he pushes my skin this way and that way. It's the warm water as he cups it and lets it fall over my sex. It's the way his fingertips feather ever so lightly over my seam to wipe away the excess shaving cream that doesn't wash away with the trickle of water.

These things add together, build into an intense experience I never would have expected and yet don't want him to stop. We've been disconnected this week, so stressed about the video and the repercussions, that we haven't even paused to pay much attention to each other besides the verbal, *Are you all right?* And *How are you doing?*

He runs the pad of his finger back down the length of me. In reflex, I push my hips forward some, a nonverbal beg for him to dip his fingers between the lips of my sex so he can discover just how much I want and need him right now. I groan out in frustration when his fingers leave my skin, prompting him to chuckle.

"Is something funny?" I ask him between gritted teeth.

He just shakes his head. "Nope. Just making sure I made that little landing strip you like nice and straight," he says, tongue between his teeth as he concentrates, oblivious to the sexual torment he is putting me through. But then again, maybe that's his goal. He can't be this clueless. He knows my body all too well to know his touch is going to stoke my fires from embers to a wildfire.

"There." He hmpfs in triumph as he leans back and looks at his handiwork, a smug smirk on his face as he looks up at me. That smug smirk soon turns into a cocky grin once he recognizes the look of libidinous desperation on my face. "What's wrong?" he asks, feigning ignorance.

He's definitely toying with me. And hell, I'm all for being played by him. What better way to forget the world outside than lose myself to the skilled hands of my husband?

"Nothing," I murmur, right before he pulls the hand-held showerhead from its base and stretches the necking so the sprayer faces the delta of my thighs. He turns it on, the pressure of the water creating its own pleasurable friction that causes me to suppress a hiss of desire.

"I think I missed some shaving cream right here," he says with a concerned look before his fingers touch me again. But this time, they slip between the seam of my pussy and slide up and down the length of it, spreading me apart so the pulse of the water hits my clit. I groan from the sensation as I selfishly offer myself to him by widening my knees and trying to tilt my hips up.

"Good. Got it," he says as his finger takes a pass over my clit before all touch and water leaves me.

"What?" I yelp, catching that lightning-fast grin of his as he starts to stand up.

"All done," he says causally, picking up the extra towel on the tub's edge to pat me dry.

"No, you're not."

His amused laugh falls into the silence around us. "Your toes are painted, your pussy is trimmed," he says, ticking off the tasks on his fingers. "Whatever else could there be to do?" Our eyes lock and then mine slowly drag down the length of his torso as he pulls his shirt over his head and tosses it outside of the bathtub. He nonchalantly undoes his belt and pulls it through the loops, making a show of throwing it aside as well. When he slides his pants and underwear down his hips his dick stands at attention when he straightens up.

"I don't know," I say with a lift of my eyebrows and suggestion lacing my tone.

"Okay. I'm going to take a shower then," he says with a smirk as he starts to step out of the bathtub, making me laugh.

"No, you're not." His eyes are back on mine, hungry with desire, and for a split second I wonder why he's not taking what's laid out before him when his want is so blatantly plastered on his face—*and* his body for that matter.

"I'm not?"

"No."

For a few moments, we stare silently at each other with words unspoken but so much emotion exchanged. And finally I ask what keeps crossing my mind. "I miss you. I want you." Something flickers in his eyes I can't read, but I can tell he's struggling with. "What's wrong, Colton?"

And I figure there is no better time than right now to ask since we are both literally and figuratively stripped down. There will be nothing left but the truth between us.

"I started all of this by taking you on the hood that night. I asked you to step outside of that perfectly square box you lived in and look what happened. Fuck yes, I want you, Ry. Every second of every damn day. But with everything that happened . . . I don't know . . . I'm not touching you until you tell me you want me to," he admits. While I want to tell him he just was in fact touching me, quite easily turning me on, I also understand how hard this has been for my always "hands-on" husband to not touch and take when he wants to.

I angle my head and stare at him, a smile spreading on my lips as my chest constricts with love for him. "I believe the motto is *anytime, any place . . . right, sweetheart*?" I ask, imitating perfectly the way he says it.

His grin lights up his face, his posture changing instantly from cautious to predatory. Shoulders broaden, fingers rub together as if he's itching to touch, and the tip of his tongue wets his bottom lip. His eyes trail up and over every inch of my body; the look in them alone setting my nerve endings ablaze.

"That's a good motto," he quips. "Time to put it to use."

"Yes, please," I murmur. He bends at the waist and places both hands on the edge of the tub beside my hips. At an achingly slow pace, he leans in and brushes his lips unhurriedly against mine. The kiss is equal parts torment and tantalizing, liquefying the desire already mounting within me. A delicious ache pools in my lower belly.

"Ride me." Two words are all it takes. He says them with his lips pressed against mine, and it's all I need to hear. I place my hands on his shoulders so he can help me stand and make it to the bed.

He lies down, propping a pillow beneath his hips, as I crawl beside him. I pull my shirt over my head and take one more taste of his kiss before I do just exactly what he's asked. Asked? Who am I kidding? More like demanded, but this is one demand I have no problem complying with since I'm on the receiving end of its delirious outcome.

Our lips meet, and I can feel his desire for me in the way his hands run down my arms and over to my torso. His fingers dig into my hips as he helps me settle atop him, our bodies expressing what we need from each other without a single word uttered.

Eye contact is way more intimate than words can ever be.

Rising up on my knees astride his hips, I scoot back so the crest of his dick is just at my entrance. His hand grabs the base of his shaft and runs it back and forth to spread my arousal onto him. And when we're both slick with my desire, I sink down slowly, inch by perfect inch upon the length of his cock until he's completely sheathed root to tip. My head lolls back and a moan of appreciation falls from my lips the same time he groans out my name. It may have only been a week since we last connected like this, but in our relationship where we both use physical touch to help say the words we've left unspoken, that's a long time.

I wait a moment—revel in the feeling of him filling me. And there is something about his reaction that is even sexier than the sensation of his dick awakening every erogenous nerve within me. It's the arch of his head back into the pillow so all I can see from my viewpoint is the underside of his jaw and Adam's apple—that place I love to nuzzle into. It's watching the tendons in his neck go taut from the desire I've created. It's seeing the darkened stubble in such contrast to the bronzed skin around it. It's the feel of his hands still gripping my hips, so his biceps are flexed, and the darkened disks of his nipples are tight with arousal.

All of it—the whole package—is like a visual aphrodisiac that makes the sensation of me rocking my hips over his all that more intense. Then of course the guttural groan of, "Fuck, Ry," only adds to it.

So I begin to slide up and down on his cock, changing the angle every couple strokes to make sure his crest hits where I need it to so I can get off with him. My God, how I needed this with him. From him.

It's amazing how we can feel so very far apart, how I can feel at the end of my rope after so much pandemonium this past week, yet when we are like this I feel complete again within minutes. Connected. United. Indestructible.

One.

I rise up, let the crest of his dick hit right were I need it to, and pop my hips forward to add some intensity to my pleasure. The girth of his shaft causes my thighs to tense and tighten over his hips. My body slowly begins to swell with warmth as desire surges within me. Letting my head fall back, I reach behind me and scratch my fingers over the tops of his thighs causing his hips to jut up and fill me more deeply when I thought it impossible.

"Oh God," I moan, head lolling back, hands falling to my sides. My words spur Colton on, encourage him to grind his hips up to work his dick between the confines of my thighs. And I pull back as he thrusts causing the root of his shaft to slide up and against my clit. My eyes roll back. I moan incoherently as I ride the high of sensation from him rubbing over one hub of nerves before moving right back in to tantalize the other in a two-for-one knockout punch.

"Come on, baby. Your pussy feels so damn incredible. Fuck, I love when you ride me." His words end on a groan as I begin rocking over him again, filling me with a sense of power, knowing I can knock him breathless.

And we began to move in unison. A slow slide followed by a quick grind by both of us as we take our time moving up the ever-beckoning ascent to climax. Explicit words muttered into the comfortable quiet. Tense fingers press into the flesh of my hips. The veins in his neck taut with strain as he holds on to the control I can slowly sense is slipping from his grip. Eyes locked on each other's as we tell each other our feelings with actions. Then a quickening of pace. Our breaths begin to labor and our bodies become slick with sweat.

And yet despite that slow, sweet build, my orgasm hits me unexpectedly. The tingling in my center starts measured and steady, then explodes into a burst of electricity that pulses through my body with such intensity it knocks the breath from me. My body drowns under the orgasmic haze, causing every one of my senses to be magnified. I hear the catch of Colton's breath as my muscles contract around him, feel the sudden sensitivity my climax brings, and ride the wave of dizziness that assaults me.

And just as I'm about comatose from the bliss—my head light and heart full—Colton begins to move beneath me. His actions rouse me to respond and help pull him over the cusp and into oblivion with me. We move in sync, and when he bottoms out in me, I can feel the hair around the base of his shaft teasing my swollen clit once again to draw out the aftershocks still quivering through me.

"What I'd give to flip you over right now and fuck you senseless," he groans when I slide back up him again.

"Yes, please," I murmur. He lifts his eyebrows in a nonverbal question, and I know he's petrified he'll hurt the baby, but my comment is all the consent he needs to tell him all will be fine. Because I know as much as Colton loves the soft and slow, he does that for me. Gives me what I need to get mine.

And I know as his wife that this is what he needs. *What he loves.*

With his help, I climb off him and get on my hands and knees, ass in the air, and head looking over my shoulder to see him taking in the sight of me swollen, wet, and completely his. Our gazes meet and the carnal lust in his is so strong I'm glad I offered him this. After a week of feeling so out of control, he needed this ownership of my pussy to right *his* world. And after all this time, I know giving him complete control allows him to find it.

"Fuck, I love looking at you like this," he murmurs, as his finger traces down the line of my slit and then back up, circling over the tight rim of muscles just above it. My whole body tenses as a deep-seated ache burns bright from his touch where we've played occasionally when we want to change it up. "I love seeing how goddamn wet I make you. The pink of your pussy. The curve of your ass. The jolt of your skin as I slam into you from behind. How you arch your back and shift your hips so you can take me all the way in. Fucking addictive."

He places his hand on the back of my neck and runs it down the length of my spine. The singular touch sending my nerves, already on high alert, into a frenzy of vibrations that heighten the anticipation of *when* he is going to enter me. And yes, while I've already had an orgasm, with Colton, there is always that thrill of him being in me that never goes away. I know this tease of touch will be followed by the overwhelming onslaught of sensations. My whole body tenses as

I wait with expectant breath.

His hand slides from my spine over to my hip and down the back of my thigh before tracing back up my inseam to my apex. This time though, his fingers part me, one finger sliding in and out to be replaced by the crest of his head.

His sigh fills the bedroom. His hands grip the sides of my hips and urge them backward and onto him while he stays completely still. The guttural groan that fills the room matches the internal war my body has over whether it wants to chase another orgasm or just take the pleasure as it comes and enjoy helping him get his.

And I don't get a chance to answer my own questions, because the moment Colton is in me, he starts to move. The pace he sets is so demanding, I know this is every man for himself, and I'm perfectly okay with it. Because there is something so damn heady about being taken by Colton with such authority. It's animalistic and raw and greedy and so very necessary to the dynamic of our relationship. I wouldn't want him any other way.

"Goddamn," he cries out as the sound of our bodies connecting echoes through the room. A symphony of sex.

"Fuck me," I shout as his dick swells within me, the telltale sign he is so very close. So I reach back and scratch my fingernails over the sides of his thighs as he slams into me again. The groan he emits from the sensation is the only sound I need to know he's a goner. Within seconds his grip tightens, his hips thrust harder, and his body goes completely taut as my name falls in a broken cry from his lips.

After a few moments a satisfactory sigh falls from his lips that is so very rewarding to me. Slipping out of me, he starts to laugh and it takes me a second to sit on my butt to see what is so funny. He's looking at the sheets and the little marks of red all over their light blue color.

"Just when I thought I couldn't have made your toes look any worse, I did."

I look up from the sheet to see the love, amusement, and satisfaction in his eyes and I smile. "Hmm. Good. That means we'll have to do some of this all over again."

"Just some of it?" he asks, eyes narrowed. When I nod my head, my favorite dimple appears alongside his playful smirk. "Which part might that be?"

"The find-our-own-kind-of-normal part."

"Just that part?" he asks, head angled to the side. His dick still glistens with our arousal as he grabs the towel used for my toes earlier and helps clean me up.

"The sex part. Definitely the sex part," I say with a more-than-satisfied smile. He leans forward and seals the comment with a kiss.

"Definitely the sex part," he agrees.

Chapter Twelve

Rylee

"RY, COVERAGE JUST STARTED," HADDIE yells from the family room. My nerves start to rattle as I waddle my way out from the kitchen. I'm not feeling too great today so at least I have a reason to be off my feet and not feel guilty about it.

Besides, this race will be the first one I haven't attended since we've been married, and it's killing me not to be there. But between how far along I am in my pregnancy and the buzz still out there over the video, the last thing I wanted was to make a public appearance on national television where I could be caught off guard and asked anything by anyone.

Two weeks out from the video's release and the frenzy has only died down a fraction. All outings are still limited and heavily guarded.

Can't some socialite do something stupid to gain attention to help me out?

"Do you have the scanner?" Haddie pours herself a glass of wine that calls to my cravings on every single level, but I avert my gaze to the bowl of Hershey Kisses she put on the table for me. Gotta love having a best friend who knows all your quirks.

"No. I think you left it in the office," she says. I motion for her to stay seated, and that I'll get the scanner that allows us to listen to Colton and Becks's radio interaction while he's on the track.

I grab the radio sitting beside my cell and just as I pick it up, my phone rings. The House's number flashes on the screen and happiness surges through me because the calls have been way too far and few between the boys and me since I've had to take my leave of absence. And of course I've battled feeling like I'm not needed in their lives since when we do talk, our conversations are filled with generic niceties from boys who'd much rather be playing outside or on the PlayStation.

And I won't lie that it stings a little. Not being the one they go to. Who am I kidding? It stings a whole helluva lot.

So when I see the familiar phone number I grab it and answer immediately, the connection I crave with the other part of my life just within reach.

"Hello?"

"Hi, Rylee."

"Hey, Zander. How's it go—what's wrong?" I'm so thrilled to hear from him that it takes me a second to hear the tinge of distress in his voice.

"I . . ." he begins and stops, his sigh heavy through the connection.

"What, buddy? I'm here. Talk to me." Concern washes over me as I listen as closely as I can to hear whatever it is he's not saying.

"I'm going to get in trouble for telling you but I know you'll make it better," he says in a rush of words that has so many parts of me startle to attention.

"What do you mean?" I ask but don't have to because it all clicks into place the second the last word is out. The basic conversations, the sense the boys don't want to talk to me, the constant run around when I ask anything too detailed about their cases. Someone has told them they're not supposed to give me any information. I've been so wrapped up in my own warped world that I've taken everything at face value, taken it all personally, and didn't delve deeper to see behind the mask of vagueness.

How stupid could I be?

The knife of absolute disbelief twists deeply between my shoulder blades as various emotions flame to life. I focus on the most important: Zander is upset and I need to help him. I can seethe later, call Teddy and express my displeasure after, but right now one of my boys needs me when I didn't think they needed me anymore.

"Never mind," I correct myself, not wanting to put him in a position he should never be in and get to what matters. "Tell me what you need, Zand."

"These people . . . they want to foster me," he says in the slightest of whispers with a tremor to his voice.

And the selfish part of me immediately wants to yell *no*, reject the idea, because Zander is mine in a sense, and yet at the same time this is exactly what I'm supposed to hope for. So I'm left in that catchall of being way too attached to a little boy that came to me damaged and broken and is now turning into a damn fine young man.

"That's good news," I say, infusing enthusiasm into my voice when I don't feel it whatsoever.

"No, it's not."

"I know it's scary—"

"It's my uncle." All encouragement is eradicated as memories of way back when flicker to the surface. His case file comes to the forefront of my mind, and I contemplate Zander's only remaining family member.

How is this possible? My mind reels with this new piece of the puzzle, my abdomen clenching in a Braxton Hicks contraction that knocks the air out of my lungs momentarily. But I try to focus on Zander and not the flash of pain.

I stutter, trying to find the appropriate response and cringe because I don't have one other than to say *no way in hell* and that's not exactly something I can promise him. "Tell me what's happening," I say, needing to get a clearer picture of everything I've been shut out from.

"He . . . he saw my picture with yours in a magazine and on the news." My whole world drops out because *that* means I'm the cause of this. My job is to protect my boys, not hurt them, and that goddamn video has done just that. A picture of Zander and me taken at some event was in a national publication and now someone wants to claim him.

Or use him.

I swallow down the bile threatening to rise as my stomach twists in the knots it deserves to be tied in.

"Jax told me they—"

"Who are *they*?" I ask immediately as I pace the office and try to push away the last image in my mind of the uncle. The one I have of the man so strung out he couldn't even make it to his sister's funeral: track marks on his arms, greasy hair, dirt under his fingernails, and uncontrollable fidgeting as he tried to claim Zander for one and only one reason—the monthly subsidy for fostering a child. While it may not be much, it's still a treasure trove to a junkie. Because let's face it, the communal druggie house in the ghetto's Willow Court is the perfect place to take a traumatized seven-year-old boy and nurture him back to his new normal. *Not.*

My skin crawls, knowing he would even have the gall to come forward again and yet here we are, six years later, and Zander's new normal is having the foundation shaken out from beneath his feet.

"I guess he's married now and they saw a picture of me in People Magazine and decided they want to foster me because I'm the only family they have." His comment is followed by an incomprehensible sound that tugs at my heartstrings. I know he has to be freaked out, ready to run and at the same time too scared to stay. "My caseworker called Jax, told him they're going to give them some supervised visits to see how it goes." And even though he doesn't say it, I can hear the plea in his voice to help him and not make him go.

"I'll make some calls. See what's going on, okay?" I try to sound hopeful, but fear I have no control over what the machine does. All I can do is assert my one, hopefully still powerful and relevant, voice since I was his caretaker for longer than anyone.

"Please, Rylee. I can't . . ." The damaged little boy's voice rings through loud and clear, a sound I thought I was never going to have to hear again. One I worked so hard to overcome and get rid of.

"I know," I tell him as tears burn in the back of my throat. "I know."

"I couldn't not tell you," he says, and I smile at the double negative he's fond of using. It's comforting in an odd sense.

"You did the right thing. Now go watch the race, try not to worry about it, and I'll see what I can do on my end, okay?"

"I'm scared."

And there they are. Two simple words that weasel their way into my heart and create fissures.

"Don't let them take me."

"I will do everything in my power to stop them," I say. Just what that is, I'm not sure yet besides raising hell. "I promise. I soccer you, Z," I add to reinforce his place in my life and heart.

"Yeah. Me too." And the phone clicks without him saying what he always says back to me.

I stare out the window and fear this may be one promise I might not be able to uphold. Visions fill my head of the first time Zander came to me—a broken boy, lost and afraid. Of the sleepless nights I spent beside his bed, building his trust, creating that bond, and now in one fell swoop I've let him down by not being there when he needs me.

And yet someone, somewhere, has handcuffed me so I *couldn't* know.

I tap my cell against my chin, my mind lost in thought as I try to figure out why after all this time his uncle would actually step forward and why social services would even entertain the idea. Because there are just too many kids, not enough caseworkers, and when the unwanted become wanted, it's so damn easy to dust your hands of one and get them off your caseload.

I hate my bitterness. Know that not all caseworkers are this way but right now I have the voice of a scared boy ringing in my ears and doubt niggling in my psyche.

Dialing, I shove away the doubt whether I should call Teddy or not. I wouldn't have thought twice about it before and hate that I am now. Corporations and their board of directors and all of the bullshit can kiss my ass right now.

They are to blame for this. Forcing me to take a leave of absence. Handcuffing me so I can't take care of one of my boys. Letting Zander down when he needs me the most.

Anger riots within me. I'm primed for a fight when Teddy answers the phone.

"Rylee," he greets me, just as I start to worry my wedding ring around on my finger.

"Teddy. I know it's a Sunday but—"

"Colton's racing, right? Is everything okay?" he asks immediately, concern lacing his tone.

"Colton's fine," I state coldly, not wanting to warm to him because he's worried about Colton. I squeeze my eyes shut, pinch the bridge of my nose, and hold on to the disbelief that he's been keeping this from me. And I know it sounds stupid, but all of a sudden, my disoriented emotions latch on to the fact someone has ordered I be kept in the dark about Zander. And that someone is most likely Teddy. "Did you think it wasn't important to tell me what's going on with Zander?"

Silence fills the line. I visualize him picking his jaw up off the ground. Insubordinate Rylee is rare and yet he shouldn't doubt I'd go there instantly when it comes to my boys.

"Rylee." My name again said with detached frustration.

"After working for you for twelve years, you didn't think I was important enough to let know that—"

"I was protecting you."

"Protecting me?" I all but yell into the phone, temper boiling, and body trembling with disbelieving anger. "How about you do your job and start protecting those who matter the most? The boys? Zander?"

"I was," he says, his voice barely audible. "If I'd told you without all the information, you'd act in haste, rush to The House before all facts are straight . . . and then that leave of absence would be permanent, Rylee. And that would not only hurt you, but the boys too. You are their number-one advocate, their fighting force, and so I was protecting Zander by not telling you. If you get fired, you're not going to be there when he needs you the most."

His words knock the whipping winds from my otherwise stalwart sails. They should shock me from my funk but almost plummet me further into it because it makes me realize how much I miss my boys, and how lost I feel right now without being able to champion for them even when I know it's best all around with the baby coming sooner rather than later.

"Teddy," I finally say, a cross between disbelief and gratitude mixed in my tone because he's right.

"I wanted to talk to his caseworker at social services first, get the answers before I called you."

"Okay. I just . . ." My voice fades off as I shake my head and try to figure where to go with this conversation when I was so sure of my knee-jerk reaction two minutes ago. "Why step forward now?"

"Opportunity? Obligation?" He fishes for the right answer when I know deep down it's none other than a self-serving agenda.

"Zander called me, Teddy. He's scared to death." *And I am too.*

"I know he is, Rylee, but this is what we strive for. To find good homes for these boys and give them the life they deserve. I know you're close to him and worry but social services is doing their job and vetting this couple—"

"Not just any couple," I say, incredulity in my voice, "but his uncle who used to be a hardcore drug addict. They want money." There's no other reason in my mind that someone would ignore their own flesh and blood for almost seven years and then suddenly want him.

"We don't know that. People can change." The laugh I give in response is so full of disbelief that it doesn't even sound like my own. My stomach tightens and acid churns in my gut.

They don't love him. So many thoughts race and circle but that's the one I cling to the most.

"Perhaps, but I'm a little leery of accepting he wants more than just the monthly living subsidy that comes along with fostering Zander. It's been so long Teddy, and voila, he sees a picture on TV of Zander and me, and all of a sudden he feels this deep-seated need to be an uncle again? I don't buy it."

It's bullshit is what it is.

His audible sigh is heard through the line. I feel my stress levels rising, not great for the blood pressure, no doubt. "Let's just see what happens, shall we? They're going to have a monitored visitation, see how things fare, and go from there."

"But Zander doesn't want to," I shout.

"Of course not, Ry. It's scary for him, but this is our job. Get them back with a family unit, and have the most normal life possible."

"I still don't believe for a minute that Zander's best interest is on anyone's mind but mine."

"I take offense to that, Rylee, and am going to chalk it up to you being upset." The stern warning is noted and yet a part of me doesn't care. "Trust me to do my job."

"Yes, sir," I state, trying to contain the sneer in my voice that I feel in regard to the reprimand. "I'm upset, Teddy, because he's upset and I can't do a damn thing about it."

"I know, kiddo. And that's why you're their number-one advocate. I'll keep you abreast of the situation. Now I've got to go before Mallory gets in a tizzy that I'm working on a Sunday."

"I'm sorry for bugging you," I apologize, acknowledging that he has a life to lead beyond the boys. Just like I do. I recall Colton's words about how I need to start taking care of our family too.

I blow out a breath as I sink down into the chair behind the desk and try to process the past ten minutes.

And I don't think any amount of time will help any of it make sense.

If someone steps forward and wants him because they love him, wants to give him a traditional home life with the white picket fence and Zander falls in love with them back, I'll be all for it. One hundred percent. But the scared tone and the broken waver in his voice scream unease and fear. They tell me so much more than any words could ever express.

Everything is tumbling out of control so fast around me and there is absolutely nothing I can do short of take him as my own. And as appealing as that sounds, then that would mean I'd leave six other boys to feel like I chose him over them. And I'd never do that. I love them all.

I clutch my stomach as a sharp pain contracts around it and tell myself to breathe deeply and try to calm down. The problem is that I know calm is not a damn option anymore, because it seems lately, everyone is out for something.

And that makes me worry how exactly I'm going to bring a baby into this world, and be able to protect him or her as fiercely as I'd like.

"Ry? Are you coming?" Haddie's voice breaks through the haze of disbelief and concern that weigh down my every thought.

"Be right there," I say. I'd much rather sit here and try to figure out what I can do to make this all right again.

"And it seems Donavan can do no wrong on the track this season, Larry. Let's just hope all of his extra-curricular activity off it doesn't prevent him from finishing strong here today," the television broadcaster says as the camera pans to a wide shot of Colton's car on pit row with the crew standing around it. I blanch at the commentator's statement, but my skin is getting thicker and thicker with each passing day.

It doesn't make it any easier but rather more my new normal. And I'm not really sure I like this new normal at all.

In my periphery I see Haddie watching me to see my reaction to the comment on the TV. I don't want to talk about it so I concentrate on the images on the screen. I'm able to make out the back of Becks's head, Smitty's face tight with concentration as he adjusts something on the wing, and then I find Colton in the back, shooting the shit with another racer. The sight of him calms me instantly and has me reaching for my cell in anticipation of his promised pre-race phone call. His voice is exactly what I need to hear right now.

"Fuck them," Haddie says, holding her middle fingers up to the television, making me laugh. I can tell that was her intention with the comment when I look her way.

"You could have gone, you know. I would have been fine by myself," I say, knowing full well I'd rather have her here with me to help calm my nerves since I can't be at the race.

"What? And leave your pregnant ass behind? Nope. Not gonna happen." She smiles as she lifts her wine glass to her lips. "Besides, someone had to stay here and guard the wine cabinet."

"Guard it or deplete it?" I ask with a raise of my eyebrows that gets a laugh from her followed by a guilty shrug.

"What good is it if it's not consumed?"

"True," I muse, shifting on the couch when a sharp pain hits my lower back. As much as I try to hide the wince, it doesn't go unnoticed by Haddie. I grit my teeth and ride it out as my stomach rolls again and fight the wave of nausea that temporarily holds my body hostage.

"You okay?" Haddie asks. She shifts to get up and move over to me, but I stop her with a wave of my hand as I take a deep breath and plaster a fraudulent smile on my lips.

"Yeah. The baby's not too thrilled about something I ate, I think," I lie, talking myself into it when I know it's most likely the stress over everything: the tape, Zander, the race. Too many things at once.

"Uh-huh," she says in that way that tells me she's not buying my story. "It doesn't have anything to do with the phone call about Zander or the—"

The ring of my cell cuts her off and I scramble to answer it, fumbling my phone even though it's in my hand. I just really need to hear Colton's voice to quiet everything in my head.

"Colton?" I sound desperate but I don't care.

"Hey sweetheart. I'm just about to get strapped in but I wanted to call real quick and tell you I love you," he says, voice gruff, the sound of chaos all around him in the background.

"I love you too," I murmur into the phone followed by an audible sigh.

"You okay?" he asks. It sounds as though he is searching to understand the caution in my response.

The tears sting the backs of my eyes as I nod my head before I realize he can't see me. I swallow over the lump in my throat. "Yes. It's race day. You know how nervous I get." And technically I'm not lying to him. I do get nervous, but it's the other things about Zander I desperately need to share that I can't before he gets on the track.

Things I can't have mulling around in his head when he's supposed to be concentrating on the race.

"I'm going to be fine, Ry. In fact, I'm going to win and then rush home to get my victory kiss from you and claim my checkered flag."

My mind flashes to my cache of checkered-flag panties—my unofficial yet Colton-approved race day uniform. The underwear I have worn every race day since that first one in St. Petersburg so very long ago.

Just like the ones I'm wearing right now.

"Smooth one, Ace." I laugh, feeling a tad better even though his words do nothing to abate my unease when I see him on television going two hundred plus miles an hour, wedged between a concrete barrier and another mass of metal.

"You like that?" He chuckles. "You wearing them?"

"You better win and rush home so you can find out for yourself."

"Hot damn."

"Be safe," I reiterate as I hear Becks call his name in the background.

"Always." I know that cocky grin is on his face, and his certainty allows me to breathe a little easier.

"Okay."

"Hey Ryles?" he says just as I'm about to pull the phone away from my ear.

"Yeah?"

"I race you." And I can hear his laugh as he hangs up the phone, but the feeling those words evoke stay long after the line goes dead. I sit there with my phone clutched to my chest and send a little prayer into the universe to let him come back whole and safe to me.

"You okay?" Haddie asks softly.

"I'll tell him about Zander when he gets home," I say as if I need to justify my actions.

"Radio check, One. Two. Three." The radio comes to life as Colton's spotter calls out and immediately distracts us from our conversation.

"Radio check, A, B, C," Colton says, and for the first time in what feels like hours, a smile lights up my face.

But the low ache deep in my belly stays constant. The ball of tension sitting in my chest only increases as the familiar call is made on the television, "Gentlemen, start your engines."

Chapter Thirteen

COLTON

FUCK, IT'S HOT.

My fire suit is plastered to my skin. Sweat soaks my gloves. My hands cramp from gripping the wheel. My body aches from fatigue.

But victory is so damn close I can almost taste it.

Get out of the goddamn way, Mason!

His car is slower, his lap time slipping by a few tenths, and yet every time I try to swerve around him to move up from third place position, he moves to cut me off.

Fucking prick.

"Patience, Wood." Becks's voice comes through the radio loud and clear.

"Fuck that. He's slower. Needs to move," I say as the force of the backside of turn four exerts pressure into my voice.

I pass the start/finish line. Four more to go.

"He's low on fuel," Becks says, his way to try and calm me down, buy some time so I don't push the car too hard, too fast, and burn it up with the endgame in sight. And he knows I know this. Knows we both want the same fucking thing. But he also knows I'm getting amped up on the end of the race adrenaline and might lose sight of the specifics.

"We good?" I ask referring to our fuel supply.

"We're cutting it close but yeah, we're good."

I whip out to the right, try to slingshot past Mason but he blocks me and the ass end slides way too fucking close to the wall. "Asshole," I grit out as I fight to gain control back of the car.

"Watch the loose stuff," my spotter says into the mic. I bite back the smartass comment *I know it's there* because I'm busy fighting its pull on the wheel. Hitting the concrete barrier beside me at two hundred miles per hour because of loose debris on the top of the track isn't on the agenda today.

Three laps to go.

My arms burn as I fight the wheel into the next turn. My eyes flicker to the traffic ahead of me, to the car right in front of me, and to the ones on either side of me so I can find a sliver of space to try to pass.

I see it just as Becks yells into the mic. "He's out! He's out! Go. Go. Go. Wood!"

Split seconds of time. Luke Mason beside me. Luke Mason on the apron at the bottom of the track as I pass him.

Gotta have gas to go, asshole.

Fuck yeah. One car down. One car left to go. *C'mon, baby.* I press the throttle and check the gauges to make sure I push her to the brink because there's one lap left. I refuse to leave anything left in the car when I can lay it all out on the start/finish line.

Steady, Colton. Steady, I tell myself as the tach edges the red line just as I get up behind Stewart's ass end. Getting sucked into his draft helps conserve my gas. And thank fuck for that because I'm sure Becks is busting a nut on pit row questioning if I'm going to burn her up.

White flag. One lap left.

Turn and burn, baby. Turn and burn.

"Traffic is coming up in two," the spotter says as I come out of turn one and see the cluster of lapped traffic clogging the track. "Go low," he instructs, causing Becks to swear into the mic. Means I'll have to let up a little, and I can't let up when I'm chasing the one spot.

"You sure?" Becks asks. He never questions this kind of shit. I don't have time to wait for an answer because I'm already moving down to the white line of the apron praying to fuck this works since lapped traffic usually stays low to make way for the lead cars.

And just as I start to question him a hole opens up between the top of the track and the middle in front of me and it's only big enough for one car: Stewart or me. I slingshot around the car I'm behind, use the conserved energy from the draft to help give me the boost. Our tires rub. Stewart from the top line. Me from the bottom line.

It's like a game of fucking chicken. Split-second reactions. Who's going to back off? Who's going to keep their foot on it? And I've faced a whole shitload of fear in my life so I'm not letting it own me right now. No way. No how.

I hear the squeal of tires as the car begins to get loose again when we connect. Forearms straight and hands gripping, I fight to keep the wheel straight as we fly an unheard of four wide out of turn two.

And I know it's crazy. Has to look like a suicide mission to those watching, because there are four of us and not enough track to keep this up, and yet no one backs off. Something's gotta give and it sure as fuck isn't going to be me if I can help it. Fear is temporary. Regret lasts forever. And another press on the gas pedal ensures I'll have neither.

We barrel into turn three as the two outside cars fall off. It's Stewart and me, nose to nose, coming into the track's final turn.

And the final stretch to clinch the win.

I slingshot out of the turn and give her all she's got: throw the car into the red and pray it pays off. I can't tell who's ahead, our noses seem even, our cars testing the barriers of machine's ability against man's will.

C'mon, one three. C'mon, baby.

The checkered flag waves one hundred yards out. Keep the car straight, Donavan. Out of the wall. Away from Stewart. Don't touch. If we touch, it's over for both of us.

"C'mon, Wood!" Becks shouts into the mic as the checkered flag waves and a whelp comes through the radio. I have no idea which one of us won. Split seconds pass that feel like hours.

"Goddamn right we won!" Becks yells. Elation soars through my tired body, reviving it, and bringing it back to life as I pump a fist in the air.

"Fuckin' A straight!"

Victory lane. People and cameras are everywhere as I pull the car into it. Becks and the rest of the crew greet me. Funny thing is I'm still searching for the one face I want to see the most and know isn't there.

And I don't think I realized how much that would fuck with my head—how much it mattered she was there every race—but pulling into the checkered victory lane without seeing her feels a little less complete. She's so much more than just my wife. She's my goddamn everything.

And then I laugh when I look up as I take the pin out of the wheel to see Becks standing there. "Motherfucking victory, Wood," he says. He takes my helmet and balaclava, handing them off to someone else as he helps me stand from the car. My legs are wobbly and I'm hotter than fuck, but when my best friend pulls me in for a quick hug, it sets in that I've finally won the elusive title on this track

I've been chasing for so damn long.

"Great job, brother," I tell him as I grab a baseball hat Smitty hands me and put it on, body dead tired but fueled on the adrenaline of victory.

The next minutes pass in a blur: confetti raining down, speeches thanking sponsors, interviews, the cold Gatorade that has never tasted better, the spray of champagne onto the crew. I'm riding that high, so goddamn glad to have this monkey off my back in winning this race. I do my proper dog and pony show, thank the sponsors, talk well of the competitors, thank the fans, but all I really want to do is get back to the pits, call Ry, take a shower, and sit back with Becks and have a stiff drink before facing more media circus.

Interview number five finished. I roll my shoulders, take a sip of Gatorade, and prepare myself to answer the same questions again for the next in line.

But when I look up and see the look on my dad's face, the next in line is forgotten. The victory not so sweet. My heart leaps in my throat. My mind spins. My feet move on autopilot as I make my way to him.

"Dad," I say. The dread and worry in my tone match the expression on his face.

"It's Rylee."

Chapter Fourteen

Rylee

I'M LOST TO DREAMS.

To darkness and warmth and a little girl with cherubic curls and a heart-shaped mouth. To her pudgy hand holding my pinky on my left hand. My eyes are mesmerized by her as she giggles, the sound warming my soul, filling my heart, and making them ache all at the same time.

There's a tug on my right hand that startles me. I'm so transfixed on my lost baby girl I never realized someone else was beside me. I look down to the top of a dark head of hair just as he looks up to me. I'm greeted with a row of freckles, a lopsided grin, and green eyes that look so familiar.

"Are you lost?"

"Nope," he says as he swings our joined hands back and forth some, a dimple flashing as his grin widens. "Not anymore."

Arms slip around my waist. The welcome warmth of a body pulling me from the dream I already can't remember. I snuggle into him, the scent of my husband unmistakable—a mixture of soap and cologne—and a calm falls back over me.

Then I hear the monitor beep, the whoosh of the baby's heart-beat filling the room, and I'm shocked awake to the here and now. I'm in a hospital bed being monitored rather than in the comfort of our home.

"It's just me," he murmurs into the back of my head. My hair heats from his breath as he pulls me tighter against him. Our bodies spoon and our hearts beat against each other's in a lazy rhythm.

"You're here," I say, voice groggy.

"Special delivery," he says, and I can hear the smile in his voice. "All the way from victory lane."

"Congratulations. I'm so proud of you and so sorry you had to leave your celebration." All those years chasing the win at the Grand Prix and of course, because of me, the one time he does, he doesn't get to revel in the glory of it all.

"Hmm." He presses another kiss to my head as his fingers lace with mine. "I'd rather be here. It wasn't the same without you. I missed you, Ryles."

How easy it is for him to make me smile and chase away the fear.

"I missed you too . . ." I wait for him to start the questions and as if on cue, the sigh falls from his mouth in resignation of ruining this moment.

"You two trying to give me a heart attack?" he asks, so many emotions overlapping in his voice in the single sentence.

"No. Everything is fine now. Just a few contractions they were able to stop. An ultrasound. Some fetal monitors. All routine things to make sure everything is okay," I explain, attempting to hide how freaked out I was when being hooked up to machines to monitor the two of us. How the room was filled with a sea of scrubs, and even though Haddie held my hand and kept my anxiety at bay, all I want-ed was Colton.

"Common things?" he asks, skepticism in his voice. "You're still having issues with your blood pressure. That's far from fucking com-mon when we're talking about you and the baby."

Shit. I close my eyes momentarily, sucking up my cowardice, and prepare to tell him the truth.

"Want to fill me in here, Ry?"

My mind flickers to the many warnings we've been given about my pregnancy: The high risk, the damaged arteries from the accident and the miscarriage that could pose a problem with heavy bleeding during labor, the stress on my uterus that will increase the bigger the baby gets.

"You have every right to be mad at me," I whisper, because for some reason it's easier to say it that way. "I had the stress under control, attempting to keep my blood pressure in the range it's supposed to be in . . . and then between the race and . . ." My words fall off as I replace them with a sigh representative of the heaviness in my heart about Zander.

"And what?" he prompts. "What else happened to push you too far?" The minute the words are out of his mouth I know he regrets them by the quick tensing of his body against mine.

Should I count the ways multiple things are causing stress right now?

"Zander called before the race started. He was scared, confused. A wreck. His uncle is trying to foster him." My words are so quiet. I try to keep my emotions in check since the constant rhythm of my heartbeat is visible on the monitor beside us.

"Okay," he says slowly, and I can sense his mind working, trying to figure out where I'm going with this. "You gotta give me more than that to make me understand why it put you in the hospital."

"It's his uncle." I swallow over the anger in my throat and continue. "The druggie asshole who wanted nothing to do with him when he first came to us."

"Why come forward now?" His simple question, and the confusion in which he says it, expresses exactly how I feel. I breathe a sigh of relief, thankful for his identical response, because it adds validation to my gut reaction over this.

"Why do you think?" Disgust laces my tone and even though it's not directed at him, I know he takes it that way.

"The video. Your work promo pictures splashed all over the fucking place," he says as everything clearly clicks into place for him.

"Mm-hmm." Because there is nothing else I can say without making it sound like I blame him in part for this turn of events.

"Money?" he asks.

"The monthly foster stipend isn't a ton but—"

"But it's enough to support your habit should you have one," he muses.

"Or better yet," I say as the thought hits me—staggers me even though I'd prefer to not even entertain the idea, "sell an interview with Zander to spill all kinds of juicy details on the woman helping run Corporate Cares who just so happens to be currently on leave from her job due to the release of a sex tape."

"That could explain the sudden urgency."

"Could." I shrug, closing my eyes and concentrating on the feel of security I have with his arms wrapped around me.

"People will do anything for money."

"And some people don't even need money as a motivator." The comment falls out without thought, but I know Colton knows I'm referring to Eddie. That damn video has become the catalyst to cause all of this: invasion of privacy, loss of normal freedoms, embarrassment, losing my job, Zander's situation, me in the hospital, our life unraveling. *Too. Many. Ripples.*

"Ry . . ." My name comes out in a resigned sigh as he rubs the stubble of his chin against the back of my neck, causing my entire body to stand at attention. "You need to put you and the baby first."

"I know. I do need to. I'm trying to . . ." And Colton is one hundred percent right . . . but in a sense, Zander is my child too. "But you didn't hear him, Colton. He was terrified. Scared. Lost. *And I didn't know.*" I take a deep breath and focus on the whir of the machine monitoring the baby's movements. I focus on that and feel centered.

"Teddy gave me some kind of explanation—the corporate song and dance that this is what we strive for. It's all bullshit. He doesn't have the connection with the boys I do . . . doesn't know the ins and outs of their stories like I do."

"He'll fight for them though if it comes down to it," Colton says softly, a quiet reassurance and an unintentional slap in the face to me all at once. But I don't feel the slap's sting. I know Colton's comment comes from a place of love.

Those are my boys. My heart. No one will fight as hard for them as I will. I know this much to be true.

"It should be me," I murmur, my heart hurting, my body exhausted. "But I don't think it will do an ounce of good. If the system does the half-ass job they usually do and don't vet them properly, then they'll get him."

"Unless he's adopted," Colton states plainly. He pulls me in tighter and I nod my head.

We settle in the silence of the sterile room that is now so much more bearable with Colton's presence. The heat of his breath, the scent of his cologne, the feel of his body against mine—all three things center me from that out-of-control feeling of fear I entered this hospital with.

The baby's movements I can and can't feel are broadcast through the room, my own reminder of priorities and unconditional love. Lulled by the sound and Colton being here, I slowly begin to drift off.

"We could adopt, Zander."

Colton's words snap me awake. My breath hitches, my body jolts, my heart hopes momentarily before the reality of the situation sets in. Tears prick the backs of my eyes over the enormity of the heart of the man behind me. One who swore he couldn't love, and yet day after day the capacity and way in which he does, makes me fall more in love with him.

"The fact you've said that means the world to me but . . . but I can't just choose one boy to adopt," I say with a conflicted heart because yes, it would fix everything, but doing that would tell the other boys I love Zander more than them and that's not the case. "But thank you for saying it. The fact you'd even consider it means the world to me."

"I think we should do more than consider it." I just nod at his comment, the resolve in his voice so strong there's no point in arguing since I know he's speaking from the experience of what it's like to be an orphaned little boy. "Don't count it out, Rylee."

"I won't," I say for good measure, "but I can't do that to the others who want to belong to someone just as much as Zander does."

"They belong to each other," he says, "and that's what matters most."

His words throw me. They're unexpected and yet so very true. And contradictory. How would adopting one not ruin that bond?

"Turn your mind off, Ryles. Shut it down for a bit. For me. For the baby. For you." He rubs a hand up and down my arm, sliding it over my belly between the two monitors resting there. I'm sure it's pure coincidence but within seconds the sound of the baby moving beneath his hand fills the room. Hearing the hitch in Colton's breath in reaction makes my heart swell.

"I'm sorry I took you away from your victory celebration," I murmur, "but at the same time I'm not because I'm glad you're here."

"There's nowhere else I'd rather be," he says as he rests his chin on my shoulder and presses a kiss to my cheek. "I lie. There's definitely somewhere else I'd like to be." Suggestion laces his voice and since sex is my only pregnancy craving, I groan.

"I have a feeling this victory lane is closed for business for a while," I say.

"Good thing I just claimed it in Alabama."

"You better be talking about a trophy, Ace."

"Nah. That's right here in my arms."

Chapter Fifteen

Rylee

"I NEED YOUR HELP, SHANE," I say, sounding desperate and not caring a single bit that I do.

"Rylee." He chuckles, sounding so much like a grown man rather than the awkward teenager that once came to me alone and traumatized. The irony I'm now turning to him for help is not lost on me. "Colton said you were going to call and try to bribe me to help you escape your house."

Damn it! He's thought of everything to keep me stuck at home where the walls of this house feel like they are closing in on me more and more every day. Sure paparazzi have died down but they are still present, still perpetuating the sensationalism. They might not all be sitting outside, but the covers of the rags still show the grainy image of me in the garage. However, now it's next to one of me leaving the hospital in a wheelchair two days ago with titles that are equivalent to the conversation Colton and I had on our first date: Chupacabras and three-headed aliens.

"I'm not trying to bribe you to escape. I'll sit here, not be stubborn, and listen to doctor's orders so long as I know Zander's okay,"

I confess. "I've talked to him and he seems fine, and Colton and Jax are telling me he's fine, but Shane, *he'll talk to you.*" The last words are emphasized so he understands I'm referring to the brotherly bond they've formed over the years. The connection between two battered souls that have healed together, shared experiences no one should ever have to, and came through it on the other side, is something that has allowed them to be the odd couple of closeness in The House.

And I'm hoping I can call on that bond right now to help find out how he's doing.

"On one condition," he says, throwing me for a loop.

"Mm-hmm?" I respond, curious if Colton has anything to do with this one condition.

"That you let me handle this. I don't want you stressed out and back in the hospital. I'll tell you everything I find out as long as I know you're going to put you and the baby first." I hear his words, and as much as I'm irritated with the ultimatum, pride overrides it and allows me to listen to what he's saying. To the concern in his voice, the compassion in his words, the remarkable man he's become.

It tells me I've done my job. And I hold tight to that idea since right now I can't continue to care for them. I have to trust in the time I've invested thus far with both of these boys and that their bond will remain steadfast when one needs the other the most.

"Can I trust you to do that, Rylee?" he asks, breaking through the emotion clouding my mind and clogging my throat.

"Yes," I say, feeling like a scolded child and yet it's hard to feel anything but love for him.

"He's struggling. He's scared and worried. We're the only good he knows. He fears going back to that constant life of not knowing what's next . . . and I can understand that," he murmurs, no doubt lost in his own memories.

He tells me exactly what I assumed but what no one else would confirm.

"Thank you for telling me." My mind races, wanting to rush over and see Zander face to face to reassure him, and wanting to beg Teddy to get back to me even though I know he's waiting on the case-worker to get back to him.

"I'm coming home next week for a few days. I'm going to stay at The House, already talked to Jax about it, and hang with Zand to make sure he's okay."

"Thank you," I say softly into the phone with my eyes closed and my heart full of love. "That's a really cool thing for you to do. He'll like hanging with you."

"He's family," Shane says. In my mind's eye, I can see that boyish smile on his face and the casual shrug that's typical of him. All I can do is smile and acknowledge that, yes, I've done a good job.

"He's family."

It seems so surreal to be folding baby clothes. Yes, my belly is so big I can't see my toes and a mountain of yellow clothes surrounds me, but with everything going on, it still feels so very far off and just around the corner simultaneously.

"While the idea of you being tied to the bed is rather hot, I'd prefer to do it with you as a willing candidate and not because you won't listen to the doctor," Colton says from the doorway. I turn to find a smirk on his face but the warning loud and clear in his eyes.

"Cute. Very cute," I say drolly.

"Well, you'd be even cuter flat on your back in our bed." We stand, a visual battle of wills war between us, and when he finally breaks eye contact and looks around, I notice his startled expression. "You put stuff away?"

"I figured it was about time," I murmur, slightly embarrassed at how long I've let my anxiety hold this process up. "It's safe enough that if he's born now, she should be okay."

"Nice change of pronouns there," he says with a laugh as he walks up to me and wraps his arms around me from behind, resting his chin on the curve of my shoulder.

"I couldn't let you think I knew BIRT's sex."

His laugh rings out, the vibration of it going from his chest into mine as I finish folding some of the receiving blankets I had pre-washed. "BIRT, huh? You've come over to my dark side and are calling him that now?"

"I've always liked your dark side," I say, intending one thing but when I feel his hands that have slid over my belly falter in their movement, I realize he took it in a completely different way. We stand there in silence momentarily as I let him shake the ghosts off his back that my comment caused to resurface.

"Did you feel that?" I ask, my hands flying to land on top of his so I can direct them to where the baby has moved beneath his palms.

"It's so bizarre," he murmurs. There's a sense of awe in his voice that tells me the darkness in his thoughts has passed for now. He presses his hands against my belly to try and will the baby to move again.

"BIRT likes his daddy's voice," I say softly, absorbing this moment we'll never get back once he's born. He presses his lips to the side of my neck and holds them there. It's almost as if he knows what I'm thinking and feels the same way, so he is trying to suspend time to make the here and now last as well.

"I have something for you. Will you come with me?" he asks.

"Is that something handcuffs and restraints?" I tease.

"Not unless you want them to be." With a laugh, he takes my hands and leads me down the hallway and into our bedroom.

I give him a look as he pats the bed for me to hop up. "And I fell for it," I say as he helps me up onto the mattress, my mind already wondering what exactly is going on since Dr. Steele said to hold off on sex for a bit. And as strict as Colton's been following her rules, he's either going to force me to rest or plan to exert himself.

I vote for the exertion.

"It's not what you think, you nympho," he says as he props pillows behind my back and under my knees before leaning in and brushing a kiss to my lips. And of course, because I can never resist him, I bring my hand up to the back of his neck and hold him there so I can steal one more from him.

"A girl can hope," I murmur against his lips. When he pulls back, a smile lights up his face and a mischievous glimmer is in his eyes.

"Not until this girl gets clearance from the doctor," he says. He walks around the edge of the bed and grabs something off his nightstand, holding it behind his back so I can't see it. And the cutest part about the action is that in the sequence of movements, I've watched my confident, demanding husband morph with discomfort so I know whatever is behind his back pushes his comfort zone.

"So I have something for you," he says and then stops with a shake of his head that's reminiscent of when one of the boys is embarrassed. It tugs at my heartstrings and gives me an exact picture of what BIRT will look like if he is a boy. He looks down at a crudely wrapped rectangular box in brown paper as he reaches it out to me. I close my hand over his and don't let go until he looks at me.

"Thank you, but I don't need anything."

"I thought it was a good idea at the time . . . but now I feel like it's lame so you can laugh at me all you—"

"I'm going to love it," I say with complete conviction, because if this present is making him this unsure then I know he's the one coloring outside of his already messy lines.

With the weight of his stare, I slowly unwrap the gift to find a picture frame made of thick rustic wood void of a photo in it. I stare at it for a moment because while it is actually quite beautiful, I sense there is a deeper meaning here than just a gift so try to figure out what it is that Colton's telling me.

"It's empty," he states, drawing my eyes up to his while my hands run over the texture of the wood. It's weathered but refined, rough but smooth, kind of like the two of us. The idea brings a smile to my lips.

"I see that."

"It's been a rough couple of weeks for us," he says as he climbs on the bed beside me. He lies on his side, head propped on his hand as I nod and try to figure how this all fits together. "Kelly is trying to find my dad." My mind slams on the brakes at that because I'm so confused and lost how we got from a frame to a person Colton has never spoken about before.

"*What*?" I look at him while he concentrates on his hand on my stomach. My mouth is opening and closing like a guppy because I don't know what to say or how we got from point A to point B in this conversation. I can tell he's just as confused as I am so I rein in my need to know and let him find the words to explain everything.

"I'm scared about being a dad," he says and continues the confession. And it's not like I don't get the fear, because I have it too, but I'm starting to connect the dots in the sense that he fears he is going to be like the father he never knew somehow. "And I thought maybe if I knew about my sperm donor then it would ease the fear that I'll be like him."

As much as I want to shift to take his face in my hands so he's forced to look in my eyes, I allow him the space he needs. "You will be *nothing* like him, Colton. There's not a doubt in my mind."

I've seen him with the boys at The House. I've watched him help them overcome adversity only he could understand. Does he not have any clue how important that is? How that interaction more than just hints at the incredible father I know he will be? I wish he could see the same man I see every single day when he looks in the mirror.

He just nods his head yet doesn't say anything for a moment. I wish there was something I could say or do to reassure him further when only time will prove the truth in my statement.

"I don't know," I say with a shake of my head. "I think it's a bad idea . . . I don't see how finding him is going to help you at all." And I probably should keep my opinions to myself, let him deal with his past how he needs to, but at the same time we've had so many things crash into our reality recently, I don't know how much more we can take. "What are you hoping to achieve if you find him?"

"A clean slate." He then clears the emotion from his throat. "This frame is empty because I want to start this next chapter of our life with a completely clean slate. Our family deserves this. It's . . ." His voice fades off. I reach out and link my fingers through his. His words—his thoughtfulness—are so damn overwhelming that I can't find the words to speak just yet. "Never mind," he says again.

"No. Please, finish. I'm quiet because I'm touched and stunned you thought of this and did this for us . . . especially after everything that has happened this month."

"I sound like a fucking chick here but this empty frame is also my promise to you that from today forward I don't want to just take pictures with you, I want to make memories. Good ones more than bad ones. Funny ones. Memorable ones. Precious ones. They will shift and change over time, each stage of our life together dictating what goes here, but more than anything, this empty frame with be filled with our new normal . . ." His voice trails off. Tears flood my eyes. The depth of emotion in this incredible gift from a man who thinks of himself as unromantic—despite the grand sweeping gestures he shows me time and again—is so very poignant and fitting.

"I love it," I whisper, my eyes meeting his as I look at him through a kaleidoscope of tears. "It's absolutely perfect." I hug the frame, my empty treasure box in a sense, and revel in how much Colton has grown since we've met.

I shift so I'm on my left side, facing him, our bodies mirroring one another's. We stare at each for a few moments, our visual connection so very intense as feelings are exchanged without any words being spoken.

"I don't have anything to give you," I finally say.

A shy smile turns up the corners of his mouth. "You've given me more than I've ever wanted."

It's silly that even after all this time I still react viscerally to praise from him, but it's undeniable. As I draw in a shaky breath, his eyes narrow and my fingers trace over the grooves in the frame lying between us.

"Sometimes I play the 'I'm game' with the boys . . . want to play with me?" His grin grows, and I realize the innuendo.

"You know I'd never turn down the chance to play with you," he says, nodding his head for me to continue. "How do you play?"

"I tell you something that starts with 'I'm' and then you go. You don't get to ask questions though . . . That way you're forced to listen to what you think the person is saying. It's an I go, you go, type thing." I'm shocked that in all our time together, I've never explained this to him, but I feel this is an absolutely perfect moment. "I'll go first. *I'm scared too*," I say in a whisper, as if the lower voice will help my confession somehow seem less.

He starts to say something that doesn't begin with "I'm" and I shush him and bring a finger to his lips. "No reassurances. Sometimes that makes you feel like your fears are invalid. Your turn."

I watch him struggle finding the words to express whatever it is weighing heavily on his mind. He takes a deep breath, looks over my shoulder for a few moments, and his fingers pluck at the sheet. In the last five years, he's grown leaps and bounds in not only identifying but in the ability to articulate his emotions. And yet right now I can tell he's at a loss on how to phrase them.

The silence stretches. My concern over what has him so tongue-tied grows.

"I'm afraid you'll never forgive me for the video and that I couldn't fix it." He won't look at me.

I close my eyes momentarily, letting the apology in his voice be the balm to the open wounds that video has caused and nod my head to let him know I heard him. Given the number of times he has apologized, I shouldn't be surprised this was his first confession. At the same time, I appreciate his need to tell me it again.

"I'm worried that when people see us now, all they'll be able to think of is the video. I can only hope it will die down and go away at some point." Colton closes his eyes momentarily and gives a subtle nod. His reaction is all I need to know he feels the same way.

"I'm hopeful Eddie will get what he deserves," Colton says, disgust and spite lacing his tone.

"I'm in agreement," I say with a laugh, because I didn't give a confession but I didn't exactly break the rules either.

"Rule breaker," he murmurs with a shy smile on his lips.

"Not hardly," I say. "Your turn."

"I'm worried you're going to be so focused on Zander that it's going to put you back in the hospital again," he says with a lift of his eyebrows and a glance down to my belly.

"I'm concerned I'm going to let him down and not be able to help him when he needs me the most." I fight the unease my confession brings, and try to staunch its very real side effects. I worry it will end up doing just what Colton fears, too.

"I'm certain that somehow we'll make everything right for him," he says, shaking his head to stop me before I even open my mouth. He knows me so well.

"I'm positive my husband likes this game because it prevents me from saying too much and arguing with him," I confess matter-of-factly, causing him to bark out a laugh in agreement. The sound of it puts a smile on my lips before the quiet falls back around us as Colton figures out what to say next.

"I'm afraid I'm not going to be man enough to give you what you need when you need it most." He licks his lips and forces a swallow down his throat. His eyes never waver from mine despite the absolute swell of emotion riding its way through them.

Wow. Well I guess he's bringing out the deep confessions now. I so did not expect that comment from him. It knocks me back a second while I wrap my head around it. Does he mean in all aspects of life or just with the baby coming? I wonder what it is he thinks I need that he's not giving me.

Doubt is the chisel that causes the fissures to drive a solid relationship apart, and I hate he feels like I have any when it comes to him.

"Colton," I begin to say, breaking my own rules, because I have to tell him he's more than man enough in all aspects for me, but he reaches out and puts a finger to my lips.

"Uh-uh." He shakes his head. "Your turn."

And I just stare, desperately wanting to tell him he's so very off base to worry about that and yet I don't. Can't. I need to allow him to say what he needs to say. I blow out a breath in frustration and discomfort because we may know each other inside and out, yet this is more soul-bearing than anything we have done in such a long time, and as cathartic as it may be, it's also scary as hell.

"I'm afraid you won't find me sexy anymore after I have the baby."

He may not speak, but his head shakes back and forth to tell me I'm crazy. "I'm afraid that every time you look at me, you think you've made a mistake in marrying me."

Is he crazy? His words stab my heart. It's so unbelievable the world sees Colton as an arrogant, self-assured man. Yet with me—*especially* right here, right now—he reveals the insecurity all people have but keep close to the vest.

"I'm afraid you are going to pull away when the baby is born," I say without thinking and realize that my deepest fear has been spoken out loud. The quick hitch in Colton's breath tells me without him saying a word that he fears the same thing. I panic momentarily, fear lodging in my throat. I know I need to fix this somehow so I keep talking like I was going to finish the sentence, ". . . but need you to know that I can't do this without you."

Silence settles between us. Our eyes lock. My heart hopes he really hears what I'm saying. "I'm afraid that I'm going to panic in the delivery room, see things I can't unsee, or not be able to handle watching you in pain."

And hearing him say something so many men fear makes me feel better. Like we're normal in a sense when our relationship and everything surrounding us is far from it.

"I'm afraid of labor." *Who wouldn't be?* The unknown pain and the absolute unexpected followed by the beautiful ending. Colton just raises his eyebrows and nods his head.

"I'm afraid I'm going to be like *them*," he says, the term *them* unmistakable in its meaning: his mother and father. His eyes burn into mine, and it kills me that he has even put himself in the same category as them. Yes, their genes run through him but that doesn't mean his heart isn't different.

Blood makes the body, not the man.

"I'm scared I'm going to make too many mistakes as a mother."

Colton rolls his eyes, prompting me to reach out and wipe his hair off his forehead. He grabs my wrist and brings the palm of my hand to his lips and presses a sweet kiss to the center of it before bringing it down to rest over his heart. "I'm sure I'm going to make way more mistakes as a father but I know that with you by my side, our baby will grow into an incredible human being . . . just like his mother." He whispers the last words, causing tears to sting my eyes, which is in complete contradiction to the soft smile on my lips from the way he changed his confession to make it a positive.

I should have known he'd find a way to make me feel better about my fears by skating under the radar and breaking the rules without actually breaking them.

"I'm sure BIRT will have your green eyes, your stubborn streak, and your incredible capacity to love," I say as Colton clears his throat. His fingers tighten over mine on his chest. I know he wants to refute my comment, the one I put out there to try to lessen his fear about him being like his biological parents, but he doesn't.

And that's a good sign because hopefully if I say it enough, he'll eventually start to believe it.

"I'm afraid that everything was going so well for us. But first it was the video . . . and now . . ." he blows out a breath and I try to figure out what's eating at him, "now . . . the other shoe is going to drop."

I stare at him, so perfectly imperfect and full of fear just like I am, and yet he walked in here tonight and gave me a gift most husbands would never even think of. Yet he still doubts us, still worries the other shit will affect us when all we need is each other.

All we've ever needed is each other.

"I'm certain that even if the other shoe drops, it'll be off an octopus with a lot of shoes so we'll be able to handle it, because I married the only man ever meant for me. We can handle anything that comes our way, shoe by dropping shoe."

Colton just falls onto his back and starts laughing, deep and long. I can tell he needed something humorous to release the stress clawing him apart from the inside out. I find comfort I can use a game I invented for little boys and still affect the grown man in my life.

Then again, boys, men, they're really no different from the other.

After a moment he rolls back onto his side and scoots up against me so my belly hits his. He cradles my face in his hands. "Octopus shoes?" He laughs again with a lift of his eyebrows and a flash of that irresistible dimple.

"Yep. They've got eight feet. Lots of shoes to drop," I tease, wanting to keep the moment now that our hearts are a bit lighter.

Colton just shakes his head with a soft smile on his lips, love in his eyes, and tenderness in his touch. How in the hell did I get to be so lucky to be the one sharing my life with this contradiction of a man?

"God, I fucking race you, Ryles," he says, sealing the sentiment with a kiss and stealing my heart once again.

With my eyes closed, our lips touching, and hearts beating as one, I think back to our wedding day, to the vows we made, and the promises we made and have kept. The "You know that's permanent, right?" and I know there's nothing I would ever change because he's here, he's mine, and no matter what life throws at us, he'll be here for me. He's protected me. Put me first. Made me consequential. Made me whole.

With every beautifully scarred, bent piece of him.

Chapter Sixteen

COLTON

"**D**ID YOU BEAT THE SHIT out of him?"

I look up from the stacks on my desk just as Becks takes a seat in front of me, propping his feet up on its edge. "Please. Make yourself at home."

"Don't mind if I do," he says in that slow even drawl of his that's equal parts irritating and comforting to me. "So?"

"He didn't show," I explain with a shake of my head. "I sat outside the damn office for an hour before and an hour after his appointed meeting with his parole officer and the fucker never showed."

Such a waste of time. Staking out the probation office during the two hours around Eddie's appointment time. Watching drug deals go down and a hooker giving a guy head in his car, while I waited to have my moment with Eddie. Draw him out to give him a little payback of my own.

"Can't you get in trouble seeking him out with the restraining order?" he asks.

"Restraining order was filed on Ry's behalf. Not mine," I say with a smirk. I want him nowhere fucking near her. Now me on the other hand? I have no problem coming face to face with him. In fact, there's nothing I'd like more.

"So you can approach him, kick his ass, and . . ."

"And no one's worse for wear," I say with a shrug. "Well, besides him that is."

"Can take the man out of the trouble but can't stop the boy in him from looking for it," he says with a shake of his head.

"Damn straight."

"But wait. He didn't show, so now what? Will he be hauled back to jail for violation or some shit?" He laces his fingers and brings his hands behind his head.

"No clue. Possibly . . . but I have a feeling he's a helluva lot more scared of the loan sharks and their thugs than missing a parole appointment. Getting put back in jail might be the safest place for him, considering the amount of phone calls I've received asking me if I know his whereabouts."

"Well played, brother," he says with a shake of his head. "Giving his name up like that to the press."

"It hit me that night at the bar. The loan sharks came knocking when we fired him. Then he fucked us by stealing the blueprints to sell so he could pay them back. So why not fuck him over by using them to pay me back?"

Full circles. They're everywhere I look.

"Scary fucking shit, dude," he muses. I glance to the garage down below. "So . . . how are things? Ry good?"

"Yeah. Good."

"That doesn't sound convincing."

I lean back in my chair and prop my feet on my desk like he did, lace my fingers behind my head, and look at the ceiling. "What if I told you I was looking into adopting Zander?"

Becks doesn't say a goddamn word, yet I can tell by the jerk of his body to attention in my peripheral vision that he heard me. "Subtlety isn't something you know how to do, is it?" he coughs out.

"Nope. So?"

"I'd ask you if you're fucking crazy on many fronts. Especially since you're using the term *I* and not *we.*"

Fucking pronouns.

I roll my eyes. "Semantics."

"You don't sound so sure about that," Becks says as he pokes holes through my story.

"Rylee said she wouldn't think of it. That she can't choose one boy over the others. I get it, but I told her I was looking into it anyway. The whole Zander thing is really eating her up."

"Eating her up or you up?" he asks, eyes daring me to lie to him.

Shit. He's calling me on the carpet and there's no way I can deny it since he knows my history. Because fuck yes, a part of me wants to give Zander the opportunity I had. Save him like I was saved.

And yet at the same time, I understand Ry's stance because I couldn't pick him and not the other boys.

"You told me once, fight or flight. I chose to fight," I say, thinking of that night a long time ago after Ry lost the baby. Becks had snapped me to attention, and forced me to be the man I feared being and of truths about myself I had to face. The ones that made me realize Ry was worth the goddamn effort and then some. "Well, I'm fighting."

"For what though, Wood? What exactly is it you're fighting for now?" He leans forward, puts his hands on his knees, and looks me in the eye.

I shove up out of my chair and walk over to the wall of windows that looks down to the shop below. It's easier to watch the guys than deal with this shit.

Memories I thought I'd forgotten hit me out of nowhere: The fear with each knock on the front door that my mom was coming to take me away from Dorothea and Andy. Hands that high-fived and didn't hit. Lights left on in the hallway because horrible things happened in the dark. Superhero posters on the walls I'd stare at when the nightmares hit. Fear turned to hope. Hope gave me life.

That life gave me love: Rylee.

"I'm fighting because like you said, she's the goddamn alphabet, Becks." I turn around to face him, hands out to my sides and a shrug of my shoulders. "Those boys are her life, and she's mine."

This conversation, this confession, and these feelings, all make me anxious. Uncomfortable. Vulnerable.

Add feelings on top of feelings when I don't want them to.

My cell phone rings and thank fuck for that because shit's getting heavy. And the only kind of heavy I like is Ry's weight on top of me.

"Kelly."

"I've found your father." I freeze. Mind misfires thoughts. Hand stops midway in the air and then drops.

What the fuck did I do this for? Doubt rears its ugly stepsister of a head to let me know she's still there. Still waiting for me to fuck all of this up.

I can't speak. All I can do is clear my throat.

"Confirmation should come within the hour. When it does I'll shoot you over his address in an email."

"Yeah. Thanks." I let the phone slip from my hand and land with a thud on my desk. I stare at it for a minute. Deciding. Wondering. Avoiding.

You got what you wanted, Donavan.

What are you going to do about it?

Chapter Seventeen

Rylee

Heading to The House. Zander is meeting with his uncle. Just found out and am speeding to get there in time.

SHANE'S TEXT REPLAYS IN MY head over and over as I search my purse for my car keys before moving to the laundry room that connects to the garage to see if they are hanging on the rack of keys. They're not. My body vibrates with anguish and my heart lodges into my throat over the need to get to Zander so I can walk him through this.

And to pick apart every one of his uncle's nuances so I can make the claims I want to make about why he can't be approved to foster.

I know I'm breaking my promise to Shane about not reacting off the information he feeds me when it comes to Zander, but . . . it's one of my boys. I need to be there. If it were Shane in distress I'd do the same thing.

"Sammy!" I yell, not sure if he's in his office off the main floor or outside doing any of the various things he does that continually remain a mystery to me. I'm smart enough to know Colton has conveniently had him staying around the house lately to keep an eye on me. That doesn't sit well with me. "Sammy. Do you know where my keys are?" I try to keep the panic out of my voice but it's no use because I need to get to The House ASAP.

"Everything okay?" he asks as he jogs down the hallway toward me, the concern in his tone matching the look on his face. And I realize he thinks I'm in labor, hence the slightly panicked widening of his eyes.

"Yes. I'm looking for my keys."

"Do you need me to run to the store for you?" he asks, his eyes narrowing.

"No, thank you. I need to get to The House," I tell him as I cross my arms over my chest and just stare.

"Sorry. You're not supposed to be going anywhere. Colton sa—"

"Did he hide my car keys?" I ask, voice becoming shriller with each word. Reality sets in that I'm not being forgetful with pregnancy brain like I thought when I couldn't find my keys, but Colton actually hid them. "Are you fucking kidding me?" I yell, throwing my hands up, my misdirected anger aimed at Sammy.

"He wanted to make sure you stayed safe," he states quietly, knowing not to cross my temper.

I start to walk away from him, mentally trying to figure out how to get there, when I turn back around. "Drive me then."

Sammy startles at my directive, considering I have never asked him for anything let alone demanded him to do something since Colton and I have been married. "Let me call Colton," he says as he goes to step away.

"*No.*" He stops and turns to look at me like I've lost it. The funny part is I have and can't bother to care that I have. "I'm as much your boss as he is. I'll take the blame, Sammy, but one of my boys needs me." I know I'm putting him in a horrible position—piss off the husband or face the wrath of the pregnant wife—but at this point, I don't care. All I can think about is Zander.

"Rylee," he says, my name a resigned sigh.

"Never mind," I say as the idea hits me and I start to walk past him to where Colton keeps his stash of extra keys. "I'll just take Sex then." By the way he sucks in his breath I know I've just delivered the coup de grace by threatening to take Colton's baby. My husband may be a generous man, but when it comes to his beloved Ferrari, that's another story.

My mind flickers back to the last time I asked to get behind the wheel. *Nice try, sweetheart, but the only place you're allowed to drive me is out of breath on the hood.* I can still see his telltale smirk and the salacious look in his eyes, before I begrudgingly moved away from the door of the driver's seat.

That was three years ago. I'm smart enough not to come between a man and his car, but I sure as hell know how to use it as leverage to get what I want.

With the weight of Sammy's presence at my back, I open the middle drawer of the desk and make a show of rifling through it to prove my point.

"I promised Colton I'd make sure you stayed here."

"I'll deal with him if you drive me, Sammy. Not taking me is ten times worse for my health and the baby than taking me. *Happy wife, happy life,*" I say with false enthusiasm. "And if not, voila!" I turn around with the key dangling between my fingers.

Our eyes meet momentarily before his dart back to the key fob. "Fuck," he mutters under his breath through gritted teeth. That single word can mean so many things, but right now for me it means I've won.

Power to the pregnant woman!

I enter The House with my key, not caring if I'm going to be in trouble or not, because judging by the strange cars in the driveway, someone is here already. I feel thankful seeing Jax's and Kellan's cars on the street. I know they are more than capable of handling the situation, but *it's Zander. My Zander.* The boy I've spent endless hours with to heal his broken heart. The boy who *soccers* me.

When I clear the great room, I hear startled gasps. The boys look up from doing their homework at the table and run over to me with Racer following excitedly on their heels. Auggie sits back with a soft smile on his lips as I'm greeted with desperately missed hugs and a mind-spinning spew of words as they all try to tell me what's been going on with them at the same time. Tiny hands run over my belly and tell me how much bigger it seems, and ask when is the baby going to come because they can't wait to meet him. Because in a house full of boys, they know the baby *has* to be a boy. A girl is not an option. My heart swells and hurts simultaneously because although it's only been a few weeks, it feels like I've missed years of their lives.

I bite back my anger toward Eddie for taking this away from me. The incessant chatter, the sticky hands, and the dirt-smudged smiles. The things that make my world go round and my heart happy. Hell yes, I'm pissed at him, but right now I'm with my boys and don't want his vindictiveness to tarnish the small amount of time I'll get with them.

Later I can stew. Later I can I punch my pillow in anger. But right now, I'm going to soak this up and ignore that I'm going to miss every single thing the minute I have to leave again.

"Rylee?" Kellan says as he clears the hallway, eyes wide, and grin welcoming.

"Hey. Sorry I didn't call but—"

"You're here for the same reason as Shane, who keeps calling, saying he's going to be here any second, yeah?" His voice is deceptive in tone—not letting the boys on what his eyes are telling me—but it's clear he's concerned about Zander too. At the mention of Shane, the noise starts up around us again from the boys, excitement that their older brother is on his way to roughhouse and tell them stories about how cool college is.

"Yes." I nod. "He needs me," I mouth to him above the fray and he motions with his chin toward the back patio that I can't see through the angled blinds.

"Okay guys, how about you finish your homework," I say, stepping right back into the role I was born to play, knowing Kellan won't take offense to me taking over momentarily. "I need to go check on Zander and when I come back in, if your homework is done, I'll stay for dinner."

Cheers fill the air around me followed by the scraping of chairs and elbowing of boy against boy as the fight to regain their position at the table begins so they can finish.

Kellan meets my eyes again now that the boys aren't watching, and I can tell he's just as upset by all of this as I am. "How long have they been here?" I ask as I reach down to scratch Racer behind the ears.

"Jax is out there with them, watching. The caseworker, the uncle and aunt, and Zander," he adds, answering the questions I would ask next.

"Thanks." Our eyes hold momentarily and suddenly it hits me how nervous I was to come face to face with him and Jax. They are the ones feeling the effects of my dismissal—extra shifts, upset boys, curious questions. And yet instead of shaking his head and walking away at the mess I've created for all of us, he gives me a gentle but sincere smile. I don't see the resentment or pity I feared. Rather I see camaraderie, as if he knows I'd move heaven and earth to fix the situation if I could because I'm not oblivious to the toll it's taken on not only me, but everyone involved.

I smile in return, my thank you for not passing judgment. He nods his head as I slowly slide open the door to the backyard and step out before closing it behind me. I see Zander and my heart breaks instantly. I'm transported back to six years ago when he first came to us, broken and traumatized. His knees are pulled up to his chest as he sits on a chair with his side to me, his arms wrapped around them, his face looking blankly toward the wood panel fence. From what I *can* see, there is a look of complete detachment on his face. All that's missing is the stuffed dog he used to tote around for comfort, which now sits up in the closet somewhere.

In a single afternoon, the two people sitting opposite him—his uncle and aunt—have potentially erased the crucial years of work, the countless, grueling hours gaining his trust, helping ease the nightmares that had owned his psyche. *Have I lost the hopeful, sweet boy I love so much?*

Zander lifts his head and vacant eyes meet mine, crushing my cautious hope about anything positive coming from this situation. It takes everything I have to force a smile on my lips and nod my head in encouragement for him to talk to them. He stares at me, the look of betrayal blatant on his face, but it's necessary for the caseworker to see I'm trying to help facilitate this connection. When I approach him after the meeting to tell him he can't let this happen, then I won't look so unprofessional.

I shift my eyes from Zander to the uncle and aunt. The uncle glances over to me. *Fuck.* I see recognition in his eyes before they suggestively slide up and down the length of my body in a not-so-subtle show that says he knows exactly what I look like naked.

My skin crawls and stomach churns with revulsion and the little smirk he gives me—just a hint of the curl of his lip—tells me he knows how it's making me feel and is enjoying it. He tucks his tongue in his cheek before giving me a slight nod of the head and looking back toward his wife.

I watch them try to interact with Zander. They attempt to talk about things he has no interest in. Because he's a thirteen-year-old boy now, not the seven-year-old they once might have known. SpongeBob isn't cool and Xbox is no longer the coveted game system

I want to scream at them. He loves soccer and building Halo Lego sets and reading Harry Potter and Percy Jackson.

You don't know a thing about him! All you want is the money that comes with him.

I can see beneath their brushed hair and best clothes. I can see the wolves in sheep's clothing. I'm certain they have no concern for Zander or his best interest. And it all becomes more than obvious the longer Zander remains silent and unresponsive, because the two of them shift their fidgeting and attention toward each other with raised eyebrows and shrugged shoulders, silently asking each other what to do now that he's not answering them.

I glance over to the caseworker sitting on the other side of the yard with his legs crossed, ankle resting on opposite knee, and a clipboard balanced on his leg. And while he may have a pen in hand and paper he's supposed to be taking notes on, his phone sits atop the paper. He's so busy texting someone he hasn't once looked up to watch the interaction—or rather lack thereof—nor notice the ever-disappearing presence of Zander losing himself to the safe world he created in his mind so very long ago. That same world I spent months pulling him out of, showing him not everyone is bad and evil—out to hurt those they love—and that it was safe to step outside.

My body vibrates with anger, my teeth bites into my tongue because all I want to do is go to him, pull him into my arms, and reiterate the promise I made him all those years ago: I'm never going to let anything bad happen to him ever again.

Lost in my observation, I forget Jax is there until he motions with his hands to silently get my attention. And when I look at him, his eyes express the same thing as Kellan's, indicating he feels the same disbelief.

No way in hell are they taking Zander from us.

Now I just have to figure out how to prevent that.

"Zander?" I call as I enter his room. The shades are pulled closed and the light remains off, but through the light of the open doorway I can see him curled up on his side in his bed.

When he doesn't respond, the sense of dread that has been tickling the back of my neck and making my stomach churn exacerbates. I glance over to Shane opposite me in the hallway and the concern in his eyes mirrors how I feel.

We move into the room together. Shane lived here long enough to know the drill, so he stands against the wall to observe while I step forward to engage Zander. And my immediate worry is that Zander has closed off even more. Jax and I spent five minutes with the caseworker, providing valid reasons why the uncle is not a good fit to foster Zander. I feel like our arguments fell on deaf ears. Now, looking at Zander rocking on his bed with his beloved stuffed dog held tight to his chest, I'm more worried than ever. I can't remember the last time he climbed up to the top shelf of his closet and pulled the sacred dog from its box. The only tangible reminder of his old life.

I sit on the chair next to the bed and feel a whisper of hope when he scoots back as if to make room for me. "May I?" I ask, as I reach out to touch him, hating feeling like we are back to square one. When he nods his head, I breathe a little sigh of relief. He isn't closing himself off from me completely. Silence weighs heavily around us. The smell of his fear almost palpable, and unfortunately one I know all too well when it comes to my boys.

God, how I've missed them.

I use my touch to soothe because I know words won't do anything for him right now. And then the idea comes to me.

"I have an idea." I scoot off the chair and very slowly lower to my knees. I rest my arms on the comforter with my chin atop my hands so we are face to face. I take in his downturned mouth and wait for him to look up to me so he can see I'm here and not going anywhere.

"I think we should play the 'I'm' game," I say, hoping he goes along with it, as it would afford me a glimpse into how far he has relapsed.

His eyes flash up to meet mine, and I see something flicker in them but wait him out, knowing that patience is so very important right now. I reach out and put his hand in mine, needing to ease some of the loneliness I can feel emanating from him.

He opens his mouth and then closes it a few times before finally speaking, his voice a whisper. "I'm scared."

Two words. *I'm scared.* They're all it takes to make me close my eyes and take a deep breath, because in that moment, I'm reminded of Colton's confessions a few nights ago. I realize that no matter how old they are, the fear will always be there. It will morph and change over time, but the invisible scars of their youth have left an indelible mark and will always have a profound effect on how they process emotion and deal with changes.

"I'm scared too," I tell him, causing his eyes to widen and prompt me to explain further. "I'm scared you're going to pull away and not realize how much I'll fight to keep you safe and sound."

"I'm worried that it won't matter to them, because I'm just a number in a broken system and they're going to want to tick me off as done," he confesses, and it amazes me how very intuitive he is with regard to the systematic process we have worked so very hard to shield him from.

"I'm positive you're so much more than just a number, and in fact are a smart, funny, compassionate teenager as well as an incredible soccer player," I say, hoping the positive might break through and help the negative. A ghost of a smile plays at the corners of his lips as his eyes hold mine, tears glistening in them that he blinks away.

"I'm ..." He pauses as he tries to figure out the rest of his thoughts.

"I'm sure that my uncle cares more about the monthly payment he'd get for fostering me than he does having a thirteen-year-old boy in his house." He breathes out long and even. I scour my mind to decide what to tell him next that might help to draw out more of his feelings and get him to talk, so I'm startled when he continues without any prompting.

"I remember his house," he murmurs. "The cigarette smoke, the bent spoons, lighters, and tin foil on the coffee table next to the needles I was forbidden to touch. The couch that was supposed to be brown, but was almost white on the seams, and stained everywhere else that I could see even when all the shades were drawn. I remember sitting in the corner while my dad and him would slap the inside of their elbows before turning their backs to me . . . and then they'd sit back on the couch with their heads looking at the ceiling and creepy smiles on their faces." His eyes focus on our hands where I'm rubbing my thumb back and forth over the top of his. And yes, he broke the rules, didn't start his confession with "I'm", but he's talking and that's ten times more than I ever thought I was going to get when I knelt down beside him.

"I'm sorry you had to go through that." I try to add strength to my voice so he doesn't realize how much his words have affected me. "And I'm so very proud of the person you've become in spite of all of that."

His eyes flash up to mine again on those last words, his head shaking back and forth a few times like he wants to reject them as my statement sinks in. "You did two 'I'ms," he says.

"So I did." I shift, feeling a tight pang as my stomach twists with worry. I suddenly feel like I'm going to be sick. I try to take a deep breath and push it down. "You can go again if you want."

"I'm going to run away if I'm told I have to go live with them." My mouth shocks open and I immediately start to refute him, but when he shakes his head to tell me I can't speak. I bite my tongue, which is laced with so many pleas for him to have faith.

"I'm going to do everything in my power to ensure neither of those things happen." The sadness and resignation returns to his eyes. Tears well in my eyes and my chest constricts. This is one promise I *have to* follow through on.

"I'm certain that..." he says, and then shakes his head. "Never mind."

"No. Please tell me," I urge, because the break in his voice worries me. *Shit.* Another painful twinge. Zander's eyes are closed and his lips are pulled tight in thought.

After some time he draws in a long, uneven breath, and when somewhere in the house laughter erupts, he opens his eyes to find mine again. "I'm certain that if they're allowed to foster me, I'll die."

And yes, he's a thirteen-year-old boy and most people would write the statement off as melodramatic, but he's not one to say something for attention. So as his statement hangs in the air and suffocates us, I struggle with a response so he knows I hear him and haven't disregarded him. And yet I have no clue what to say because his comment can have so many connotations, and I'm not sure which one he means by it.

"Zander . . ." A sharp pain knocks the rest of the thoughts from my head and has me doubling over instantly. I try to hide the grimace on my face and fight the immediate need to curl up in the fetal position. Another pang hits me, causing my whole body to tense and my fingers to grip the comforter beneath them. I cringe when I feel the wetness between my legs; Full bladder, baby resting upon it, and a tense body is not a good mixture.

Seconds pass as I try to register the pain, and how I'm going to explain to a bunch of boys—who are obsessed with bodily functions—what just happened. Then I realize that the wetness keeps spreading.

Another sharp pain hits, this time drawing a gasp from my mouth. My mind spins as elation mixed with fear vibrates through my body on a crash course of adrenaline-laced hormones.

"Rylee?" Shane is at my side in an instant. Zander shifts to sit up, his face a picture of panic, and his eyes ask Shane for help. *His* face looks just as freaked out.

"My water broke," I say with a laugh tinged with hysteria.

"*What*?" Shane exclaims, eyes wide with panic. "You can't be— it's not—oh shit. What do you need?" He walks to one side of the room and then back unsure what to do as I breathe deeply and slowly push myself up from the ground. And then he stops abruptly, eyes lighting up and mouth shocking open. "This is because I brought you here, isn't it? The stress. Zander. Holy shit!"

"No." I shake my head, trying to hide my own fear.

"Yes, it is. You promised," he shouts, worry controlling his thoughts. "Oh my God. Oh my God!" His hands are in his hair; his feet are walking the floor. "Colton's going to kill me. Frickin' kill me."

"Shane," I say softly. "Shane!" He stops and turns to look at me. "No. He's not."

"It's too early," he whispers, eyes wild with fear.

"Go get Sammy." Oh shit.

It's too early.

The thought runs through my head, paralyzing me with a mixture of anxiety, fear, and worry, until a sniffle behind me snaps me to the here and now.

The baby's not full term yet. In a pregnancy that has left me in a constant state of worry and fear, the thought is downright unnerving.

"I'm okay, Zand," I say, hoping it's the truth, fearing it's not.

I look back to meet eyes welled with tears. "This is my fault," he whispers.

No. No, that's not true.

But for the first time in my life, I reach back and put my hand on top of his and don't say a word to assuage his fears.

Because mine are greater right now.

And when I squeeze his hand, I'm not sure who I'm reassuring more, him or me.

Chapter Eighteen

COLTON

SWING. WATCH. WALK. SCRATCH YOUR head and contemplate. Repeat.

Why anyone plays golf on a weekly basis beats the shit out of me. I'm so bored that watching paint dry would be more fucking interesting.

There's a reason I race for a living. Adrenaline. Speed. Excitement. Too bad I can't take the golf cart and open that baby up. Lay down some rubber on this boring green. Now *that* would be fun.

But sponsorships call. The dog and pony show must be performed. The ass-kissing must commence.

I slide a glance to Becks standing behind the head of Pennzoil and notice him giving me a lopsided smirk that says, "Quit being such a little bitch." And he's right. I need to, but I have so much shit to do and not enough time to do it in. Using my middle finger, I scratch the side of my head and give him the bird on the sly, causing his smirk to widen and his head to shake, obviously enjoying my misery.

The shrill sound of my cell disrupts the silence just as the Pen-

nzoil rep is mid swing. He shanks the ball into the rough and immediately shoots me a glare for committing the cardinal sin of not
silencing my cell on the green.

Fuck. Guess I screwed the pooch on that one.

I mumble an apology as Becks walks over to smooth over my
error, and I pick up to see what Sammy needs.

"Sammy."

"It's time!" Rylee's voice fills the line. Confused, I hold the phone
out so I can look at the screen. Yep. Sam's number all right.

"Time for . . . WHAT?" I shout, disturbing the silence on the
green once again and not giving a fuck because my head is spinning
and my heart is pounding.

"The baby," she whispers, her voice a mixture of so many emotions I can't place any of them.

"You sure?" I ask like a dumbfuck. Of course she's sure.

"My water broke."

Can't get any more sure than that. *Oh fuck.* This is like real, real.
"I'm on my way."

I start to walk one way off the green and then stop and head
the other way, hands shaking, mind reeling, and absolutely clueless
about what to do now. The adrenaline I was begging for just moments ago is now coursing through me like jet fuel to the point I can't
focus on anything and yet need to do everything.

"Wood. You okay?" Becks asks, as I look like a goddamn ostrich
walking back and forth with my head stuck up my ass.

"I gotta go." I put my phone in my pocket. Take it out. Grab my
club. Put it in my golf bag upside down. Start looking for my glove
and can't find it only to see it's on my hand.

"Colton." Becks's stern voice breaks through the mosh pit of
chaos in my head so that I stop pacing aimlessly.

"The baby . . . Ry's in labor. I gotta go," I say again as Becks throws
his head back and starts laughing.

"Not so calm and collected now, are you?" He chuckles.

If looks could kill he'd be in a body bag right now as I start rifling through my golf bag for my keys before realizing we're on the back nine and way too fucking far from the country club's parking lot.

"Chill, dude." He puts his hand on my shoulder and squeezes it. "I'll drive you to the clubhouse and then come back and deal with the suits," he says, reading my crazed actions to know what I'm thinking. "Just promise me you're stable enough to drive."

That comment isn't even worthy of a response.

Push the up button. Push it again. Pace three steps. Grumble. Push it again.

I'm not nervous. Not at all.

Door dings. Enter the elevator. Push the number three button. Smile politely to the man in the car, but keep my head down.

Scratch that. I'm freaking the fuck out now.

A stop on the first floor. The man walks off. Push close door. Push close door. Close the fucking door!

A baby. Holy shit.

Door closes.

I'm coming, Ryles.

Doors open just as my cell rings. I answer as I walk toward the nurses station.

"I don't have much time, Shane. What's up?"

"Is she okay?" he asks.

"Not sure yet. I'm almost there. I'll text—"

"I'm so sorry. It's all my fault."

Come again? "What's your fault?"

"I told Rylee I'd take care of Zander and then I called her and told her I was going there because the foster douchebag was meeting him and she was there. Zander told her lots of things and said he'd die if he went and that made her go into labor and now I'm worried I caused all of this—"

"Whoa! Slow down," I say to stop his word vomit. What the fuck is he talking about? His words irritate my temper like an itch. How? Why?

Missing pieces fit together in my mind. Ry was at The House. Sammy was driving her to the hospital. Goddammit! Sammy drove her to The House to begin with. Against. My. Orders.

That itch turns into a full-blown scratch. I'll be having words with Sammy. No doubt there.

"Colton?" I can hear the fear in his voice that I'm angry.

My mind is scattered as I make a wrong turn and get lost down the wrong hallway in this monster of a hospital. "I'm not mad," I lie through gritted teeth because, hell yes, I'm pissed but it's not at him. It's at my wife.

"She was just trying to help Zander," he says quietly, and my heart goes out to the kid. Kid? Shit. He's a man now. *When the fuck did that happen?* I'm still trying to wrap my head around the notion—around the fact I'm here for her to have our baby—but it's not lost on me Shane's trying to protect Rylee from my anger.

Even now, when I'm frazzled and lost in this goddamn hospital trying to get to her, it's impossible not to recognize the incredible job my wife has done to instill compassion for others in her boys.

Our baby's going to be one lucky kid to have her as a mom.

"Colton?" Shane's voice pulls me back from my thoughts just in time to prevent me from going the wrong way down a hallway.

Get a grip, Donavan. Pay attention. Get to Ry.

"Is he okay?" I finally digest his words from a minute ago about what Zander had said. My shoes squeak on the polished floor as I rush down the hallway and look for signs to direct me.

"I'm with him. Yes. But Ry was so upset and—"

"Look. I'll fix it somehow, okay?" I then pass what feels like the same exact place for a second time. I'm anxious. Worried. Need to get to Rylee and yet couldn't find my way out of a wet paper bag right now if I had to.

"There is no fixing it," he says with resignation.

"There is if we adopt him," I say off the cuff, distracted, overwhelmed, trying to get to Rylee, navigate this place, and carry a conversation that I shouldn't be having right now.

"Oh."

And then it hits me what I've said and who I've said it to. Fuck! Ry's concerns flood my head and yet I just went and opened by big fucking mouth and did exactly what she didn't want to do—hurt one of her boys. Let them think we'd pick one over the others.

"Shit!" I say through gritted teeth as I make myself stop and pinch the bridge of my nose. I need to figure out how to make this right. I've been there. Unwanted. Feeling slighted. Jealous. On the wrong end of the schoolyard pick. *Fix this, Donavan.* "That's not what I meant. I'm doing too many things at once: talking, walking, and trying to get to Ry. I suggested the idea just to fix the situation but we'd never really do it because there's no way we could just adopt one of you and not all of you. And social services—"

"Would never allow you to adopt all of us," he says, finishing my sentence for me. But then nothing else.

Silence hangs on the line as I grimace at what I just said. At talking without thinking. Fuck. Fuck. Fuck. Talk to me, Shane. *Cuz, dude, as much as I want to make sure this is right, I also have somewhere else I need to be like ten damn minutes ago.*

"Shane?"

"Of course. Makes sense," he says. And goddammit, I'm torn between making sure I believe he's not upset and getting to where I need to be. I look up and fucking kick myself when I see the nurses station to my left.

"I'm here. I gotta go. We'll talk later. I'll keep you up to date, yeah?"

"Yeah." I don't hear anything else because I hang up as I impatiently wait for the nurse to look up. And when she does I get the usual response: wide eyes, big gasp, flushed cheeks.

"Hi. Wh . . . How . . . What can I help you with?" she stutters as her hand automatically goes to pat down her hair in a move I've seen more times in my life than I care to count.

"Room number for Rylee Donavan, please." My smile is forced, my patience nil. Because now that I'm here I need to see her, touch her, know she's not in pain.

That's brilliant, Donavan. Labor. The word means it's not going to be easy. Pain is inevitable.

"Three eleven is the room, and you'll need this," she says as she pulls out a visitor's badge from a stack sitting on the ledge next to her. "What name do you want?" She winks. "Your secret is safe with me."

"Ace Thomas." The name is off my tongue without thought. *Where'd that come from?*

"Ace Thomas, it is," she says writing it out and handing me the badge. "Good luck, Mr. Donav—Thomas."

I flash her a smile and jog down the hall to where Sammy sits in a chair outside the door to her room. He lifts his eyes and locks them on mine. He knows I know, knows I'm pissed, and stiffens his spine.

"Her. Safety. Comes. First," I say through gritted teeth. "Always. Understood?"

The words he wants to say as my friend are written clearly in his eyes, but his obligation as my employee and lead security keep them from coming out of his mouth. "Understood."

It's all he says. All I need to hear from him. Discussion over. Point made.

I push through the door and into the room anxious about what awaits me. *No turning back now. This is real as real can be.*

Ry's back is to me and Dr. Steele is just walking out. She smiles when she sees me. "Everything looks good, Colton. Be prepared to be a daddy within the next twenty-four hours," she says, then shakes my hand.

"Colton!" Relief. I can hear it in her voice and breathe a little easier now that I'm here.

"I guess we didn't have time to repaint those toes," I say as I walk to her side of the bed and press a kiss to her lips. That's what I needed. A little bit of Ry to calm me.

"Or do other things," she murmurs with a smile.

"I got here as fast as I could."

"Ace Thomas, huh?" she says, her eyes flickering down to my nametag and then back to mine with amusement. "I seem to have heard that somewhere before."

"Hmm. I'm not sure what you're talking about." I feign ignorance.

"Just don't tell my husband you're here. He's got a mean right hook."

I laugh. *God, I fucking love this woman.* Framing her face with my hands, I take in the feel of her skin beneath mine and breathe in a huge sigh of relief. "You okay?" She nods her head, her eyes searching mine, and I know what she's looking for, knows I've connected the dots. "Yes, I'm mad at you . . ."

Furious. Livid.

But I love you more.

"Don't be mad at Sammy. I made him drive me," she says with a cringe, and I hold back the snort I want to give because Sammy's a badass motherfucker. I doubt she *made him* do anything but at the same time, I know how Rylee gets when it comes to her boys.

"Have you talked to Zander? I need to make sure he's okay."

The saint. In a moment that's all about her, she's thinking about them.

"Rylee," I say with a sigh but know she won't give up or relax until she knows they are okay. "I just talked to Shane."

"What did he say about Zander?"

"We talked. Shane's still there with him. I'm sure he's fine. Let's worry about—"

"No. He's not. He was scared and said some things that—"

"I'll call him, okay? Make sure he's all right. If I promise to do that, will you stop worrying about everyone else and start thinking about yourself right now?" Her huge violet eyes look up at me, searching to see if I'll really make sure, and when she likes what she sees, she worries her bottom lip with her teeth and nods reluctantly. "Good, because I wasn't taking no for an answer." I flash her what she calls my panty-dropping smile. She rolls her eyes.

"Did you forget that this is my show, Ace?" She laughs as she reaches out and fists a hand in my shirt to pull my lips back to hers for another kiss. By all means. Kiss away. "No need to give me that smile, considering I'm not wearing any panties to drop in the first place."

I laugh long and hard over that. The hospital gown, the monitors on her belly, the rubber gloves. They all scream sexy. *Not.* "So there's no chance—"

"No chance in hell," she says, pushing against my chest and as silly as it seems, this banter makes me feel a bit more relaxed about what it is that's about to happen to us.

"You in pain?" I ask, unsure exactly what to ask or do.

"Only when I have contractions," she says with a smirk. Smartass.

"So we sit and wait?"

"We sit and wait," she agrees. I link my hand with hers and sit in the chair beside her bed.

Hours pass.

Minutes tick. Seconds lag.

Anticipation riots. Boredom reins. Doubt lingers.

I'm excited. Can't wait to meet this little person.

Contractions come.

What am I doing? Fuck. Fuck. Fuck. I'm not ready to be a dad yet.

Contractions go.

Suck it up.

I'm brash and moody and selfish and I say *fuck* way too much.

Quit being such a pussy.

Contractions come.

I've never changed a diaper. Never even held a newborn. *God, what am I doing?* I'm completely clueless. Inept. How could I think I could do this?

Contractions go.

It's a little too fucking late to turn back now, Donavan.

Panic claws at my throat. Fear tightens around my windpipe. I stand, pace the room to abate my nerves while Ry sleeps.

Breathe, Donavan. Fucking breathe. Ry's the one in labor and you're the one nervous? Think of her. Worry about her.

The after part you're worried about will just happen.

Relax.

Chill the fuck out.

I call Shane to eat up time. Try to right my wrongs and make sure he's cool. Make sure Zander's better. Hang up. Send Sammy to get some decent coffee downstairs. Wait some more.

I look out the window to the city beyond just as night begins to eat the daylight. Deep breath in. Exhale all the bullshit out. I glance up, surprised to see Ry awake in the window's reflection.

Our eyes meet as a sleepy smile forms on her lips and my world clicks back into its place. How could I doubt this? Our connection? Our love? Our future? She's my Midas. Everything she's ever touched in my life has been made better, fucking golden, including me as a man.

I turn back around. Ready to do this.

Wheels on the track.
Hands on the wheel.
It's time to add our first memory to the frame.

Chapter Nineteen

Rylee

"YOU'RE DOING GREAT, BABY," COLTON murmurs in my ear. My head's back on the pillow, eyes closed. He brushes my hair from my forehead, kisses the top of my hand clasped in his.

"I'm tired," I whisper, my body feeling exhaustion like I've never felt before. Bone-deep. Dead-tired. And yet there is this underlying current like a livewire buzzing through me. Fueling me.

"I know, but you're almost there," he says, words laced with encouragement. He feels helpless. I know he does. My big bad husband who can't rush in to save the day for me. Who can't do anything really but hold my hand.

I open my eyes and meet his green ones. "Are you okay?" I ask, noting the guarded emotion in his eyes and figuring he's a little freaked out.

"Shush. I'm fine. Don't worry about me. Let's meet BIRT," he says with a reassuring smile that gives me just what I need.

A laugh. A moment to relax, albeit brief. This man who is so full of contradictions and owns every piece of my heart. "You're relentless."

"And you're beautiful."

Tears well. I'm sure it's the hormones surging through my body or just the connection I feel with him right now in the midst of bringing this life we've created into the world, but all of a sudden the tears are there. He reaches out, thumbs on my cheeks, and holds my face in his hands, shaking his head very slowly.

"Thank you," he says. That shy smile I love ghosts his lips as his emerald eyes swell with unfathomable emotion. And I'm not sure what it is he's thanking me for—those simple words could mean so many things—so I just nod my head ever so subtly because he has no idea how much those two words and the intention behind them mean to me.

"Another contraction is coming, Rylee. I need you to be strong. A couple more pushes and I think we are going to meet your new little miracle," Dr. Steele says, interrupting the moment and reinvigorating my depleted energy.

"Okay." I nod my head as Colton's hand squeezes mine.

"Give me a good push," she says.

A deep breath in. My whole body taut as I hold my breath and push. Dizziness hits as the ten-second count slowly comes to an end. The world fading to black as every part of my body is exhausted.

"There's the head," she says, pulling me from the darkness and making this all more real, more urgent than I ever could have imagined. "Lots of dark hair."

And when I open my eyes, Colton has shifted so he can look down to see the baby. His expression when he looks back at me? Fear and inexplicable emotion in his tear-filled eyes. His jaw is slack and awe is written all over his face. Our connection is brief but intense before the mesmerizing sight of our baby pulls his eyes away from mine once again.

And as envious as I am that he gets to see our miracle first, I also know I'll never forget his expression. The pride and astonishment etched in the lines of his face have forever imprinted in the space of my heart.

Chapter Twenty

COLTON

MY HAND IS SQUEEZED IN a goddamn vise-like grip. My heart is too but for a completely different reason. The sight in front of me. Incredible. Indescribable. Grounding in a way I never thought possible.

"This is the hard one, Ry. Last push and you're done," Dr. Steele says, as she looks up at her and then back down to where my eyes are glued. "And go."

My hand is squeezed. Rylee's moan fills the room. Her body tenses. "*Spiderman. Batman. Superman. Ironman.*" The words come from out of nowhere. I'm not even sure if I whisper them aloud or just in my head. But the only other thought that flickers is that they belong here.

Full circles.

And then all thoughts are lost. Emotion rules. Pride swells. A tiny pair of shoulders emerge followed quickly by a little body.

Snapshots of time pass. Seconds that feel like hours.

My breath is stolen. Hijacked. Robbed. And so is my goddamn heart because there's no other way to describe what I feel as Dr. Steele says, "Congratulations, it's a boy!"

"Oh shit." My whole world picks up, moves, flips upside down, and reverses on its axis. And I couldn't be happier about it.

Soft cries. Dark hair. Cutting the cord. A blur of disbelief as my eyes lock on the baby. My son.

Holy motherfucking shit.

My son.

I'm a dad.

The moment hits me like a goddamn sucker punch—every part of me reacting to the impact—as Dr. Steele places him on Rylee's belly. Nurses wipe him off as Ry's sobs fill the room when she gets to see him for the first time.

I'm looking at fingers and toes and ears and eyes and trying to figure out how this completely perfect little person is a part of me.

How is it even possible?

Swimming in emotion, I lean down and press a kiss to Rylee's forehead. Her eyes are as focused as mine on our son. "I love you," I murmur with my lips still pressed against her skin.

His crying stops instantly the minute Ry cradles him in her arms. *He knows.* How simple is that? And if I thought I was sucker-punched before, the sight of her holding our son is the knockout punch. I'm looking down at his little face and hers next to each other, and shit I never expected to feel in my life surges through me, wraps around my heart, and fills it in a way I never thought was possible.

My whole fucking world.

My Rylee. My son. My everything.

"He's beautiful," she says, awe in her voice and tears sliding down her cheeks. She presses a kiss to the top of his head, and for some reason the visual hits me hard.

The future flashes: first steps, skinned knees, first homerun, first kiss, first love.

Tears sting. My chest constricts. All I can think is that this little boy may get kissed by a lot of women during his lifetime but this first kiss is the most important.

He's taken from her. Cries fill the room. He's measured and weighed. Tested and looked over. I can't take my eyes off him for a single second.

I glance back and find Ry. Her eyes match mine—both so overwhelmed with everything that we don't have words. I feel like such a sap—the tears in my eyes, the inability to speak—like I should be the arrogant bastard I normally am. It seems even assholes like me have a soft spot. Yeah. Ry's always been that to me, but I have a feeling I just found another that aces all the rest.

If it's in the cards.

My heart stumbles in my chest. The memory flickers and dies in seconds. One I can't place, can't remember, and yet somehow know it means something. And I don't give it a second thought when the nurse holds him out to me, wrapped tightly in a blanket.

I freeze. Like arctic-chill freeze because all of the sudden I'm afraid I'm going to hurt him. Thank fuck the nurse sees my reaction because she shows me how to hold him and then places him in my arms.

And then he looks up. And this time I freeze for a completely different reason.

I'm mesmerized, lost, and found again. By bright blue eyes, little lips, and a soft cry. By dark hair and perfect ears. By his untouched innocence, unconditional trust, and love: all three given without asking the first time I look into his eyes.

I go to speak. To reassure my son I won't let him down. I open my mouth. I close it. I can't lie to him right off the bat. Can't tell him that when I know I'm going to screw up sometimes.

But I sure as fuck am going to do everything in my power to be what he needs.

Chapter Twenty-One

Rylee

PINCH ME.

This can't be real. This beautiful baby boy in my arms can't possibly be mine.

But if this is a dream it's so incredibly real I never want to wake from it. Sure my body is exhausted, and despite my legs still being slightly numb, I ache all over the place. But the one ache I don't think will ever go away is the one in my chest from my heart overflowing with love.

I can't stop looking at him as he sleeps soundly against my chest. The nurses suggested putting him in his bassinet but I can't bear to part with him just yet. I've waited way too long for this moment. I'm fixated on every single thing about him and can't get over how much he looks like what I think Colton would have looked like as a baby.

When I look across the dimly lit room toward Colton, his phone is up and he is taking another picture in an endless line of photos of us. It's adorable how he wants to document every moment. His need for his son to have tangible memories of being a baby since he has absolutely none is both moving and bittersweet.

I smile softly as the flash goes off and then raise my eyebrows and wait for him to lower the phone. When he does, our gazes meet, and there's the slightest flicker of something I can't quite read. He blinks it away as quickly as it comes and grants me an exhausted smile in exchange.

"Is he sleeping?" he asks, leaning forward so he can see for himself.

"No. Do you want to hold him?" I ask, knowing damn well I don't want to give him up, and yet also feel I've been hogging him. It's only been two hours since we moved into the maternity suite and between trying to get the baby to latch on and the nurses coming in and out constantly, Colton hasn't had another chance to hold him.

"No." He shakes his head. "Leave him be." He stands and comes to sit on the edge of my bed and leans forward to press a gentle kiss to our son's head before granting me one as well. Our lips linger momentarily before he leans back, a large sigh falling as he shakes his head again. I get it though, because I keep shaking mine too, trying to wrap my head around the fact the one thing I never thought I'd ever get to experience has just happened.

And I was able to share it with him.

"Well, I guess I can't stall any longer on the name thing unless we want to make BIRT the official one on the birth certificate."

"No," I whisper, harshly contradicting the smile on my lips. "So we're really going to say our first choice at the same time and go that route?" The whole idea makes me nervous. And I hate that such a lasting, important decision is going to be made on the fly.

"Yep. Perfect plan."

"No." He's going to give me hives if he keeps this up. And he knows it. I can see it in the little smirk on his face and gleam in his eyes. Damn, Donavan.

"Or we could just call him Ace Thomas Donavan and call it a day," he murmurs, head cocked to the side, lips pursed as he waits for my reaction. My eyes flicker down to his visitor's badge, where the two names are spelled out, and for a moment I'm hit with utter clarity amidst the haze of drugs and fog of fatigue.

Ace Thomas.

Looking down at my sweet baby boy, I roll the name on my tongue as it repeats over and over in my mind. It's nowhere close to the unique and trendy names I'd narrowed down on my numerous lists, and yet as I stare at his tiny fingers curled around my pinkie, I can't believe I didn't think of the name myself because it couldn't be more perfect.

Those two names hold so much significance in our relationship so why not put them together? My nickname for Colton and his endless attempts to know what ACE stood for. Allowing my son to have a part of my identity by giving him my family's last name as his middle name. Our first date at the carnival when Colton used the name as his alias and confessed he used it because he wanted me all to himself. And of course, Colton's own definition of the acronym that fits so poignantly now: A chance encounter.

And look what we have now as a result of that chance encounter.

"Ace Thomas," I murmur softly, liking the sound of it more and more with each passing second.

"I had other names in mind but as I was sitting watching you sleep between contractions, I couldn't get it out of my head. It fits, doesn't it?"

"It does," I say hesitantly. When I look from our son to Colton and then back to our son, I know it makes absolute perfect sense. "Hey Ace," I say to the snuggling baby in my arms. My heart skips a beat as I feel like all the stars have aligned and our little world we've created becomes complete.

The soft suction of his mouth on my breast is strangely the most comforting feeling I've ever experienced. Almost as if my body knows this was meant to be. And as I look down at him it hits me that this little being depends on Colton and me for absolutely everything. It's a humbling and overwhelming feeling, but one that warms me completely.

"Are you two going to catch any sleep?" the nurse asks as she checks my vitals yet again on what feels like the ever-constant rotation through our room. And it always seems like the interruption is immediately after I fall asleep.

"We're trying to," I murmur softly as I look down at Ace as he eats.

"I know it's hard with nurses coming in and out constantly but you should consider putting him in the nursery so you can get some sleep."

"Absolutely not." Colton's voice is resolute when he speaks from the recliner in the corner of the room making both the nurse and my head turn to look at him. "There's a reason Sammy's sitting outside on a chair. The last thing we need is paparazzi snapping pictures of him, selling it to the highest bidder, and then plastering it all over the place. No. End of discussion."

I stare at him, eyes blinking over and over as I come to terms with what he's just said. After the clusterfuck of the past month with the media's intrusion on our lives, how could I be so ensconced in our little bubble that the thought never crossed my mind? That people will be clamoring to get pictures of Ace to sell and make money from?

"He's right," I say, caught off guard as I look at the nurse staring at us like we're crazy.

"Okay," she says with a sympathetic smile, "if you change your mind, let me know. We do deal with this fear quite a lot here so I assure you we have safety measures in effect to prevent that from happening. If you end up needing some sleep, just buzz me at the nurses station."

"Thanks," Colton says, the muscle in his jaw clenching and un-clenching as he stares at her.

She finishes checking my vitals and then reaches to check Ace out since he's fallen asleep and is no longer latched on. She looks at her temporal thermometer and frowns some. "His body temp is a little cold. It's normal for a newborn to have trouble keeping their body heat but let's help him a bit and get him skin on skin with you." She starts unbundling him and taking his white T-shirt off so I'm left with a tiny ball of pink who's dwarfed by the white diaper.

I know this is normal but it's a little different when it's your baby. She hands Ace to me, lifts down the shoulder of my hospital gown so I can slide Ace inside, and his smooth skin is resting against my bare chest.

"We'll let him be like this for a bit and see if that helps or else we'll have to bring a warmer in, okay?"

"Okay," I say as she collects her things. I don't even pay attention because the feeling of him against me is all-consuming. He tries to suckle my collarbone and I laugh quietly at the sensation and how very surreal this feels.

When I look up, Colton's eyes are locked onto the two of us, expression completely stoic. "What are you thinking about?" I ask, knowing damn well it could be a loaded question but needing to ask it nonetheless.

"Nothing. Everything." He shrugs. "Everything has changed and yet nothing is different. I don't know how to explain it."

I nod my head ever so slowly understanding and not under-standing what he's saying and needing so much more of an expla-nation from him but having a feeling I'm not going to get one. Ace moves and I'm drawn back to watch him for a bit as I fight the ex-haustion and the fear of hurting him if I fall asleep while he's lying on my chest.

"I feel like I'm hogging him," I murmur, my lips kissing the crown of his head, reveling in that scent of a newborn baby, before looking over to Colton as I scrunch my nose up in an apology.

"No. You're good," he says with a gesture to reinforce his words before he leans back in his reclining chair and closes his eyes, effectively changing the subject.

"You sure you don't want to hold him?"

"No," he says, eyes still closed. "The nurse said he needs skin to skin with you to help his body temperature."

"He can be skin to skin with you and get the same thing," I explain, my tired mind trying to understand how on earth Colton could say no when I don't feel like I ever want to let him go.

"No. No. I'm okay." He rejects the idea quickly with eyes still closed and arms crossing over his chest.

He's afraid of Ace. Big man. Teeny baby. Lack of experience. Fears of inadequacy. The notion flickers and fades through my mind: his history, his staunch refusal, the way he's seemed busy when I've needed him to hold Ace, add validation to my assumption.

I'm scared. Colton's confession from the 'I'm game' float through my mind.

"He needs you too," I whisper softly, my voice breaking with enough emotion to cause his head to lift so our eyes meet. "Your son needs you too, Colton."

"I know," he says with a slow nod of his head. And even though there is guarded trepidation in his eyes, I don't back down this time from our visual connection. Instead I let my eyes ask him everything I can't say aloud or push him on further. "You two look so peaceful and perfect together. I just don't want to disturb you."

And as much as I know he's being honest in his response, I also know he's using it to distract me from delving deeper into his nonchalance.

Talk to me, Colton. Tell me what's going on in that wonderful, complicated, scarred, scared, beautiful mind of yours.

I want to reassure him, tell him he's not going to drop Ace, harm him, or taint his innocence, and yet I don't think there is anything I can say that will lessen his unease.

Give him time, Rylee.

Chapter Twenty-Two

COLTON

THIS CAN'T BE REAL. *I know it can't be.*

She's dead.

Kelly proved it to me. So why is she calling to me from inside that room? The one that fills me with such a vile, visceral reaction. Bile's in my throat. My mouth feels like the morning after I've drunk a fifth of Jack. My stomach a bath of acid.

Run, Colton. Put one foot in front of the fucking other and escape while you can.

"Colty, Colty. Sweet little Colty," *she says in a singsong voice. One I've never heard her use before. It calls to me. Draws me in. Makes me want to see and fear to know.*

Goddamn ghosts. Even sound asleep they come back to haunt me.

I clear the doorway, the smell of mildew and must hits my nose and pulls the nightmares I thought were dead and gone from my mind. The problem: they're not nightmares. They were reality. My reality.

And when I look up I'm knocked back a step to see the woman in the rocking chair. I know her but don't remember her looking like this at all: dark hair pulled back, a pink tank top on, and the softest expres-

sion on her face as she looks down at the baby cradled in her arms. *She's sitting in the stream of moonlight, a smile on her face, and the baby's hand is wrapped around one of her fingers.*

"Colty, Colty. Sweet little Colty," she sings again and all I can do is blink and wonder if what I'm seeing is really real, if it really happened, or is just a figment of my imagination.

That's not me. Can't be.

This is me.

I pat my chest. See the glint of my wedding ring against the light. And yet I can't help but stare at my mother looking so real and normal and . . . nice. Not the strung-out, crazy-haired, high monster who used to trick me, trade me, and starve me for her own benefit.

"Stop calling him that. He'll get a complex." *A deep voice to my right startles me. I catch a glimpse of the man in the shadows: tall, broad-shouldered, dark hair, jeans hanging low on a shirtless torso.*

But I can't see his face.

My heart races. Is it my dad or the monster?

Is he one and the same?

The bile comes up—fast and furious—and I throw up all over the carpet as the thought rips me apart in a way I never thought possible. Was the monster my dad?

I throw up again. My body rejecting the idea over and over, dry heaves of disbelief, but no one in the room moves or notices me.

It's a dream, Colton. *A goddamn fucking dream. It's not real. It is not.*

And yet when I look up again, the man coming out of the shadows seems different, more familiar than moments ago, but it's my mother's voice that whips my head her way.

"Acey, Acey. Sweet little Acey."

No! I scream but no sound comes out as she looks up at me. Her eyes are bloodshot and ragged now. Her mouth painted red like a twist- ed clown. She starts to lift the baby, my son, up and out to the man in the room.

"No!" *I yell again. I can't move, can't save him. My feet are stuck to the floor. The darkness of the room is slowly swallowing me whole.*

"Yes," *the man growls as his meaty fingers reach out to take Ace from her.*

The hands. Those hands. The ones that fill my fucking nightmares. The ones that stained my soul.

I fight against the invisible hands holding me in place. Need to get to him. Have to save him.

And then he steps out of the darkness and into the light. My shout fills the room and hurts my ears. But no one looks. No one stops. It's the monster from my childhood's life taking my son, but he has my face.

My face.

My hands.

I'm going to abuse my son.

Spiderman. Batman. Superman. Ironman.

I'm shocked awake from my struggle when my ass hits the floor as I fall out of the hospital recliner. I lie where I am for a few seconds in the room's silence. My breathing harsh. My mind fucked. My heart racing out of control.

Fucking Christ.

I close my eyes and let my head fall back onto the floor. My body tense, mind reeling. Thoughts, images, emotions crash together like the rubber debris scattered on the topside of the track: always where you're afraid to touch them for fear you'll spin out of control.

But this time I need to touch them. Need to know what has scared the fuck out of me more than the normal nightmare.

It doesn't matter because I'm already spun. Crazed. There's only one thing I remember and it's the one I wish I could forget: I'm the one who hurt Ace.

Or rather, I'm the one who will hurt Ace.

Get a fucking grip, Donavan.

Shake it off.

It was just a dream.

Then why does the fear feel more real than anything I've ever felt before in my life?

Chapter Twenty-Three

Rylee

"CAN YOU TAKE HIM FOR a second?" I ask Colton. He's busy on his iPad in the corner of the hospital room. "I want to brush my teeth before everyone gets here."

Colton's eyes flicker over to me and then to the bassinet the nurse moved across the room and out of the way beyond my reach. I wince as I try to scoot up a little, and he slowly gets up and approaches the bed. I'm not one for games but I know the longer Colton fears Ace, the harder this transition of having a child will be for him. And while my body aches all over, the dramatic grimace on my face was for good measure.

He reaches out hesitantly and I place Ace in the cradle of his arms. I hear him suck in a breath.

"Thanks. I'll be just a sec," I say as I push myself off the bed and slowly make my way to the sink area. I take my time, brushing my hair and teeth, and apply a little makeup while watching father and son out of the corner of my eye.

Colton stands there looking down at Ace, his features softening as he takes in his spitting image and I wonder what's going through his head. Is the connection stronger than the fear or is he still just trying to come to terms with this life-changing moment?

I glance in the mirror's reflection to see Colton slowly sit down with Ace cradled in his arms, and I swear to God my heart can't swell any more with love at the sight of the two of them together. And he's completely focused on Ace so I'm afforded the moment to watch the two of them together unhindered.

There must be something about the sight that makes my mind recall what I thought I heard him say yesterday. When I was slowly blacking out in one of my final pushes, I thought I heard Colton quietly say the names of his beloved superheroes.

The longer I watch this awkward dance between new father and baby, I know he did. But the question is *why*?

Moving into the room, I purposefully sit back on the bed without taking Ace from him. And the funny thing is, he's so absorbed in our son, he doesn't notice.

"Why did you say the superheroes before he was born?" I ask softly. He may be looking down, but I can see his body tense and know there's a reason behind it.

Silence stretches and either he didn't hear me, or he doesn't want to answer. Regardless, he's still holding Ace and that's what matters. I lay my head back and just as I close my eyes he speaks.

"Because I figured if I called to them then, he might never have to call to them himself. And I wanted to welcome our baby into the world with the strength of those who gave me hope—kept me alive—on his side."

His words, the raw grit in his tone, tell me he still has so many fears I don't know about yet. When I open my eyes to meet his, I hate the lingering shadow of a past I thought we had put behind us. It hasn't been there in so very long.

"Colton . . ." His name is a plea, an apology, an endearment simultaneously, and before I can say another thing, there is a knock at the maternity suite's door and the moment is gone.

"Come in," I say.

Within seconds the room is a whirlwind of sound, people, balloons, and oohs and aahs as our family and friends descend upon us.

"Let me see my grandbaby," Colton's mom, Dorothea, says as she leads the charge into the room, her hands outstretched and smile wide as she reaches out to take Ace from her son.

"You'd think you were royalty or something with all the press outside," Haddie says above the fray, and even though I can't see her yet, I can hear her.

I look over and meet Colton's glance, and give him a nod in acknowledgement. He was right in making the call to keep the boys away from here and out of paparazzi's lenses' crosshairs. And God yes, I want to see them all. Look Zander in the eye to really make sure he's okay like he told me he was on the phone, and thank Shane for staying with him last night. Have them come here to the hospital—a place most of them still associate with where they had to lie to doctors about why they were hurt—and see it's not always a bad place. So they could meet the newest brother in their family, and see for themselves that I'm perfectly fine.

The last thing I want to happen though is to deliberately put them in the public eye. That should be avoided for Zander at all costs. Besides, Teddy might have turned a blind eye to my visit to The House and interference in Zander's visitation there yesterday so the board doesn't know, but I don't think he'd be able to do the same if pictures of the boys at the hospital were plastered on the Internet.

"Oh my God, he's adorable," Dorothea says, pulling me from my thoughts. I glance to Colton and back to where Andy, my mom, and dad gather around her as she holds the newest member of the family. I watch them all for a second, enamored by how my always-regal mother-in-law has been reduced to a bunch of expressions and sounds as she revels in her first moments as a grandmother.

"We figured we'd all bombard you at once so you could get this all over with in one shot," Quinlan says as she leans forward and gives me a tight hug. And for some reason—probably the hormones running in overdrive right now—I hold on a little longer than necessary and just breathe her in.

"Thanks," I say as she pulls back and looks at me closely.

"You doing okay?" she asks, prompting a nod from me as emotion forms into a lump in my throat and lodges the words there.

"Yeah," I say with a soft smile. "I'm just tired." She reaches out and squeezes my hands, my thumb running over the tiny pink heart tattooed on the inside of her wrist.

"Congrats!" Her rockstar boyfriend Hawke says from behind her before he steps forward and presses a kiss to the top of my head. "We can't wait to spoil him rotten."

"Don't get him started," Quin says with a roll of her eyes. "He already has a mini guitar for him. And microphone. And—" Hawke's hand covers her mouth in a mock attempt to shut her up and save him the embarrassment, but I think it's a little too late.

"Outta the way." I know there's no ignoring that voice nor do I want to. "I need to see my girl."

Hawke and Quin step back so Haddie can barrel through and launch herself at me. Within seconds I find myself squeezed so tight I can barely breathe.

"You're a mom," she says into my ear with such love and affection that tears sting the backs of my eyes. I don't care either because we've been through a lifetime of ups and downs together so I love being able to experience this up with her. "Do you know how hard it is for me not to push the grandparents away so I can hog him all to myself?"

"I think you'll lose that fight," I say, pulling back and looking at the smile on her face and the tears in her eyes.

"And Ace, huh?" she says with a quirk of her eyebrows, earning her a smirk of mine in return, considering she is the one who started the whole acronym with me way back when.

"What am I, chopped liver?" Becks asks as he squeezes into the room and along the wall toward me, since everyone else is focused on where my mom is now holding Ace at the foot of the bed.

"No . . . but I'd easily trade you for the warm chocolate chip cookie and milk this hospital gives you," I tease, causing him to laugh and shake his head.

"I see how you are, Donavan," he says as he leans in and presses a kiss to my cheek. "You did good, Ry. We're so damn happy for you."

"Thanks, Becks." My God. Where are all the emotion and tears coming from right now? You'd think things were sad the way I'm leaking like a faucet instead of being the exact opposite: perfect.

"And of course he looks just like his Uncle Becks. Damn handsome." Haddie rolls her eyes beside him and then gives him the "I'm innocent" face when he looks at her and that makes me laugh.

"Nope. I'm pretty sure his good looks take after his Uncle Tanner," my brother says, stepping beside Becks and shaking his hand with a good-natured squeeze, kissing Haddie on the cheek in greeting before looking at me. "Hey Bubs. How're you handling all of this?"

"It's indescribable," I say softly because there really are no words to accurately describe the feelings, emotions, and sensations that are a constant high in my body and mind right now.

"You look gorgeous." I roll my eyes at the comment. "And he definitely does take after me."

"Bullshit, Thomas," Colton says, as he steps to the other side of the bed and reaches out to shake his hand. "I get to claim this one."

Tanner gives him the hands up motion like it's no contest and Colton laughs. Colton glances down at me and squeezes my hand. I can see the pride in his eyes over Ace and that gives me more hope than I thought I was even looking for that he'll overcome his fear. Look at what those few moments of holding Ace did already.

"Where's your better half?" I ask my brother.

"She had an event to work and is super bummed but she's going to try to drive up tomorrow to meet him." He leans in and gives me a hug that brims with love and whispers in my ear, "Mom's in fricking heaven having a new little baby to spoil. She's already telling Dad she's not sure how she's going to live so far away from him, so be prepared for her wanting to spend the night a lot."

"Thanks for the warning, but I might just need the help."

"Ha. You needing it and accepting it are two different things," he says with a doubtful lift of his eyebrows. He's so very right but I can't let him know that. I glance over to where Ace is nestled gently in my mother's arms and the need to hold him is so strong right now I have to tell myself he's okay. And of course he is. I trust every single person in this room but when you have something be a part of you for nearly nine months, it's a little hard to not need that connection.

My eyes shift to the sight of Andy and Colton in a quick but heartfelt embrace. I watch as Andy steps back, one hand still on the side of Colton's cheek, and his eyes searching his son's in that way he always does to make sure he's okay. It's the look of unconditional love, and I hope that when people watch me interact with Ace, they see the same thing.

Their connection captivates me. As I watch Colton accept love from his dad, my concern over Colton's lack of engagement dissipates. By demonstration, Andy has given Colton all the tools he needs to know how to be a good father. My fears fade as a vivid picture forms in my head of how Colton will love Ace: absolute, unequivocal devotion.

Just as he has loved me.

Andy glances my way. "And there's the woman of the hour!" His voice booms through the room and then he immediately winces when he realizes how loud he was.

"Andy . . ."

He swoops down and gathers me up in one of his bear hugs you can usually feel all the way to your toes, but at least he's a little gentler this time around. "Rylee-girl, you've made me so damn happy. All over again. You are such a blessing to this family," he says. He pulls back and does the same thing I was just admiring with Colton to me—hand on my cheek, eyes searching mine—and I feel blessed to be completely loved by my in-laws.

"You good?" he asks, eyes double-checking to make sure the smile on my face is real.

"I'm incredible," I whisper back with the smile spreading on my lips. How lucky was Colton to have sat on this amazing man's doorstep? A patient man capable of teaching him what it means to love so completely. For that, I will forever be grateful to him. "Congratulations, Grandpa."

He throws his head back and laughs that full-body laugh of his that reminds me so much of Colton's, even though he is adopted, that I squeeze his hands and wonder if Ace will have the same mannerism when he laughs like that when he's older.

"Move out of the way, Andy, I need to hug this new momma who just gave me my first grandchild," Dorothea says. She all but pushes her husband out of the way so she can hold my cheeks in her hands and kiss both of them.

"Hi." Surprise flickers through me when I see tears in her eyes.

"Thank you," she whispers, her usually resonating voice unsteady and laden with emotion. "He's absolutely adorable. You must be over the moon."

"No need to thank me—"

"Yes, there is," she says with a nod of her head to tell me not to argue. I'm smart enough to know by now when to pick my battles with her and this is not one of them. She leans in and gives me what feels like the hundredth hug in as many seconds before standing back with a soft smile on her lips and adoration in her eyes.

My gaze shifts over her shoulder to my dad. I'll never forget the look on his face: awe, pride—discomfort at being packed like sardines in the room—but more than anything, love.

"Hi, sweetie." He steps forward and presses a kiss to my head. But I don't let him off that easily because I wrap my arms around him and hug him tight.

"Hiya, Daddy. What do you think?"

"I think I couldn't be more proud of you and in love with him and I haven't even gotten to hold him yet," he says with a laugh. "You're going to be a fantastic mother."

And this time I don't fight the tears but let one slip over and down my cheek, because that's a huge compliment coming from a man I've idolized my whole life.

"Your turn," my mom says, softly nudging my dad from the side as she holds out Ace for him to take for the first time. I watch the transition from one of my parents to the other and instantly know I'm going to enjoy watching them be grandparents to my son. And not that Dorothea and Andy won't either, but it's *my* parents, so the notion hits home a little more, knowing the same arms that rocked me as a newborn are going to rock him too.

I look to the right and notice Colton also watching them and realize he will never be able to have that same thought, and a part of me hurts for him because of it. And for the first time, I truly understand his hesitation, feeling like he's on the outside here because not a single person in this room shares the same blood running through them with him like I do. It's a humbling thought that opens my eyes all at the same time.

My dad looks up from Ace in his arms and asks Colton something, so my mom's attention shifts to me. "Hey baby girl," she says as she sits on the edge of the bed and reaches out with her fingers to move the strands of hair from my face. "You look tired. You in a lot of pain?"

"Just sore, but the pain was definitely worth it," I say as she leans forward and presses a kiss to my forehead.

"Yes, he is most definitely worth it. You two sure know how to make a beautiful baby."

"It's in the genes," I say.

The conversation continues on around us as my mom asks me

to retell everything I've already told her about on the phone: how my water broke, the labor, how Ace is eating, about his health, about my recovery. At some point I scoot over and she sits in the bed beside me. I put my head on her shoulder, and she plays with my hair like she used to when I was a kid and was sick. It's comforting and soothing and just the right person I need right now to bridge that gap for me from pregnant to now being a mother. She knows I don't need words, just her silent support, and it means the world to me as I look around this room crammed full of our friends and family.

There's barely any room for anyone to move and everyone is watching Ace get passed from person to person and complimenting on what an easy baby he is to not be scared by all of this. And suddenly I'm overwhelmed with the thought that as many heartbreaking lows as I've been through trying to have a baby, it couldn't have turned out more perfectly.

My heart is absolutely the fullest it has ever been in my life.

Time passes, the chatter subsides, and at some point Ace begins to cry. My body reacts to the sound of him. Panic sets in as Tanner tries to soothe him by bringing him up to his shoulder. And it's not that I don't want my brother to hold him but rather I *need* to hold him more. My body vibrates to hold my son again with a strange new mix of maternal instinct and hysteria.

"I can take him, Tanner," I say, trying to subtly let him know.

"I can handle it, Ry," he says. As I meet Haddie's eyes she knows I'm starting to freak out.

"Tanner," my mom's voice rings above the chatter in a warning, "we've got a new momma here who is a bit overwhelmed by all of us swooping in on her at once. She hasn't held Ace in a bit, and I'm sure she's getting a little frantic, so why don't you hand him over?" And even though I can't see her face, I know the exact look she gives him from my own experience.

He responds immediately but by the time he gets Ace to me I'm sweating and heading toward a full-blown panic attack. "Here you go," Tanner says as he slips him into my arms and plants a kiss on both of our heads. "He really is beautiful."

And I can breathe again. He's crying and I have no clue if it's because of all of the stimuli or if he's actually hungry, but I don't care because he's back in my arms. I look up to find Colton through the crowd of people, and he can tell I'm flustered and overwhelmed. When he mouths *I love you*, it puts a little more right in my world.

"Okay, guys," he says after winking at me, "it's feeding time and not for me." Laughter rings through the room. "Thanks for coming to meet Ace, but it's time to say goodbye and head out."

The room explodes in a hurried frenzy of hugs and congratulations and promises to stop by the house later in the week or phone calls to check in before Colton ushers them all out. The women linger a little longer, asking the questions they couldn't with the guys around before they begrudgingly leave the room with just my mom left.

"Thank you," I whisper to her with a sigh as I unbutton my hospital gown and let Ace latch on. That instant surge of calming hits me. *All better.*

"It may have been a long time ago for me, but I remember that feeling of panic and *give me my baby back* and being overwhelmed."

"You've got that right," I murmur, both of our heads angled downward as we watch Ace fall into bliss.

"Just remember that your hormones are going to be out of whack for a while so expect the sudden hot flashes and mood swings—"

"Great," I say with a laugh.

"How's Colton doing with all of this?" she asks.

"He's fine," I say hesitantly, and I'm not sure if I'm trying to fool her or want her to delve deeper into my comment. But being my mother, I'm pretty sure it's the latter.

"Fine can mean a lot of things," she murmurs as she leans her head on top of my head resting on her shoulder.

I'm quiet for a few moments. As involved in our lives as our families are, I usually don't relay the details of every issue. Part of me feels kind of alone right now. Part of me also needs the reassurance that what I think I should do about it is the right thing.

"Fine as in, he's present, but I know he's scared for so many reasons. Afraid to do too much, not enough, to drop him, that he might not connect with him, that he might be like his parents . . . I don't know." So much for keeping my thoughts private. But at least I've said them to the one person I know won't judge me and won't repeat them elsewhere. Thank God for our mother-daughter bond.

"Men are fickle creatures," she murmurs. "Of course he has fears. And his are probably a little more justified after all he's been through. Give him time. He looks at his hands and sees how big they are against Ace's head and thinks how he might accidentally hurt him somehow." I murmur a sound of understanding. The soothing feeling of Ace nursing and my lack of sleep, cause my exhaustion to catch up with me. "Your body was made to do this, to be this . . . It has gone through all sorts of changes over the past nine months. Plus you've raised the boys so you're more comfortable with kids than he is."

"True," I say softly.

"This is all new to him. A shock to the way he's lived his life. The one thing he never wanted or expected until he met you. Men have a hard time adjusting to change when they have no control over it. He'll come around, sweetie. He has no choice."

But he does, I think to myself. I know the old Colton who used to close himself off with impenetrable steel walls. He wouldn't do that to his son, though. There's no way he would. Because that would make him too much like his birth parents.

"I know. I just don't want him to pull away."

"He might for a bit, but here's the thing, Rylee: the connection between you and Ace, and Colton and Ace is completely different. Perfect example is what just happened. You don't want to part from Ace. He's the air you breathe right now. It's rarely the same for men."

"I never thought of it that way."

"I know the idea of having to be apart from him causes your heart to race. And if you had to, you wouldn't give a second thought to driving onto sidewalks, over people if need be, to get home to him as quick as you can. That's normal," she says with a chuckle. "I used to feel the same way with you guys. I'd need a break . . . but the minute I had it I needed to be with you as soon as possible. But for Colton? It's a different type of feeling for him. There's this huge change in his life right now. A bonus, yes, but at the same time it's scary as hell for him. Not to mention he worries he's being replaced in your life by the one man that's probably more handsome than he is."

I snort a laugh at the comment but her words of wisdom hit home more than I thought they would. "Thanks, Mom. You always know what to say."

"Hardly, but thank you."

The door to the room opens with perfect timing and Colton walks in at the same time my mom rises from beside me on the bed. "There's my cue," she says as she leans over and presses another kiss to Ace's head before looking up into my eyes. "I'm always here for you. Always. Any time."

"Thank you. I love you."

"Love you too," she says as she gives Ace one last glance and turns to face Colton. "I'll leave you with your family now, Colton. Take good care of my babies." She steps forward and gives him a long hug before kissing his cheek.

"I will. Let me walk you out."

They leave the room and the comforting silence surrounds Ace and me once again.

Chapter Twenty-Four

Rylee

I'M SWITCHING ACE FROM MY left side to my right side when the door swings open into the room. "Thanks for walking her out," I say distractedly. When Colton says nothing back I look up and let out a little yelp at the man standing near the foot of the bed.

"I'm sorry. You scared me." I do a double take and notice the blue scrubs, the top of a surgical cap covering his hair as he looks down at the clipboard in one hand and a pen poised to write with the other.

"Shift change paperwork check," he mumbles, keeping his head down and even though I can't see his face, I suddenly have an uneasy feeling begin to crawl over my skin that burns its way up my throat. "How's that sweet little baby of yours?" His voice and the question cause the hairs on the back of my neck to stand up.

Where are you, Colton? Did Sammy go with you?

"What do you need?" My voice is even and calm despite the alarm bells sounding in my head as I subtly try to look at his nametag that is flipped upside down.

"Now that you have him," he says, lifting his head a little to indicate Ace resting against my breast, "could you imagine if you lost him?"

Discord vibrates within me at the extremely odd question and yet when I stare at him, he seems completely normal and focused on what he's writing on the chart in his hand. I try to move Ace to cover my exposed breast, while I slowly inch my hand down toward the nurse call button. And of course it's located on the bedrail right near where he is standing, so I try to be ever so discrete as uncertainty overtakes me.

"No. Never," I finally answer.

"I lost everything. My wife. My kids. All by the hands of someone else," he says, his voice hollow and even. I stare at him now, wanting him to lift his face from where he's focused. I realize he's scribbling furiously but hasn't asked me a single question to take notes on.

My finger hovers over the call button, not wanting to make a scene, and yet my gut instinct is telling me something's off here. My mom's words flicker in my mind about how crazy a new mom can feel, and I wonder if that's what is going on here: hormones surging and taking over my rational mind.

Ace must sense my discomfort because he starts crying. "I'm so sorry," I finally respond, distracted, trying to watch what he's doing while trying to tend to my son. "How horrible."

"I thought it was only fair he knows how it feels. To feel vulnerable. To be exposed. To think he might lose it all. Jeopardize his happiness."

I shake my head. That eddy of unease returns for one more whirl as I try to figure out what in the hell he's talking about as Ace's wails escalate in pitch. "I'm sorry. I'm not following you, and you're making me uncomfortable. I'd appreciate it if you'd leave my room."

He looks up for the first time and meets me with crystalline blue eyes that hold a hint of humor oddly matching the slight smirk on his lips. "Of course. I just need your autograph on this form I have to turn in, and I'll be out of your hair," he says as he walks forward and places the manila folder on the table beside me. And as much as he makes me uncomfortable, I glance up one more time to look at him, trying to place why he looks familiar, but his head is already back down and focused on what he's fumbling with in his pocket.

"Sure." Anything. Just get the hell out of here. I set Ace down in the dip between my thighs as I grab the pen he hands me.

And then I open the folder.

My mouth drops open.

My mind is shocked.

My privacy invaded.

My little bubble popped.

Everything clicks all at the same time when I see the still photo of me from the video, spread-eagled, and every part of me unmistakable.

I look back up. His hair's a little longer and there's a goatee covering his facial scar that would have given him away instantly. But there is no doubt this is the man who has turned our world upside down in the past month.

Eddie Kimball.

I think I hear a click. I'm not sure. I force my eyes from his face to the phone he's holding up and just before the flash goes off, I bend my body over, hiding my face and exposed breast and start screaming. My finger jabbing at the call button over and over as Ace's cries rise with my burgeoning panic.

"Help!" I scream. Ace's wails escalate. "Help!"

"*Why so camera-shy now*? Donavan stole everything from me. Revenge is a bitch." He runs from the room just as the nurse comes through on the intercom.

"Everything okay, Mrs. Donavan?"

"Security!" I shout into the room. I pick Ace up and hold him tightly to my chest, rocking him as my body shakes, and my mind tries to process the fear that's clouding my judgment.

The door flings open as my nurse runs in the same exact time as a loud crash is heard in the hallway followed by a fire alarm of some sort that shrieks through the hallway of the hospital wing. "Are you okay?"

"Yes. Yes. We're fine." I keep rocking. "It's okay," I repeat to Ace over and over, as I try to reassure myself I am okay. But I'm not.

Far from it.

The nurse picks up the phone in the room and starts speaking words I don't hear because my pulse is thundering in my ears. And the minute she lowers the phone the wailing alarm stops.

But the one in my head and heart screams even louder. I'm afraid it will never shut up now.

Fear like I've only known a few times in my life—the accidents that made me lose one man and almost another—owns my soul right now. We're supposed to be safe. Supposed to be happy. And yet the man who has wreaked so much havoc in our lives just caused it to implode again.

"Tell me what happened," the nurse says at the same time Colton comes barging into the room completely out of breath, his posture defensive, and eyes wild with fear as they scour over Ace and me to make sure we are okay.

"Rylee? They were shouting for security to the room."

"*Eddie.*" It's the only word I need to say for him to understand why I'm crying tears I didn't even know were coursing down my cheeks, and holding Ace to me so tightly, that if it weren't for his crying, I'd think I was smothering him.

"You're okay?" he asks through gritted teeth. The muscle in his jaw pulses as he waits for my response. A quick nod of my head and he charges out of the room.

The old me would have yelled at him to come back. Tell him I need him more. *Which is still partially true.*

But I don't say a word.

I. *Am.* Okay. *For now.*

Eddie Kimball just fucked with my son.
I hope my husband fucks with him.

Chapter Twenty-Five

COLTON

"THE POLICE HAVE IT UNDER control."

"Like hell they do!" I growl into the phone at CJ and Kelly as I pace the hallway of the hospital like a caged fucking animal. "He was in HER room. ALONE. The fucking bastard was within a foot of her and Ace. Taunting her. That is a huge goddamn problem!"

"Did he get a picture?" CJ asks, prodding the sleeping dragon within.

"Do you think I fucking know?" I grit through clenched teeth. "She doesn't know. Doesn't think so, but isn't sure. It all happened so quickly." My skin crawls, thinking how fucking close he was to her. To Ace.

The heavy sigh on the connection grates even more on my nerves because I feel like I'm not being told something. "What are you not telling me?"

Anger eats at me. Ire like I've never known before scratching through my resolve and testing my restraint to not go take that eye for an eye right now because he's already taken way too fucking much from me.

"Nothing," CJ says and before I can question him further, he continues, "the hospital security—"

"Is for shit," I finish for him. "They let a random man dressed in scrubs and a surgical cap, which he probably bought at Scrubs-R-Us or some shit, lift an I.D. off the nurses station, and waltz into her fucking room the moment Sammy helped me manage the vultures outside when I walked our family out. He had to have been hiding if Sammy didn't see him. Probably watched and waited for me to leave. *Fucking bastard.*" My hands fist. The urge to punch a fucking wall so goddamn strong I have to stand in the middle of the hall so there's nothing within reach I can destroy. "They'll be lucky I don't sue their asses for—"

"Calm down—"

"Don't tell me to calm the fuck down!"

"I'm already filing grievances with Cedars, and Kelly has notified the police of the violation of the restraining order that—"

"It's not going to do a fucking lick of good, but go right ahead. Just be ready to have bail money to post when I come face to face with him because you're going to need it." I glance over to the door of Rylee's room, knowing I need to get this rage out before I can face her and not scare her.

"Colton. Let the legal system—"

"I'm getting Rylee out of here right now." I don't need to hear his pacifying bullshit that's not going to do a damn bit of good. Not like my fist hitting Eddie's face will. "I'll hire a nurse if I have to, but we're leaving within the hour. Fuck their protocol with discharge papers. I'll have Sammy wait if need be, but I'm not putting them at risk out in the goddamn open like this."

"Understandable," Kelly speaks for the first time.

"Find him or you're fired."

I end the call. The urge to throw my phone so intense that I squat down on my haunches for a second with my head in my hands and force myself to breathe. To do exactly what I told CJ not to tell me to do: calm down and be rational. But rational went out the goddamn window the moment that bastard went after my wife.

Rational is way the fuck overrated.

God, I wish I had found him. Caught up with him somewhere in the hospital grounds and beat the shit out of him until he lost consciousness.

But nothing. He disappeared into the goddamn wind. *Fuck.*

Just like the ghosts of the nightmares that are sitting in the back of my mind laughing at this. Chiding me and telling me this is proof I can't take care of my own wife and son. That I'm no better than my mother. That I let the same man threaten my wife and now my son as I sit on the other side of the fucking door, wrists handcuffed, unable to do a goddamn thing to stop him.

Acey, Acey. Sweet little Acey.

I scrub my hands over my face as I rise to my feet and tell myself the mixture of rage and exhaustion are playing tricks on me. I need to shut out the voices in my head. I need to tell the doubt to fuck off and die.

What I need is the crunch of his nose against my knuckles.

I sigh and head toward the hospital room. Five minutes ago I couldn't wait to get out of the room so I wouldn't have to look her in the eyes and see the fear there, or look at Ace and know I already let him down within the first thirty hours of his life. And yet now all I can think about is getting to them, packing our shit up, getting the fuck out of here, and going home to our own little world.

Chapter Twenty-Six

Rylee

MY BODY BREAKS OUT IN a sweat. It's a different kind than I've ever experienced before. This kind is that whole-body heat that causes your limbs to tremble, heart to race, and head to become dizzy. I swallow over the unease as Sammy drives us out from the protected cover of the hospital's parking garage into the driveway where paparazzi swarm us instantly.

All in a shoving match to try to get their lenses to see through the dark tinted windows of the Rover and get the first picture of Ace. The coveted shot they could sell and make a year's salary with a single frame.

Fists bang on the windows. My body jumps. I lean over the baby carrier buckled in between Colton and me. With my back to the window to block the view of Ace and my eyes closed, I fight back the threatening tears.

"Don't, Ry. Please don't," Colton murmurs as he reaches out to take my hand with one hand and smooth over my hair with the other. I clear my throat and blink the tears away and stare at Ace—this sweet, innocent baby who doesn't deserve any of this.

I chose to step into this lifestyle because I love Colton, and yet now I've brought this baby into it. I know it's too late but I don't like it. Eddie waltzed into that room to make a point and to taint this perfect moment in our lives just like he did with the video.

"We'll never get this back," I whisper. Hands thump the rear window as Sammy turns into the traffic and away from the vultures looking for scraps.

"What do you mean?"

"This moment. Our time in the hospital where we get to bond before everyday life gets in the way. He took that from us. He took that feeling away. We'll never get that back."

"Yes, we will," Colton answers immediately. He releases my hand and frames my face so I'm forced to look up and meet his gaze filled with so much concern and guilt over what happened. "Remember that empty picture frame? This was the first memory we put in there. No one will ever be able to take that away from us, baby. It's just you, Ace, and me. Our first memory slid into that frame without us ever doing it. Eddie was there for a split second of time. I'm so sorry I fucked up and wasn't there. But this—this moment, this memory, this life-changing event—overshadows it by miles."

He runs his thumb over my bottom lip as if he's trying to re-inforce his words with his touch. And it does work. His whispered words and reassuring touch calms me so I'm able to shut out the external factors and focus on what matters most: *us.*

Solidifying this notion further, he presses a kiss to my nose and then to my lips before resting his forehead against mine. "Thank you for the greatest gift I've ever been given besides you. This memory doesn't even need a frame though because the look on your face when you held Ace for the first time will forever be burned in my mind."

His words anchor my tumultuous psyche and the foundation that's been shifted beneath my feet. His touch reinforces our undeniable connection and irrevocable love. The baby sleeping peacefully in the carrier between us the greatest proof of that love.

"I don't blame you. Never. I'm just . . . we just have more than us to worry about, and it scares me because I feel like we have no control over anything."

"No one has control of life, Rylee. That's the beauty and fear in living it. We take each day as it comes, try to maintain our little piece of it, and enjoy every goddamn moment we're given."

"I just want our little piece to have peace."

The gates at home are just as crazy with paparazzi as the hospital. Probably even more so because they all knew where we'd be going when we left, and so we go through the routine again of thumping on the windows and shouting through the glass for us to give a statement.

Desperate to regain some kind of privacy and keep our son free from this absolute madness, I demand Sammy pull into the garage to let us out, which means he first has to move Sex out while I sit in the car so he can pull the Range Rover in.

I know I am being ridiculous and yet every part of my life and body has been exposed to the public beyond—my nonexistent privacy ever so easily invaded as shown by Eddie's demonstration today—that I desperately need to keep Ace as ours before sharing him with the world.

Screw the offers to our publicist, Chase, from People Magazine and US and Star offering ridiculous amounts of money for the first pictures with Ace. This isn't a matter of money to me, but rather the gaining back of some of our privacy. Our normalcy. Not feeling so goddamn exposed. The vulnerability that comes with living in a fishbowl surrounded by prying eyes.

I need our burst bubble back to whole again. Colton and I worked so hard to keep that bubble around us—cocoon our marriage and us in its early days. The one that told the press to back the hell off because no matter how hard they tried, we weren't going to bend to their gossip or tricks.

And we haven't.

Even with the release of the video, we didn't. And yet I still feel like they stole something from us. The part of us that makes us feel like every other couple in America, trying to make their marriage work and live their day-to-day life. It's not the anonymity so much but rather the constant state of being bared and vulnerable to the prying eyes and public scrutiny that caused me to lose my job, put Zander at risk, and took a special moment in our lives and turned it into Internet ecstasy.

It's just too much. All at once. So much so I'm hoping Ace helps us find that peace again. The piece of peace I told Colton I need.

My nerves are frayed. My body beyond exhausted. My mind in a mental overload so much so that everything I try to focus on becomes harder to concentrate on instead of easier. It's been such a long time since I've felt this way, Mrs. Always-in-Control. Yet right now I'm so drained I don't have the strength to care.

We walk into the house and as tired as I am, I feel restless, antsy, wanting to close myself off in a room with my two men and let the world fall away. Instead, I pull Ace against my chest and pace, letting the unsettled feeling rule my movement.

"Ry, you need to sit down," Colton says as he comes down the stairs from putting the bags and gifts away. All I can do is shake my head and try to figure out why I'm feeling so restless even in our own house. "You just had a baby. You promised me you'd take it easy until you heal more. This," he says motioning to my pacing, "is not resting."

"I know. I will," I murmur softly, my mind distracted elsewhere and locked on an idea.

"What is it, Ry? I can see your mind working. What's going on?"

"Do you ever wish we could just shut the world out? Make this our own little space and ignore everyone else?" I stop moving as I utter the final words, but my mind keeps going.

Colton angles his head and stares at me, trying to decipher what it is I'm getting at. "Yeah. All the time." He smiles softly. "But I kind of think you'd get sick of me if I was your only company."

I force a swallow down my throat as the huge pocket sliding glass doors behind him loom larger than life, my eyes flicker to the expanse of them that never bugged me before but now all of the sudden seem like this huge beacon advertising our life and allowing people to see in.

"No one can see in here, Rylee. In the fifteen years I've lived here, not a single photo has been taken from the beach." His tone is serious, eyes full of concern. I should love that he can read me so well. Appreciate that he immediately tries to assuage my anxiety before I even express it.

But I can't. I'm too focused on the large windows and thoughts of long-range lenses that might somehow be able to see us through the tinted glass.

"What about rogue reporters? Or drones? Drones are the newest thing," I say, risking sounding like a crazy woman, but the need to keep this space in lockdown is more important.

"You know the windows are tinted. We can see out but no one can see in, unless they are open, okay?" He has a placating tone in his voice that pisses me off at first and then snaps me out of the moment of hysteria, bringing me back to myself.

"Sorry." I shake my head and press a soft kiss to the top of Ace's forehead. "Today rattled me. I don't mean to sound crazy. I'm just tired and—"

"Today rattled me too, Ry. It makes me thank God I overhauled the security system last year." He walks toward me and pulls Ace and me into my safe space, his arms, and presses a kiss to both of our foreheads. "You guys are my everything. There's not a thing in the world I wouldn't do to make sure the two of you are safe."

The next twelve hours pass in bouts of sleep followed by blurry-eyed moments of shoveling food in, changing diapers, and trying to stay awake while Ace nurses so I don't hurt him somehow. It's a brutal cycle I'm sure I'm doing all wrong. I can't for the life of me bear to hear Ace cry, so when he does, I try to nurse him or lie on the couch with him on my chest so I can sleep when he does. The minute I set him down in his bassinet, he wakes right back up.

I'm mid-slumber, blissfully so, and yet sleeping so lightly out of partial fear I won't hear Ace if he wakes up and needs me. So when I startle awake with my heart in my throat and with a body full of aches, what scares me most is the reality I've fallen asleep on my side with Ace beside me nursing.

That panicked feeling doubles as I immediately put my hand on Ace's chest to make sure he's breathing and that I didn't roll over on him in my sleep. Just as my mind is back at ease, Colton thrashes beside me, yelling out in a voice sounding hollow and scared. Was this why I woke up in the first place?

"Colton!" I gasp out to try and wake him. At the same time I hurriedly gather Ace into me so somehow, some way, Colton doesn't hurt him while in the throes of his nightmare. "Colton!" I try to push myself up against the headboard with Ace pressed against my chest when Colton's protests and harsh grunts fill the silence of the room around us.

"No!" he shouts again, but this time shocks himself awake. Without seeing his eyes through the moonlit room, I know whatever he dreamt about has left him shaken. I can smell the fear in his sweat, hear the grate of his voice, and sense how disoriented he is.

"It's okay, Colton," I say, jarring him again as he startles at the sound of my voice. It unnerves me, considering I can't remember the last time he had a dream like this. When I reach out to touch him he jumps, and I just keep my hand on his arm to let him know he's with me and not in the dark room with the musty-smelling mattress that still controls his dreams from time to time.

Or maybe more often than that and he hasn't told me.

"Fuckin' A," he grits out as he shoves himself off the mattress and starts to walk back and forth at the foot of the bed, trying to work off some of the discord rioting through his system. He rolls his shoulders to come to grips with whatever it was that marred his dreams.

After a few moments with his fingers laced behind his head in a complete inward focus he stops at my side of the bed and rests his hips against the mattress. "I'm sorry."

"Nothing to be sorry for," I say, eyeing him cautiously as I study his body language to figure out his state of mind. If he's freaked, moody, scared . . .

"Goddamn fucking dreams." He makes the statement more to himself than to me. Since I can't remember how long it's been since Ace last nursed, I let him latch on as Colton sifts through his emotions.

"You want to talk about it?"

"No!" he barks into the room before sighing when he realizes the bite in his voice. "Sorry . . . I'm just in a bad spot. Okay?"

All I can do is nod my head and hope he'll talk to me, get out whatever it is into the open so it doesn't eat at him like I know his past sometimes does. He doesn't know I can see when the ghosts move in, how the demons of his past try to ruin his happiness, haunt his eyes, and etch lines in his face.

As much as I hate asking this question, I need to. "Is it Ace?" I ask in the softest of tones almost fearful of the answer.

"No." He sighs deeply. "Yes," he says even softer than I did. And as much as I'm internally freaking out over this, as much as it's supporting the theory I thought was happening in the hospital, I also know Colton well enough that I need to sit back and listen because he deserves a minute to explain. "It's not him, Ry. It's not you . . . it's just me being a dad is stirring shit up I thought I'd come to terms with."

"That's understandable."

"No, it's not. It's fucking bullshit. You can sit there and carry our son for nine months, go through all that labor pain like a goddamn champ, looking no worse for wear, and hell if I'm not the asshole so fucked up with nightmares, I'm afraid to sleep in the bed in case you have Ace in here." His words hang in the silence as it expands angrily in the space between us.

"Kelly found your dad, didn't he?"

Colton looks over at me and even though it's dark, I can see his jaw clench and the intensity in his eyes, and know the answer before he nods ever so slowly in response. Everything clicks into place for me.

"Yeah, and between that and the dreams, my head's one goddamn patchwork quilt of bullshit." The pain in his voice is raw, the turmoil within him almost palpable, and while I rarely press him to talk about things, this time I am.

"How so?"

"*How so?*" he mocks me, sarcasm lacing the laugh he emits after it.

"Tell me about your dreams."

"No." The quick response unnerves me and tells me they are worse than the normal ones he usually has no problem sharing. And that in itself worries me.

"Do you plan on going to see your dad?" I ask, knowing full well what happened the last time I made a suggestion like this to him. How he'd sought out his mom and that night at the track where he'd bared his past, let go of the demons that had spent a lifetime weighing him down. It had allowed him to begin the journey forward. When he doesn't answer, I respond in a way completely contradictory to the way I did when he first told me about this. "I think you should."

Colton startles at my comment, confusion over my about-face

written all over his handsome features. "Come again?"

"Maybe you need to look him in the eyes, see that you are absolutely nothing like him. Maybe you'll find out he knew nothing about you or—"

"Or maybe I'll find out my dad was my abuser and not only is *her* blood running through me but so is his." His anger causes my mind to spin in a direction I'd never considered before.

"What are you saying, Colton?" I push gently for more because I hadn't expected *that* response.

"My dreams," he begins and then stops momentarily as he shakes his head. He reaches out to hold Ace's tiny hand that has escaped from the blanket. "I've been having this dream that I walk in that room and my mom is there. She's younger, prettier, not at all how I remember her, and she's holding a baby. I think it's me. She sings to me and there's a man in the corner I can't see. I think he's my dad. When I look back to her she's how I remember—strung out, used up . . . It's so real. I can smell her, the stale cigarettes. I can hear the drips from the apartment faucet I used to count. See the superheroes I tried to draw in crayon on the wall so I could focus on them when . . ." His words break my heart for the horror he endured and survived and is now reliving due to circumstances beyond my control.

I wish there was something I could do to help him, comfort him, anything to help take this pain and conflict from him. *But I can't.* All I can do is stand beside him, listen to him, and be here for him when or if he decides to face this ghost head-on.

"Fuck," he curses as he shoves up from the bed again. Baxter lifts his head to see if it's time to go out as Colton walks to the wall of windows looking into the darkness of the night to his beloved beach down below. "The fucking problem is *it's me* in the dream. His body. His hands. His stench. But my goddamn hands reaching out to take Ace and do God knows fucking what to our son." My stomach rolls as I look down at Ace's angelic face. I can't even fathom how much I'm going to hurt for him when he gets his first set of shots, so I can in no way comprehend the horrors Colton's mom made him endure for a five-minute high.

"Oh, Colton," I murmur to his back, needing him to come closer so I can wrap my arms around him and reassure him. But I know even my touch won't calm the stormy waves crashing against each other inside him.

"You know . . . I asked Kelly to find my dad so I could come full circle with my history and put it to bed. I sure as hell don't want a Kumbaya session with him that's for sure. Wasn't even sure I'd speak to him, but deep down I think I wanted to see if we were alike in any way. Stupid, I know, but a part of me needs to know." He turns to face me now and in a sense I get he's asking for me to understand something he doesn't even understand.

"And now?" I prompt in the hopes he'll keep talking, that voicing aloud his fears will allow him to overcome them.

"Now it's like," he sighs and runs a hand through his hair, such a striking silhouette against the moonlight coming through the windows at his back, "now I wonder if the dreams are true. Was that fucker my dad?" he asks, voice full of distraught disbelief. "I never once thought that as a kid. Never once made that connection. I knew I had *her* tainted blood in me, have dealt with that, knowing the other half of me was at least okay . . . but what if he's just as bad? Even worse? What if I go to see my dad and it's true? Then what, Ry?"

The look on his face and sound in his voice tears me apart because all I can offer are words right now and words won't help. They won't take away fear or mitigate the unknown. But I offer them anyway. "Then we deal with it. You and I. Together." I reach out for his hand and link my fingers with his. He blows out a breath. "Parents give you their genes but don't make the person you become."

Will he ever be free of this torment? See the amazing man inside of him that we all see?

"Still, Ry. If it's true, every time I hold Ace will I . . .? I don't know." His voice fades off as he looks down at our linked hands, the silence heavy in the air around us. "Since I've been eight years old, there hasn't been a single person in my life I have had a blood connection with. That's what being adopted is like. And it's not like Andy, Dorothea, or Quin made me feel any less because they were related and I wasn't . . . but a part of me wanted to have that connection with someone. *Desperately.* I used to watch Andy, memorize everything about him so I could learn to laugh like him, talk like him, gesture like him. Just so I could be *like* somebody. So people might see us together and from our mannerisms alone think I was his son."

"Colton." It's all I can say as pain radiates in my heart, digs into my soul, and brings tears to my eyes for the little boy hoping to belong *and* for the grown man still affected by the memories.

Still conflicted by the memories.

"Do you know what it's like to know that for the first time in almost thirty years I'm connected to someone? Blood. Genes. Mannerisms. All inherited. That Ace is a part of me?" The incredulity in his voice resonates louder than the words.

"You're not alone anymore." I squeeze his hand, a silent affirmation.

"You're right. I'm not," he says. I watch his posture change—spine stiffens, shoulders straighten—to be more defensive. A man's vulnerability only lasts for so long after all. "But at the same time I was naïve in thinking that this—the blood connection with Ace—would override the rest of this shit."

I narrow my eyebrows. "What shit?" I ask, trying to figure out which one of the myriad of things can be considered as *shit*.

"Nothing. Never mind," he says as he stands back up and presses a kiss to my forehead and Ace's. "Just some things I need to work through on my own. I promise I'll try to be quick."

Our eyes connect under the cover of night, and I worry about what the darkness is hiding that I'd normally be able to see. I thought it was just the idea of becoming a dad but now I worry it's more.

I've been so absorbed in my own world with everything that's happened over the past few weeks that now I feel like an ass. I can worry about Zander, be upset over my job, and yet not once did I stop to look at the man beside me, my rock, to ask him what other shit he was dealing with.

I want to tell him, just not now. Can't he deal with this all in a bit? Hell yes, it's a selfish thought but at the same time, when I look down at Ace he trumps all of this. He is the perfect moment in our lives and we need to stay just like this, all together, as a unit. Colton promised me this moment and now we've found it, all I want to do is hold on to it for as long as I can.

But when I look back up to Colton and see the stress in his posture, I know that while the moment is perfect for me, he's just taking a little bit longer to find his.

"Get some sleep. I'm going to go sit out on the patio for a bit and clear my head," he says. I know that means the nightmare is still there, still lingering in the fringes of his mind and he's not ready to go back to sleep again for fear it will return.

I bite back what I really want to say. *Don't go. It's lonely in bed without you. Talk to me.* Instead I say, "Okay. I'm here when you need me." *Because we do need you.* But I also know Ace and I need the him that is one hundred percent and if he needs some time to get there, then I'm resigned to give it to him.

For him. Anything for him.

And for *us.*

This is marriage; being who you are while being what your partner needs when they need it the most. Stepping up while they need to step out.

"Night," he says as he heads toward the door.

"Colton?" His name is part plea, part question because I know he is shutting down and possibly shutting me out.

He stops in the doorway and turns to face me. "It's going to be fine, Ryles. All of it."

Chapter Twenty-Seven

COLTON

THE MOTHERFUCKER IS DEAD.

My feet pound the sand. One after the other. My cadence: *Fuck. You. Eddie.*

Angry strides eating up distance but doing absofuckinglutely nothing to lessen the rage. All they do is put more distance between paparazzi sitting at the public entrance to the beach and me.

My lungs burn. My legs ache. My eyes sting as sweat drips into them. I pick up the pace. Needing the exhaustion, the sand, the space to clear my head before I turn around and head back.

Fuck. You. Eddie.

I push myself to the brink of exhaustion. As far north as I can go before I'm bent over, hands on my knees, gasping for air. And even fatigued the image doesn't go away. Won't go away.

The picture he took.

Ry's face is in the corner, mouth open in protest, one hand reaching to cover her breast, and the other reaching out to cover the camera lens. But the joke's on us. It wasn't Ry he was taking a shot of. Nope. She was just the frame around what Eddie wanted more: Ace sitting between the dent of her thighs. White diaper. A mess of dark hair. Mouth open crying. Face beat red.

One day old and already thrown into the goddamn inferno of chaos that is my life. Used. For money. For revenge. To hurt us. Take the purest thing in my life and use it to hurt me.

Not fucking cool. That's sleazy. Unacceptable.

Fuck. You. Eddie.

I turn back south. My feet move again. Arms pump. My leave from reality only temporary.

I sure hope that cool half a million he just pocketed was worth it. When I get done with him, he'll realize that damn photo cost him so much more.

Now I have to face Rylee. Tell her the man who took our moment, our piece of peace, has stolen from us again. Took the control to introduce our son to the world in our own way. Made Ace a pawn in this fucked-up game of his.

Fuck. You. Eddie.

Rylee's face fills my mind: eyes wide with panic, voice wavering, paranoia over the windows consuming her. And now I have to go add a little more crazy to her chaos.

On top of everything else I've already heaped there.

Too much. Just too goddamn much. Open ends. Unexpected surprises. Forced hands. Uncontrollable situations. The never-ending unknown.

Fuck. You. Eddie.

CJ's words were gasoline added to a wildfire already out of control. What had his answer been when I asked him how that little fucker keeps getting the upper hand in this goddamn game of payback? *The only power Eddie has over you is the reaction you give him.* My response? A curt *Fuck you.*

He holds no power over me. *None.* I'll let him think he does, but his hand's been dealt. Cards are on the table. He may have the wild card.

But I'm carrying all the aces.

Chapter Twenty-Eight

Rylee

"SHH! DON'T BE SO LOUD. You're going to scare him," Aiden shouts in a whispered voice to the rest of the boys gathered around him. Or more like gathered around Ace.

Seven heads—blond, brown, and one red—form a phalanx of overeager boys all vying to watch him sleep in Shane's arms. All but one.

Zander sits on the couch, just outside of the circle and watches from afar. A slight smile is on his face but there is a distance in his eyes I recognize and detest. I watch him observe but make no move to get closer. And instinct tells me he's doing what he knows, putting up a wall around him, distancing himself from his brothers, so if he's fostered out, the blow won't be as hard to take.

Defense mechanism 101.

Why do I suddenly feel the need to take this course?

I look up from watching Zander to find Shane's eyes above the heads of the other boys. Our gazes hold and I can't read the look in his. He's getting so old now, graduating from college next semester, and has gotten so much better at guarding the emotions in his eyes.

I can't read what they say, and it's not like this is the time or place to ask him what he's not telling me.

An elbow is traded between Auggie and Scooter. The interaction surprises me, and even though my reprimand is automatic, a small part of me smiles at this small step in Auggie's marathon journey to fitting in. And then the other part of me is saddened I haven't been there to know of this progress.

"Easy, boys," Colton warns from where he's talking to Jax in the kitchen when elbows bump again.

Questions ring out left and right. Does he sleep all the time? Is it my turn to hold him yet? Are his diapers nasty? Is it my turn to hold him yet? Does he really come out of your belly button? Is it my turn to hold him yet? Is it true he eats milk from your boobies?

That one earns some snickers and a few pairs of blushed cheeks.

"Zander, you want to come sit next to me?" I ask, needing to draw him out of his shell some.

"Okay," he mumbles as he rises from the couch and shuffles over. He sits next to me, and I put my arm around him and pull him in close. Needing and trying to offer some comfort, and pull some from him even in his silence.

"I missed you," I murmur as I press a kiss to the top of his head that I'm sure embarrasses him, but I don't care. Affection is something that never goes to waste no matter how much the other person thinks they don't need or want it.

"Me too," he says. I rest my cheek on the top of his head and just hold him there as the boys continue to stare at Ace, mesmerized by how little he is.

And a part of me is slightly surprised I'm not as freaked out as I imagined I would be watching all of these typically not-so-gentle boys crowding around him. But I shouldn't be; these are my boys— my family—and I trust them because I know they'd never hurt something so dear to me.

Then again, I'm so exhausted I think the only thing that pulls me wide-awake instantly is the sound of Ace's cry. Other than that I feel like I'm walking through a fog.

I'm talking to Zander, asking about school and simple things, trying to draw him out of his shell, when out of the blue a flash goes off.

Something in me snaps and takes over me.

"No!" I shout, flying off the couch as fast as my sore body can go. Heads turn to look at me as shock silences the room. "No pictures!" My voice is shaky but firm. My heart races and fingers tremble, as anxiety owns my body. I'm on panic-riddled autopilot as I jerk Connor's phone from his hand and delete the picture he took of Ace immediately.

I see the shock in his eyes, the lax jaw, the shake of his head, and yet all I can think of is Ace. All I can feel is the rage I've kept in check after losing my shit yesterday when Colton told me about Eddie's ultimate invasion of our privacy. How it's eaten at me bit by bit. Made me feel like our life is spinning out of control and will never get our bubble back.

I need our bubble back. Desperately.

I'm standing in the middle of the family room, Connor's phone grasped in one hand, and the boys looking at me, unsure what to do. My body begins to shiver as a hot flash of dizziness engulfs me. Sweat beads on my skin. My stomach turns. I look from boy to boy, unable to explain, and worried because I know I just scared them and yet I can't help it.

The panic attack hits me like a flash flood—instant and yanking me under its pull—magnifying everything I was feeling and then some. But just as my knees start to buckle, Colton's arms wrap around me from behind and pull me against him.

"Breathe, Ry," he murmurs into my ear, his warm breath on my flushed skin, a grounding sound when all of a sudden I feel like I'm losing it. And when I can focus again, the looks on the faces around me tell me as much. "You're okay. Just a little panic attack. I've got you."

His words and the feel of his body against mine calm the anxiety seizing me, limb by limb, nerve by nerve to the point it's hard to focus or catch my breath. My clothes stick to me as I break out in a cold sweat.

"I've got you," he says again, his voice the only thing I can focus on. The one thing I need. I can see the concern on the boys' faces but my emotions are paralyzed. I can't feel, can't bother to care to explain I'm okay, that they shouldn't worry. I have a momentary ability to focus. The fact I'm not thinking of the boys first means something is off with me. That's not me at all.

And that realization—that snippet of reality—causes a second wave of anxiety to hit me harder than the first.

"Something's wrong," I whisper so softly I don't even know if Colton hears me.

"Ry's okay," I hear Jax say as he steps forward and reassures the boys like I should. But I can't. Words are locked in my throat. "Just a panic attack."

"Let's go upstairs," Colton murmurs. His body is still behind mine, and just as he turns us, I lock eyes with Shane. I can see the fear in his eyes, his own panic written all over his face, and yet Colton pushes me to walk toward the hallway before I can unlock the apology in my throat.

"I can't," I murmur, lost in a daze. "I'm sorry. I don't know . . ."

"C'mon, baby." His voice is soothing as he gently lifts me into his arms once we clear the boys' line of sight. "I've got you." I start to wriggle, unsure, uneasy, un-everything. "I'm not gonna let you fall, Rylee. I'll never let you fall," he murmurs against the side of my face.

I sink into him, hear his words and let him take the reins. Knowing he's right but don't want to admit I'm having a hard time dealing with everything right now. Each step he takes is like the hammer reinforcing everything that's been piled onto my buckling back.

"It's just all too much, too fast," he murmurs.

Step.

The video release. Invasion of privacy. Exposed. Embarrassed. Violated. Helpless.

Step.

Taking a forced leave of absence from my job. Lost. My purpose gone. Betrayed.

Step.

Zander's uncle stepping forward. Handcuffed. Inadequate. Taken advantage of.

Step.

Ace's birth. Emotional overload. Intense joy. Unconditional love.

Step.

Eddie in the hospital room. Fear. Panic. Betrayed.

Step.

First night home as a new mom. Overwhelmed. Exhausted. Changed.

Step.

The reappearance of Colton's nightmares. Unsettling. Disruptive. A wild card.

Step.

Eddie selling Ace's picture. Violated. Used. Exploited. Helpless.

Step.

Zander today. Distant. Scared. Reticent.

Step.

The flash of Connor's camera. Out of control. Protective. Scared.

Too much, too fast. Colton's words keep repeating in my head.

"Stop thinking, baby," Colton says. "You keep tensing up. Just shut it all out for a while."

I close my eyes as he clears the landing, my pulse racing and body still trembling, but I feel a bit calmer with the staccato of his heartbeat against my ear. He lays me gently on the bed, the softness of the mattress beneath me nowhere as calming as the warmth of his body against mine.

"A little better?" he asks as he brushes my hair off my face.

I nod my head, hating the sting of tears and the burn in my throat. "I'm sorry." It's the only thing I can manage to say as I attempt to find myself through this panic-laced fog.

"No . . . don't be sorry," he says, pressing a kiss to my forehead. "You're exhausted. I know you're used to being so strong but stop fighting it. Allow yourself a couple hours not to be. Okay?"

I open my eyes and look into the crystalline green of his. I see love, concern, compassion, and more than anything I see *his* need to take care of me. So as much as I'm feeling a little less shaky, I sigh and nod my head. "I need to apolo—"

"I've got everything under control." He presses a finger to my lips to quiet me. "Just close your eyes and rest."

And I do. I close my eyes as I hear his footsteps retreat down the hallway. Follow them down the stairs and onto the tiled floor below. I force myself to relax, to try and quiet my head.

For some reason I don't think it's going to happen.

Ace is crying.

I just shut my eyes.

The crying is getting closer.

Then why is it dark outside?

And it's getting louder.

How long have I been asleep?

And louder.

Please leave me alone.

I squeeze my eyes shut tighter. Roll on my side away from the doorway. I just need to sleep. Don't want to think. Just want to drift back into the blackness of slumber and shut everything out.

"Ry? Ry?" Colton's hand pushes gently on my shoulder. Ace's cries hit a fever pitch.

"Yeah," I murmur, eyes still closed, but my breasts tingle with the burn of milk coming in as my body reacts instinctively to the sound of my baby.

"Ace is hungry," he says, pushing my shoulder again.

And even though he says the words and I can hear Ace cry, that innate instinct isn't there. There's cotton in my mouth. I can't tell him no. I'm not sure that I want to either. But at the same time the only word I can use to describe how I feel is listless.

You're just tired. You got an hour's sleep when you really need twelve. Your body is sore, changing, working overtime to produce milk and heal, and is making you more groggy than ever.

That's all.

"'Kay." It's all I say as I roll on my side and lift up my shirt on autopilot. My breasts ache they are so heavy with milk. Colton lies Ace down beside me in the middle of our bed as I guide my nipple into his mouth.

Ace latches on, and I wait for that feeling to consume me. The one I've gotten every other time we've connected like this in the most natural of actions. There's usually this soothing calm that spreads throughout me, like endorphins on speed. And this time when Ace latches on, all I want to do is close my eyes and crawl back into sleep I desperately need.

"I'll be right back," Colton says, causing panic I don't quite understand.

Don't go! I shout the words in my head and yet my lips make no sound. My throat feels like it is slowly filling with sand. My chest feels tight. Sweat beads on my upper lip.

Get it together, Ry. It's just your hormones. It's the adjustment period. Mixed with exhaustion. And feeling like I don't know what in the hell I'm doing even when I do.

Tomorrow will be better.
And the day after that even more.

Chapter Twenty-Nine

COLTON

"YOU WANT TO TELL ME what we're doing here, son?" I glance over to my dad and then back to the garage across the street from us. I don't say a word. And even if I wanted to tell him, I'm not sure exactly what to say. My body vibrates with uncertainty. Head and heart an ocean apart on this decision. My leg jogs up and down where I sit in the passenger seat. Jet Black Heart conveniently plays on the radio and all I can do is hum the words that hit too close to fucking home.

My dad's car stands out like a sore thumb in this neighborhood. Sleek and red, subtle as far as my standards, but flashy for this rundown part of town. Guess I should have thought about that when I called him up and said, "I need you to drive me somewhere."

No other details given.

And of course within an hour he was at my house, passenger door open for me to scoot in. No questions asked. Almost as if he knew I needed time to work through all the shit going on in my head.

No small talk. No bullshitting. Just a turn of his steering wheel when I indicated to take a right or a left as we drove.

So why am I here? Why am I chasing this goddamn ghost when the man beside me is all I've ever needed?

It all comes back to full circles. Eventually everything connects. Now I just need to see the connection for myself before I leave it there and walk away for good.

My elbow rests on the doorjamb, my hand rubbing back and forth on my forehead as I stare at the dilapidated storefront. The mechanic's bay is open on the side, a late model sedan up on a lift, rusted parts just to the outside of the door, but it's the pair of boots I can see standing on the other side of the car that holds my attention.

Buck the fuck up, Donavan. It's now or never.

"Be right back," I say as I open the door, realizing I never answered his question. With my heart in my throat and a pocketful of confusion, I walk across the sidewalk and up to the open bay, wondering if I'm about to come face to face with my worst nightmare or a man who has no clue I even exist.

Flashbacks hit me like a car head-on into the wall: fast as fuck, out of the blue, and knocking the wind out of me. Memories so strong I feel like I'm back there in *that room*, full of shame, shaking with fear, and fighting the pain.

My feet falter. My pulse pounds. My conscience questions me. My stomach rolls over.

And just as I'm about to turn around and retreat, the man comes walking around the front of the car. I freeze.

"Get the fuck out of here!" he growls. And at first I think he's talking to me but then I see him kick the flank of a mutt standing just inside the door. Its yelp echoes through the garage and fades but tells me so much about this man in the few seconds I've been in his presence.

Only assholes kick an animal.

He sees me the same time I see him. Our eyes meet, green to green. Just like mine. Curiosity sparks. His greedy eyes flicker to the expensive car behind me, to my watch, and over my clothes

My first thought: *It's not him.* He's not the fucker who haunts my dreams and stole my childhood. The exhale I thought I'd give doesn't come. Relief mixed with confusion adds to the pressure in my chest.

We stare at each other like caged animals trying to gauge the situation. Figuring out why it feels like there is a threat when none has been made.

I take in every detail about him: hair slicked back, cracked hands stained with grease, a cigarette dangling from his lips, a teardrop tattoo at the corner of his left eye, and the unmistakable stench of alcohol. A sneer is on his lips and a chip weighs visibly on his shoulder.

My second thought: *I know your type.* Your lot in life is everyone else's fault. Bad luck. Hard time. Never your fault. Entitled when you don't deserve shit.

I stare at him—jaw clenched, eyes searching—and wait for a reaction. Anything. Something. The little boy in me figuring that in some fucked-up way he'd know I was his son. Some kind of recognition. A sixth sense.

But there is nothing. Not even a flicker in his dead eyes.

Seconds pass. But the emotions rioting within me make it feel like an hour. And I'm not sure why all of a sudden my temper is there. Fuse snapped. Confusion rising.

But it is. My temper is front and fucking center. Anger is alive.

He takes a step forward, gaze still flicking back to the car and my watch, mind still figuring how much he can take me for in bogus repairs. Because that's what he sees: rich guy, expensive car, and a chance to fuck me over. Nothing else even computes. He looks down at the red rag he's wiping his hand on before meeting my eyes again. Cocky bastard of a smirk on his lips.

"Can I help you with something? Car having some trouble?" His voice sounds like years of cigarettes ground into the gravel.

I can't tear my gaze from him. Hate that I keep waiting for something to spark in his eyes when I don't want it to. Just something to tell me I mattered at some point. A flash of a thought. A pang of regret. A question of what-if over time.

There's absolutely nothing, just his words hanging in the air. He narrows his eyes, broadens his shoulders.

I shift my feet. Swallow. Decide.

"No. I need absolutely *nothing* from you."

One last look. A first and last goodbye. Circle completed.

Fuck this shit.

I turn on my heel and walk away without another look. With my hands shaking and my heart conflicted, I slide into the passenger seat. I can't bring myself to look at my dad. *My real dad.* The only dad I have.

"Just drive."

The car starts. The world zooms by as I move back into the comfort of the blur. The place I haven't returned to in so very long. My dad doesn't say a word, doesn't ask a thing. He just drives and leaves me alone with the motherfucking freight train of noise in my head.

Regret. Doubt. Confusion. Anger. Hurt. Uncertainty. Guilt. Each one takes their time in the limelight as we drive. *Shut it down, Colton.* Lock it up. Push it away.

The car pulls to a stop. The blur fades to clear. The beach stretches before us off Highway 101. *It's my spot.* The place I go when I need to think.

Of course he'd know to bring me here. That *this* is what I needed.

I sit for a moment, quiet, unmoving, before the guilt eats up the air in the car until I can't breathe anymore. I shove the door open and stumble from it, needing the fresh air, the space to think, and the time to grieve when there's nothing really dead to grieve over.

And that's the goddamn problem, isn't it? Why in the fuck am I upset? What did I expect? A reunion? An *attaboy*? Fuck no. I didn't want one either. And yet that teeny, tiny piece of me wanted to know I mattered. Wanted to know that the blood we shared tied us together somehow.

But it doesn't. Not in the fucking least. I'm nothing like him. I know that from the two minutes I came face to face with him, looked him in the eyes, and felt only indifference.

Does he even know I exist? The thought comes out of nowhere, and I don't know if it makes the situation worse or better. Ignorance over abandonment.

Fuck if I know. Hell if I care.

But I do.

My chest hurts. It's hard to breathe. I sit down on the seawall separating the asphalt from the sand and tell myself this is exactly what I wanted. To prove he's nothing to me. To close the circle. And walk away.

So what in the hell is wrong with me?

It's the man in the car behind me. That's who. How could I betray him? How could I let him drive me there? Would he think I didn't believe he was enough for me when he's given me *everything*?

I'm such a selfish prick. To think I was looking for more when I've had it right in front of me since the day he found me on his steps.

The ocean crashes on the beach and I lose myself in the sight. Find comfort in the sound. Use the one place I've always escaped to, to quiet the shitstorm in my head.

I hear him before I see him. The fall of footsteps. The scent of the same soap he's used since I was little. The shuffle as he swings his legs over the wall to sit beside me. The sounds of his thoughts scream in the silence.

"You okay, son?"

His words are like poison lacing the guilt I already own. All I can do is blow out a breath and nod my head, eyes staring straight at the water.

"Was that your father, Colton?"

I take a moment to answer. Not because I have to think about it but because how I respond is important. Was he my father? By blood, yes. And yet when I hold Ace, even though I'm scared shitless and don't know what the fuck I'm doing and still fear I'm not going to be the man he needs me to be, I still feel connected with him. An indescribable, unbreakable bond.

I didn't feel it with the man at the garage.

But I do feel it with Andy.

I look over to him. Our eyes hold, grey to green, father to son, superhero to saved, man to man, and I answer without a single fucking ounce of hesitation.

"No. *You are.*"

Chapter Thirty

Rylee

"**A**RE YOU SURE YOU'RE ALL right and don't need any help?"

No. Yes.

Silence fills the space where my answers should be. "Yes. We're all fine, Mom. I'm just . . . I'm just trying to get him on a schedule and want to do that before people start coming over."

I grit my teeth. The lie sounds so foreign coming from my mouth. Like an echo down a tunnel that I recognize but can't place as my own voice when it comes back to me.

"Because it would be perfectly normal for you to need help, sweetheart. There is no shame in needing your mom when you become a mom."

"I know." My voice is barely above a whisper. The only response I can give her.

"You know I'm here for you. Any time. Day or night. To be there with you to help or just to sit on the other end of the phone line."

"I know." The emotion in her voice—the swell of love in it as she searches if I'm being truthful—almost undoes me.

Almost.

"Okay, then. I'll let you get back to my handsome grandson now."

Silence.

"Mom?" Fear. Hope. Worry. All three crash into each other and manifest in the desperate break in my voice.

Tell her something's wrong with you. That you don't feel right.

"Ry?" Searching. Asking. Wanting to know.

No. You're perfectly fine. You can handle this. Your hormones are just out of whack. This is normal.

"You still there, Rylee? Are you okay?"

"Yes. I'm fine." A quick response to mask the unease I feel. "I was going to . . . I forgot what I was going to ask. Bye, Mom. I love you."

"Love you, too."

Silence again.

The music from the baby swing where Ace sits floats in from the family room. He begins to cry and yet I sit and stare out to the beach beyond, lost in thought. Convincing myself that I'm fine. Telling myself that empty void I suddenly feel is normal. Wondering if I'm not hardwired correctly to be a mother.

That maybe, just maybe, there was a bigger reason as to why I lost my other two babies.

That's crap and you know it.

But maybe . . .

"Ry?" Colton calls out to me as the front door slams.

Ace's cries pick up a pitch at the sound of his dad's voice, and all I can do is close my eyes from where I'm still sitting, lost in staring at the clouds out the window. I open my mouth to tell him I'm in the living room but nothing comes out.

"Rylee?" Colton's voice is a little more insistent this time, concern lacing the edges, and it's just enough to break through the fog that seems to have a hold over me. I put my hands on the arm of the chair to stand but can't seem to get up.

There is a change in Ace's cry. It's garbled at first and then muffled, and I sag in an unnatural relief, knowing Colton has given him his pacifier. And the relief is quickly followed by an intense wave of self-loathing. Why couldn't I have done that? Pick up Ace. Why did I have to wait for Colton to walk in the front door to take care of him? That's my job. Why couldn't I make my legs walk over there to do it myself? I'm failing miserably at the one thing I've always wanted and always knew I was born to be: a mother.

The tears well in my eyes and my throat burns as I shake my head to clear it from thoughts I know are ridiculous but feel nonetheless. *Snap out of it, Ry.* You're a good mom. You just need a little more time to recover. It's your hormones. It's the exhaustion. Possibly a touch of the baby blues. It's the need to do every little thing for Ace yourself because you don't think Colton can at this point with everything he's going through. You're just trying to step up to the plate and do it all when you can't and that's driving your type A, controlling personality batty.

"Rylee?" Colton shouts my name this time, panic pitching his voice.

"Coming," I say as I force myself to stand up and swallow over the bile rising in my throat. I close the fifty or so feet to the family room to find Colton awkwardly holding Ace, trying to keep the pacifier in his mouth so he stops crying.

I look at the two of them together and know I should feel completely overwhelmed with love but for some reason all I want to do is sit down and close my eyes. So I do just that. And even with them closed, I can feel the weight of Colton's stare. The silence that is usually comforting between us is suddenly awkward and uneasy. Almost as if he's passing judgment on me because . . . because I don't know why but I feel it anyway.

"Everything okay, Ry?"

Is it okay? I open my eyes and stare at him, not certain how to answer him because it sure doesn't feel okay right now.

"Yes. Yeah. I was just . . . uh . . ." I don't think even if I could put into words how I feel, he'd understand me. I fumble for something to say as I watch him try to figure out how to undo the onesie to change Ace's diaper.

Has he even changed a diaper yet? Or have I always jumped up and taken care of it, needing to be the supermom I think is expected of me and I expect of myself? I can't remember. Five days worth of sleepless nights and endless diaper changes and feedings run together. It's like my mind and body have been thrown into the washing machine on spin cycle and when the door opens everything is upside down and inside out.

When I come back to myself, his hands have stopped fooling with the snaps between Ace's legs and his eyes are locked on mine, waiting for me to finish my answer. "Ry?" I hate the sound in his voice—love his concern but hate the question in it. *Am I all right? Is everything okay?*

NO, IT'S NOT! I want to yell to make him see something feels so off. And yet I say nothing.

And then it hits me. Lost in this haze of hormones and exhaustion, I totally forgot about where he went, what he did today. The whole reason I was lost in thought in the first place was because I was worried about not having heard from him yet.

I cringe at my selfishness. At sitting here feeling sorry for myself when I know the courage it just took for him to come face to face with his dad.

"Sorry. I'm here. Just . . . I was in the office, worried because you hadn't answered my texts. I was . . ." This time when he looks up from Ace, I can see the stress etched in the lines of his handsome face and know without him saying a word that he did in fact find his biological dad. "You found him?"

He sighs as he looks back down to a fussy Ace with a slow nod of his head. I give him time to find the words to express what he needs to say, watch him reach out and run the back of his hand over Ace's cheek. The sight of him connecting to Ace like that tugs at my heartstrings. That feeling I felt like I had been missing moments ago—of utter love seeing my two men together—fills me with such a sense of joy that I cling to it, suddenly realizing how absent it was before.

And the thought alone makes me choke back a sob, feel like I'm losing my mind. *Keep it together, Ry. Keep. It. Together.* Colton needs you right now. It's not the time to need him because he needs you.

"Did you?" I ask, trying to regain my schizophrenic focus.

"He's hungry," he says abruptly as he lifts him off the floor and carries him to me. We've been together long enough that I know avoidance when I see it and yet for the life of me when he places Ace in my arms for me to nurse, I blank for a second. My mind and body not clicking together on what I need to do.

And as loud as Ace is crying, the last thing I want to do is nurse so in a move I register as callous but don't quite understand, I tune Ace out and focus on Colton as he walks across the room and into the kitchen. I hear the cupboard open, close, the clink of glass to glass, and know he's poured himself a drink. Jack Daniels.

Crap. It must have been really bad.

I wish he had let me go with him today. I wish we didn't have Ace so I wouldn't fear leaving my own goddamn house because of the cameras and never-ending intrusion into our privacy. Both of those things prevented me from being there for my husband on a day he needed me the most. Guilt stabs sharply, consumes my state of mind, as I wait for him to return and hopefully talk to me.

Out of nowhere and without a trigger, a sudden wave of sadness bears down on me in a way I've never felt before. Oppressive. Suffocating. So stifling it's significantly worse than the darkest of days after losing Max and both of my babies. And just as my shock ebbs from the onslaught I feel, a ghost of a thought becomes stronger and knocks the wind out of me: I just want our life back to when it was Colton and me and no one else.

Oh my God. *Ace.*

The unspeakable thought staggers me. Its ludicrousness takes my breath momentarily but is gone as quick as it comes. The acrid taste of it still lingers though but thankfully the rising pitch of Ace's cries breaks its hold on my psyche.

I try to get a grip on myself, remorse and confusion fueling my actions as I gather him closer to me and kiss his head over and over, begging him to forgive me for a thought he will never even know I had.

But I will remember.

With shaky hands, I go through the motions of getting him latched onto my breast as quickly as possible, needing this moment of bonding to quiet the turmoil I feel within me. When his cries fade as he starts to suckle, I close my eyes and wait for the rush of endorphins to come. I hope for it, beg for it, but before I feel it I hear Colton enter the room and stop in front of me.

I open my eyes to find his and have to fight the urge to look away, fearful if he looks close enough, he'll see into me and realize the horrible thought I just had. Panic strikes, my nerves sensitive like bare flesh on hot coals. I just need something to ground me right now—either the soothing rush from nursing or to be wrapped in the arms of my husband—to prevent me from feeling like I'm slowly spiraling out of control.

And just as my breath becomes shallow and my pulse starts to race, it hits me. That slow rush of delayed hormones spreads their warmth through my body and dulls the erratic and out-of-control emotions. All of a sudden I have a bit of clarity, can focus, and the person I need to focus on most is right in front of me.

Our eyes hold in the silence of the room, the intensity and confusion in the green of his makes my heart twist from the unmistakable pain I see in their depths. His eyes flicker down to Ace at my breast and hold there for a moment before lifting back up to meet mine with a touch more softness in them, but the hurt still plain as day.

"Do you want to talk about it?"

Colton clears his throat and swallows, his Adam's apple bobbing. "I saw what I needed to see, know what I need to know. Curiosity satisfied," he says as he sits down on the coffee table in front of me.

And I know that sound in his voice—guarded, protective, unaffected. There is a whole storm brewing behind the haunted look in his eyes, yet I'm not sure if I should draw it out of him or leave it be and wait for the eye to pass on its own.

My own curiosity gets the best of me. My innate need to fix and soothe and help him when he's hurting controls my actions. "Did you get to—?"

"He's a piece of shit, okay?" he explodes, startling both Ace and myself. "He didn't give a goddamn flying fuck who I was. All he saw was a nice car, nice clothes, and was totaling up dollar signs in his eyes for how much he could take me for. He reeked of alcohol, had the tats to show he'd earned his prison cred . . ." The words come out in a complete rush of air, the hurricane within him needing to churn. The muscle in his jaw pulses with anger, his muscles visibly taut as he lifts the glass of amber liquid to his lips. He pushes the alcohol around the inside of his mouth trying to figure out what to say next before he swallows it. "I am nothing like him. I will never be anything like him." He grits the words out with poisoned resolution.

"I never thought you were or would be." Still unsure of the right thing to say, I take the direct approach with him. He doesn't need to be coddled right now or treated with kid gloves. That would only diminish the validity of his feelings and what he's going through.

"Don't, Ry," he warns as he shoves up from the table, his anger eating at him. "Don't give me one of your speeches about what a good man I am because *I'm not*. I'm the furthest fucking thing from it right now, so thanks . . . but no thanks."

He turns to face me, eyes daring me to say more, the defensive shield he carries at the ready, up and armed. Our gaze locks, mine asking for more, needing to understand what happened to rock the solid foundation he's been standing on for so very long.

"You know I went there today with no expectations whatsoever. But a small part of me . . . the fucked-up part obviously," he says with a condescending chuckle, "thought he'd see me and shit, I don't know . . . that he'd just know who I was. Like because we shared blood it would be an automatic thing. And even more fucked up than wanting to know I was a blip on his fucking radar, was at the same time, I didn't want him to realize it at all." His voice rises and he throws his hands out to his sides. "So yeah . . . tell me how I'm supposed to explain that."

The anger is raw in his voice and there's nothing I can say to take away the sting of what he went through. I just wish I'd been there with him.

"You don't owe an explanation to anyone," I state softly. His legs eat up the length of the living room and he moves like a caged animal. "Everyone wants to feel like they belong to someone . . . are connected to another. You have every right to be confused and hurt and anything else you feel."

"Anything else I feel?" he asks, that self-deprecating laugh back and longer this time around. "Like what a fucking prick I am for asking Andy to go with me? For asking the only dad I've ever known, the only man who has ever given a rat's ass about me, to drive me to find a man who hasn't given me a second thought his entire life? Yeah . . . because that screams son-of-the-fucking-year now, doesn't it?"

His verbal diatribe stops just as abruptly as it starts, but his restraint from saying more manifests itself in his fisted hands at his sides. And I can see his internal struggle, know he feels guilty over needing to close this last door to his past at the expense of possibly making Andy feel less in all senses of the word in his life.

I want to shake him though and assure him Andy wouldn't see this as betrayal. Find a way to make him see that he'd see it as his son taking the final step to lay the demons to rest. Find peace in the one constant that has been his whole life.

"Your dad has always supported you, Colton." His feet stop, back still to me, but I know I've gotten his attention. "He encouraged you to find out about your mom. You're his son." He hangs his head forward at the term, the weight of his guilt obvious in his posture. "He's proven he'll do anything for you . . . I imagine he's glad he was the one with you when you faced the final unknown of your past."

I hope he really hears my words and realizes that as a parent all you want is your child to be whole, healthy, and happy, and that was exactly what Andy wanted for him today. I thought I understood that concept. Now I have Ace—albeit for a brief five days of motherhood—I know I'd move heaven and earth for him to have those same exact things.

He walks toward me without saying anything and sits back down in front of me. He reaches out and tickles the inside of Ace's palm so he closes his hand around Colton's pinky. There is something about the sight—huge hand, tiny fingers holding tight—that hits me hard and reinforces the notion that Ace depends on us for absolutely every single thing. That we are his lifeline in a sense. I wonder if a baby senses when one half of that connection is absent.

"I look at Ace," he says, his voice calmer, more even, "and I feel this instant connection. I figured it was because I have blood ties to someone for the first time in my life. That it was an automatic thing you feel when you're related to someone. I can't tell you how many times over the years I've felt like a fucking outsider, cheated out of having this feeling." He pauses for a moment, runs a hand through his hair and clears his throat, the grate in his voice the only sign of the emotion wreaking havoc inside him. "But today I was standing there looking at this bitter man with eyes just like mine, who couldn't be bothered to give a shit about me, and I felt *absolutely nothing*. No click. No connection. No anything. *And his blood runs through me*." His voice breaks some, but his confession causes every part of me to bristle with guilt for my feelings moments ago. The ironic parallel of how I desperately needed the connection with Ace when he latched on to nurse to make me feel whole and centered again.

"It freaked me the fuck out, Ry," he confesses, pulling me from my thoughts. "That connection I thought I was missing for most of my life, I've had all along with my dad. *Andy.* Today, I realized that blood ties mean shit if you don't put in the time to make them worth it. So yeah, I'm connected by blood to Ace . . . but in a sense, I've been no better than that sperm donor was to me."

I start to argue with him, my back up instantly, but he just shakes his head for me to stop. When he lifts his gaze from Ace to meet mine, there are so many emotions swimming in them, but it's the regret in them I take notice of.

"Look, I know I haven't been very hands-on with Ace. I'm still petrified of hurting him or doing the wrong thing because I'm absolutely fucking clueless. But standing in that driveway, looking at that piece of shit, I realized Ace doesn't care if I'm perfect . . . all he cares is that I'm there with him every step of the way. Just like Andy has been for me. Shit, Ry, I've been so busy trying to figure out what kind of dad he needs me to be that I'm not really being one at all."

My tears are instant as I look at the little boy become entirely eclipsed by the grown man I've loved all along.

"You're going to be an excellent father, Colton."

We both lean forward at the same time, our lips meeting in a tender kiss packed with a subtle punch of every emotion we share between us: acceptance, appreciation, love, and pride.

"You are nothing like him. We've known that all along. Now you finally know it, too. I'm so proud of you, Colton Donavan," I murmur against his lips. He brushes one more kiss to my mouth before pressing his signature one to the tip of my nose.

We sit there for some time in silence. The three of us. My new little family.

I fight fiercely against that undertow of discord that seems like a constant so I can revel in this moment. Memorize the feel of it and the sense of completeness I have with them by my side.

And all I keep thinking is that the storm has finally passed.
I just hope there are no new clouds on the horizon.

Chapter Thirty-One

Rylee

I STARE AT THE OPEN email from CJ on the screen. At the five magazines listed down the page with ridiculous dollar figures next to them. Their offers for the first photos of the new Donavan family. The tamed ex-bad boy racing superstar, his sex-crazed wife, and their little piece of perfect between them.

My muscles tense. My eyes blur. My mouth goes dry at the thought of anyone getting his or her sights on Ace. The mere thought of taking him out of the house causes me to break out in a panic attack. Thankfully Colton was able to get the pediatrician to make a house call for his first check up or else I'm not sure what I would have done.

I close the email. No way. No how. Publicity pictures are not even an option.

Any pictures for that matter.

Because even though the public got Eddie's picture of Ace—scrunched-up red face, mouth open, hands blurred in movement—to obsess over, it wasn't enough. Not even close. It almost gave the reverse effect. They are now hungry for more. Staking out the house, trying to bribe Grace to sneak a picture while she's cleaning the house. You name it, nothing's off limits.

And I refuse to give it to them. They've taken enough from me, so I refuse to give them any more.

My phone vibrates again from where it sits on the desk beside me. I glance at the screen. This time a text from Haddie instead of the five I've received from my mom today, telling me that pretty soon she's not going to take no for an answer. That she's going to come over without asking so she can see her grandson and help me in any way possible.

I clear the text from the screen and send it to the vortex of the bazillion other texts from family and close friends asking when they can come over, if they can bring us dinner, or if I need them to stop at the store for diapers.

Take the offer, Rylee.

The last time someone came over—the boys—I had a breakdown. And I've had plenty more on my own in the silence of this house; the last thing I need is to show everyone else how unstable I am.

Just tell her to come.

No, because then she'll know how much I'm struggling. I can't let everyone know the lie I'm living. That the woman they all said would be such a natural mother can't even look at her son some moments without wanting to run and hide in the back of the closet. How more and more I cringe when he cries, have to force myself to go get him when I'd rather just lie in bed with my hands over my ears and tears running down my cheeks.

Type the words, Ry. Ask her to get here.

I have the baby blues. That's all this is. A goddamn roller coaster of emotion, extreme joy interlaced with moments of soul-bottoming lows, all controlled by the flick of the hormonal switch.

She wouldn't understand. These feelings are normal. Every new mother goes through it, but no one else understands it unless they're in the midst of it.

I can get through this on my own. It's just my need to control everything that makes it feel like it's uncontrollable: the outside world, my emotions, our everything. I can prove I can handle this, that I'm good at this. It's only been seven days. I can handle this on my own.

Take the break she'll give you. It's exactly what you need.

How can I let someone else watch Ace, when I'm having a hard enough time allowing Colton? I know I'm the only one who can nurse him, but there are still diapers and burping and rocking left for others to help with. And it's not because I don't think Colton can handle it, but if I get there first, prove to myself I've got a handle on this, then maybe it will help me feel less haywire.

Get a few minutes to yourself. Let her come over. Take a shower without rushing. Brush your teeth without staring to see if his chest is moving. Eat some food without a baby attached to you.

I pick my phone up, hands trembling as I stare at Haddie's text. Every part of me is conflicted over what to write.

We're good. Thanks. Just settling in. Maybe next week when we're in a better routine.

I hit send. Will she see through that response? Will she come over anyway and in five minutes know something is wrong with me?

Maybe that's what I want.

I don't know.

I close my eyes and lean back in the chair. Lost in my thoughts, I try to find some quiet in my head since Ace is asleep in the swing right now while Colton is outside the walls of my self-imposed prison.

The first tear falls and slides silently down my cheek. Thoughts come and fade with each tear that drops, but for some reason my mind fixates on the empty picture frame on the bookcase beside me. The one that's supposed to be filled with the new memories we make together as a family and yet when I open my eyes to look at it, its emptiness is all I see.

Just like I feel.

I came in here with the intent to do so many things and now for the life of me, I can't remember what they were. I swear that pregnancy brain has turned into postpartum brain with how groggy and forgetful I feel when I'm wide awake.

Check on Zander. Take a shower. Reassure Shane I'm all right after the other night. Pump breast milk. Ask Colton if the police have gotten any closer to finding Eddie. Eat. Must remember to eat something. Email Teddy about status of Zander's caseworker. Respond to the texts on my phone.

It all makes my head hurt. Every single item. And as important as each item is, I don't want to do any of them. All I want to do is pull the blankets over my head and sleep. The only place I can escape my thoughts and feelings that don't feel like mine.

I go to close Outlook on the computer when an email closer to the bottom of the screen catches my eye that I didn't notice before. It's from CJ and has the subject: LADCFS process started.

What the hell? What process was started with the Los Angeles Department of Child and Family Services? Colton's comments flicker back into my mind from a few weeks ago but I refuse to listen to them. Refuse to believe he did what I think he did.

I open the email and read:

Colton,

As per your instruction, I have started the initial legwork to qualify you and Rylee as suitable candidates to adopt Zander Sullivan. I'd like to reiterate that this can be a tedious and often cumbersome process and might not end in your favor. Attached you will find the completed forms submitted on Rylee's and your behalf to get the ball rolling.

I reread the email, emotions on a merry-go-round in my mind: shock, disbelief, pride, and anger on a constant circle.

How could he do this without telling me? How could he force my hand and make me choose one boy over the others?

For some reason I can't grasp onto the positive side of it. I can see it, realize it, but I can't hold on to the thought long enough that one of my boys means enough to Colton to want to do this. All I can see is that he acted without me.

This is not even an option.

Can't be.

It may help save one but it would alienate the others.

I lose my grip on the edges of the rabbit hole I felt I was slowly clawing my way out of and slide back down into its darkness. It's sudden and all-consuming. The feelings are so intense, so inescapable, that the next time I come up for air, the shadows in the room have shifted. Time has passed.

I'm freaked. Ace is screaming. Blood curdling screams that call to my maternal instincts and aching breasts overfull with milk. And yet all I want to do is escape to the beach down below where the wind will whip in my ears and take the sound away. Give me an excuse not to hear him.

"Goddammit, Ry! Where the fuck are you?" Colton's voice bellows through the house, disapproval and anger tingeing the echo when it hits me.

Is that what snapped me out of my trance? Colton calling me?

Déjà vu hits. Same place, same situation as yesterday, and yet this time the tone in Colton's voice speaks way louder than the words he says. And before I even set foot into the family room, I'm primed and ready for a fight.

I walk into the room just as Colton's lifting an absolutely livid Ace out of his swing and pulling him to his chest to try and soothe him. He lifts his eyes when he hears my footsteps and the look he gives me paralyzes me.

"That's twice I've walked in the front door in two days to find Ace screaming and you nowhere to be found. What the fuck is going on, Rylee?" His voice is quiet steel and ice when he speaks, spite and confusion front and center.

I stare at him dumbfounded. I know I deserve the reprimand, that he has every right to ask the question, and yet I don't have the words to explain to him the why behind it.

"Answer me," he demands, causing Ace's cries to start again, his pacifier falling from his mouth.

"I . . . I . . . I can't . . ." I fumble for the words to express what's going on when I don't even know myself. So I change gears. Use my emotions to throw the whole kitchen sink into the argument I can see brewing and do so knowing this is going to be nasty. He's on edge from the emotional overload of seeing his dad yesterday and I'm overwhelmed with the constant free fall of my emotions. "How dare you submit adoption paperwork on our behalf for Zander and keep it from me! I told you I couldn't pick one boy and not the others!" I yell at the top of my lungs, combining two completely unrelated topics—and it feels so damn good. So damn cleansing when I've been holding so much in for so long. And yes, I'm fighting a battle to distract him from the truth, but I can't stop myself once I start. "You went behind my back, Colton. How dare you? How dare you think for one goddamn second you know what I want or what Zander needs?"

Colton stands there, slightly stunned, eyes wide and jaw clenched—our baby on his shoulder—and just stares at me with absolute insolence. "*I don't know what Zander needs*?" he asks, voice escalating with each word. "You want to fight, sweetheart, you better come at me with something stronger than that because you and I both know the truth on that one." Hurt flashes in his eyes and as much as I hate myself for it, it does nothing to stop the tsunami of anger taking over me.

"You. Hid. It. From. Me," I grit out in a barely audible voice.

"I did?" he says incredulously, taking a few steps in my direction as Ace continues to cry, feeding off the room's atmosphere. "I told you I was going to look into it. The email is sitting on the fucking computer clear as goddamn day. If I was hiding it from you, don't you think I would have deleted it? Or better yet, tell CJ to send it to my work email so you wouldn't see it? I was just getting our names in the system, trying to show interest in Z to maybe fuck with the social worker and have him stop the process. Get a grip, Ry—"

"Don't you dare say that to me," I scream, hysteria unhinging at the simple statement because I don't want to see the truth in it. Can't. "Don't you waltz in here like you have a fucking clue what's going on and treat me like I'm your goddamn nanny."

He startles his head from the whiplash in my change of topic. "What in the fuck are you talking about? I've told you twenty fucking times to let me help and you won't. It's like you're on some goddamn mission to prove you're supermom. Last I checked this isn't a competition, so stop making it one. *Nanny*? Jesus Christ, have you lost your mind?" He looks at me, chest heaving, head shaking, like he doesn't even know me and the sad thing is, I don't even know me right now.

I despise this woman who picked a fight with her husband because she's scared and confused and not sure what is going on inside her. However, I can't seem to stop for the life of me. We stand ten feet apart but there is nothing but animosity vibrating in the air between us.

There's so much I want to say to him. So many things I need to try to explain and yet I can't find the words, and Ace's constant crying is like rubbing gravel in an open wound that just seems to agitate me more.

Colton closes the distance between us, his eyes searching my face for answers I can't give him. "When you want to fight about something worth fighting about, Rylee, you know where to find me." His eyes dare me to come back at him, press those buttons of his he wants me to push. When I don't say a word, he holds a crying Ace out for me to take. "Until then, your son is hungry and has been for who knows how long before I walked in the fucking door."

I look down at Ace and then back to Colton as my body freezes and words fall out of my mouth I can't even believe I'm saying. "Feed him yourself."

No. I don't mean that.

"What?" Confusion like I've never seen before blankets his face.

Help me snap out of this, Colton. Please help me.

"Feed him formula." My voice doesn't even sound like my own.

Something's wrong with me. Can't you see it?

"Rylee . . ." Ace's cries escalate as Colton holds him in that space suspended between the two of us. I know Ace can smell the milk on me, know he's hungry, but that goddamn veil of listlessness falls like a lead curtain around me to the point that it's taking everything I have not to turn and run. And at the same time to *not* fight to the death on this single point I am still shocked I'm even fighting over.

Take my shoulders and shake me. Tell me to snap out of this funk.

My thoughts, my breath, my soul all feel like they are being suffocated to the point that the room starts to spin and my body starts to feel like I've stepped into an oven. The air is hot, thick as I suck it in, making it hard to breathe and my head to be fuzzy.

He eyes me, frantic flickers from Ace to me as he tries to figure out what's going on. He's scared. Worried. Freaked.

I am too.

"I thought you wanted to only nurse for the first two months, that—"

"I'm not producing milk," I lie, as I struggle to wade through this viscous veil of darkness that feels like it's taking hold of me, seeping from my feet up my legs.

No. No. No. Fight, Rylee. Fight its pull on you.

"Quit lying to me."

"I'm not lying." He points to my shirt. I look down to see two wet patches staining my red shirt dark where my breasts have leaked through my nursing pads from Ace's continual crying.

This is not you. Ace. Think of Ace. He needs you.

My mind is utterly exhausted and depleted from this civil war inside me that continues to rage regardless of whether I want to step on the battlefield or not.

"Give him to me," I sob. Suddenly, the tears come harder than before as I reach out to take Ace. And the thing that affects me even more than my own thoughts is the look on Colton's face and the slight way he pulls Ace back, searching my eyes to make sure I'm okay, before handing him over to me.

I turn my back to him and sit down on the couch, grabbing my nursing pillow and within seconds Ace is latching on, greedy hands kneading, and little mouth frantic for food. My sobs continue uncontrollably, but I refuse to look up and meet Colton's eyes. I can't. I need to do my job. Be the best mom I can be to Ace while fighting this invisible anchor slowly weighing me down and pulling me under.

"Rylee?" Colton says calmly, restraint audible in his even tone as he tries to figure out what in the hell just happened.

It takes me a second to stop crying long enough to be able to speak. "Can you please run to the store and get some formula. I just really need formula." My voice is so quiet I'm surprised he hears it. But I need him to go so I can have a moment to pull myself together so he doesn't think I'm losing it, although I really feel like I am.

"Talk to me, please."

"I'm fine. Everything's fine. I just have a little case of the baby blues and what would really help me is if you went to the store right now and got me some formula so when I feel like this you can help me by feeding Ace." I try to gain back my business-as-usual attitude with slow and measured words asking for help the only way I'm capable of right now.

Please just go and give me a few minutes to have this breakdown so when you come back I'm better.

I can sense his hesitation to leave by the way he starts to move and stops a couple times before blowing out a loud sigh. "Are you sure that—?"

"Please, Colton. I'll be right here feeding Ace the ten minutes you're gone."

"Okay. I'll hurry." And the fact he hesitates again is almost too much for me to bear. The tears burn my throat again.

But he goes and the minute he's gone, I welcome the unsteady silence that wraps itself around me like a warm blanket fresh out of the dryer. I want to snuggle in it and pull it over my head until I can't see or think or feel. Lose myself to the nothingness around me.

I look down at Ace and hate myself immediately. I have this beautiful, healthy baby I know I love very much, but I can't seem to muster up that feeling when I look at him. This love is the most natural of instincts, the most simplest and complex form of love—from mother to child—and yet somehow something is so broken in me. When I look at him, all I feel is the ghost of it, instead of that all-encompassing rush I felt just days ago.

And knowing it and losing it is incomparably worse than never knowing it at all.

"Now that you have him, could you imagine if you lost him?" Eddie's taunt flickers through my mind. It haunts me. Make me question myself.

He did this to you, Rylee. He's responsible.

How is that possible? He can't be the cause of this.

It has to be me. Something has to be wrong with me.

My mom told me most new moms would drive on sidewalks to get home to their newborn. What does that say about me if I just want to drive the other way?

All I want is that connection to be back. For it to not feel so damn forced, because that's exactly how I feel right now, sitting in this empty house. I'm nursing him because he needs to be fed, not because I want to. *I'm just going through the motions.* I'm watching my life from behind a two-way mirror, and no one knows I'm hiding there.

I close my eyes, a contradiction in all ways, and try to quiet my head. And the minute I feel relaxed for the first time in what feels like forever, I'm scrambling up as fast as I can, Ace still latched on, and running for the office. I grab my phone and frantically dial Colton as that black veil of doom and gloom slips over my sanity.

Ring.

Images of Colton lying dead on the side of the road somewhere fill my head. Car smashed. Thrown from the car because he was in such a rush to help me he forgot to put his seatbelt on.

Ring.

Colton lying shot dead on the floor of the local minimart just up the road where he walked in and interrupted a robbery in progress.

Ring.

Tears are burning. My mind like a horror slide show telling me that Colton isn't coming home again. Panic claws at my throat, claustrophobia in wide-open space.

Ring.

"Pick up the phone. Pick up the phone!" I scream into the receiver, hysteria taking over as I move back into the family room, one hand still cradling Ace, the other on the phone.

Beep. Colton's voice fills the line as his voicemail begins.

No. Please no.

I pace the floor, nerves colliding with anxiety, panic crashing into fear. Working myself into a frenzy as I wait for the knock on the door from the police telling me something has happened to Colton.

The problem this time though is I can't step outside the emotions holding my thoughts hostage and realize I'm losing my mind like I was able to a few days ago. No, this time I'm in such a state of agitation that when Colton opens the door from the garage into the house I almost tackle him with Ace in my arms. "Oh my God, you're okay." I sob, wrapping my free arm around him, needing to feel the heat of his body against mine so I can believe it's true.

"Whoa!" he says, thrown off guard by my sudden attack. He drops the bag holding the can of formula and tries to comfort me as best as he can without smashing Ace between us. "I'm okay, Ry. Just went to the store for formula." I can hear the placating tone in his voice, the confusion woven in it, and I don't really care because he is here and whole and came back to me.

"I was so worried. I had this horrible feeling that something happened to you and when you didn't pick up your phone, I thought that—"

"Shh. Shh," he says, using his free hand to smooth over my cheek as he looks into my eyes. "I'm okay. I'm right here. I'm sorry about my phone. I've had it on do not disturb so if it rings it doesn't wake Ace up if he's napping."

I use the clarity in his eyes to soothe the uncertainty in me. "I'm gonna go put Ace in his swing, can you give him to me?" he asks, eyes alarmed as he looks down to where Ace is asleep in my arms and then looks back up to meet my gaze. I force myself to take a deep breath, hand him over, and then watch as Colton buckles him in the swing's bucket seat and turns it on.

Within seconds he's back in front of me, pulling me against his chest and wrapping his arms around me tightly. I breathe him in. Try to use everything familiar about him to quiet the riot within me: that place under the curve of his neck that smells of cologne, the rhythm of his heartbeat against my cheek, the scratch of his stubble against my bare skin, the weight of his chin resting on my head.

I sag, letting him hold up the weight that's been bearing down on my shoulders. "Ry . . . you're scaring the shit out of me. Please talk to me. Let me do something . . . anything to give you what you need. Helpless doesn't look good on any man, least of all me," he pleads, his arms only holding me tighter as his words make me want to pull away and dig my hands into his back simultaneously.

"Something's wrong with me, Colton. *I'm broken.*" My voice is barely a whisper, but I know he hears it because within a second his hands are on my face guiding it up to look at the concern heavy in his.

"No. Never. You're not broken, just a little bent," he says with a soft smile, trying to replicate that moment so very long ago. Bring back a piece of our past to try and fix the current situation, but this time I'm not too sure it's going to help.

"I feel like I'm going crazy." The words are so difficult to say. Like I'm pulling them one by one from the pit of my stomach. When they are finally out, I feel instant regret and relief concurrently. The continual contradictions seem to be the only thing my mind can keep consistent.

His head moves back and forth in reflex, immediately rejecting my comment as his hands run over my cheeks, eyes looking deeply into mine. "What can I do? Do you want me to call Dr. Steele?" I can tell he's panicked, lost in my minefield of hormones, unsure what to do to help me.

"No." I reject the idea immediately, shame and obstinacy ruling my response. "It's just the baby blues. It's just going to take me a few days to get over it." I hope he's fooled by the resolution in my voice because I sure as hell am not.

"Then why don't we get some help? Your mom or my mom or Haddie—"

"No!" The thought of someone else knowing is almost as suffocating as the emotion. Even my own mom. That would mean I've failed. That I'm not good enough. The thought causes more panic. "I don't want anyone to know."

An admission I can't believe I've made.

"Then a nanny. Someone who—"

"I'm not trusting Ace with anyone." This is a non-negotiable option for me. My body starts trembling at the thought, panic vibrating through every inch of my body at just the thought of someone we don't know touching him.

"Rylee," Colton says, exasperated. "I want to help you but you're not giving me any way that I can."

"I just need time," I whisper. *I hope.* My head shaking in his hands, my eyes blurring with tears, and my heart racing, as another swell of panic hits me and takes me for its ride. "Just hold me, please?" I ask.

"There's nothing I want to do more," he says as we sit on the couch and he cradles me across his lap so my head is on his shoulder, legs falling over his thighs.

I use his touch to calm me. Need it to. Let the warmth of his body and the feel of his thumb rubbing back and forth on my arm assuage the wrong inside me that I can't seem to make right or fight my way out from.

Snuggling into him, I realize how much I depend on this tie between the two of us. That connection we feel when we make love— the one we haven't been able to have since I've been on bed rest and know won't have again for several more weeks—has been lost. It makes me feel farther away when more than anything, what I really need is to feel close to *him*.

My heart aches in a way I can't explain. Almost as if it's in mourning. There has been no loss. Just a gain. A huge one. Ace.

I start to apologize again but stop myself. Apologies are only good if you can stop doing what you're sorry for. The problem is I don't know if I can.

But I've got two huge reasons to fight like hell.

Hopefully, they'll be enough.

Chapter Thirty-Two

COLTON

"I'M ALL OUT OF PATIENCE." That and a lot of other fucking shit but Kelly doesn't need to know that.

"I know you are. I've got two lines on him. I'm staking out one place—sitting in my car in front of it right now—and I've got Dean on the other. Twenty-four, forty-eight hours tops . . . But I've gotta tell you, Colton, if a man wants to get lost in a city, Los Angeles is a good place to do it." He pauses, unspoken words clogging up the line. "Are you sure, though? I mean—"

"Don't question me, Kelly. If you want out, walk now. I'll get Sammy to do what I need if you can't." There is no mistaking the threat in my tone.

"Relax, Donavan." Those words are like nails on a chalkboard to me. Piss me off. The irony since I think I said something similar to Ry to set her off. "I'll set everything up. Get it all in place but I still think you need to let the police handle this."

My laugh is low and rich. And lacking any amusement. "Eddie is a blip on their radar. Not mine. He's done enough to my family. I'm done fucking around with this. Get. It. Done."

"Understood. Just remember you can lead a horse to water but you can't make him drink."

"This horse is thirsty for revenge. I'm sure he'll drink."

"I'll call when I have him. Now go spend time with that hot wife and cute baby of yours." I know he's trying to cheer me up with the comment but it does anything but.

I murmur an incoherent goodbye because I'd love to do just that—spend time with my hot wife. But I can't. She's hidden beneath who knows what, and I can't do a goddamn thing to help her.

Give her time, she said earlier. Time my ass. Each hour she slips farther away from me.

Even now as I walk into our bedroom and see her on the bed with Ace, I can see her struggling—eyes scrunched tight, crease in her forehead—as she tries to feel that connection with him while he's nursing. She says it's the only time she doesn't feel completely numb. And thank fuck she's keeping her head above water. *Barely*. But luckily it's above the surface enough to nurse Ace because trying to get him to drink from a bottle has been a goddamn nightmare.

Useless seems to be my new middle name.

It's just the baby blues. That's it. *About ten days to two weeks.* That's how long Google tells me it can last. A topic that's a long fucking way from my typical search history of good porn sites, Indy Weekly Magazine, and surf reports.

We're eight days in. *Halfway through.*

This wasn't supposed to be this hard. We were supposed to have Ace—the baby we never thought we'd ever have—and be blissfully happy. Get the unexpected cherry on top of our happily-ever-after sundae.

Not this bullshit.

I thought the hard part would be coming face to face with my dad. That would be our biggest challenge. That I would be the one to fuck this all up. I had no clue that while I was closing the damn door on the skeletons in my closet, Ry would slowly come undone.

The other shoe most definitely has dropped.

Humpty fuckin' dumpty. The thought's there instantly of another time, another place when I felt this goddamn helpless. This time though . . . man, I'm not sure what it's going to take to put things back together again.

I walk over to the bed, to my whole fucking world, and hate that it doesn't feel so whole. I press a kiss to the side of her shoulder and just leave my lips pressed there for a second as I breathe her in. *Fight, Ry. We need you. I need you.* I'm not sure if she's asleep or not because she doesn't react, and man, how I want her to react. I know she's doing everything she can to keep herself together right now—for all of us—when it seems all she wants to do is fade away.

My scrappy fighter, who is so goddamn beautiful even now with circles beneath her eyes, will find her way. I just can't pressure her regardless of how much I want to.

Or at least that's what Google says. *Her mind is betraying her.*

Reaching down, I scoop up Ace, who thank fuck is completely content with his full belly, and carry him out of the room.

What the hell do I do with him now?

My hands feel like clubs when I change diapers.

My lullaby game is non-existent.

The blanket thing? How in the hell do you get it to look like a burrito? It's not that fucking easy. So what if I used a four-inch piece of duct tape to keep it closed? Call me resourceful.

Or an idiot.

It's taking everything I have not to cry uncle and call in the cavalry: our moms, Quinlan, Haddie. But then that's admitting defeat and fuck if I want to admit that. Plus I can't do that to Ry. She's already so fragile. Asking others for help without her consent would be a slap to her face. Push her farther under water when she's already drowning. Prove to her that I don't think she's capable of handling this.

And that's not what my intention would be. But with Ry right now? Shit, I know that's just how she'd take it.

Yet my cell sits on the counter and looks so damn tempting.

I'm a fish out of water. It's not pretty. I've paced, I've rocked, I've swayed, and no goddamn dice. Ace won't have any of it.

Just go to sleep!

"Look, little man," I say, holding him up so I can look in his eyes as he continues to fuss. "I'm new at this. Have no clue what the fu—er, heck I'm doing here. Can you give a guy a break and go easy on me? Please?"

I can't believe I'm pleading with a newborn—that I've been reduced to this—but desperate times call for desperate measures.

"It's just you and me, dude. *Boys club.* Your momma's having a tough time so you're stuck with me. I know I suck . . . don't have boobs like she does. Believe me, I miss them too. One day you'll understand. But for now . . . you have to man up. I'll show you how. First step, go to sleep for me."

Please. I close my eyes for a moment, unsure what to do now. My mom's not too far away and could get here quickly at this ungodly hour of night. When I open them back up, his eyes are closed.

Thank fuck for that.

Chapter Thirty-Three

Rylee

THE DARKNESS CALLS TO ME. Pulls me. Drowns me in its welcome warmth. It's like a lover's kiss, addictive, all-consuming, and irresistible.

I don't want to leave it.

But I have to.

I'm going to be better today. I'm going to look at Ace and want to wrap my arms around him and pull him in close to me, breathe him in, love him till it hurts.

Connect with him.

Be a mother to him.

My sweet Ace. My miracle baby. My everything.

The constant merry-go-round continues. Colton brings Ace in. He nurses. My head hurts, my heart aches, and my soul tries tirelessly to be what I need to be for him. For them.

It kills me when I can't.

Colton watches, gauges if I'm better today. Or worse. If he should leave Ace with me a little longer. If it's helping or hurting. There are lines etched on his face. Concern. Worry. Disbelief.

My mom. Short texts. Avoided phone calls. Unanswered messages. I know she's worried. I know I can talk to her. But I can't bring myself to pick up the phone.

Colton talks to me. Spends endless hours trying to pull me toward his light.

"I think I'm going to skip the next race or two. Denny deserves a shot at driving the car. Besides, I'll miss Ace too much if I'm gone."

You're lying. You're afraid to leave me here alone with him.

And yet I don't respond. Can't. Because I'm afraid of being alone with Ace too.

The silences screams around us.

"I talked to Zander today." He tries again.

My Zander.

"He sounds better."

If I could feel relief, I would. But I won't believe it until I see it for myself.

"I told him when you're feeling better you're going to have him come back over. He misses you. The boys miss you." I can see the look in his eyes that says, *I miss you.*

I miss you, too.

But Colton doesn't stop, doesn't dwell on the fact I don't respond to his unspoken words. He just walks slowly back and forth with Ace on his shoulder and rambles on about nothing and everything until his cell phone rings or our son falls asleep.

Or Ace needs to nurse again.

The endless cycle. One I abhor and crave desperately. Because it means he hasn't given up on me.

Guilt eats at me. Niggles in the back of my mind. Confuses me. I try. I really do. I fight the pull of the water over my head, drowning in the numbness that ebbs and flows before I can resurface from its hold. I fight to come up for air for my burning lungs, before plunging back down into its depths.

A text from Colton even though he's just downstairs:

Remember this one? It still holds true. I'm here. Keep fighting. I'll wait. All of Me by John Legend.

A flashback of our earlier times. An attempt to lift me up. A challenge for me to remember the feeling. The love. *Myself.* But I'm so buried I can't even lift my head. Or take a breath.

I'm so sorry, Colton. I'm so sorry, Ace.

I'm trying.

I'm fighting.

Don't give up on me.

I really do love you. I just can't feel it. Or show it.

But I will.

It's just the baby blues. I'm stronger than this. Than it. I just need a bit more time.

Tomorrow will be better.

Chapter Thirty-Four

COLTON

"I CAN'T WAIT TO GET my hands on this little guy." Haddie rubs her hands together as she leans forward and hugs me distractedly, already reaching out to grab Ace from me.

"Thanks for getting here so quickly. I didn't know who else to call." Who Rylee wouldn't freak out over, I add silently, because she sure as fuck is going to go ballistic when she wakes up to find Haddie here.

"Anytime. Besides I should be thanking you," she says, lacing kisses on Ace's head. "Ry's been so set on getting his routine down before having visitors that I thought I'd never get to see him."

"About that . . ." I say, taking a deep breath, knowing I'm crossing some kind of marital boundary I shouldn't be, but am past caring. "She's struggling a bit. Baby blues." I nod my head to reinforce my words, to try and relay the rest of what Rylee has forbid me to say. Haddie narrows her eyes at me.

"Oh, that's normal. Everyone I know goes through it a bit. No worries, Donavan, I'll cheer her up," she says with a wink.

I know I need to move. Get to Kelly ASAP but fuck is it hard to leave Ry when she's like this. This could go so wrong on so many fronts. Ry is going to kill me. She's not going to be able to hide from Haddie what's going on. And a tiny little piece of me feels relieved because I don't know what to do anymore.

I'm lost. Like on-a-deserted-island lost and don't have a clue how to help her.

This could push her over the edge or help reel her back. I hope to hell it's the latter.

"Now go. Get. I know you're in a rush. I've got it covered here," Haddie says, interrupting my thoughts.

"She's napping upstairs. I didn't tell her I was going."

"GO! I've got it under control. You're starting to eat into my auntie and Ace time." She starts to shut the front door, and I walk toward the car where Sammy is waiting in the passenger seat when she calls to me. "Hey, Colton?"

I turn, my hand resting with the car door handle, anticipation humming in my blood. "Yeah?"

"Kick Eddie extra hard in the nuts for me, will ya? He deserves it for fucking with my bestie."

"Only if he's still standing when I'm done with him." I slide into the driver's seat. Sammy's chuckle fills the car, and my mind races.

"We're good to go?" I ask, my eyes flickering back and forth from Kelly to Sammy to make sure we're all on the same page.

"Yep. Dean's got him inside. Everything else is in place." Our eyes meet, his unspoken warning I don't want to see is loud and fucking clear within them: cool my jets, my temper, and let the plan work.

And as much as I know he's right, I turn my back to him and start up the walk without acknowledging I saw it.

No one's going to tell me how to run my own show. I know the fallout for my actions. They're clear as fucking day. But I also know Eddie's fucked with my wife and my son, and if a man doesn't stand up for his family, he shouldn't be standing at all.

Going to jail isn't an option. And not because I care about having a record or the media frenzy it would cause. I just can't do that to Ry with how she is or to Ace with how little and helpless he is. But it sure as fuck doesn't mean I'll toe the line.

Bring it, fucker. I'm ready for you. Pumped and primed. Push my buttons. *Pretty please.*

Without knocking, I open the door to the rundown apartment. Kelly's cohort, Dean, is standing just inside. Our eyes meet. A mutual understanding is passed between us—my *thanks*, his *take your time*—before he steps out without another sound.

I take three steps in. I don't hear the door shut. I don't notice that Sammy's back is pressed against it, because my eyes are focused on the man sitting on the ripped couch in front of me: elbows on knees, head hanging down, leg anxiously jogging up and down.

Rage like I've felt very few times in my life roars through me. A fucking freight train of fury I need to keep on track before I let it derail.

I clear my throat. When Eddie realizes someone else is in the apartment, he whips his head up with eyes wide as saucers and mouth open. He looks like shit. *Good.*

"What the . . .?" he asks at first, looking startled, eyes blinking as he shoves up from the couch to stare at me again. And then he belts out a long, low condescending laugh that does nothing but confuse me and piss me off further.

"Something funny?" I ask, fists clenched, curiosity piqued why this is so amusing to him.

"I should have known," he says with a shake of his head, his body visibly relaxing.

Give me a reason, you fucker. Just one.

"Were you expecting somebody else?" I know my threat is nothing compared to the others he will face. That unexpectedly works in my favor.

"Yes. No." That taunting smirk is back front and center. "Your pretty little wife, perhaps."

Bingo.

I'm across the room in two seconds. Arm cocked. Fist flying. The give of flesh against my knuckles. The thud of bone connecting against bone. The crunch that is nowhere near satisfying enough after what he's done to my family.

The sound of glass shattering as his arm hits the lamp and knocks it over breaks through my silent rage, brings me back to the here and now. Reminds me that I want some answers before I finish what he started.

I don't worry about the neighbors hearing us and calling the cops. In places like this no one pays attention. They all keep their head down and stay in their own trouble. I should know. I grew up in a place just like this. No one came to the rescue of the little boy screaming in pain on the other side of the wall.

The thought fuels my anger. Adds strength to my resolve to not be that person. To not stoop to the level of the man in front of me.

But God, how I want to stoop.

"Look at me," I yell. My voice fills the room. He lifts his head up from where he's landed askew on the couch, a red welt swelling on his cheek. "Don't talk about my wife, again. This is between you and me, you fucking bastard."

That chuckle of his is louder, and it takes every ounce of restraint I have to not unleash the fury I feel.

Because I want what I came here for. Answers first. Vindication second. And, oh how sweet that last one will be. He doesn't have a clue what's about to hit him.

"You want to settle a score? Go right ahead. You think you scare me, Donavan? Think again. *You. Can't. Touch. Me.* You're such a pussy you have to bring your goddamn henchman over there," he says, pointing to Sammy standing silently at the door, "to do your dirty work for you."

"I think your black eye will prove I can do my own dirty work just fine." I look over my shoulder and lift my chin to Sammy to tell him to leave. It's better this way. No witnesses. No *he said, she said*. Just my word against Eddie's. Kelly's so damn convinced that Eddie'll sue if I touch him anyway.

Oops. Guess I already broke that rule. My bad.

"Is everyone in your life that tight on your string? One pull on it and they dance?" He raises his eyebrows as his eyes follow Sammy out the door. I glare at him. Bide my time. He's so fucking arrogant I can see him itching to gloat about how he pulled this all off.

"You don't know shit about my life, Eddie."

"I know I won't dance. So how does it feel to pull a string and get back a big giant *fuck you*, huh?"

"Is that what this was all about? Proving you're better than me?" I ask, feigning indifference when I'm anything but.

Take the bait, Eddie. Feed your ego. Prove. Me. Wrong.

He rises from the couch and steps toward me with eerie calm. "I *am* better than you," he says as he steps right into my wheelhouse. Tempting me like never before. "And I'm not stupid either. Lift your shirt up. I bet your pansy ass is wearing a wire. Trying to hook me on something I didn't do."

Is he fucking crazy? Like I'd let the police be in on this little get together we're having. Shit, he's going to wish I went with a wiretap.

"Prison was that good to you, huh?" I taunt as I lift my shirt up and turn around for him to see I'm not wired. "You into guys now?"

"Fuck you," he spits.

"No thanks," I say, taking a step closer. "I want nothing more from you than answers. Everything else you've got coming to you is of your own making."

He quirks his head, arrogant smirk spreading wide. "Thanks to your son, nothing else is coming to me. Sold that picture of him to the tabloids." He sneers. "Made a mint and paid off old debts. *Thanks to Ace*, I'm free and clear."

Fucking pompous bastard. Joke's on him though. That's the only reason I'm not throwing another fist into his face.

"Bravo," I say as I clap my hands slow and deliberately. His eyes narrow, his jaw clenches. Good. I'm pissing him off. "You could have made more money with the video though." The lie flows off my tongue, but I have to force the words out. "Bet you didn't think of that now, did you?"

There's the hook, fucker. Take a big bite so I can set it.

"Prison has a way of putting things on hold." He glares at me. "But it also allowed me a lot of time to plan, to figure out how to get the fucker back who put me there."

"Get me back? *For what*? Because I didn't let you waltz out of my office with the blueprints, sell them to someone else as your own, collect the royalties, and get away with it? Are you out of your fucking mind? Did you think I was going to let you take what was mine and use it?"

"*Seems like I took what was yours and did it anyway.*"

The quiet comment's double meaning—the stolen blueprints and exposure of Rylee on the video—calls to me like a goddamn moth to a flame. This time I can't resist.

He sees my punch coming and gets a quick one into my rib cage before my knuckles meet his jaw. His head snaps back. His body slams into the wall behind him. The sound of him grunting overrides my quick sting of pain from where he landed his.

My body vibrates with anger. Pure unfettered rage as I stare at the waste of space and talk myself out of finishing this right now. And of course because he's a cocky fucker, when he lifts his head back up, that curl to his lips tests my restraint.

Jesus Christ. This is so much fucking harder than I thought it would be. To keep my shit together when all I want to do is show him the rage I feel. Throw punch after punch. Relieve the stress and pain he has caused us.

But that won't solve anything.

"You're a useless piece of shit. Deserve everything you get."

"What I get? Like I said, Donavan. You can't touch me. I did nothing illegal. The video wasn't yours. I didn't steal it. It was in a safety deposit box while I served my time. Shit, it gained in value."

"Did that eat at you, Eddie?" I ask, stepping back into his personal space. "Taunt you every fucking day while you sat in a six-by-ten cell? You felt entitled to fuck with my family because you're a useless piece of shit who can't control his own gambling habits, so to save his own ass, has to rob Peter to pay Paul? It's so much easier to place the blame somewhere else than realize you did this to yourself." I poke my finger in his chest as I laugh under my breath. Taunt him. "Talk about being a pussy."

Dangle the carrot.

"A pussy?" he asks, voice louder as he stands taller. Little-man complex front and center as he puffs his chest out. "You cost me everything!" His voice thunders into the empty apartment, spittle flying from his mouth, as he slowly becomes unhinged. "My wife. My kids. *Everything!*"

"Cheaters never prosper," I say in a singsong voice. He starts to come after me, nostrils flared, fists clenched, but stops when I just raise my eyebrows at him. My empathy is nil. "You. Can't. Touch. Me," I whisper back to him in the same voice he used with me.

"Fuck you!" he screams, rage winding with each and every word. "You're the one who caused all of this. Not me. You want to point a finger? Point it at yourself, you arrogant son of a bitch."

"I caused this? You're out of your goddamn mind!" *Come at me. Please.* Give me a fucking reason to go against my promise to myself. *Motherfucker.* My fists are clenched, my blood is on fire, and it is taking every ounce of restraint I have to not knock his teeth out. But I don't. He's baiting me. Doing a damn fine job of it. But a black eye is one thing. Knocking his teeth out is another.

But damn is it tempting.

His jaw clenches. Hands fist. His body physically bristles at my criticism. His ego so large he's dying to correct me. "You're such an arrogant asshole. I knew you wouldn't part with your money. Even planted some seeds with the tabloids to put pressure on you. But fuck, you're the goddamn golden boy so you figured you'd take the hit in stride. Get an ego boost from the attention it sure as fuck was going to get you. But not once did you think about that precious wife of yours, did you?" His words serve their purpose. Dig at me. Carve into the guilt. "Threw her to the goddamn wolves rather than pay me the money. You proved me right. You're all about you and could give a fuck less about Rylee or her reputation—"

"Don't you fucking say her name again," I yell. I connect with him, forearm against his throat as I pin him against the wall behind him. And he doesn't resist. Knows damn well he's pushing my buttons and he's having way too much fun doing it because he thinks I can't touch him. His lack of reaction a non-verbal, *fuck you.*

"Why? Does it bug you, Donavan, that I called it right? That when I knew you weren't going to pay, I chose to fuck your wife over anyway. Prove to her what a piece of shit her husband is. That he chose money over her?" I press my arm harder into him, needing to shut him up yet wanting the torture of hearing more. "How did it feel when she pushed away from you? When she blamed you for losing her job? I hoped it ripped you apart inside. Fucked with your head because it's nowhere close to how I felt when you took my wife from me."

"Go to hell," I grit out, unable to move because I know if I do, I'm not going to be able to stop myself. My fury has a mind of its own and all it's waiting for is any little thing to set it off. "I'm not playing into your mind games. Because you're leaving out that you're the one who fucked up. You were so goddamn thirsty for revenge that you forgot about the loan sharks waiting to crawl up your ass. You let your temper get the best of you, uploaded the video without even negotiating, and were shit out of luck because your bargaining chip just went out the goddamn window. You lost your money and knew the bill collectors were coming." I let the smirk play the corners of my mouth as my fists beg to finish the talking for us.

"I get the last laugh though, don't I?" he taunts in his calm, even voice despite the pressure on his chest. "That little video made you the 'it couple' for the media. Caused a frenzy. Frenzy means more money. Upped the price of the photo of your son to a pretty penny. Killed two birds with one stone: paid off my debts and got a final 'fuck you' in with your kid." He leans his head forward as far as he can so his face is inches from mine. He whispers but I can hear it clear as fucking day. "You're not such a badass when every man in America is watching that wife of yours come and fantasizing it was them with her, now are you?"

Restraint snapped.

Promise to myself reneged.

The fucker deserves it.

This one's for Rylee

My fist flies. The impact is bittersweet as his head snaps to the side, blood spurting from his nose, a groan falling out as he brings his hands to his face and slides down the wall. I'm only allowing myself one.

Fuck it's going to be hard to walk away. *So I don't.* I step closer, rein in the fury and take the high road when all I want to do is crawl in the gutter with him. I reach out and yank his hair so his head snaps up to look at me.

"Don't *ever* come near my family again." My threat is plain as day. I let go of his hair, shoving his head back. "What is it they say about revenge? Before you try to get it, make sure to dig two graves?" I grate out, voice shaking, body amped up on adrenaline. "Maybe you should have taken the advice." He looks up, confusion flickering in his eyes as to what I mean. His mind only focused on the grave he dug for me, and not the one he should have dug for himself.

Well, if he doesn't get it now, he sure as fuck is going to understand in about two minutes.

"Fuck you," he says as I walk toward the door.

I stop and hang my head down as a chuckle falls from my mouth that clearly says the same thing back to him. I let the silence eat up the room. Allow him to think this is all there is going to be.

And then I drop the hammer.

"You may have paid your debts back. But I think you forgot about the interest you owe them. I guess I'll let someone else do my dirty work for me after all."

I open the door and walk out of the apartment, a part of me wishing I could see the expression on his face, the other part of me never wanting to see him again. Holding my hand up, I ask the guys standing a few feet away to give me a minute. A goddamn second to catch my breath and figure out how the fuck I feel about getting but not getting what I wanted.

Because yes, I got my answers. Got them tied up with a nice little bow that normally I'd question the ease in which he confessed them. But I know that fucker inside out. I worked with him for years, watched him across the table from me in mediation and on the stand during the trial, can read him like a fucking road map. Do I question the answers' validity? Not enough to care because he was so itching to one-up me. Desperate to prove he stuck it to me in the end—got me back—that he was so amped up on the high of it, there was no way in hell he'd be able to spin the truth.

So yes, I'm good with his explanations. But fuck if I'm not struggling with giving him what he deserves by my own hand. *Rylee.* The reason. The answer. The goddamn everything. *That's why* I have to be okay with this outcome. With someone else doing my dirty work to reach the same endgame.

And when I look up, they are there, ready and willing to do it for me. And for them. Three fuckers solid as tree stumps. Scary shit to owe money to these guys.

"You have five minutes to collect your interest before Kelly calls the cops. Make sure he's alive when they get here. He seems to be in violation of a restraining order."

Fucker has no idea what's about to hit him. Fairly sure it'll wipe the smarmy smirk off his face.

I think he'll welcome going back to jail after they get done with him.

I meet Sammy's eyes. I see the question there. *You've wanted a piece of Eddie for so damn long, why are you walking away now*?

But Sammy knows why. Probably can still hear the fury in my voice from the hospital all these days later. *Her. Safety. Comes. First.*

And if not, it doesn't matter. I don't need to justify shit to anyone. I have two perfectly good reasons at home. They're what matters. My end all, be all.

The reason I'll never stop trying to be the man deserving of *them.*

I just shake my head and slide into the waiting car. I've wasted enough time on Eddie fucking Kimball.

Eddie will not be bugging you again. He's in custody.

My feet stop as I look at the text. I need a minute.

Fuck, I need more than a minute. I need to drown myself in a fifth and take a whole goddamn evening to swim in it. So I can brood. Be that cocky asshole I used to be and not give a fuck about anything or anyone.

But I can't.

So I sit down on the step to the front door and sigh, close my eyes, hang my head, and give myself sixty seconds I can't afford to take. Because once I walk in the door, I need to be the same man who just walked away from Eddie without throwing another punch. Responsible. Mature. Selfless.

Right now I want to be anything but.

Or is it that I'm a pussy and fear what I'm walking in on? A goddamn powder keg of unknown. Will my wife be here? Because I miss her so fucking much. Or just that shell of her that I've grown to despise?

Yeah, you've been pussified, Donavan. Needing a woman to complete you when you used to not need shit. My, how the player has fallen.

I chuckle. Not for relief but because I need something to take the edge off all this pent-up emotion. And because I know what else I need to do when I go inside, what I need to tell Ry is going to happen, and I just hope the news about Eddie helps take the sting out of it.

The door opens behind me. It closes. And I wait for it. Know it's coming.

"You okay?" Haddie asks as she sits down beside me and holds out a beer and a bag of ice to me. I look over to her, wondering how she knew I needed both. "Call it a lucky guess."

"Thanks." I take them and hiss when I put the ice on my knuckles. We sit in silence for a few moments.

"Shane stopped by unexpectedly. He's in with Ace right now," she says, surprising me. But I shouldn't be. Shane's one of Ry's boys. He knows something is wrong just like I do. "Ry's out on the upstairs patio. I talked her into getting some fresh air."

"She is?" Hope tinges my voice. She must be feeling better. I knew she'd come around.

"Colton?" By the way Haddie says my name, I know: Rylee isn't better at all. In fact, it reinforces what I have to do even more.

"I'm calling the doctor in the morning." I answer the unspoken question she left hanging out there, bring the beer to my lips, and take a long pull on it. And I hate myself for saying it because now I've put it out there, I have to admit there is something wrong with Rylee.

And I don't want there to be something wrong with her.

"At first I was pissed at you, at her . . . You didn't tell me and I'm her bestie. I should know this. But I get it. I understand how proud Ry is. How she thinks she can handle everything and if she admits she can't then it makes it even worse. But, Colton, this is about her getting better. Not about her being weak." She leans her head on my shoulder and sighs.

I shake my head. Emotions fucked. Head more so. "I thought that dealing with Eddie today would help. I could come back and tell her he won't bother us anymore. Maybe knowing that worry was gone might be what she needed to help her break through . . ." I stop when I realize how fucking stupid that sounds.

"It might help some," Haddie says softly, "but it's not going to fix her. We're back to Matchbox Twenty on repeat again but there's no music this time. *In fact, there's no sound at all.* She needs help, Colton."

I scrub my hands over my face. "I know, Had. I know."

"She tried to keep it together for a while but I know her well enough to know better," she says as I stand up.

"Thank you . . . for everything." Our hug is brief, my need to see Ry ruling my thoughts.

"Always," Haddie says as I open the door and walk into my house.

I hear voices, my hopes rising to be dashed once again when I see Shane on the couch talking to Ace. And fuck, for some reason seeing Ace hits me hard, validates the reasons why I walked away from Eddie.

My end all, be all.

Shane looks up when he notices me. "Hey," he says as he stands immediately, eyes locked on mine. I know a threat when I see one but for the fucking life of me can't figure out why Shane's the one giving it to me.

"What's wrong, Shane?" I ask, mind spinning as he hands Ace off to Haddie without letting me see him first.

"Can we talk?"

And if he wasn't so dead serious, I might laugh at the sudden growl to his voice and stiffening of his spine. "Sure," I say as I fire a look at Haddie and get a shrug in response. "Why don't we head into the office?"

I lead the way, let him walk in first, and then shut the door. We take seats on opposite sides of the desk, and this time when he looks at me I see so much more than the threat from a moment ago. I see a scared kid trying to be a brave man and I'm not sure of the footwork of how to go about this.

Well, I'm scared too. For different reasons. But scared nonetheless.

"What'd you want to talk about, Shane?"

He shifts in his seat, fidgets his hands, and before he even speaks, I can see we need to spend some more time together so I can help him look controlled when he's not feeling it. That's a must for a man and I've dropped the ball in teaching him that.

"You're supposed to be the one who takes care of her," he accuses with more certainty than his eyes reflect, suddenly nervous now that he's actually standing his ground. "I mean, you can see something's wrong with her, right?"

I bite back the flippant comment I'd normally give—how I sure as shit know how to take care of my fucking wife. The exhaustion and the shit with Eddie make it so goddamn tempting, but I'm able to find my restraint. To realize this is Shane in front of me trying to make sure Ry's okay.

I lean back in the chair and roll my shoulders, put myself in his shoes. "She's having a tough go of it, isn't she?" I meet his gaze. I don't shy away from it, because I want him to see I understand Rylee needs help.

"If you're not going to get her a doctor, then I will," he states, voice resolute but then throws me for a fucking loop when his eyes well up with tears before he quickly looks down.

"I'm calling one tomorrow. She asked me for time to try and get through it," I explain with more patience than I feel. But it's one of her boys, a part of her family. "But she's not getting any better so I'm going to get her some help. She's going to be okay, Shane."

"Don't say that," he says between clenched teeth. He squeezes his eyes closed and his face transforms. "That's what they said about my mom. And look what happened to her." His voice breaks as he delivers the words.

Fuck. How could I have not seen this coming? How could I have not realized Shane would compare Rylee's postpartum depression to his mother's depression? The illness that caused her to take her own life in an overdose of pills. Or the fact he is the one who found her and is forever scarred by the memory.

"Look at me, Shane." I pause, waiting for him to lift his head and meet my eyes. The courageous man who walked in here is gone. The broken boy who lost his world when his mom died has replaced him. I scramble to fix it. Him. Use words that won't do shit but will sound like it. "She will get better." And I'm not sure if the strong resolve in my voice is to convince him or me. "I am going to have a doctor see her tomorrow. It might take some time, but we'll get our Rylee back, okay?"

He stares at me no doubt deciding if he believes me or not. He nods his head slowly as he begins to speak. "Rylee is the only mom I have. I'll do whatever it takes to make sure she gets better."

I nod my head, the words he doesn't say are reflected in his eyes: *I can't lose another person.*

I understand that more than you know, kid.

"That makes two of us."

Chapter Thirty-Five

Rylee

"RY?" Colton's voice shocks me from the darkness of my mind into the blinding light of the patio.

Everything wars inside me: relief against spite, fear against hope, numbness against pain.

He stands in the doorway. Vitriol-laced accusations scream in my head but don't form into words. Can't. It's too much effort.

"You left me." My voice sounds hollow, unaffected. Numb.

I missed you like a drowning person misses the air.

The baby monitor clicks as he sets it on the table. The cushion whooshes as he sits beside me. His eyes give an apology I don't want to accept.

"I had to take care of some things, Ry." He sounds tired. Rough. Something's going on and yet I can't find enough energy to care.

My body begins to hum. The ghost of the panic attack I had when I found out he had left comes back to haunt me. I wring my hands. Try to hold on to my control even though I can feel it slowly slipping away from me.

I can't breathe.

"I went to see Eddie."

Air feels like water, slowly filling my lungs with each inhale. Closing over my head and pulling me under.

"It was the first time he'd surfaced so I had to go."

The deeper I fall the more my body begins to burn with heat from the inside out.

"He won't be bugging us ever again."

I fight back. Break the surface. My lungs heaving for the air his words bring me.

My eyes open wide and meet his, a moment of clarity amidst this haze.

"Thank you," I say, voice hoarse as I try to elicit the emotion to match my words. *But I can't feel.* When I don't want to it's all I can do, and when I do want to, I can't.

I keep my eyes locked on his. Hope they'll be the lifeline I need to keep me afloat, and sustain this feeling of normalcy for a little longer. The span of time seems to be less and less as the days go on.

Colton reaches out and runs the back of his hand down the side of my cheek. Tears well. I fight them back. I open my mouth to speak, but the words don't come out.

I need help.

He moves to sit next to me, pulls me in close to him. I try to find comfort, try to use that hum of our bodies touching to tell me I'm still alive. And if I'm alive I can keep treading water until I can get to the edge.

I close my eyes. A tear slides over. A little piece of me leaving with it.

"Shane is really worried about you."

I saw it in his eyes: the fear, the memories of his mom, the worry. I couldn't stop them. I couldn't reassure him. He saw right through it.

Guilt. The one constant I feel is back, swims in my head.

"Your mom. I'm not going to be able to keep her away much longer, Ry. She's worried." *I am too.* I can hear the unspoken words in his voice but don't have the wherewithal to respond. "I've kept her happy with pictures and videos. Telling her you're sleeping when she calls. She's going to come up this weekend."

"No!" It's the only show of emotion I can give. The need to keep this under wraps from those who would be disappointed in my failure the most.

"I'm going to call Dr. Steele then." His voice is soft but slams into my ears like the harshest of noises.

"No!" My voice cracks with panic—the word on repeat in my head—as I try to shove away from him. Struggle as he pulls me hard into him to stop my resistance against the idea.

I fight because I can handle this.

No, I can't.

And because I'm scared. What if I can't ever find my way back?

Yes, I can.

The darkness is so much more tempting than the fight. Less work. Less struggle. But Ace and Colton are worth fighting for. I'm so sick of the dark. So sick of its loneliness. I do the only thing I can: cling onto Colton, my light.

"I'm holding tight so you can let go, Ryles," he says into the crown of my head, the heat from his breath warming the cold lingering inside me. "Let go, baby. Deal with what you need to. And just know that Ace and I are here for you when you come back to us. Then we'll get our little piece of peace."

He still loves me.

He still wants us.

He's fighting the fight for me.

Even when I can't.

Chapter Thirty-Six

COLTON

"HADDIE MUST HAVE CALLED IN the troops."

My mother's laugh is deep and rich through the phone. The concern is there though. I can hear her hiding it.

But it's okay. I am too.

I glance to the extra bedroom where the door is shut and wonder what is taking them so long.

"You have no idea. She only means well." Then silence. *Fuck.* Here we go. "You should have told us, Colton. It's nothing to be ashamed of. We're here to help you." I can hear the hurt in her voice, get that she thinks I didn't trust her coming into our private life enough to tell her what was going on. And if my own mother feels this way, I'm going to have to steel myself for how Ry's mom is going to handle this.

I clear my throat, unsure what to say. "It's not like that, Mom. It's complicated." Tread lightly, Donavan. She's not intruding; she just wants to be a mom.

Just like Rylee does.

"I know it is." Her voice is softer. Her hurt feelings back in check. Being a mom again—pushing away her hurt to help me deal with mine. "Has the doctor finished talking to her yet?"

I glance at the door again. "No."

"I'm sure she's just reassuring Rylee. Sometimes when you hear things you don't want to hear and they're spoken by someone else, you actually listen to them."

"I miss her, Mom."

God, I sound like such a pussy. You can't miss someone who is right in fucking front of you twenty-four/seven.

"Of course you do. You've all had a lot of changes over the past few months."

"Changes?" I snort and then press a kiss to the top of Ace's head. Use him to calm me. "I feel like we've had the shit beat out of us so much in the past month I'm surprised we're not black and blue." Sarcasm she doesn't deserve is thick in my voice.

"You're only alive if you bruise," she says softly.

Then I must be thriving.

"Yeah." I sigh. My eyes are back on the door but her comment sticks in my mind.

"You can't do this all yourself, son. Let all of us help you. We're setting up a schedule so we can come and—"

"I don't know about that, Mom. I appreciate it, but Rylee—"

"Sorry. This is what family does. We rally the troops and take care of our own," she says, the no-nonsense tone in her voice taking me back twenty years to when I was a punk kid getting reprimanded. "You don't have a choice. Ry's mom, Quinlan, Haddie, and I will take shifts if need be. Anything it takes. And you'll take the help and not argue. Understood?"

Yep. Right back there to being ten and getting caught trying to light firecrackers in the backyard.

"Yes, ma'am."

"And you need the break too. You'll burn yourself out. A proud

312

man is a good man. But he can also be a stupid one."

I can't help the laugh that falls from my mouth. My blunt mother telling me like it is. One of very few women who can.

"Mom, I have to go," I say as the door opens.

"Let me know what she says so I can let everyone know and—"

I hang up the phone. Cut her off. I need to know.

"Dr. Steele?"

"Walk me out, please?" she asks.

"Sure." We head to the front door. This doesn't sound good. My dread builds with each footstep. My heart is in my throat by the time we walk outside and shut the door behind us.

"He is an adorable little guy, isn't he?" she says as she focuses on Ace when all I want her to do is tell me about Rylee.

"Doc?" I finally ask, hoping she'll have pity on me.

"You were right to call me, Colton." The breath I'm holding burns in my lungs. "She's definitely struggling with more than the typical baby blues."

I feel a flicker of relief. I don't know why. She hasn't said she's going to be okay, but at least I'll know the beast we're facing.

"Okay, so what do I need to do for her?" Something. Anything. I'm a guy. I need to fix things and this not being able to fix Rylee is fucking me up.

She smiles softly at me. "To be honest, there's no clear-cut answer here. I talked with Rylee. Explained how she's not alone. That a lot of women go through this and that getting help does not mean she's failing as a mother." She reaches out and plays with Ace's hand as she continues. "Sometimes, postpartum depression is triggered by a sequence of events that seems out of the person's control. Add in the rush of hormones. Then there's the pressure of trying to get a newborn—who couldn't care less about a schedule—to be on a schedule because every book you've read says that's what you should be doing or you're not doing it right. All of those combined are like the perfect storm of uncontrolled chaos. In Rylee's case, her mind has internalized it all and has fallen into a little downward dip of depression."

I blow out a breath, hear her words and know it's not my fault. But I'm a guy so I blame myself nonetheless. "Is she going to be okay?"

She nods. "I've written a prescription for some anti-depressants and—"

"Can she still nurse?" I ask, knowing that nursing is the only time she feels somewhat connected to Ace.

"Yes. There is much debate on this. In my opinion the trade-off is worth it: getting Rylee on the road to recovery versus a trace of the drugs passed on through the milk."

"Okay."

"She's a fighter, Colton. Get her out in the fresh air. A walk on the beach. A drive in the car. Anything you can think of doing to get her up and about without triggering her panic attacks."

I chuckle. She does realize who we are, right? Did she forget there's a reason she's making a house call and we're not going to her office?

"I know. It's difficult in . . . your situation, but the more stimuli, the better."

"Thanks," I say quietly. "I appreciate you making the house call."

"She's going to be fine, Colton. She just needs a little time. It's not going to happen overnight. The drugs take some time to take effect, so be patient like you've been so far, and soon enough you'll have your wife back."

The words cause my heart to pound. Fucking stupid since she's been here all along. And yet my pulse is racing at the mere thought of getting my best friend back. Hearing her laughter. Watching her eyes light up with joy over staring at Ace. Listening to her sing off key to her beloved Matchbox Twenty. It's the little things I miss. The day-to-day. The insignificant.

Desperate may not be something a man should wear but fuck if

I'm not swathed in it wanting her to come back to me.

After the gates close behind Dr. Steele, I head inside, uncertain which Rylee I'm going to find: The fighter I've grown to admire or the lost woman I can't even recognize.

"Let's go, little man. Let's see if we can make your momma smile."

Chapter Thirty-Seven

Rylee

FADING IN.

My moments with Ace, the ones I can feel, I try to hold tight to them. Try to use them to keep me afloat. Soak them in.

A text from Colton: **Photograph by Ed Sheeran.**

A rush of warmth. A flash of happy. The recollection of that night. Of sweetness. A picture frame waiting to be filled. Memories to make.

Panic I won't be able to make it. A struggle to hold on to the good from the song, and not the bad. Please help me hold on to the good.

Falling out.

Thoughts come. Thoughts go.

The house a constant revolving door: my mom, Haddie, Dorothea, Quinlan. Frustrating me. Reviving me. Holding me up so I can fall, but not be alone when I do.

My mom. Opening blinds. Zipping through the house like Mary Poppins infusing her cheer to try and make me smile. Except I can't smile. I can't feel anything. Watching her hold Ace, coo over him, connecting with him should make me happy, jealous—anything— and yet I feel absolutely nothing.

The clock ticks. Time in Ace's life I can't get back.

My Colton. I watch him with Ace. Day after day. Night after night. Moments I capture, file away, and pray can keep. Colton asleep with Ace on his chest, tiny fingers curled against his muscles. Made- up lullabies that dig into the fog and make me feel something . . . lighter. A flicker of warmth. A strand of hope. A moment I can em- brace.

Before the lead curtain falls again.

Seconds spent.

A tug of war of inner wills.

Hours gone.

And every night, Colton pulls me against him as we lie in bed and murmurs in my ear the wonderful memories we still have to make to put in our picture frame. The warmth of his body against mine is his subtle reminder to his wife, who is still lost in her own mind, that she's not alone.

Days lost.

"Teddy called today," Colton says. The ocean breeze is cool. The soothing surge from Ace nursing a little stronger today. The fog a little lighter.

"Hmm?" Afraid to hope. Wanting to know but fearing the worst.

"The board voted to keep him on as director." An unexpected flutter. A tinge of excitement. "You'll be reinstated if you choose to go back to work after your maternity leave."

A deep breath in. Exhale out.

"Mm-hmm." A bit of inflection.

Colton's smile at my response. *I love his smile.* The feel of Ace's hand kneading my breast. *I love his little hands.* A glimpse of hope.

A pile of jumbled jigsaw pieces. Two finally fitting together.

A text from Colton: **I'll Follow You by Jon McLaughlin**

He tries so hard to keep me above the fray. To do anything to help me hold on a little longer than last time. A message to tell me I'm not alone. That it's okay.

A pinprick of light at the end of the tunnel.

You can do this.

Change is never easy.

Fight to hold on.

Fight to let go.

Fight because they're your whole world.

Chapter Thirty-Eight

COLTON

"I STILL CAN'T GET OVER it."

"Get over what?" I ask as I look from where Ace is passed out on my chest—mouth open, hands up, legs apart. Content as fuck. And thankfully asleep since he's been running me ragged.

"You. A dad." Becks chuckles with a shake of his head.

"Yeah well, he looks sweet right now . . . but don't let him fool you. He's a stubborn little cuss. He had me up to my elbows in shit earlier. Not a pretty sight." Fucking disgusting. But shit, I'd do it a hundred more times if I could be rewarded by the soft smile on Rylee's face when I looked up and saw her standing in the doorway watching us.

Becks throws his head back and laughs. "Fuck. I would have paid to see that."

"No. You wouldn't," I deadpan, "but you do what you have to do."

Becks nods his head and lifts his chin toward the pool deck where Rylee is reading. Baby steps. Tiny bits of her returning to me.

"Haddie says she's doing better?"

"One step forward. Three back." I shrug. "But at least we're moving, right? Just trying to figure out our new kind of normal or some shit like that."

"And you're hanging in there?"

"Most days," I say with a laugh. "But God I'd kill to get on the track. I need some speed to clear my head and give me a chance to not think for a bit."

"Not thinking is what you do best. You don't need to hit the track for that."

"Fuck off," I say with a laugh. And regardless of my response, I welcome the dig. Need a bit of our typical banter to get a little part of my normal.

"Dude, you better watch your mouth or else Ace's first word is going to be fuck. And while it would be funny as fuck," he says, raising his eyebrows at the intended pun, "I think that might earn you a spot in the doghouse."

"True . . . but fuck—"

"There you go again." He laughs, causing me to just shake my head and sigh.

"This is going to be harder than I thought."

"Most good things in life are," he says with a lift of his eyebrows. And I stare at him for a beat, hearing what he's saying. That shit's tough right now but it's all worth it.

Damn straight it is.

"Like I said, just say when and I'll get the track time reserved for you," he says as he stands. His unspoken, *I've got your back*, comes through loud and clear.

"Thanks . . . for everything."

"No problem, brother. That's what I'm here for."

They're gone.

I'm thankful the vultures have packed up shop and gotten the hell out of Dodge, but I still can't believe it's true. I check the live feed on my phone from the security camera mounted on the front gate one more time. The street's still free and clear of paparazzi scum who had been camping out there for what felt like for-fucking-ever.

Thank God they listened for once. Chased the story I hand-fed them about Eddie. Uncovered truths behind his actions: his desperate and fucked-up act to exact revenge on my wife because he was found guilty. Paparazzi's apologies mean shit to me. They're just covering their asses from getting sued for slander. Besides, I know it won't stop them from doing the same thing with their next story, their next lead, their next chance to fuck up someone else's life.

Of course, I'm not blind to the fact they're all playing nice in the hopes of getting first crack at pictures of Ace if we ever decide to go that route and sell the rights. So I'll take their printed retractions. Use their hope to clear our street and rid our lives of their constant presence. But more than anything I'll hold tight to the fact that their apologies have helped restore Rylee's reputation.

Too bad she's so lost in her depression she doesn't know it.

Because while their apologies may have restored calm outside the gates, they've done nothing to quiet the storm still brewing inside them.

From my chair on the patio, I set my cell down and watch the set of waves roll in, immediately itching to grab my board and get lost in the ocean. My mind wanders. Thoughts run. Will Ace want me to teach him to surf some day? Will he be interested in racing?

Or will I just be the authority he resists until he gets old enough to understand the why behind my rules? *Like father, like son.*

The baby monitor crackles on the table beside me. I give him a sec, wait to see if he's awake, but nothing. I lean back in my chair and get lost in thoughts about the next race. My everyday world that feels so fucking far away from the one I'm currently living in.

"Shh. Shh." Ry's voice comes through the monitor and startles me. My heart races. My eyes burn with emotion I don't want to feel but can't stop as I bring it to my ear to hear more.

Silence. Nothing else. Should I go upstairs or stay here and see what happens? If I'm there, does it add more pressure on her as she takes a step forward when so many we've taken have been backward?

And then those dark thoughts in the back of my mind take hold. The ones I haven't wanted to acknowledge but linger nonetheless. The ones that make the evening news headlines about what mothers with postpartum depression have done to their children.

I'm up and on my feet in a second. A war of emotions battle over what to think and what to do. I stand in the hallway, frozen in indecision with what feels like the weight of the world on my shoulders.

Hope surges through me. I hate it and love it at the same time.

I choose to love it. Need to.

C'mon, Ry. Give me something to tell me I'm right.

"My sweet boy. You hungry?" I exhale the breath I didn't realize I was holding, pissed at myself for doubting her but knowing I have every right to.

Joy, relief, fear, concern, caution. Too many fucking feelings hit me at once. The biggest of all of them is relief that I can see the light at the end of this long-ass tunnel. Our life has been put on hold for what feels like forever, and it's time to get it back.

She's not better yet. We still have a long way to go. Hell yes, this moment is a baby step, but fuck if I won't take it because we weren't even crawling a few days ago. This step may be on wobbly legs, but it's a step all the same.

When I enter the bedroom, Rylee is lying on the middle of the bed, and Ace is nursing beside her. It's the first time I haven't had to bring him to her. The thought sinks in and takes hold as I watch the two of them together. A visual sucker punch of love.

Leave her be, Colton.

Good in theory, but not in my reality. I don't know why I resist the pull when I know in the end it's futile. It always is when it comes to Rylee.

I cross the room, pull my shirt over my head, and slide into bed behind her without saying a word. Careful of disturbing Ace, I put my arm around her hip, and line our bodies up. And just breathe her in.

God, I've missed her.

"Sorry. I didn't hear him wake up. I didn't mean for you to have to get him." I give her the lip service, soft words that won't upset her, when I'm not sorry at all.

Silence greets me. I hold back the sigh I want to breathe out. Push down the disappointment she's lost again. Accept that the power of her own mind is ten times more powerful than any love I can give her. Fight the fear I won't be able to pull her back again.

So I begin the routine. My nightly process. My way of telling her I'm not giving up on her. I tell her about a memory I can't wait to make with her.

"I thought of another one today. Memory two hundred thirteen that I can't wait to put in our picture frame. We should rent a private island. Or a secluded beach somewhere. Sand, sun, and our family left all alone to do as we please. Silly, right?" My own voice rings in my ears but her body relaxes against mine and I know she's listening. "It's not though. Because the island rules are that you're required to wear very skimpy bikinis. Or go topless. Topless is preferable. And yes, to make it fair, I'd have to wear that loincloth thingy so we have clothing equality on the island. Oh shit," I murmur as I press a kiss into the back of her hair. "I'm still getting used to this baby thing. I forgot topless doesn't bode well with a kid. So I guess topless would only be allowed when Ace is napping. I'm sure we could find a few ways to occupy our time during those hours anyway."

I lose my train of thought. Get lost in the feel of her body against mine, and how much I miss physical intimacy between us. Because physical is my barometer. Makes me feel closer to her and at the same time tells me we're okay. And without it, I hate not knowing if we're okay.

"Sorry," I say, pulling myself from my thoughts. "I was daydreaming about being on the beach with you."

"Thank you."

Her voice is so faint but I hear it immediately. I squeeze my eyes shut, overwhelmed from those two simple words.

Gathering her a little tighter, I rest my chin on the curve of her shoulder. I look down in front of her where Ace has fallen asleep, and I know I need to put him in his bassinet but I don't. Not yet. This feels a little too normal when we've had anything but, so I want to make it last a little bit longer. Just the three of us.

There are so many things I want to say to her, so many reasons why she doesn't need to thank me, but I don't. I was given two glimpses of my wife tonight. That's enough to tell me more is coming soon.

So I do what I think is best. I continue on. "Don't thank me yet, Ryles. This island doesn't have any indoor plumbing. Or Diet Coke. And I know how you love your Diet Coke. But they do have . . ." I continue on. My rambling evening entertainment.

Anything for my Ry.

Chapter Thirty-Nine

Rylee

Hi sweetheart. Just checking in to see how you're doing. I love you. I'm here for you. I'll be up later this week.

THE TEXT FROM MY MOM sits on my phone. The screen is lit up. My insides are still so very dark.

I miss the outside world.

Lazy walks on the beach. Trips to the farmers market in town where I get to laugh at Colton with his hat pulled low to avoid attention. The roar of the racetrack and vibration of the engine in my chest as I sit in the infield and answer emails while Colton tests the car. The incessant chatter, sound of kitchen chairs scooting over worn linoleum, complaints about homework, and sly smiles given behind one another's back that are a constant at The House from my boys.

I miss everything that makes me feel alive.

But I'm not ready yet. I miss the idea of everything but not the reality. Because with the reality comes the chaos. The intrusive cameras and judging eyes. The scrutiny and the exposure. The lack of any control or privacy. The never-ending sense of vulnerability.

Besides, how can I begin to want any of *those* things when I can't even look at my beautiful baby boy and feel that soul-shifting love I should for him? Sure it's there, hidden deep down and buried beneath the haze. I know it is. I've felt it before. And that almost makes it worse. To want something and never have it is one thing but to have something, lose it, and know what you're missing is brutal.

And I'm missing Ace. Not him, per se, because he's here and I feed him, but rather the emotion. Brief moments of intense joy and overwhelming love peek through every now and again. The want to have them return consumes me to the point they drive me back into the warped and silent comfort of the darkness.

And then when I resurface, there is Colton. The songs he texts to help me remember. And to help me forget.

It's when the sky is the darkest that you can tell which stars are the brightest. There's only one star I see: Colton's light shines the brightest to me. Maybe because he's the one saving me.

I wish I could feel the amusement I know is beneath the surface when I watch him deal with Ace in his adorably awkward way. The made-up lullabies about car parts and superheroes he sings to stop Ace from crying are so sweet. I try to dredge it up, hold on to my smile, but it's a constant battle between the darkness and light.

Then there's the night. When he pulls me into him and tells me about the silly places he is going to take me, the memories we are going to make, and lifts that lead curtain for a bit so I can lose myself in his voice and humor. I can look down to Ace at my breast and have Colton's body against my back and know I can beat this.

And so I fight, winning little pieces of myself back day by day. Moment by moment. Because it's the things we love most that destroy us. Break us down. Tear us apart. But they are also the things that build us back up. Heal us. Make us complete again.

"Hey, man!" Colton's voice rings down the hallway, interrupting my thoughts. I immediately start to rise from the couch, bothered I was actually enjoying sitting beside Ace in the bouncer, and start to head upstairs because the unexpected usually triggers uncontrolla-ble anxiety. And that anxiety inevitably leads to another trip down the rabbit hole.

"I'm sorry I didn't call first, but I was driving back to school and needed to stop by. Can I speak to you and Ry for a moment?"

Shane's voice echoes down the foyer and makes me falter. And it's not what he says that stops me from standing but rather the tone in his voice—formal, businesslike, and anxious—that makes me sit at attention.

"Not a problem. Let me go tell Ry that you're here first," Colton says, followed by the lowering of their voices. They say something I can't hear but can assume it is the typical question of how I am doing that gets asked when they arrive. "Be right back." Footsteps. "Hey, Ry?"

"Yeah?" My voice is shaky as I answer, and I hate that the anxi-ety surges within me when it's just Shane. He's the boy who has been with me the longest. The one I have watched grow into a man.

"Shane stopped by. Okay?" Colton's eyes hold mine. They're tell-ing me that Shane's coming in and to prepare for it. My two-minute warning. I force a swallow down my throat as I try to reason with myself that this is Shane; he poses no threat to Ace or me, or my little world.

I nod my head.

"Come on in," Colton yells as he stands there with eyes locked on mine and waits for Shane to close the distance.

C'mon, Ry. You scared him last time. Show him that you're not his mother. That this beast can be conquered. Be the you he knows. Try, baby. Please.

And as much as I prepare myself, when Shane walks into the living room, my heart races out of control and body breaks out in a cold sweat. And I detest that I can't muster up more than a forced smile when our eyes meet. I open my mouth to say hi, but the word doesn't come out.

I see concern in his expression, and he glances over to Colton, blatantly telling him he lied, that I'm not better like he'd said moments before at the door. Colton nods to trust him.

"So you're heading back to campus?" Colton says, saving me from having to speak as he leads the way into the living room and motions for him to sit down.

"Yes. Yeah. I spent the night at The House with the gang." His eyes flicker back and forth between the two of us as he sits down on the edge of the chair before landing on Ace sleeping contently in the bouncer. "He's getting so big."

"Yeah. It's crazy," Colton says. He stares at Shane as he watches Ace, and I can see him narrow his eyes to try and figure out the same thing I am: why does Shane seem so nervous?

I want to ask so many things: how is school, how is Zander, is Auggie hanging in there? Do you miss me? But my restlessness only adds to the awkward silence filling the room. Colton finally speaks. "That was cool of you to hang out with the boys. I was thinking maybe in a week or two when Ry is feeling a little better, we'll have all you guys over for a barbecue."

And as much as I know Colton is trying to make Shane feel more comfortable, it feels like hands are squeezing my lungs at the mere thought of so many people being in my space at once. He said a few weeks, though. Maybe by then . . .

"Yeah, uh . . ." Shane shifts and rubs his palms down the thighs of his pants. "Well, I stayed with the boys because we had a little house meeting and um, I came here because I wanted to let you know about it."

I vaguely hear him over the roar of my heartbeat. My curiosity is piqued and internal instinct overrides the depression's pull trying to yank me back from the edge and protect me from whatever it is that is making him so nervous. Colton's eyes meet mine and something flashes in them—a moment of unexpected clarity—that worries me.

"Go on," Colton says cautiously.

"I've been thinking about what you said, Colton, and after look-ing at Zander's situation from all sides, I think you're right." Shane wrings his hands and keeps his eyes focused on them as Colton sighs loudly.

"*What thing did I say*, Shane?" he asks, voice searching, body language pensive as if he fears he already knows.

"About Zander."

Colton scrunches up his nose in a show of regret and I'm com-pletely lost. My body wants to shut down but my mind fights the allure to find out what's going on. I look back to Shane, trying to find the words to ask an explanation when I catch Colton mouth out of the words, "Not now," with a shake of his head.

Panic, my one constant, returns, jolting through my system as I look back and forth from Colton to Shane, both of them realizing I saw the exchanged warning. Something's going on, and it's about Zander. I need to know now or else I'm going to go crazier than I already feel. I open my mouth, shut it, then open it again, willing my frenzied thoughts to find the voice that's been silent for so very long.

"No," Shane says, standing up to Colton, causing us both to snap our heads to him. "She deserves to know that we've voted, and we're okay with it."

I blink my eyes rapidly as I try to understand his cryptic com-ment. I feel like I've just walked into a movie halfway through and I'm lost in the plot. As much as I want to be angry at Colton, he obvi-ously fears that whatever Shane has to say is going to knock me back a few of the steps I've gained these past few days.

"What?" My voice breaks. It sounds foreign to my ears. My eyes widen as I search their faces for answers. Now it's their turn to both look at me.

"I'm just trying to fix everything I started," he says, and I don't understand what he means. He looks at me with little boy's eyes in a grown man's body, begging me to let him help me. "It's my fault."

"*What* are you talking about?" Colton asks, voice demanding yet sounding just as confused as I am.

"I told you about Zander's meeting with his uncle at The House that day when I shouldn't have. I should have known better. But how was I to know Zander was going to say things that would cause you to get so upset you'd go into labor? And then we came here to meet Ace. You were fine one minute and then you talked to Z and . . ." His voice drifts off, and I strain to remember bits and pieces from when the boys came. But I can't—just flashes of wide eyes and scared faces—and I know I obviously frightened them somehow. "I just want you to get better, Rylee. And I want Zander to stay in our family where he's safe. *We all want these things.* And I kept thinking if you knew Zander was safe then maybe you'd get better."

A part of me awakens when I hear his words. I want to tell him it's so much more than that but the love and concern lacing his tone somehow weave into and wrap around me, warming up the places this postpartum depression has left so very cold. It's scary and foreign and exciting to feel these things even if it's just a fraction of what is normal.

"Then I remembered the comment you made, Colton. The one about how you'd adopt Zander if it would fix the situation and—"

"No!" I shout, standing up in protest. Both of them stare at me as I struggle to make my point and understand why that sudden flicker of warmth I felt moments ago is now gone. In seconds, my mind spins in a tornado of thoughts with clarity sharper than I've felt in weeks.

Shane's not nervous; he's upset. Upset and hurt that in his darkest hour I never thought to adopt him, *choose him,* and now all of a sudden Zander's in this situation and Colton obviously told him his suggestion when never in a million years would I even consider it.

The twister spins out of control. Anger, betrayal, compassion, despair, love. They all whirl inside me. I can't catch my breath. I can't speak. And yet the feelings within me are so violent, crashing into one another without recourse, that I can't process them. I begin to shut down. Crawl with my tail between my legs into the darkness because obviously I thought I was stronger when I'm not.

I need my bed. To pull the covers over me and to try and quiet the riot in my head, but I don't move. Instead I start to hyperventilate, my lungs convulsing as panic takes over my body, so all I can do is sag back down into the couch to try and catch my breath.

Colton's at my side in an instant. His eyes are alarmed, but hands are gentle as he rubs my back and tells me he's there. My body burns for oxygen, my blood on fire, and my head starts to become dizzy. I clutch my head in my hands, desperate for some kind of control.

"No peeking, Scooter!" Shane's voice sounds off. How can it be in front of me when he's beside me? Regardless, the sound of it pulls me to the present. I open my eyes and he's holding his cell phone so I can see a video playing on the screen. The camera pans across the room and six heads are bowed down: Connor, Aiden, Ricky, Kyle, Scooter, and Auggie. Curiosity pulls my head above water; the sight of my boys keeps it there as my breathing slowly evens.

"Okay. You ready?" It's Shane's voice on the phone, his hand recording, as an array of yeses sound. "We all know that Zander was told today his uncle has been approved to foster him."

"*What?*" Colton says in shock, hand stilling on my back, the same time the breath I just got back catches in my chest. My eyes, mesmerized by the sight of my boys again, sting with unwanted tears. Disbelief courses right alongside the panic.

Spiral. Twist. Slide. Back down into the dark.

"Just listen," Shane urges, his voice giving me a focal point to cling to.

The video continues. "Who is in favor and completely okay and know that it has nothing to do with playing favorites—"

"Jesus. We got it, dude!" Aiden says. "We all know we're Donavans. We don't need a formal adoption process or the official name change to tell us that. It's a given. Just take the vote, Shane."

Colton sucks in a breath beside me. My pulse starts to race again.

A little at first. Then a lot. But this time it's not from anxiety. The lack of panic and the presence of disbelieved hope pull me a little closer toward the surface.

"Shut it, Aid!"

"Always the boss," Aiden says, eyes rolling, as Connor elbows him.

"Who is in favor of Rylee and Colton filing a petition to adopt Zander?" Six arms rise in the air without a moment's hesitation. Shane flips the camera lens onto him to show his hand in the air. "And it's a landslide," he says, angling it back to my crew where they've all raised their heads, smiles on their faces, and patience gone.

I'm transfixed with the images as a few of them give a shout out to me until a scuffle ensues over hogging the spotlight and then the video stops. But when Shane goes to pull his hand holding the phone away, I reach out in reflex and grab it, my eyes lifting up to meet his.

I don't know what to say. All I know is how I feel. And how I feel is that I actually feel *something* when there's been nothing in so long. A sudden rainstorm in an arid desert.

My hand squeezes his wrist as I scramble to mouth the words backing up like a dam in my mind. Nothing comes out but I can't let go of him. And I can't look away.

Colton runs his hand up and down the length of my spine in reassurance as Shane lowers to his knees in front of me and puts his free hand on top of mine, holding steadfast to his. Eyes laced with concern and swimming with love meet mine.

"We know you're not choosing Zander over us. You're doing what you've always done. You're trying to save him just like you have done for each one of us." His voice breaks and tears well, despite him trying to hold it together. "We didn't tell Zander about the vote, didn't want to get his hopes up if you guys decide not to pursue it . . . but we also didn't want you to throw the idea out because you thought it would upset us."

"I don't even know what to say," Colton says, his voice thick with emotion.

"There's nothing to say." He shrugs, bringing back thoughts of the little boy I first met. "I'll admit when you first told me about it, I was a little shocked. Surprised. But at the same time, it's what you said *after* telling me you'd adopt Zander that I heard the loudest."

Colton looks back and forth between us and shakes his head as he tries to recall what Shane's talking about.

"You told me Ry nixed the idea because it would make the rest of us feel bad. That spoke louder to me than anything. She was willing to hurt him to spare our feelings. It didn't sit right with me. Ry, you raised us to look out for one another, take care of each other. Be a family. Well, Zander's our family. So I mentioned it to Aiden. Played it down. Pretended I'd had a dream about it happening to see what he'd say. He thought it was brilliant. Didn't have a problem with it. We went from there." His voice fades off, but I hear hope in his tone and see optimism in his eyes.

"Shane." It's the sound of Colton's stilted voice that causes the first tear to slide over.

"*I just wanted to try to make things right.*"

The curtain lifts. Huge body-wracking sobs take over my body as the curtain lifts to the highest it's been since my mind fell into this depression. And I still can't speak. All I can do is show them that the smile on my face is not forced anymore—a break in the black clouds. A ray of light flooding me with the knowledge there is still good in the world. That I've raised seven boys who came to me damaged and beyond hope—with all odds stacked against them—and have turned them into compassionate, loving individuals who have formed a family.

My family. Their family.

"Ry? Baby, look at me." It's Colton's voice that pulls me out of this storm of emotion. I actually want to stay in it though, because it feels so damn good to feel something other than the weight of sadness. But I look at him anyway. I want him to see the glimpse of the real me peeking through because I know as good as this feels, as long as it has lasted, it will probably be gone soon. In my compromised psyche, I know you don't snap out of postpartum depression so easily.

But it gives me hope. Tells me I can do this. That the glimpse will turn into more. Baby steps as Colton says.

"These are happy tears, right?" he asks as I glance over to Shane and then back to him. Both of their eyes hold a cautious optimism.

"Yes."

I might not be broken after all.

Chapter Forty

COLTON

FUCKIN' BECKETT.

He knows just how to push my buttons. Get me where I need to be. Even if it takes a few *fibs* as he calls them. More like bald-faced lies.

But who's the fool? I fell for them. I'm right where he wants me. On the track. In the car and just hitting my stride on my thirtieth lap after some new adjustments.

God, I needed this. Everything about it: the routine, the camaraderie with the crew, the vibration of the car all around me, the control and response when everything else has felt so chaotic.

The freedom.

I shift, coming into turn one. Let my car own the track since I'm alone on it, getting a feel if the last adjustment was right or wrong.

"Wood?" No other words need to be said to know what he's asking me.

"Feels good. Ass end's not sliding as I come outta the bank." I take a sip of water from the tube. It's piss-warm. Fuck.

"Okay. Open her up then for a few laps once you hit the line.

Push to pass. Let me see what the gauges say when we do that."

"Open her up? You get some last night, Daniels? I don't think I've ever heard you say those words." Hands grip the wheel, body braced for the force as I come out of turn four toward the start/finish line.

"Wouldn't you like to know?" He chuckles. That's an affirmative on getting laid. "Let's see what she can do."

I drop the hammer. Race the motherfucking wind. Let the vibration of the car and the fight of the wheel own my mind and body: escape from the worry about Rylee—the constant responsibility of Ace, the *everything* that feels like it has been on my shoulders—and just be.

The car and me. Machine and man. Speed against skill. Chaos versus control.

Each lap peels away the world around me a little bit more. Pulls me into the blur. Lets me become a part of the car, hear each rattle, feel every vibration, and listen to what she's saying to me.

If she's going to be a whore or a wife for the next race: let me use her, abuse her until I get mine at the start/finish line, or if I need to praise her, stroke her with foreplay, and hope she gets off by the time the checkered flag is waved.

"Gauges are looking good. How's she feel?"

"A good mix." He knows I mean she's a little bit of both—whore and wife—the perfect mix to win a race.

"We need a little more whore for the next race. Push her harder. See if she sucks or swallows."

I laugh into the open mic as I head into turn three. Routine entry, down shift, gaze drops down to the gauges one last time before the track and car own them with the concentration the turn takes.

The ass end slides high, fishtails at the topside of the curve. Rubber tires hit a rash of pellets. I hydroplane across them, slick tires over balls of rubber.

FUCK!

Split seconds of time. Increments of thoughts. Routine of movements.

The nose end turn turns high. Arms tense fighting the wheel. A flash of concrete wall.

Ace. An image of him flashes before my eyes. A slideshow of frames. His cry is in the whine of the engine.

Releasing the wheel. Crossing my arms so I can hold onto the harness.

Ryles. Soft smile. Big heart. Incredible strength. Just when she's coming back to me.

Shoulders shoving into the seat. The car spins. Nosecone hits the wall. Metal sparking as it shreds.

"*Wood!*"

Spinning. Hands grip seatbelts tight. Waiting for the second impact.

Nothing.

C'mon. C'mon. C'mon

Spinning.

Slipping down the track.

Spinning.

Grass flying as I hit the infield.

Coming to a stop.

Taking a breath.

Hands stiff from holding tight to the seatbelts.

"Goddammit, Colton! Answer me."

Sound comes back. Adrenaline takes over. My heart pounds. My mouth is dry.

But I'm fine.

"I'm good. Fine," I rasp as my body starts to tremble from the aftereffects. "Fucked up the nosecone and front right side."

"You're good?" His voice is shaky.

"I'm good." *Well, I will be.* After I have a stiff drink.

"Fuck, Colton! I told you to open her up, not tear her up and slam her into the goddamn wall!" he yells through the mic as I unpin the wheel to get out.

My chuckle fills the connection—the tinge of hysteria in it clear as fucking day.

I'm grateful for his comment. For getting me back to the norm when a part of me is so lost in my own head over shit I never allow myself to think about.

And yet sometimes when you're forced to close your eyes, everything else becomes so much clearer.

"Colton?"

"Can I come in?" I look at my dad. There are so many things I want to say. No, *need* to say to him.

My mind hasn't stopped since I left the track. The wreck made my mortality front and fucking center like never before. I have a kid now. Responsibilities. People that matter to me when before the only person I cared about besides my parents, Quin, and Becks was me, myself, and I.

I got out of the car needing to call Ry. Talk to her. Hear her voice. Get home so I could hold Ace. But know I can't.

It was just another day at the track. I spun out. A job hazard. I couldn't call her because even though she's making huge strides, she's still not one hundred percent, and I didn't want to do anything to trigger her to pull away.

So I drove. *Aimlessly.* Ended up at the beach. Then drove some more. Checked in with Haddie to make sure Ry was good and ended up here. Fucking full circles.

"Come in. Everything okay? Ry and Ace?" he asks as I follow him into the house I grew up in.

"Yes. Yeah." *Shit*. He's worried. "Sorry. They're fine. It's all good." We walk past the stairs I used to slide down on cardboard, and the liquor cabinet I used to sneak bottles from in high school. I focus on that shit because all of a sudden I'm antsy, nervous. Feel stupid for coming here but need to tell him nonetheless.

"It's good to see you out and about," he says.

"Haddie's with Ry," I explain when he doesn't ask. "I had to get some time at the track."

"How'd it go?"

"Good. Fine. Hit the wall."

Fight or flight time, Colton. Say what you need to say.

"Colton?"

I snap from my thoughts. The shit that I'm here to say but have now lost the words for. "Sorry." I sigh, lift my hat and run a hand through my hair.

"I said hitting the wall doesn't sound like it went well. Are you okay?" His grey eyes look at me in that way he has since I was a kid. Checking for ghosts he's not going to find.

"Yes. No." I shake my head. "Fuck if I know." I laugh and can hear the nerves in it as I watch him sit down and lean back on the couch, expression guarded, eyes an open fucking door that say, "*Talk to me, son.*"

I shove up out of the seat I've just sat in and walk toward the mantle where it is littered with picture frames of Q and me as kids. A house that has been featured in every style magazine known to man, and my mom keeps our homemade frames sitting on the mantle like they fit right in with the Louis whatever chair I was never allowed to sit on. I'm restless, fidgety, and just need to get this the fuck over with so I can stop thinking about it and get home.

"I had no right to ask you to go with me the other day." That wasn't what I was expecting to say but, fuck it, might as well go with it. He stares at me, father to son, body and eyes warring between asking for more and letting it come to me.

"I'm not following you."

Of course you're not going to make this easy on me, are you? *Fuck*. I sigh. Move. Pace. Hand through hair again.

"When I asked you to drive me so I could see my . . . uh . . ." Fuck. I can't say the word. Can't use the same term for that piece of shit as I do for this man in front of me, my endgame superhero.

"*Dad*. You can say it, Colton. I'm confident with my place in your life."

"I know but it was a slap in your face, and it's been eating at me. I shouldn't have asked you to go," I say as I turn around and meet his eyes again. "Or I should have told you where we were going. Given you a choice."

"It's never a slap in my face when you want to spend time with me, son. The fact you wanted me there with you tells me more than you'll ever know."

I stare at him, jaw clenched, and head a mess. I don't deserve him. Never have. But sure as shit, I'm not letting him go.

"It was chickenshit of me." It's all I can say.

"It's only natural for you to wonder. What you need to ask yourself is, did you get what you wanted out of it?"

"Yes. No. Fuckin'A straight I'm so angry but I don't know *why*." I pace again. Pissed I'm still bugged by it all.

"Why? Because you wanted him to see you, pull you into a hug, and start a relationship?" he goads, knowing damn well that wasn't what I wanted. "Have a get-to-know-you session?"

"No," I shout, hand banging down on the table beside me. The sound echoes around the room while I rein in my temper. I don't want to have emotion over the loser. None. So why do I feel so fucked up when I thought I had it all under wraps? "I didn't want shit from him other than to see him so I could look at the fucking reflection of what I never want to be to Ace. *You happy*?"

"Perfectly," he says with a ghost of a smile that taunts me. I've punched guys for less. But I force myself to breathe. Unclench my fists. Redirect my anger. *Try to at least.*

"Really? My fucked-up head makes you happy?" I grate out between gritted teeth.

"Nope. But you've been through a lot of shit this month, Colton. Taken on a lot of responsibilities and haven't really gotten to deal with any of this, so here I am. Scream and yell. That vase right next to you? *Throw it.* Watch it break against the wall. I'll cover for you with your mom. Tell her I fell or something." He pauses and lifts his eyebrows.

"What? She'd kill you. That's like some antique-ey thing we were never allowed to touch."

"Even better. Expensive shit sounds better when it breaks."

"You're fucking crazy." I laugh, not really sure what else to say because he looks dead serious. What is going on here?

"Yeah, well, you have to be crazy to be a good parent." His lips curl up, eyes flash with something, and I know I'm about to get schooled. Too bad I have no idea what the lesson covers. So I just stare at him and wait, knowing from experience that something else is coming. The difference is that as a kid, I'd let it go in one ear and out the other. This time, I'm fairly certain I won't be so blasé.

"Connect the dots here, Dad, because I'm lost." White flag is waving. Help me out.

"Being a parent is the hardest thing I've ever done. It's made me question my sanity more times than you can imagine," he says dryly, and I know many of those times were because of me. "And there are times that you have to bite your tongue so hard you're not sure if it's going to be in one or two pieces when you open your mouth. It's exhausting and you're constantly doubting yourself, wondering if you're doing the right thing, saying the right thing, being the right thing."

I look at him like he's crazy and yet every single thing he says is gold. So damn true I can't argue a single point.

"But then there are those moments, Colton, when you watch

your child do something and are so damn proud of them you are left speechless. And those moments take every single doubt and fear and heartache and moment of insanity you've ever had and wipe the slate clean. That's how I felt watching you go to see your dad. That's how I feel knowing you and Ry are going to adopt Zander. That's how I feel watching you be a father. Hell, son, when you stepped up to the plate after Rylee got sick and swung it out of the goddamn park by taking care of Ace? I've never been prouder."

My eyes sting with tears I don't want to shed from the praise I never like to receive. Yet at the same time understand completely now that I'm a father.

"I've never been more proud to be your father than I am right now. *That man*," he says, pointing over his shoulder to tell me he's referring to my biological father, "doesn't deserve to get to know the incredible person you are."

The lump in my throat feels like it is the size of a football. "Thank you." I feel like a shy little kid, unworthy of the no-holds-barred love he's given me my whole life when I haven't always been easy. Fuck. Who am I kidding? I've been a nightmare. And yet the quip that's on my tongue dies when I look back to his eyes. I see love and approval and pride and shit that makes me uncomfortable to see. I know Ace needs to see it every day of his life so he can know exactly what I feel right now.

"No need to thank me, son." We stare at each other for a moment, years of unspoken words traded in the span of silence. "Now . . . I'm sure you didn't stop by to hear me blather on. What can I do for you?"

Just like him to lay down the law and then act like we're not even in court.

"Believe it or not, you gave me the answer anyway."

And he did. Tons of answers, in fact. *He* turned wounds into wisdom.

The most important thing is that he let me be who I needed to be, guided me when I needed it, and let me figure shit out on my own when I was too stubborn to ask for help. Regardless, he let me grow, let me experience, let me chase the goddamn wind as I raced, and the fact he was by my side without judgment the whole time, made me the man I am today.

Now I can't wait to be that exact same man for Ace.

Chapter Forty-One

Rylee

I STARTLE AWAKE.

Colton's arms have fallen off me in sleep, and I struggle to remember the last time I slept this deeply. The last thing I remember was memory number who knows what that had to do with zip-lining through the forests of Costa Rica.

Naked.

I seem to think every one of his memories had to do with me being naked. It's kind of funny. Kind of not.

I sit up and look at Ace asleep in the bassinet. His hands are up over his head, lips are suckling even in his sleep. I stare and wonder what type of person he'll be. What will his future hold? Images that are so crystal clear slide through my head: first smiles, first steps, first day of school, first date. So many of them have this little boy with dark hair and green eyes and freckles over the bridge of his nose it's almost as if I've seen a picture of what he's going to look like before.

But the one thing I don't expect, don't even notice until it hits me like a lightning strike, is that the oppressive weight of dread and doom doesn't come. It doesn't drop one single time to darken my thoughts or steal my calm.

I wait for it. Hope for the best, expect the worst for a while. But the panic, the sweat, the fingers clawing at my throat and squeezing my heart, don't come.

All that does is a soft smile on my lips. Not one forced or laced with guilt that comes because I need to show I'm improving, but rather because I really feel it.

Tears well. Big fat tears slide down my cheeks. And the funny thing is the taste of the salt as it hits my lips is like a smelling salt waking me up from passing out. And I'm not sure how long this is going to last but for the first time in the six weeks since Ace's birth, I feel optimistic, hopeful . . . *like me.*

So I sit in this mass of a bed with my sweet baby boy beside me—who I desperately want to pick up but was fussy and difficult for Colton to put down tonight. I want to pull him tight to my chest and tell him he's been my heartbeat throughout this mess. Apologize to him. Say words about events he's never going to even know or remember but that will make me feel a little better.

I'm transfixed by him, feeling like I'm looking at him for the first time and in a sense I am, because he's already grown and changed so much. I feel like I have to make up for lost time, although I know I have a whole lifetime to do that with him. Hesitantly, I reach out to touch him and then pull back when he squirms, smelling the milk on me.

And even though I shift back onto the bed, I can't take my eyes off him. He's so beautiful. Everything I've ever wanted. My ace in a loaded deck of cards.

The thought makes me smile. Memories colliding of that first encounter between Colton and me—jammed closets and first kisses and fear over how strong the chemistry was between the player and this good girl—when I first called him Ace.

A chance encounter that lead to this moment. Right here. Right now. Where so much love fills me that I'm swamped by it. And I'll take being swamped by love because I've been drowning in sadness for what feels like forever.

I look at him now. My achingly handsome husband. His dark hair is a little longer than normal, falling over his forehead. Dark lashes fan on bronze skin. That perfectly imperfect nose of his. And those lips that have murmured memories he wants to make with me every single night over the past five-plus weeks.

Rogue, rebel, reckless. Those words still apply to him. As do so many others that would make him blush, roll his eyes, and play them off because they make this stoic man uncomfortable. My *rock* is the one I can't seem to get out of my head. Because that's exactly what he has been to me.

My everything.

Just like with Ace, I reach out my hand and pull it back. He deserves a good night's sleep. Some peace and quiet since he has been the one handling all of my noise. And yet I can't resist. Never can when it comes to him.

I lean forward and press a soft kiss to his lips, wanting nothing more than this connection with him. My body is still recovering, and the thought of sex is the furthest thing from my battered mind, and yet this simple touch, lips to lips, completes the sensation that something is still missing.

It's probably bogus, my mind still playing tricks on me, and yet the spark that hits when I kiss him jumpstarts every part of my body drugged by the postpartum depression back to life.

My hands frame his cheeks as I brush my lips to his again, need becoming want, want becoming all-consuming. The desire to feel his touch in a way that's not to soothe but rather to sate a need.

A gasp of breath. A flash open of startled eyes. A reach of his hands to grab onto mine holding him.

"Rylee." His voice. That sexy, sleep-drugged voice that calls to me as he says my name and owns my soul.

"Yeah. It's me." And I mean it in every sense of the word. His emerald eyes widen and lips part in shock as he pulls me into him. One arm wraps around my back and the other cradles the back of my head as he presses me into his chest.

Our hearts connect. His feels like it wants to jump out of his chest and collide with mine as it beats an erratic yet familiar rhythm that is one hundred percent ours.

His hands hold me tight and don't let go. He's already lost me once, and I love the knowledge he's going to make damn sure I'm not going to leave again.

The scrape of his stubble as he rubs his cheek against mine, a subtle sting of coarse to soft tells me this is real, this is him, and I am loved. Irrevocably.

The scent of soap and shampoo still lingers from his shower. The smell of home, of comfort . . . of safety as I breathe him in.

Everything seems so new and yet so familiar all at the same time. Whoever said the only way to find yourself is to get completely lost, knew exactly what they were talking about.

His hand fists my hair and pulls my head back. Emerald eyes own my soul when they meet mine. They ask if this is a dream, if I'm really here, and I do the only thing I can. I lean forward and take a sip from his lips—the taste of his kiss is seared into my soul, one I'll never forget—and it reawakens my senses the minute it hits my tongue.

We move in the darkness.

Two soulmates reuniting.

Two best friends grateful to have their other half.

Two lovers rediscovering each other in an intimate dance of tongues and the slide of fingertips over thirst-starved flesh.

Two parts of a puzzle finally realizing their piece of peace they've been missing has been found.

Once again.

Epilogue

PART 1

COLTON

Eight months later

THE TURBULENCE JOLTS ME AWAKE.

Well, that's what I'll tell the twenty or so people on the other side of the door. Because it sure as shit isn't the turbulence that wakes me up. No. It's Ry's hand sliding into my pants, fingernails tickling my nuts, and soft-as-fuck lips, kissing the underside of my jaw.

"Ry . . ." I sigh.

"Be quiet," she warns against my skin, my body already fully alert at this unexpected wake-up call. Her other hand slides up beneath my shirt. Nails against bare skin. Teeth nipping my earlobe. Hot breath against my neck. "Your mom has Ace. You were asleep. And I was horny."

Well, damn.

Alright, so...

I glance at the cabin door, visually make sure the latch is set to lock before I lay my head back and close my eyes. Her tongue then does something to me that sends a jolt of electricity straight down my spine connecting to where her fingers are slowly stroking me.

"Horny is good." Her lips meet mine as she climbs astride me. Tongues and teeth. Greed and need. Wet against hard. Goddamn she's hot. Sexy fucking hot. "But it's going to take a whole helluva lot more to get me to tell you where we are going."

The stutter in her movement tells me I'm right, know her angle: confession by orgasm. Not a bad way to be tortured but my lips are sealed.

Maybe I'll wait to tell her though. I've been to a lot of places with her, but the mile-high club isn't one of them.

Maybe it's time to venture there.

She sits up, a taunt in her eye and determination on her face. But that pout on her lips tells me she's game to change my mind.

Change away, Ryles.

"Guess I'll just have to take care of myself then."

Don't you dare. My eyes say it but lips don't. I'm too goddamn focused on her hands traveling over her tits, hard nipples visible through the thin cotton, down to where her fingers pull up her loose skirt inch by fucking inch. And then they disappear beneath the flowy fabric so I can't see shit.

But I sure as fuck see her head fall back, lips fall open, and hear the sigh fall from her lips as her hands begin to move in a motion I know all too well. Quick strokes of her finger to add friction to her clit.

Motherfucker.

Another quiet moan. Her back arches. Tits push forward. Hands move quicker, harder. Her skirt inches up farther so I can see the slick arousal on her fingers.

She's playing me and I don't even have a ball in her court. Playing with fire when I want to be the only one striking the goddamn matchstick.

My stick's out all right. Now I just need to light the flame.

Within a beat I have Rylee flipped over, hands cuffed beside her head, and our faces inches apart. "You're playing with fire, sweetheart," I tease between teeth gritted in restraint.

The scent of her arousal on her fingers fills my nose. Temptation at its fucking finest. *Two can play this game, sweetheart.* I lower my mouth, take the tips of her fingers between my lips and suck. Tongue laving over them, savoring her addictive taste. Her body squirms beneath me. A moan hums in the back of her throat.

"Don't make a sound," I whisper around her fingers.

One final suck. One last taste. One last hit. I look down at her beneath me. Her lips are parted, cheeks are flushed, and her eyes are heavy with desire. Goddamn sex personified.

And thank fuck for that because I'm digging in and taking what's mine. Her orgasm. Her moans. Her scratch marks. And every damn thing in between.

"Burn, baby, burn," she taunts with a gleam in her eyes as I release her hands so I can free my dick. And before I can pull my pants down far enough to free my thighs, her hand is pulling up her skirt, and bringing herself back to the brink of climax.

It's such a turn-on. Watching her own her sexuality. Getting herself off. But it's too damn much—the need to have, to take, to claim—and so I do just that.

With one hand on her throat and my dick in her pussy, I dive head first into the addiction that is everything about her. And at thirty-eight thousand feet above the middle of nowhere, she comes quickly—legs tensed, eyes locked on mine, and lips pulled tight—with my hand over her mouth to muffle her moans. The look on her face and her pussy pulsing around my dick pulls me over the edge so I can chase her.

When I catch my breath and look down at her all I can do is shake my head. "That's one hell of an effort," I whisper, leaning down to press my lips to hers, "but even your voodoo pussy isn't magic enough to get me to tell you."

She laughs. That's all she can do.

Goddamn, I'm a lucky man.

Epilogue

PART 2

THE AIRPORT WAS A THATCH hut. We walked straight from the private jet to the awaiting cars, and the road we're on is rutted dirt that requires serious suspension. Ben Montague plays on the radio as I take in the foliage, thick and green around us, causing my curiosity to grow with each passing bump along the road.

Where in the hell is he taking me?

I think back to the look on our boys' faces when we deplaned on the tarmac. Their incessant chatter filled the air. My parents' laughter as they became caught up in Colton's mysterious family vacation. The knowing glance between Becks and Colton, and Haddie's squeeze of my hand before we all loaded into our waiting vehicles. The shower of kisses rained down upon Ace by his adopted brother and his six other brothers—who claim him simply because we unceremoniously claim them—before we separate in three separate car arrangements. The happiness in my heart when Zander looked up and met my eyes. Unspoken words passed between us. *Thank yous* to Colton and I for saving him and at the same time allowing him to still be a part of the family he'd made with the boys. The slight smile on his lips and lift of his head to ask if it's okay to ride with them instead of us was all I needed to know we made the right choice. That we didn't harm the others by saving Zander.

And off we went.

Two vans: one driven by Becks and Haddie with the boys, and the other driven by Andy with the rest of our family. A whole lot of smiles as the doors closed and not much explanation by Colton on the two-way radios other than "we're almost there."

And then there's the three of us in our Jeep. The SUV jostles in the terrain and pulls me back to the sights around us, all the while reminding me how fortunate I am to have everyone here. My boys. My family. My husband.

My everything.

Well, everything except for not knowing where we are, why we've been divided, or where we're headed.

I glance over to Colton. I know it's useless to ask again because he's not going to give me an answer.

Live dangerously with me, Ry.

His words to me flicker through my memory, and I can't help but smile. I want to tell him I'll live dangerously a million times over so long as he never gives up on me. But I know I don't have to worry about that happening. He's already proven he won't. So I do the only thing I can. I shake my head in disbelief and accept how full of love my heart is for him.

We've been through so much in the last year. Things I never thought we'd have to face hit us head-on, blindsided us, and knocked us flat on our asses. Yet here we are, stronger because of it. And I'm not oblivious to the fact we survived when so many other couples wouldn't have.

How could we not have? *It's permanent, right?*

And I glance back to check on Ace, the reason we fought so hard to find our piece of peace again. He seems completely unfazed by this rough ride. I take in his dark hair with a bit of a wave at the ends—the perfect combination of Colton's color and my texture—and my smile is automatic. Green eyes look up and steal my heart like they do every single time they meet mine. Just like his father's.

He babbles something incoherently, chubby cheeks bulging and hands waving in emphasis. I may have no idea where we are going, but I know he's going to be in heaven having all of his brothers, his grandparents, and aunts and uncles here to play with and give him nonstop attention.

"We've lost them," I say, as alarm moves through me when I glance up from Ace and notice the vans aren't behind us.

"Becks knows where he's going. They're fine." It's all he says. Nothing else. I'd love to wrap my hands around that sexy neck of his and force him to tell me where we are and where he's taking me.

"You sure?"

"Yep."

Gah! I tried sex on the plane, sweet-talking, and just about any-thing else I could imagine but nope, the man won't budge. I just hope wherever the hell we are, my clothes are suitable, because it's not like he gave me a chance to pack. Who knew Colton would surprise us all after the first race of the season by flying us from St. Petersburg to wherever we are now?

Definitely not me.

I look back at Ace to see his eyes closing. The rocking of the car has lulled him to sleep. When I turn around, the view out the windshield hijacks my breath: white sand, palm trees swaying in the breeze, and a small hut on stilts stretched out over the crystal clear water.

"Colton!" I glance over to him and then back to the sight before me, and then back to him. A slow, shy smile turns up one corner of his mouth—dimple winking—but it's the look in his eyes that holds me rapt.

And something fires in my mind, covered somewhere in cobwebs but I must be crazy trying to figure it out when all of this is in front of me.

Colton opens the door and I glance back, deciding to leave Ace sleeping for a moment while I admire the view. I get out of the car as Colton comes around the front, a knowing smile still on his lips, and love in his eyes.

"Do you know this place?" he asks, head angled, hands reaching out to pull me against him.

"What? Colton! This is just . . ." I'm shocked, curious, floored, and grateful as I look up at him with confusion in my eyes.

"I wanted to take a family vacation. We all deserve it after this year, don't you think?" he asks. I know him well enough to know he's holding something back. What it is though, I don't know.

"This place is incredible." I'm still in his arms but my head swivels from side to side to take it all in.

"And secluded," he adds, causing my focus to turn back on him.

"I like secluded," I murmur.

"And bathing suits are optional."

The laugh comes freely. "I'm sure they are," I respond as my mind fires again, but this time it all comes back to me. Knocks me flat on my ass. Takes hold of my heart and squeezes so damn tight my chest hurts from love.

My eyes flash up to his—violet to green—and the words fall from my mouth in a whisper. "This . . . this is from . . ." He nods his head, smile spreading, and waits as my words pause and mind recalls. "When I was sick. This is one of the memories you said you wanted to make with me." Awe owns my voice as I try to comprehend that he did this for me.

"Yes," he whispers and brushes his lips against mine in the most tender of kisses. The kind that owns your soul and completes your heart. "It's the first of many of those memories I plan to make come true for you. We're going to have to buy a lot more frames to put them in."

"Colton . . ." Tears well in my eyes as I pull him closer, the moment so poignant I'm at a loss for words.

"And yes, there is a very skimpy bikini on the bed in there for you that is for my eyes only. Or you can skip it and just run around naked."

"Run around naked?" I say as I look back toward the car where Ace sleeps.

"And that's why our family is at a huge house about three miles down the road. Babysitters," he says with a quirk of his eyebrows.

"You've thought of everything," I murmur against his lips.

"Mm-hmm," he says as he presses a kiss to my nose.

"I can't wait to see you in that loincloth."

He throws his head back and laughs, the vibrations of it echoing in my chest, and all I can do is stare at him. And then laugh with him. Because if we've learned one thing in our marriage it's that we need to laugh as much as we breathe and love like we are the air that allows us to do both.

I stare at him—stubbled cheeks, emerald eyes, and dark hair—and all I see is happiness. All I feel is love. All I know is completeness. All I want is forever with him.

My husband.

My rock.

My piece of peace.

My memory maker.

My happily ever after.

THE END

Acknowledgements

Thank you to the women in my life that make me a better author, friend, mother, daughter, and most importantly, person: to Brook, CJ, Willy, Wendy, Jeni, Susan, Christine, Laurelin, Lauren, Amy, and YOU. Because I include YOU – the readers, bloggers, admins, VP Pit Crew members – in this group of incredible women who continuously challenge, support, teach, and empower me. Without you, none of *this* would be possible.

About the Author

New York Times and *USA Today* Bestselling author K. Bromberg writes contemporary novels that contain a mixture of sweet, emotional, a whole lot of sexy and a little bit of real. She likes to write strong heroines and damaged heroes who we love to hate and hate to love.

She's a mixture of most of her female characters: sassy, intelligent, stubborn, reserved, outgoing, driven, emotional, strong, and wears her heart on her sleeve. All of which she displays daily with her husband and three children where they live in Southern California.

On a whim, K. Bromberg decided to try her hand at this writing thing. Since then she has written The Driven Series *(Driven, Fueled, Crashed, Raced, Aced)*, the standalone Driven Novels *(Slow Burn, Sweet Ache, Hard Beat)*, and a short story titled *UnRaveled*. She is currently working on new projects and a few surprises for her readers.

She loves to hear from her readers so make sure you check her out on social media.

51217632R00209

Made in the USA
Lexington, KY
15 April 2016